A QUESTION OF IDENTITY

A Question of Identity

A Chief Superintendent Simon Serrailler Mystery

Susan Hill

THE OVERLOOK PRESS
NEW YORK, NY

This edition first published in hardcover in the United States in 2012 by
The Overlook Press, Peter Mayer Publishers, Inc.
141 Wooster Street
New York, NY 10012
www.overlookpress.com

For bulk and special sales, please contact sales@overlookny.com

First published in Great Britain in 2012 by Chatto & Windus,
a division of The Random House Group

Cataloging-in-Publication Data is available from the Library of Congress

Typeset in Palatino by Palimpsest Book Production Limited
Manufactured in the United States of America
FIRST EDITION
ISBN 978-1-4683-0050-5

1 3 5 7 9 10 8 6 4 2

For LGHR
30 May 2012

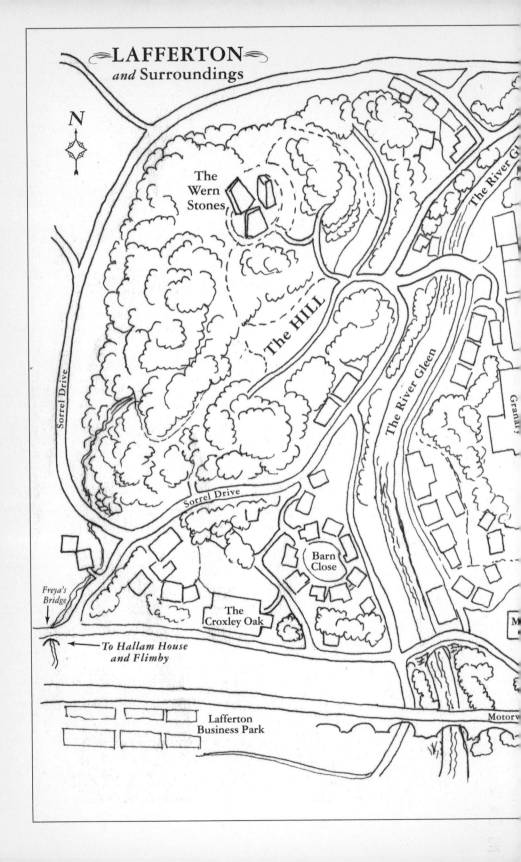

Acknowledgements

I am greatly indebted to Brian Hook for his detailed information and guidance on a number of specialist police subjects and also for his inventiveness and ingenuity in advising me on several scenarios.

Barrister Anthony Lenaghan has again been most helpful in giving me the benefit of his professional expertise in legal matters and trial procedure and I am also grateful to him for allowing me to take over his Yorkshire terrier, Wookie, for a role in this book.

Barbara Machin has helped me to unravel several plot-knots and come up with some clever suggestions about criminal psychology and behaviour and Dr Jill Barling has helped by talking through medical details and practice with me on many occasions.

PART ONE

YORKSHIRE, 2002

It's like your brain's bursting. It doesn't happen all at once, it builds up. And then your brain's going to burst until you do something about it. You do it. You have to do it. Then it's all right again for a bit, 'til it starts again.

One

'Members of the jury, the defendant has answered an indictment containing three counts. On count one he is charged with murder. The particulars of the offence are that on or before the seventeenth day of July 2001, he murdered Carrie Millicent Gage. On count two he is charged with murder. The particulars of the offence are that on or before the thirtieth of July 2001, he murdered Sarah Pearce. On count three he is charged with murder. The particulars of the offence are that on the fourth of August 2001 he murdered Angela Daphne Kavanagh.

'To each count he has pleaded "Not guilty", and it is your duty, having heard the evidence, to say, in respect of each count, whether he is guilty or not.

'Would the defendant please stand?'

Alan Frederick Keyes, thirty-two, a self-employed builder of 33 Westway Road, Crofton – wearing dark trousers and a blue open-necked shirt – stood.

23 MAY, 2002

'Would the next witness please take the stand?'

A small woman. Brown coat, beige felt hat. She looked frail, walked slowly, as if in some pain, eyes huge in a bony little face darting about the court, skin the colour of an old candle.

'Will you please state your name?'

She leaned on the wooden ledge of the witness box, eyes still fearful, catching her breath.

'When you're ready.'

Silence. She looked down in panic at the clerk.

'Are you feeling unwell?'

His Honour Judge Malcolm Palmer, notoriously kind to witnesses, relatives, court attendants, women and babies. Notoriously harsh to prosecution or defence not on top of their game, cocky police officers, unprepared expert witnesses and members of the press.

But she pulled herself up. Shook her head, looking anxiously at the judge, who gave her his best encouraging smile. Satisfied that she was ready to attest, he nodded at the clerk.

'Will you please state your name?'

'Gwendolyn Violet Phipps. Mrs.'

'You must speak up a little so that the jury can hear you. Would you mind saying it again?'

'I'm sorry, I'm . . .'

'That's quite all right. Just once again, please.'

Pause. She cleared her throat. Spoke up loudly. 'My name is Gwendolyn Violet Phipps. Mrs.'

'Thank you, Mrs Phipps, that was perfect.'

Mr Anthony Elrod, for the Prosecution: 'Mrs Phipps, would you tell the court please where you were on the night of 17 July last year – 2001?'

'Well, I was at home . . .'

'And your home is?'

'Number 8 Meadow View Close – the bungalows. I was in bed, only then . . . I heard something . . . and I got up.'

'Can you explain to the court where exactly your bungalow, number 8, Meadow View Close is, in relation to the bungalow in which Mrs Carrie Gage lived?'

'Opposite. Right opposite, across the grass.'

'So you have an unobstructed view of number 20?'

'Oh yes. Very clear. I could see Carrie – Mrs Gage – when she was alive . . . I could see her going in and out or if she was at her front window . . . and she could see me. The same.'

'Quite. Now, on the night of 17 July, you say you were awakened by a noise?'

'No, I didn't say that. No. I said I heard something . . . I didn't say it was a noise, or that I was asleep.'

'Well, whatever it was, what did you do?'

'I got up. I knew it wouldn't do any good just lying there. I got up to make a cup of tea.'

'Did you put a light on straight away?'

'No, I went to my bedroom window and looked out.'

'Why was that? Wouldn't the first thing anyone would do would be to switch –'

Mr Jeremy Brockyear, for the Defence, getting to his feet: 'Your Honour –'

Judge Palmer: 'Yes. Mr Elrod, this is very elementary you know, you are trying to ascertain what the witness and only the witness would do, she cannot know what "anyone" else would have done.'

'I beg your pardon, Your Honour. Mrs Phipps, why didn't you put a light on immediately?'

'I must have wondered what had disturbed me and gone to look out first . . . if there had been someone out there, I always think it's safer to see and not be seen, if you follow. If I'd switched on a light whoever it was could have seen me and then what?'

'So you were disturbed by a person making some sort of noise?'

'I must have been. Well, obviously, after I saw him, I realised that, didn't I?'

'"After I saw him"? Who or what was it you did see, Mrs Phipps?'

'The man.'

'One man?'

'Yes, one. Only one.'

'Will you describe the man for us please?'

'Well, it was the man I saw in that line of them, the one I pointed to.'

'That would be in the identification parade at the police station?'

Judge Palmer: 'A step too far ahead, Mr Elrod.'

'Yes, Your Honour. Mrs Phipps, just let's go back to the night on which you say you saw a man outside number 20 Meadow View Close . . . Was it a dark night? Was there a moon?'

'It was dark, but there's a security light, that came on. They come on when anyone moves, only sometimes it's a nuisance, a stray cat or those bloomin' foxes run past and it goes on.'

'Did you see a cat or a fox?'

'No.'

'But you saw a man.'

'Yes, I definitely did.'

'Did you recognise him?'

'Well, I said before, it was the one I –'

'We'll come to that in a moment, Mrs Phipps. Did you recognise him when you looked out of the window that night and saw him? Was it someone you knew?'

'I don't think I knew him. No, I didn't.'

'Are you quite sure?'

'I think I am, yes. Only it was dark of course.'

'Except for the security light that came on, and in which you could see the figure of a man?'

'Yes.'

'Thank you. So now let us move on to the afternoon of 14 October when you attended Crofton Central Police Station. You were shown photographs of a number of men.'

'A lot of photographs. It was quite confusing actually.'

'Did you recognise any of them as being the man you saw that night, outside Mrs Gage's bungalow?'

'Not really. They were photographs of faces close up and I didn't see him like that.'

'Quite. You saw him across the grass from your own window. Let us now move on to 4 November, when you went to Crofton Central Police Station again, and this time you looked at an identity line-up of eight men. You saw them standing, not just their faces. Now did you recognise any of them as being the man you saw on that night from your window?'

'Oh yes. I recognised him.'

'You recognised the defendant?'

'Yes.'

6

'You're quite sure about that?'

'I was . . . I thought it was him. The others weren't anything like him. Well, not much anyway. No, it must have been him.'

'Thank you, Mrs Phipps. No more questions, Your Honour.'

Mr Jeremy Brockyear, for the Defence: 'Mrs Phipps, do you wear glasses?'

'Yes. For reading and sewing.'

'So, you're long-sighted. You have no problems with distance vision?'

'No. I'm very fortunate in that regard.'

'How far can you see clearly without any blurring of vision? Ten yards? Twenty-five yards? One hundred –'

Mr Anthony Elrod: 'Objection, Your Honour – the witness can hardly be expected to know the exact measurements of how far she can see.'

Judge Palmer: 'Point taken but most people have a general idea of their visual extent.'

Mr Jeremy Brockyear: 'Do you drive a car, Mrs Phipps?'

'I did, only I gave it up when I moved into Meadow View.'

'Because you could no longer see clearly?'

'No, because I could no longer afford the running of it.'

'Well, the distance it is necessary to read a number plate clearly, in order to pass the driving test is 25 yards, with glasses if worn. How long is it exactly since you last possessed a driving licence?'

'Seven . . . no, nearly eight years.'

'And do you think you could still see well enough to pass the driving test?'

Mr Anthony Elrod: 'Your Honour . . .'

Judge Palmer: 'Yes. Mr Brockyear, you cannot ask the witness to speculate in that way.'

'Mrs Phipps, will you please tell the court, in as much detail as you can, what or who you saw exactly when you looked out of your window that night?'

'A man. It was definitely a man. That man.'

'How can you be so sure of that?'

'I . . . well, I think . . . no, I mean, I just know. It wasn't quite dark and it isn't far across the grass. I might have seen his reflection in the window.'

'In which window?'

'The one opposite mine, number 20. Carrie's window.'

'Are you saying you definitely did see this man's reflection?'

'I think I might have, yes.'

'But you cannot be absolutely sure? Mrs Phipps?'

'I don't know . . . I'm saying . . . well, I don't know how else I'd have seen him, is what I'm saying.'

'Might you have been mistaken?'

'No. I saw something.'

'Something or someone? Something, as in an animal, or even a shadow – perhaps a tree threw its shadow across the grass?'

Judge Palmer: 'Take your time, Mrs Phipps. Remember you are under oath. You must be sure about what you remember and if you aren't sure you must say so. Do you understand?'

'I do, but it's – it's quite confusing.'

Mr Jeremy Brockyear: 'Mrs Palmer, did you see a man standing in the garden on that night?'

'Yes.'

'You are quite sure.'

'I was sure.'

'You *were* sure or you *are* sure? You see, what I think happened is that you saw something . . . and possibly it was indeed someone. Possibly it was a man . . . but a few minutes ago you said it was almost dark. You're quite correct. There was indeed no moon that night. There was heavy cloud. Behind it, the moon was only one day from new. It would not have been visible behind such cloud. So in fact it was pretty dark in the garden when you looked out, wasn't it?'

'Yes, but I saw someone. I definitely saw – well, I saw something, anyway.'

'But you're not sure it was a person at all, let alone a man?'

'You're making me think I'm not. But the light came on. The security light.'

'You're sure it did?'

'It must have done, mustn't it? It always comes on when something moves and I saw the man, so he must have moved and then the light came on.'

'Now I think we are all confused. Mrs Phipps, I'm trying to get

8

you to be absolutely sure, and it seems to me that the more you think about this extremely important incident, the less sure you are. But let's leave the garden and move on to the identity parade at the police station. At this parade you picked out one man as being the man you are certain you saw that night, didn't you?'

'I suppose I did.'

'Did you or didn't you?'

'I feel . . . I don't know. I just don't know anything, you've confused me so much.'

'I'm sorry if that's how you see it because I am not trying to confuse you in any way. On the contrary, I am trying to get at the truth. I am trying to be clear and to make sure you yourself are clear, about what or who you saw that night. And you're not sure, are you? About what you saw –'

'I am sure about that. I was and I am. It was a man. I saw a man.'

'So now let us again move to the identity parade at the police station.'

'They confused me there too.'

'Who confused you?'

'The detective. The policeman. One of them, maybe the other . . . the woman detective.'

'Mrs Phipps, we need to be absolutely sure about this. Are you saying that one or possibly two members of the police "confused" you during the identity parade? How exactly did you feel they were confusing you?'

'It wasn't confusing me so much as . . . I don't know . . . pushing me. Making me say it was him.'

'The defendant?'

'Yes. I looked at them all and at first I didn't recognise any of them, I'd never seen any of them before. But then I looked again and I really did think it was him – the one in the . . . that man. And they sort of hurried me . . . I felt they . . . oh, I don't know. I'm sorry.'

Judge Palmer: 'Mrs Phipps, would you like some water? It's very important that you finish answering the defence questions but you should take as long as you need.'

'I'm all right, thank you. Thank you, Your Honour.'

Mr Jeremy Brockyear: 'When you were viewing the identity line-up, what made you hesitate and then look again at the accused?'

'I just recognised something about him . . . maybe the way he was standing and his – well, his shape.'

'His shape?'

'People have a shape, don't they?'

'Was his shape the shape of the man you saw in the garden?'

'I think it was, yes.'

'So was there something unusual about his shape?'

'Not really . . . only it was . . . I recognised it.'

'You will have to do better than that, Mrs Phipps.'

Mr Anthony Elrod: 'Your Honour . . .'

Judge Palmer: 'Indeed, Mr Elrod.'

Mr Jeremy Brockyear: 'I'm sorry, I withdraw that remark, Your Honour. Mrs Phipps, look at the accused now. Look at him carefully.'

Judge Palmer, to the accused: 'Will you please stand?'

Mr Jeremy Brockyear: 'Mrs Phipps?'

'Yes. He's got a – a sort of particular shape. It's up here – his shoulders. They slope.'

'So, solely on the basis of his shape – the way his shoulders slope – you identified the accused as the man you saw in the garden that night. You positively identified him as the same man, is that correct?'

'I suppose it is. Only I'm still telling you that they pushed me . . . the detectives. They persuaded me I was doing the right thing.'

24 MAY, 2002

'Will the next witness take the stand please?'

A thin woman, early thirties, worn-looking. Hair tied back, blonde with streaks. Strong black eyeliner.

Clerk to the court: 'Will you please state your name?'

'Lynne Margaret Keyes.'

Mr Anthony Elrod: 'You are the wife of the defendant, are you not?'

'Yes.'

Eyes on anyone, anything, but not once on him.

'Will you please tell the court where you were on the night of 17 July 2001 between the hours of midnight and 6 a.m.?'

'At home in bed.'

'Do you know where the defendant was at the same time?'

'I've said to the police. It's in my statement. He was at home in bed with me.'

'So the defendant's alibi for the night of 17 July was that he was at home, in bed, with you? Do you also confirm that you were at home in bed with the defendant on the nights of 30 July and 4 August 2001 between midnight and 6 a.m.?'

'Yes.'

'Do you and your husband share a bed?'

'Of course we do.'

'Always?'

'What do you mean, always?'

'Sometimes married couples have a spare room and one of them may sleep there if, say, they are ill or returning home very late? It's not uncommon.'

'I wouldn't know.'

'Are you a sound sleeper, Mrs Keyes? Or do you wake in the night sometimes?'

'No. I work hard. I'm shattered. I never wake up.'

'What work do you do?'

'I work in a dry cleaner's.'

'I suppose the fumes from the cleaning machines are likely to make you sleepy, aren't they?'

Mr Anthony Elrod: 'Your Honour, I object strongly to the implication behind this question which is completely irrelevant to –'

Judge Palmer: 'I agree. Mr Elrod, please stick to facts not speculation about fumes and machines.'

Mr Jeremy Brockyear: 'Is the defendant a good sleeper as well?'

'Yes. Never stirs.'

'How can you be sure? If you sleep so soundly yourself, as you have just told us, how do you know that he's doing the same? How can you be sure he hasn't got up and made himself a cup of tea?'

11

'Oh, I'm sure of that all right. If he wanted tea he'd wake me up and ask me to get it.'

'And would you?'

'Of course I would.'

'Isn't that a bit unusual these days? For a wife to get up in the middle of the night and make tea for her husband if he wants it, even though she has just been sound asleep? Wouldn't most men these days get their own tea?'

'He's not most men.'

'Can you explain what you mean by that?'

'Your Honour, I object –'

'Wait a moment, Mr Brockyear. Mr Elrod, I hope this line of questioning has a relevant point because it sounds dangerously like vague speculation about the nature of the population at large.'

'I'm coming to the point now, Your Honour.'

'Then please do so.'

'Mrs Keyes, have you ever refused to make tea when your husband demanded it – in the middle of the night?'

'No.'

'Has he demanded it?'

'No. I said. He sleeps as good as I do.'

'Does your husband snore?'

'Yes, like bloody roadworks.'

'How do you know?'

'I can hear him in my sleep.'

'I see. Would you be aware of it if he got out of bed in the middle of the night and went to the bathroom?'

'I don't know. No, I probably wouldn't unless he put the light on.'

'And would he do that? Put the light on?'

'Shouldn't think so.'

'So he could get out of bed, leave your bedroom, go to the bathroom, come back, get into bed again – and you would never know it?'

'I probably wouldn't, no.'

'You probably wouldn't know that he had been up? Have you ever woken because he'd gone in and out of the room?'

'Not – if I have it's not for years. I told you, I'm –'

'. . . a very deep sleeper. Yes. So if he were not only to get out of bed and leave the room in the middle of the night, but go downstairs, open the door and leave the house altogether, you wouldn't be aware of that either?'

'No. I –'

'I put it to you that in fact he did exactly that three times, on the nights in question, when you have stated that the accused was at home in bed with you. He got up and left the house and went out to commit three terrible murders of three innocent elderly women. He left you sound asleep and he returned later, got back into bed and you were still asleep – because you sleep well, as you have told us. You knew nothing else. Because you were undisturbed by his comings and goings. Isn't that why your evidence is flawed? Why there has to be considerable doubt about its reliability? I am not accusing you of giving false evidence, Mrs Keyes. You are under oath and you know it. No, your evidence is not reliable and the alibi you have given to the accused is not reliable because when he left the house and returned on those nights, you were sound asleep. Isn't this the case?'

'I don't know.'

'Mrs Keyes, will you look at the accused please?'

'Your Honour, I . . .'

Judge Palmer: 'Do you have a good reason for that request, Mr Elrod?'

'I do, Your Honour, if you will allow me.'

Judge Palmer: 'Objection overruled. There is no reason why the witness should not be asked to look at the accused. He is her husband, after all.'

'Thank you, Your Honour. Mrs Keyes, will you please look at the accused? No, not a swift glance. Please look at him steadily. You seem nervous. Are you? Are you afraid of your husband, Mrs Keyes?'

'Your Hon–'

Judge Palmer: 'No, Mr Brockyear, sit down. Carry on, Mr Elrod.'

'Mrs Keyes, you obviously have difficulty answering that question, just as you had difficulty looking steadily at the accused. I put it to you that you are afraid of him – very afraid. That you have been afraid of him for a long time and that if you had not given him an alibi for the nights of 17 July, 30 July and 4 August 2001, you were afraid – terrified – of his reaction. He told you what to say and you said it. You know perfectly well that he got up and went out on those nights. You didn't know why but you would never ask. You covered for the accused because you were and you are afraid of what he would do to you if you did not. Isn't that the truth, Mrs Keyes? You are quite safe. You can say yes without looking at him now. Isn't that the truth?'

'Yes.'

'I'm sorry, I can barely hear you, Mrs Keyes, and I doubt if the rest of the court, and especially the jury, could either. Will you please speak up and answer again?'

A long hesitation.

'Yes.'

From the *Daily Telegraph*, 28 May, 2002

Alan Frederick Keyes is alleged to have slipped out late at night, leaving his wife asleep, and made his way on foot and without use of a torch to the complex of sheltered bungalows collectively known as Meadow View Close which lies about a mile and a half from his home at 33 Westway Road, Crofton. He was familiar with the bungalows because he had worked there several times as a builder, and has occasionally been called out to them at weekends and bank holidays to do urgent repairs.

Keyes is charged with the murders of Carrie Millicent Gage (88), Sara Pearce (76) and Angela Daphne Kavanagh (80), all of whom lived near to one another in the complex. Mr Anthony Elrod QC, prosecuting, said that Keyes had known precisely where to go, how to gain entrance to the bungalows, and how to cover his tracks and destroy any traces of his presence on the three nights. He had entered the bedrooms of Carrie Gage and Angela Kavanagh and strangled them. Sara Pearcè was suffering from a chest cold and had been finding it difficult to sleep lying down and Keyes had found her sitting in an armchair in the living room.

Keyes overpowered these elderly ladies without any difficulty, but there was evidence that Angela Kavanagh had fought for her life and Keyes had to use some force to kill her.

Mr Elrod said: 'You deliberately and callously, and with meticulous planning, went out to the bungalows belonging to these elderly women who, although they all lived alone, thought they were safe in their beds in a secure environment. You used previous knowledge of the layouts to enter each one and find each of the victims. You then strangled them without reason, motive or remorse, and left them to be discovered by their traumatised neighbours the next or on a subsequent day. You took care to destroy all evidence of your presence and left the complex to walk back through the dark and deserted streets to your own house. There you let yourself in, and went back to bed beside your still-sleeping wife. These are terrible, wicked acts of which you are accused. But you have lied consistently during every questioning, you have shown not only no remorse but, unbelievably, barely any interest in these events. You ostentatiously yawned your way through at least one cross-examination, and at several points, on hearing the details of these dreadful murders which you had so calmly committed, you smiled. I hope the minds of the jury are concentrating hard upon that, as well as upon all the other facts because they beggar belief.'

The trial continues.

The best one was the one in the chair. The one who was already awake. That was the best, no question.

'What do you reckon?'

It was warm outside, sun, blue sky. The trees round the perimeter of the Crown Court building were bright fresh green.

Charlie Vogt and Rod Hawkins sat on a low wall out of the press of people near the main doors, with plastic cups of coffee and Hawkins with his usual hand-rolled. Charlie was local, Rod Hawkins senior crime reporter for the *Mail*. They went back a decade, to the dilapidated old Crown Court building in Barnsley Square and several high-profile murder trials, but this was the biggest here for some years. Television, radio, every national paper as well as the agencies and the regional press were represented, a couple were doing updates as the trial had rolled on. They were nearing the end now, prosecution and defence had put their cases, the judge had summed up and instructed the jury, who had gone out the previous afternoon, and were still out. It was twenty minutes to three.

Charlie swigged his coffee. 'I reckon the same as you reckon, don't I?'

'I reckon you do.'

'Felt sorry for the defence – but then you always do in these open-and-shut jobs. Hiding to nothing.'

'Didn't think he was that strong actually.'

17

'Oh come on, he saw the forensics woman off a treat. Love it when they pull bloody experts apart.'

'"Dr Culshaw, would you please tell the court on what basis you and your expert colleagues have decided that the odds of the DNA from samples from the accused and the cat is one in two hundred million? How many feline DNA samples have been tested?"'

'"Members of the jury, can you be certain, beyond all reasonable doubt, that you can rely on this new, emerging and so far unproven and previously untested type of evidence? If you cannot then you are under a duty to acquit."'

Rod dragged on the last of his disintegrating roll-up. 'Right, that was a good left hook on one dodgy expert . . . come on.'

'Oh I know, I know. He's guilty as hell, I just like it when I see a defence come out fighting. He had her in a corner.'

'Bugger it though, Charlie . . . you got any elderly rellies?'

'Nah. My mum died ten years ago, breast cancer, Dad remarried, lives in Tenerife. You?'

'Too right I have, my mum is eighty-one, her sisters are, what, eighty and eighty-three, something like that, and they're looking to sheltered housing, got their names on lists. We've encouraged it – there are some smashing places not far from Pete and me, we'd make sure Mum and Aunt Lil were all right – the other's up in Liverpool. But now what? The old girls are out of their minds with fretting about all this and I don't blame them. Think about it. Locked and bolted, alarm by the bed, all tucked up and he slides in through the bedroom window, not a peep . . .'

'What do you reckon about the wife?'

'Shitting herself, what else?'

'I bet there's a record somewhere – she rang the emergencies when he'd been having a go. She's terrified of him.'

'Weasely little bugger as well.'

'Not sure I agree . . . Easy to read something into how they look when you know they've murdered old ladies but he's not that bad-looking actually. He's not stupid either.'

'Psychopaths aren't stupid.'

'Is he one?'

'Murdering three defenceless old women in their beds

18

without any motive other than his own sick enjoyment? Not a psychopath?'

'Take your point. I wonder how it started? Where do these things start? Nothing – then three in a row. Come on! Got to be more to it.'

'Something back then. Always is. He had a witch for a gran. That's what he'll come up with, on appeal.'

'No chance.'

'None. You know, doing this job, you get a bit blasé.'

Rod shook his head. 'There's always one though.'

'That's what I mean. You get blasé until someone like Keyes comes along and you get the creeps just looking at him, knowing what he's done, hearing it all. You never get used to the worst of them.'

'My dad did this job. Sat through the whole Moors murderers trial for the *News and Star*. It did for him. He said he knew he'd never get it out of his head. He used to brood about it. Really did for him.'

'I bet. Jeez.'

'They're going back in . . .'

Rod crushed his plastic cup and threw it in a bin as they walked towards the steps. People were pushing back through the doors, relatives of the dead women easily picked out by the way they hung back in separate little groups, by the dead look in their eyes, the way it had left its marks on their faces. Grey-suited CID, having a last quick drag on a cigarette. The press pack, trying to stay near the back, ready to exit fast and phone in the verdict when it came.

Charlie Vogt held the door open to let in a woman he knew from CID. She nodded to the defendant who had just come back into the dock and made a face. Alan Frederick Keyes. Not bad-looking. Charlie wanted to ask her for a woman's opinion but there was no chance, she'd gone along the benches. Besides, was it relevant? He had the blood of three elderly women victims on his hands. What else mattered except that he'd be leaving that dock and going down for life? Charlie felt a spurt of bile come into his mouth. Once in a while, anger and loathing turned your stomach.

19

The door bumped to immediately behind him, deadening the murmur from outside, where the news that the jury was back had filtered out. The TV cameras were getting ready, furry mikes swaying on their extension rods. Beyond them, the crowd had filled out, the news having travelled like magic to those who had just been waiting to hear and then shout, punch the air, call Keyes every filthy name they knew. The murders of little children and old ladies – it brought the mass hatred out and roaring like nothing else.

In the street beyond, cars slowed, even a bus, faces peered out before the lights went green again. Police stood about, arms folded, watching, waiting to hold back the rush when the prison van emerged later, Alan Keyes in the back, cowering as fists thudded on the metal sides.

I read about this Russian. He was fine but then when there was a full moon – or maybe it was a new moon? – no, a full moon, definitely – when that came, he went mad inside, he had to do it, that was when his head was bursting.

The court was full to overflowing, the public benches packed. Charlie and Rod stood pressed against the doors poised like greyhounds in the slips.

You never got over it, Charlie thought, your blood pressure went up with the tension and the excitement. Better than any film, better than any book. There was just nothing to beat it, watching the drama of the court, eyes on the face of the accused when the word rang out. Guilty. The look of the relatives, as they flushed with joy, relief, exhaustion. And then the tears. These were the final moments when he knew why he was in his job. Every time.

Alan Keyes stood, face pale, eyes down, his police minder impassive.

Charlie's throat constricted suddenly as he looked at him, looked at his hands on the rail. Normal hands. Nothing ugly, nothing out of the ordinary. Not a strangler's hands, whatever they were supposed to look like. But the hands, resting on the rail, hands like his own, one beside the other resting on the rail, resting on the . . . those hands had . . . Charlie did not think of himself as hard-boiled but you did get accustomed. But nothing prepared you for the first time you saw the man in front of you, ordinary, innocent until proved guilty, however clear his guilt was, nothing prepared you for the sight of a man like Keyes, there in the flesh, a man who had strangled three elderly women. Nothing. He couldn't actually look at Keyes at all now.

The lawyers sat together, shuffling papers, fiddling with box lids, not looking at one another, not murmuring. Just waiting.

And then the door opened and they were filing back, concentrating on taking their seats, faces showing the strain, or else blank and showing nothing at all. Seven women, five men. Charlie was struck by the expression on the face of the first woman, young with dark hair pulled tightly back, bright red scarf round her neck. She looked desperate – desperate to get out? Desperate because she was afraid? Desperate not to catch the eye of the man in the dock, the ordinary-looking man with the unremarkable hands who had strangled three old women? Charlie watched as she sat down and stared straight ahead of her, glazed, tired. What had she done to deserve the past nine days, hearing appalling things, looking at terrible images? Been a citizen. Nothing else. He had often wondered how people like her coped when it had all been forgotten, but the images and the accounts wouldn't leave their heads. Once you knew something you couldn't un-know it. His Dad had tried to un-know what he'd learned about Hindley and Brady for years afterwards.

'All rise.'

The court murmured; the murmur faded. Everything went still. Every eye focused on the jury benches.

In the centre of the public benches a knot of elderly women sat together. Two had their hands on one another's arms. Even across the room, Charlie Vogt could see a pulse jumping in the neck of one, the pallor of her neighbour. Behind them, two middle-aged couples, one with a young woman. He knew relatives when he saw them, very quiet, very still, desperate for this to be over, to see justice being done. Hang in there, he willed them, a few minutes and then you walk away, to try and put your lives back together.

Schoolteacher, he thought, as the foreman of the jury stood. Bit young, no more than early thirties. Several of them looked even younger. When he'd done jury service himself, several years ago now, there had only been two women and the men had all been late-middle-aged.

'Have you reached a verdict on all three counts?'

'Yes.'

23

'On the first count, do you find the accused guilty or not guilty?' The first murder, of Carrie Gage.

Charlie realised that he was clenching his hand, digging his nails into the palm.

'Not guilty.'

The intake of breath was like a sigh round the room.

'Is this a unanimous verdict?'

'Yes.'

'On the second count of murder, do you find the accused guilty or not guilty?' Sarah Pearce.

'Not guilty.'

The murmur was faint, like a tide coming in. Charlie glanced at the faces of the legal teams. Impassive except for the junior barrister of the defence who had put her hand briefly to her mouth.

'Is this verdict unanimous?'

'Yes.'

'On the third count, do you find the accused guilty or not guilty?'

His Honour Judge Palmer was sitting very straight, hands out of sight, expression unreadable.

'Not guilty.'

'Is –'

The gavel came down hard on the bench and the judge's voice roared out: 'Order. There must be silence for the clerk to finish his question to the foreman of the jury and for him to reply. If there is not I will clear this court immediately.' Judge Palmer's eye glittered. 'These are the gravest moments of the entire trial and the court *must* remain silent. Will the clerk now please ask his final question and the foreman give his reply?'

'Is this verdict unanimous?'

The foreman had been composed. Now, briefly, he looked terrified. 'Yes.'

The court erupted.

Charlie caught Rod Hawkins's eye as they both made for the doors through the crowd, trying to beat the rest of the press pack to it. By the time they were outside, the news was ahead of them, the corridors and front lobby of the building seething with people relaying the verdict. The few police on duty outside were calling for backup and getting into position to restrain the crowd and prevent them surging into the front area.

Charlie Vogt stood on the steps listening to the sound of anger that was growing, becoming a roar, like a tide racing in towards the court building.

Rod was beside him. 'What the fuck . . . That lot are baying for blood. What's going on in there?'

Without consulting one another, they headed back down the corridor, weaving and dodging through the crowd coming out, others standing about the hall in stunned groups, briefs charging past, gowns flying.

By the time they reached the doors of Court Number 1 the mass of people had left, driven out by the officials. Alan Keyes stood in the centre of a knot of police and clerks, his defence counsel and the rest of the team behind.

'You can't stop me,' Keyes was shouting, his eyes swerving round the group, to the clerk, to the uniforms, to anyone who could hear him. 'I'm a free man, didn't you bloody hear? Not guilty, not guilty, not guilty. He said so.' He pointed to the empty jury benches, then round to the judge's chair. 'Not guilty. I'm a free man and I'm going out there to tell them so, I'm walking out those gates, I'm discharged, and you can't hold me in here.'

The police stood conferring. The barristers looked troubled.

Charlie and Rod stood by the doorway, their presence not noticed in the scrum.

'He's right,' Charlie said.

'If he goes out through those doors he'll get torn apart.'

'Get the fuck out of my way, clod.' Keyes lurched forward and took a swing at the copper. The blow made no contact, but within seconds Keyes's hands were behind his back and cuffed. In the middle of yells and curses of protest, he was cautioned by one officer and restrained by two others.

'Gotcha,' Rod said. 'Though they can't hold him for a fist that didn't connect.'

But Charlie Vogt was already sprinting for the doors.

She had sandals on with a mended strap which came apart as she ran so that she tripped and almost fell on her face, but didn't quite, recovered, ran on. She had never moved so fast; she felt like a rugby player dodging this one coming towards her, then that one, then a knot of them together. She ducked and dived, banged her arm against the corridor wall, dodged again, almost pushing over a man carrying a pile of boxes, hearing them crash to the floor as she went on, through a pair of swing doors, down a long corridor where there were fewer people, right to the end, down a short flight of steps. Then there was only the sound of her own running footsteps, the broken sandal slapping unevenly on the tiled floor. She had no idea where she was going but somehow she'd get out, even if it was much later, when they'd all gone. When he'd gone. She'd find an empty room and stay there until the place went quiet, people had all left for home, then try. Nobody would notice her.

Two doors. It reminded her of a corridor at school with classrooms on either side. Both were locked. She stopped to get her breath. From a window high up in the wall, she could hear a muffled sound, like the sea murmuring. A siren, then another came wailing towards the building.

The corridor smelled of chemical cleaner, making her sneeze, and the sneeze seemed to crash around the walls and down the corridor, echoing and re-echoing. She froze, pressing herself against the wall. Nobody came. It was quiet again.

Then, a corner and another door and when she pushed against it, it swung open. She almost fell inside with relief and leaned on the other side, catching her breath in gulps, shaking. And all she could think of was his face when the words were said.

Not guilty.

And again.

Not guilty.

Not guilty.

As they were spoken, and a second before the whole courtroom exploded, he had half turned his head and looked straight at her and the expression on his face, in his eyes, had frozen her to ice.

Now, the ice was thawing and melting, water ran through her body, and she felt herself sliding slowly down until she was a pool on the floor.

You feel as if the top of your head will blow off. Two minutes after you've done it you can do anything. You're, like, the most powerful person in the universe. You're God.

'You can't keep me here. I'm a free man, you heard, "not guilty". So I should be walking out there not in here with you. And I want my brief.'

'Listen –'

'No, you listen, dickhead –'

'You can have what you want, Keyes – tea, coffee, something to eat – you can't have your brief because he's gone home, and you don't need your brief because you're not charged with anything.'

'You cuffed me, you dragged me down here, I'm not guilty, you heard.'

'Yes,' the DI said, 'I heard.' He didn't keep the contempt out of his voice. 'You attacked a police officer –'

'I missed. Didn't get near him. You saw.'

'Right.'

They were in a small holding room in the basement of the court building. It had a metal table and two chairs. Alan Keyes sat in one, the DI in the other. A uniformed constable stood outside the door.

Alan Keyes stood up and pushed the chair over as the door opened and two more men came in.

'DCS Granger. Sit down, Keyes –'

'Mr Keyes to you.'

'Sit down,' the Superintendent said, not looking at Keyes.

The other man, who was tall and upright and had a thin

moustache, stood beside him. Said nothing. Did not give his name.

'Now listen –'

'I want to walk out of this fucking building, I have every right to walk out of –'

'I said listen. There is no way I can let you walk out. No way. Why do you think you were cuffed and brought down here?'

'I didn't bloody touch him, I missed, I only swung at him, it wasn't –'

'It had nothing to do with you taking a swing at a police officer – we cuffed you and brought you down here and are keeping you in custody *for your own safety.*'

'Piss off.'

'Because if we'd let you strut out of that court you probably wouldn't have made it a dozen yards down the corridor, you would have been set upon, battered to death – my guess is you would have lasted three minutes. You've got no idea, have you? There's several hundred angry people out there, and there'd be more arriving if we hadn't closed the road. You know why, *Mr* Keyes? That's right, you can look terrified.'

Keyes twisted his expression back into defiance.

'I'd be terrified if I was in your shoes. You still want to walk out there? You're not under arrest, as you say, and I've no power to stop you, but it's my duty to advise you that you should remain under police protection.'

'You'll get rid of them, won't you? Clear the street. Tear gas, water cannon, they'll bugger off.' Keyes smiled. 'I'm an innocent man.'

'Yes, Mr Keyes. Which won't prevent the public forming its own judgement and acting accordingly. So I'm advising you to accept police protection . . .'

'What's that mean? You put me up in a nice hotel?'

'We do not.'

'I'm not going back inside that fu–'

'Nor in prison custody. You'll be taken to a place of safety and then we'll discuss the choices you might have.'

'What choices? I'm going back home, aren't I? You can't stop me, a man's home is his castle, a man's –'

'Shut up, Keyes.'

'What is this place of safety then? How long do I have to stay?'

'As I said, you're not under arrest. We are giving you advice for your own protection. You're free to take it. Or not. I can't tell you where you'd go but you would stay until such time as we decide you would be safe to leave. Or make other arrangements.'

'What other arrangements?'

'You'll be given various options within the next few weeks.'

'Weeks? I'm not staying away from my own home for weeks. You tell the wife where I'll be, do you?'

'No.'

'She'll wonder then. She'll report me missing.'

'We'll deal with that. Right.' The Super stood. 'You'll be collected in an hour or so.'

'Now look –'

'Don't start again.' the Super said. 'I'm beginning to lose patience.'

It was cold. Her leg was numb and her arm painful where it was bent back against the wall. But she knew where she was. After a moment she began to straighten her body cautiously, to sit up, stand.

She never wore a watch. How long had she been – what? Unconscious? Asleep? Why would she be unconscious if she hadn't hit her head? Or been hit?

She hadn't. No one had been in here, no one knew where she was. He didn't. Couldn't. The toilets were somewhere in the bowels of the building – she had glimpsed them as she ran down endless corridors, through sets of doors, to get away. Get away.

She found the toilet, pulled the door to but didn't lock it, then went to the basins and splashed her face with a handful of cold water. Pulled her hair out of its band and retied it.

And then there was a clatter outside in the corridor, something metal, and the door opened.

'It's all right, I'm going, I'm going . . .'

The cleaner put down his bucket and mop and stood barring the door.

'You hold on – who are you? You shouldn't be here. This building's closed. You on the run?'

'No. Not like you think.'

'Like what then?'

Lynne Keyes told him. He was a huge man with a big belly under his overall, a thick neck, big feet, big hands. But he stood still and listened to every word and she felt safe with him. He could have reached out and strangled her without any trouble but she had no fear that he would. They were different sort of men, the stranglers.

'I hear you. Only you can't stop here. We go in an hour, place is locked and that's it.'

'I can't go home.'

'Tell you what, him getting off – it's shocked everyone rigid.'

She said nothing.

'So . . .' He pushed the mop down into the bucket and twisted it this way and that. The smell of pine disinfectant came off it. 'You must have family. You go to them. Family's better than friends, times like yours. Come with me, I'll slip you out the side door, no one'll be around, and I never saw you, all right?'

She followed him because there was nothing else she could do and because he was kind and she trusted him. The side door had an iron bar that he lifted up and a chain and padlock that he opened. She could see a passageway. Concrete steps.

The door banged and the iron bar came across it on the other side.

Just clocked what it is. They're afraid. They're terrified, of me. Everybody is. When I get to walk down that street, they'll shake with fear. But they've got no reason. Well, have they? 'Not guilty' he said, didn't he? 'Not guilty. Not guilty. Not guilty.'

So what have they got to be afraid of?

'I . . . I need to speak to someone. I need someone to help me.'

'What department do you want?'

'I don't know. Police. Just the police . . . I need help, I'm . . . I'm scared out of my skull, I daren't go home . . .'

'Domestic violence? Hold on.'

He had never let her have a mobile and she thought she hadn't really minded. Now she did. Now, after she'd walked for ages to find a phone box that worked, she was put on hold. She waited, but she wasn't put through to anyone else and the woman didn't come back.

The town was very quiet. A pub on the corner was emptying out, cabs drawing away from the rank. She slipped round the backstreets, across the bus station, in and out of the mesh of streets near the railway line. She felt better because the flat was right on the other side of town. She knew what he'd be doing – she had a sudden flash of him, sitting in the brown leather chair with a can, watching the news. Watching himself on it, smirking, raising his can to the screen.

Lynne Keyes shivered.

The only person left was Hilary. It was a long walk – she had no money for a bus fare, but the last one would have gone anyway. Her sandal strap had broken completely so she had to pinch her toes together to keep it on and there was already one blister on the side of her foot. Walk to Hilary's? She sat down on the low wall in front of a house. Drawn curtains. Glow from

33

a lamp. Flicker from a TV. She wanted to knock and ask them to let her in.

It took almost an hour to get to Hilary's because she had to keep stopping to fiddle with her sandal and try and move it away from the blister.

Cumberland Avenue. Nice houses. Not large but modern with decent gardens. She'd wanted to move out this way but he wouldn't. She'd never properly understood why, until all this had come out. He wouldn't have been able to get up in the night and slip out, do what he did, slip back, no need for the van.

She dragged herself the last hundred yards to Hilary's, all the energy gone out of her, but at least the lights were still on. Hilary was seven years younger than her, same dad, different mother. They hadn't spent a lot of time together when they were younger but they'd picked up later, got on well. She felt such relief walking up the front path it was like heat running through her.

She rang. The sound on the television went off. She waited. No one came to the door. She rang again. After a moment or two, footsteps.

'Who is it?'

'Lynne.'

Nothing. Then the door opened a few inches on the chain. She could see her sister's hand, the side of her head, her shoulder.

'Hil? It's me.'

'What do you want?'

'Can I come in?'

'What for?'

She couldn't believe what she was hearing but then she realised. 'It's OK. I'm on my own.'

'It's late and Mike's on a night shift. He's not here.'

'What's that got to do with anything? Let me in, Hil. I'm cold, my foot's hurt, and I've walked miles.'

'What for? What are you doing here?'

'I daren't go home.'

'For Christ's sake, are you daft or something? I don't care if you are my sister, you know what happened today, and it's all over the news. He murdered three women, Lynne, and how they managed to find him not guilty God only knows. So now he's

34

a free man and you're wetting yourself and in your shoes so would I be. I'm sorry for you. Only you're not coming in and staying here, I'm on my own with the kids and –'

'He wouldn't come here.'

'Of course he'd come here. Where else could you be? He'll know and he'd come and I'm not having it. Go and check into a B & B.'

'I haven't got any money, Hil . . .'

Hilary swore and pushed the door closed again, muttering to her to wait.

'Here, but that's it, don't come back here, Lynne. I'm sorry but I'm not taking the risk. Go on, you'll get somewhere if you hurry up.' Her hand, with a twenty-pound note in it, came through the opening.

She stood after the door had closed and the chain and bolts been drawn, the money clenched in her hand. The lights went out downstairs. A low one went on in the bedroom. She looked up, wondering if Hil would change her mind. But she wouldn't and who could blame her? She was right. It was one place he'd come looking, and Mike was on nights so she was on her own with two kids.

She turned away and began to walk slowly back down the road. Twenty quid wasn't enough for a night's B & B, even if she could find one to take her in at this time and without even a toothbrush. Come on.

The main road was deserted. She took off both her shoes now, it was easier than having the strap rub on the raw blister. She walked without thinking, back towards the town, not wanting to put the thought of going home into her mind. Where else? She stumbled, pain shooting up through the sole of her bare foot where she had trodden on a stone.

There was a bus stop, with a half-shelter and an iron seat, and when she sat down in the dark and put her hand on her foot to soothe it, the hand came away wet with blood. Only now did she cry.

The lights of a car washed over her. The car pulled in a few yards ahead. She didn't need that, some guy on the prowl thinking she was a tart. She got up, about to run, in spite of her foot.

Now it was a torch in her face. 'Hold on a minute.'

The last puff of energy drained away and she sat down heavily on the bench.

The copper was joined by his mate. 'Are you all right, love?'

'No,' Lynne said. 'Since you ask.'

They could have done anything, quizzed her for soliciting, checked her for drugs, asked to see ID, anything at all. What they actually did was put her in the back of the patrol car and take her to the Crofton A & E. It was empty apart from a mother and child who went into a cubicle as Lynne arrived.

No one seemed to have recognised her, not the policemen, nor the nurse who cleaned up her foot or the doctor who stitched it. One of the coppers got her a cup of tea from the machine.

The radio in the car was yattering to itself but apparently no one wanted these two.

'Right, we'll take you home and see you in. Got any painkillers? Used to give you those at the hospital. Not any more.'

She told them the address because she'd given up now, too weary to think of anywhere else. In any case, where was there?

She felt safe in the car. But when they turned into the street she began to shake. Her stomach turned over.

'This one, is it?'

'Next . . . it's one up. Thank you . . . thanks a lot.'

'All right, I'll see you in.'

'No,' Lynne said, scrambling out and almost falling as her foot hit the pavement. 'I'm fine. Thanks.'

She had to hop up the path. The copper had got out and he stood there, his torch following her all the way.

'Thanks.' But she whispered it, terrified he would hear, waiting for the light to go on.

The radio started to gabble and the copper was inside and the car was slewing round. They had had a call and they didn't pause and that had to wake him, the racket of the engine and the tyres. She waited, hand on the wall. There were no lights on, downstairs, next door, opposite. Nobody to hear. Not that anyone ever heard anything.

Her foot was throbbing. She just wanted to get in, take some aspirin, lie down.

She slid the key into the lock almost silently, used to doing it. Crept into the hall. If she could get the tablets from the kitchen cupboard without waking him, she'd lie down on the sofa. That drove him mad but she'd face him in the morning, tell a story about coming home late, Hilary giving her a lift, not wanting to disturb him.

Her heart was pounding so hard it hurt her chest.

The kitchen was just as she'd left it that morning, her tea mug in the sink. Nothing else.

The flat had the empty silence she had grown used to during the months he had been in prison waiting for the trial. She sensed it. Felt it.

She went carefully across the hall, listening, listening. Opened the door of the bedroom. He had heard her, she knew, but not let on, stayed in the dark, waiting, waiting. He had done that before.

He was not asleep because there was no snoring, no puff of breath in and out. Nothing. She edged the door open. The last time he had been behind it, waiting for her. Waiting.

It was ages before she dared reach out to the switch.

The light blazed into the empty room.

PART TWO

LAFFERTON, 2012

Two

Judith had told Richard she thought the funeral would be small. 'Not many people here knew Marie-Elise – she'd only been in Lafferton a couple of years.'

She was wrong. There were three undertakers' cars behind the hearse leaving her old friend's terraced house in the Apostles and starting the slow crawl through town and out onto the bypass to the crematorium. Several people driving their own cars followed.

It was a bitterly cold day. Snow was lying along the verges, but the sun shone out of an enamel-blue sky. The early-afternoon light was brittle. Another hard frost tonight then.

The hearse turned carefully out onto the Old Bevham Road and stopped at the red lights.

Judith was remembering summers in the Lot Valley with Marie-Elise and her family when Don was alive, holidays with their children swimming in the lakes and picnicking every day, drinking wine at a table on the veranda. They had never lost touch, and after Marie-Elise's husband died she had first come to visit and then, later, to live in Lafferton. It had seemed a strange choice, a new life in an unfamiliar place, and perhaps it had been a mistake in some respects because, almost from the start, Marie-Elise had been unwell. But she was a stalwart woman, and made friends as easily as a young child. Before

41

long, she had a wide circle of people around her. Judith had loved meeting up but never had to worry that Marie-Elise might feel upset if they didn't for weeks at a time. One thing her friend had never done after the first couple of uneasy suppers was visit Hallam House when Richard was there. They had disliked each other from the start and Marie-Elise had solved the problem once and for all by telling Judith as much. 'I come to see you and only you, Judith. We do not see eye to each other's eye, your Richard and your old friend. It happens. N'importe.'

Richard did not like many people. For a time, after their marriage, he had tried to be accepting and pleasant to Judith's friends but hadn't kept it up and she had understood, knowing that at heart he was not unwelcoming or antisocial, simply a man who preferred his own company, or hers and sometimes that of his family.

The traffic lights were slow. Judith caught a glimpse of Marie-Elise's son and daughter sitting in the hearse, Simone black-veiled.

Just then, a cyclist appeared from nowhere and dashed across as the lights were changing. As she did so, she glanced to her left, taking in the hearse. In a panic, she stopped and tried to turn back. But the traffic was already moving forward. The hearse, going at only a few miles an hour, managed to avoid running into her and the rest of the funeral procession remained stationary. Any other driver would have had the car door open and been shouting abuse at the cyclist. The hearse driver merely sat and waited. By this time, the inner lane of cars as well as those moving southbound were speeding up. The cyclist stood frozen, terror on her face beneath her blue helmet, and then Judith saw that it was Molly, Cat's medical student lodger. There was clearly something wrong and she wondered if she could safely get out and help her. Molly seemed unable to move in either direction but stood holding her bike and staring white-faced at the hearse, the driver, the coffin.

A van coming fast up to the junction seemed to startle her into a dash to the pavement, where she stopped and leaned over the saddle as if her stomach was hurting her.

*　　*　　*

42

The crematorium funeral was an even more dismal event than usual, mainly because the two hymns chosen were French, which few of them knew, and the officiating priest had not known Marie-Elise or apparently made any effort to find out much about her.

Judith left the gathering as soon as she could, not to go into town, as she had planned, but out to the farmhouse to see if Molly had arrived back in one piece.

There was a meeting of Emma's reading group that evening, and it was Cat's turn to host, so Molly usually made the cake and then put Felix to bed, helped Hannah with homework or watched television with her, so that Cat was free.

Emma's bookshop in the Lanes had been a success but would not have been so without initiatives, in the form of reading and creative writing groups, author visits and talks. Now, she had plans for a book festival over one weekend in the spring and Judith was brainstorming ideas with her and being co-organiser of the event itself. As she drove now she had ideas for both another potential visitor and a competition, and tried to keep them in mind until she could stop and write them down. If the festival was a success, perhaps they could extend it to a long weekend the following year.

'It's what Lafferton has been waiting for,' she had said to Richard, coming home from the first meeting.

'I doubt it.'

His lack of interest and support, in this as in other things, made her unhappy. She thought he had changed, always fought his corner, especially when Simon criticised him for coldness and lack of interest in whatever activities and occupations Meriel, his first wife, had had. When Judith and he had married, he had at least made a show of enthusiasm in what she was doing, even though that had not been very much, outside of home and her life with him. In the past few months, even that had gone.

The car dashboard already showed minus four and the brightness was draining out of the sky as she pulled up in the drive. The winter had been too mild. Now, in February, it had caught up on them with a week of snow and blizzards which had mainly thawed in a single day, but given way to bitter cold. Judith pulled on her coat and scarf even for the few yards to the front door. The house was in darkness, Cat's car not in the drive. It was half-term so there was no school run and Sam was away for the week.

Wookie the Yorkshire terrier had already heard her and was yelping with delight. Judith took out her key, but the front door was unlocked. She went in and through to the kitchen to switch on the lights. Mephisto opened half an eye from his deep slumber on the sofa, took her in, and closed it again.

There were no preparations under way for the evening ahead, no cake cooling on the rack, no chocolate shortbread under cling film, no coffee pot and mugs set out. Molly had always made a start by this time, conscientious as she was.

Judith went into the hall and listened but the house had the oddly hollow sound of one that was empty.

She went back to the kitchen and put on the kettle. Cat had not been expecting her of course and had probably taken the children somewhere, but what about Molly? Where was she?

Judith went to the side door and looked across the yard. Molly's bicycle was propped against the log shed.

Three

'It's times like this, you know?'

Cat had got out of her car and was watching Hannah who had flung her arms round Judith and was shouting something in her ear. Felix was still strapped into his seat playing an intricate game involving a plastic box, a tiny silver ball and nine holes on a painted golf course. Games of this demanding kind were now his passion and his skills were better than those of anyone else in the family by a mile. He was privately hoping that his presence would be overlooked and he would be left in the car all night to play this one.

Judith unwound herself from Hannah's embrace. 'Slow down, slow down . . . something amazing has happened and I can't make out what.'

'I've been asked to go *back*.'

'Back?'

'For a second audition. For the part in the *film*, duh.'

'Hannah!'

'Sorry.'

'The film? Do I know about this?'

'No,' Cat said, leaning into the car to unbuckle Felix, who squealed in protest, flailed his arms and dropped the game. Cat watched it slide under the car out of reach.

'I'll get it, I'll get it, the more good deeds I do the more I'll get the part.'

'Doesn't work like that, I'm afraid. But thanks.'

Judith took Felix's hand, and they went into the house. 'What was it you said? "Times like this . . ."?'

'Times when something good happens, even a small something, and I still want to rush home and tell Chris. Madness.'

'No. Perfectly normal and understandable. You're so hard on yourself.'

'I thought you were at a funeral. Marie-Elise?'

'I was. I went.'

'Upsetting?'

'Not exactly. But I couldn't face the bun fight.'

Cat took out the cafetière.

'Besides, it looks as if you're going to need help for tonight.'

'Oh?'

Judith told her. 'I was just going to investigate upstairs in case she was ill.'

'It would be seeing the hearse,' Cat said. 'I'll go up in a minute.'

'I can –'

'Thanks but it had better be me. She talks to me.'

Hannah came in triumphantly with the game and handed it to Felix who rushed off to the den with it.

How tall she is, suddenly, Judith thought, tall and slender and no longer really a child.

Hannah's eyes were bright with excitement. 'OK, listen, some film people came to drama class and asked some of us if we wanted to audition, people they picked out, and I was one, only loads of us were. We went into the side room and did some stuff and they talked to us and they said they'd let us know if they wanted to see any of us again and I forgot all about it and today we got the letter and they want to see ME ME ME ME again. I have to go to an audition room, in a hotel, next week.'

'That's fantastic, Hanny! Well done!'

'Yes, though of course nothing might come of it, I'm not getting my hopes up.'

Judith heard Cat's warning words being repeated.

'So what's the film?'

'*A Christmas Carol*. I'd be one of the Cratchit family. Have you ever heard of it?'

Cat left them making preparations for last-minute baking to feed the book group, and went upstairs.

A thin line of light showed under Molly's door.

'Can I come in?'

A moment's pause, then a murmur.

Molly was curled on the bean bag, wrapped tightly in a fleece, although her sitting room was warm. The previous year Cat had rearranged the west side of the farmhouse so that Molly could have a sitting room, bedroom and bathroom which led from one another. The original thought had been that when her boyfriend Rob, now a junior doctor, came to stay, they needn't feel they had to be part of the family house. But Rob had found it difficult to cope with the change in Molly since the attack on her by Leo Fison, now known locally as 'Dr Death', and he had broken up with her just before Christmas. 'Trust a man not to do things by halves,' Cat had said in fury. But Molly had shrugged. 'Who can blame him? Look at me.'

She glanced up as the door opened, but did not move.

'What happened?'

'God, just when you think it's OK, just when you think you really have turned a corner, something happens . . . life just chucks stuff at me, Cat, and I can't deal with it.'

'Judith saw you. She was driving behind the funeral cars. Panic attack?'

Molly turned her head away. Her post-trauma and anxiety state embarrassed her. Anything could trigger it – reading about a violent crime, or seeing something connected with death, like the hearse today. She had nightmares about being murdered, about lying on a bed waiting to be given a lethal syringe, about being locked in a room. Ambulances unloading bodies, bodies on slabs, bodies in freezer drawers, bodies found lying in fields and by the roadside. It had been clear that she couldn't take her final medical exams and she'd been given a year's deferral without penalty. Privately, Cat doubted if she could ever continue, unless the anxiety and its accompanying depression went away for good. Medicine demanded, among other things, a lifetime of familiarity with the dying and dead. Meanwhile, Molly was having regular counselling, talking to Cat if she needed to and helping to organise the

47

Deerbon household, without giving her future profession much thought. That could come later.

'I've been so much better. I really thought I was beginning to crack this. It's so bloody unfair.'

'The trouble is, you can't plan these things and it's the randomness you need to deal with. If you were told you had to walk into the undertaker's parlour in a week's time you could prepare yourself and do it. You'd be fine. Seeing a funeral cortège with hearse and coffin right in front of you when you're crossing the road . . . that's the sort of thing that throws you. Perfect trigger for a panic attack.'

'I know I'm not going to die, I know it. But what I know in my head doesn't seem to help at the time. I feel as if I'm dying and then I start seeing Fison everywhere. Some man on a poster looks like him, a bloke walking past me turns into him and he's seen me, he's not going to let me get away this time.' She gave a small scream of anger and frustration and pushed her face down into the blanket. Cat went and put her arms round the girl and tried to calm her.

'Moll, you are getting better, you're so much improved.'

'It's going on too long.'

'No quick fixes. We want you to get better and stay better. It's hard but it does work.'

Molly sat up suddenly. 'Oh my God, I've forgotten the book group, I was supposed to be making the cake and –'

'Don't worry, Judith's here, she's taken over.'

'Oh God, I'm a total failure. I can't go on being like this.'

'You won't. Listen, make a list of all the days this week when you've functioned normally, had no panics, nothing. You'll find it's six out of seven.'

'It doesn't feel like that inside my head.'

'Your head is giving you an unbalanced version of events, that's all.'

'You know, when I saw that . . . hearse and the coffin inside, I just . . . if I just jumped in front of it, it would all be OK. I'd have sorted it.'

'Is this something you've thought about before? Killing yourself?'

Molly winced and turned her head away.

'You thought that killing yourself by jumping in front of a car would solve everything? Who for? And suppose you just injured yourself very badly, became a paraplegic or were brain-damaged but didn't die?'

Molly sat up and looked at her. 'What are you trying to do to me?'

'Get you to face it.'

'I face it all the time. All the bloody time.'

'Do you? Molly, if you actually do want to die and plan to make it happen there's nothing I can do to stop you. But I doubt if you actually do. You want to live a full, normal life, have a career, be happy, fulfil your very great potential, and you will.'

'How can I do that so long as I feel so crap? My head's all over the place, I can't get rid of those thoughts, that memory, I can't make it un-happen, I can't pick it out of my head and chuck it away. It's there. It plays itself over and over again like a film on a loop. I need to get out of myself and I can't.'

Half an hour later, Cat had persuaded her to come down and supervise the cake-making, something she knew would make Molly feel better because she took great pride in her baking, which she claimed had kept her sane when working for her exams. The moment she went into the kitchen and saw the cooling rack on the table she took over, persuading Judith that she needed to leave the cake in for another five minutes, suggesting a different consistency for the fudge icing. Hannah had gone to start her homework with some reluctance.

'What about something savoury as well?'

'Cheese straws?'

Molly snorted. 'Parmesan crunch and paprika biscuits. I'll do them. What's the book you're discussing tonight?'

'Graham Greene. *The End of the Affair*. We avoid the latest best-sellers.'

'I've never read any Greene. But I'm pretty ill-read all round.' Molly, who was not tall, pulled out the stool to reach a top cupboard. 'Maybe I should join, but I'm not sure I'd get through the books. I'm better as Catering Manager.'

'She looks fine,' Judith said, helping Cat set out the china and glasses in the sitting room.

'She isn't but she's always better being busy and being with other people. I still have to remind her of it. She says she feels safe on her own in her room.'

'Poor girl. It's going to take a long time for her to forget what happened.'

'She never will. People don't. Damage limitation is what we're about. How's Dad?'

Judith made a face. 'Not sure. Something's ruffled his feathers lately but of course he won't tell me what.'

'I thought he talked to you. You've made him open up far more than the rest of us ever did. Mum just gave up and got on with her own life but you've been brilliant. Even Simon thinks you discovered there was a heart beating under there.'

'You know there is.'

'Yes. I do. Mostly. Not everyone agrees.'

'I'll wait a few more days for him to tell me, and if he doesn't, I'll have to tackle him. He'll let it fester on and it's making him bad-tempered and unreasonable.'

Cat glanced up from opening a bottle of wine. Judith usually sounded upbeat, even jokey, about Richard Serrailler's moods, with which she had always coped so well. Now she sounded weary.

From the kitchen came the sound of the radio, and Molly singing softly along with Bette Midler. Cat was relieved she could stop worrying about one person in the household, at least for the rest of the evening. But that storm clouds were gathering and thunder rumbling in the distance she had no doubt at all.

Four

In a rash moment, Harry Fletcher had promised to take Karen to see Will Young for her birthday, should he be performing anywhere within a reasonable distance of Lafferton. He had felt pretty safe there until Karen had pointed out a Will Young gig in Bevham.

'You couldn't bloody make it up.'

He hung back until the last minute hoping the venue would be sold out. Just his luck that there were a handful of returns when he rang up.

'It was absolutely bloody brilliant. Thanks, love.' Karen leaned over to pinch his cheek. 'You didn't hate it that much, did you? Honestly?'

'Nah, I coped. He can sing a song, I'll give him that. Just not the sort of stuff I'd pay good money for again.'

'And we know what that stuff is.'

'So, what's wrong with Status Quo?'

It was gone eleven as they drove into Lafferton, the roads quiet. Karen's friend Lorna was babysitting the boys, the first time they'd had a proper night out together since Harvey was born and Harvey was rising four. Bradley was five and they'd left him for the odd night quite early on. Bradley had slept and generally been laid-back with life. Harvey did not sleep and battled against life twenty-four seven.

'Want to stop for a drink? Might as well make the most of it.'

'Great. I'll just text Lorn, see if –'

'No you won't. If there's been any sort of problem she would have texted you.'

'I suppose.'

'And has she?'

'No, only she won't be expecting us to stop out till midnight. Maybe I should just give her a quick bell.'

'She'll be fine.'

'It's Harvey . . .'

'I know it's Harvey. It's always Harvey That's why I slipped him a double brandy in his beaker.'

He saw her face and let out a bellow of laughter.

They parked at the end of the Lanes. Reynaldo's Club was on the opposite corner.

'You can't,' Karen said.

'It's gone eleven, it'll be fine. Yellow perils don't work night shifts.'

'Coppers do.'

'When did you last see a copper around at this time? Correction. When did you last see a copper?'

Harry took her arm. Seconds later, he was dragging her back by it onto the pavement as a black 4 x 4 with a wide, ugly bull bar swung round the corner, two wheels over the kerb and all but mowing them both down.

Karen screamed. The car drove up the cobbles of the pedestrian-only street, reversed, swung round again, and within seconds was ramming backwards fast into the plate-glass windows of the jeweller's shop. The noise was sickening.

Harry spun round and as he pulled Karen, shielding her with his body, he was unlocking the door of his car. He pushed her inside, and ran round, trying to find his mobile as he did so, but Karen already had hers out, hands shaking. He was starting the car as a man with a stocking over his face was coming down the street towards them, his arm raised.

'Oh God, Oh God . . .'

'Get down, Kaz, lie down.'

The bullet hit the side of the car as he accelerated up the road, grabbing Karen's phone as he went. Behind them in the Lanes, shouting, more glass breaking, another shot, the engine of the 4 x 4 revving and revving.

'Oh God.'

'It's all right. You're safe. It's OK, Karen. Yes . . .' he said into the phone, 'In the Lanes, opposite Reynaldo's.'

The jeweller was standing on the glass-strewn pavement in shock, his dressing gown unbelted, his feet bare and bleeding. Others stood around him – the man who owned the deli, Emma from the bookshop, still in her coat after a late return from the reading group meeting at Cat's, the antique dealer and his wife, white-faced but already organising coffee from the room at the back of the shop.

PC Robin Crabbe felt someone tugging at his arm.

'You'd better listen to me. Two of them had guns, they waved them all over the place.'

'Thank you, sir, if you could just stand over there off the pavement, out of the way of the broken window . . .'

'It was like in a film. That's what I thought, you see, I thought, "This is people making a film, this is going to be worth seeing" and then –'

'I'll take statements in a minute, sir, don't go away but if you could just –'

'I knew you wouldn't listen.'

Crabbe turned his back, that being the best way of dealing with the sort of man who tugged at your elbow, didn't draw breath and smelled of drink.

'Over here.' His partner was beckoning. 'Forget him, it's Nobby Parks.'

'Says they had guns.'

'They did, two of them had sawn-off shotguns,' Laurence from the deli said.

'I'll get the tape round, someone's going to slice their foot in half on this lot. Anyway, who's Nobby Parks?'

'Pain in the arse. Hangs about town at night, turns up like a bad penny. Lives in one of the old canal cottages. Here's the backup. That guy needs the paramedics as well.'

The circus swung into action. Lights were set up, crime-scene tape run out, more blues and twos screeching up. Information went round.

'They had guns. Two of them. Should be hung.'

'Get bloody Parks out of here,' the DI said.

'Says he saw it all . . .'

'Right, and I saw the men land on the moon. Get him out of here. Someone can go round to his fleapit tomorrow but we need to get these guys sorted.'

PC Crabbe went over. 'You,' he said. 'Home. Now.'

'I want a lift.'

'You'll walk.'

He took a stringy-feeling arm beneath a greasy jacket and marched Parks to the end of the street. 'Go.'

The man went, swearing under his breath, leaving a beer and body smell on the air behind him.

'It's minus seven,' PC Crabbe said. 'Anyone realise that?'

The DI who had turned up and taken charge glanced round at him. 'And your point is?'

'Sir.'

But Nobby Parks had been right, he thought, going over to the huddle of people just inside the bookshop doorway, it was like a film set. The lights. Radios going. Sudden bursts of movement, then a pause. A film. Weird. But not a film.

What in God's name was happening to the quiet town he'd grown up in?

Slugs I worked with, creepy-crawly neighbours, bastard who was my dad. Wife. Ex-wife now. No, I haven't forgotten them. Haven't forgotten a thing. What it was like, the old biddies, cops, stir, brief, then the Big Bang. I haven't forgotten a speck of it.

Keeps me warm at night. Even now.

Five

The day before had been so cold the streets were empty at three o'clock in the afternoon. Even the teenagers who usually hung about in all weathers without a coat between them had fled to the warmth of coffee shops and, as a last resort, their own homes.

The pavements were scoured by a bitter north-east wind, the sky looked flayed, as if it had lost a skin. But just after midnight, the wind veered south-west then dropped, and clouds piled up.

'Here we go,' PC Crabbe said to his partner, turning the patrol car into the square. He flicked on the wipers as the first flakes came swirling down. Twenty minutes later, there was a covering over the pavements and the verges. An hour later, the roof outlines of the cathedral and the houses in the Close were softened by half an inch of snow.

Judith Serrailler, sleepless, looked out of the window and saw a pure white garden. Five miles away, Cat Deerbon, going to Felix who was thrashing and shouting from the depths of a nightmare, looked out of his window onto a world of dizzying flakes. It was still extremely cold but the wind no longer cut through every chink in the woodwork, roof and walls of the old house.

It snowed on, piling into drives and gateways and entrances.

'Look at it this way,' PC Crabbe said, 'it'll be mayhem in the morning but at least nobody'll be out thieving and ram-raiding.'

Dawn seeped in late with a puffy, leaden sky and snow piling upon snow upon snow.

Bradley and Harvey Fletcher were out in the back garden soon after seven, padded up like moonwalkers, throwing snow, kicking snow, rolling in snow, chasing the next door's cat through it, pushing piles of it up against the passage door, starting the foundations of a snowman, but within half an hour, inside, hands scarlet and burning, drinking hot chocolate.

'Don't mither your dad. He's got to get to work somehow through this lot.'

'He can stay at home and play.'

'Right, and that'd pay the bills. Not. Now you heard me, leave Dad alone to have his breakfast, finish your chocolate, and then either back outside or play in your room.'

The boys sped upstairs as their father crossed the landing and reached out to pull Harvey to him in a bear hug.

'AAAGGGH. Will you do a snowman with us?'

'Be dark by the time I get in, son. Saturday, no prob.'

'But –'

'You deaf now or what?'

Harvey shot into the room he shared with his brother, and banged the door. It was the big back bedroom, with plenty of room for their space-station layout and the moon-landing area they were making out of scrumpled-up newspaper and Play-Doh.

Downstairs, Harry Fletcher sat down in front of a plate of beans and sausages, toast, butter, a pot of tea and the paper. He ate, drank and read without speaking for seven or eight minutes, then looked up.

'You all right, love?'

Karen poured her own tea. She worked in the kitchens at the Sir Eric Anderson Comprehensive and was usually out of the house bang on a quarter to eight. Half-term: toast and a cup of tea with the paper when Harry had finished with it. Luxury.

She spread jam on her toast. Harry was looking at her.

'Scum,' he said. 'They want to throw away the key. They could have run you over.'

'They can't throw away the key before they've caught them.'

57

'And are they going to do that?' He made a nasty sound in his throat.

Karen wished he hadn't brought up the whole thing about the ram raid. He kept on asking her if she was all right, if she'd hurt herself, if she had nightmares about it all. But she didn't. She was fine, so long as she could put it out of her mind for good.

So long as Harry would let her.

Six

By eight thirty, Cat was half a mile out of Lafferton, having left home just before seven. The snowploughs were out and gritters had been down the bypass the previous night but off the main roads driving was treacherous and she inched along behind other vehicles. They had rung from the hospice at six thirty and she had given advice and medication changes over the phone but there was one patient she should see, though the nursing staff were more than competent. She had learned to let go, to give them a lead but then let them do their job, though sometimes instinct told her she ought to go into Imogen House herself and since her days as a junior hospital doctor she had listened to that instinct.

She had left Hannah and Felix with Molly. It was half-term, and the children would have a day of snowmen, snowball fights, baking and hot chocolate. What Molly would undoubtedly be good at, sometime in the future when her problems were behind her, was a family of her own. There would be plenty of young men where Rob had come from.

At the end of the Flixton Road Cat came to a halt. Two cars had spun into the ditch, two drivers were standing in the cold watching two police patrolmen on their walkie-talkies. All four were shaking their heads.

One of the officers came across, waving his arms to Cat. 'You'll have to go back, madam, it's – oh, morning, Doc. You trying to get to work?'

'To the hospice, yes. Which way can I try?'

'Hold on.'

Five minutes later, the patrol cars had moved and she was given a clear passage. Occasionally, it paid to be a doctor and the DCS's sister.

There were only two cars in the parking spaces of Imogen House and the snow was piled up in mounds to either side. But Lois, on the reception desk, was as cheerful as ever. 'I walked in, and I haven't walked so far for years, but you know, once I got going I loved it. I'm glad you made it, Cat – she's been asking for you.'

Cat shook her head. Often, as a palliative care doctor, she had to accept that there was little or nothing she could do for a patient, in the sense of curing them or extending their lives, though there was usually something to be done about pain relief, and almost always she could talk, listen, comfort. But once in a while, either because of the nature of the disease or the patient's temperament, she felt helpless. Redundant was a word that came to mind then. Yes, she thought, going down the corridor now, in spite of all her medical training and experience, plus her innate instinct, sometimes that was it – she was redundant.

As she tapped and opened the door of Room 9, she had the momentary sensation of moving into some other-world. The sun on the snow outside radiated a silver-white light through the windows, which touched the far wall and made it gleam in an unearthly way. To die now, in this, must surely be to die in radiant peace, no matter what else was involved.

And what was one of the first things you learned? Cat asked herself, going in. Don't sentimentalise to make yourself feel better.

Jocelyn Forbes was propped up on the backrest and pillows, breathing with the help of an oxygen mask. She was parchment-pale and her arms on the sheet were so thin the bone gleamed through the skin. She had motor neurone disease, but she was patient, uncomplaining and, above all, sanguine about her situation and apparently not unhappy. MND did not usually cause clinical depression but Cat was surprised how cheerful she was. It was her daughter Penny who had sunk into a downward spiral of misery and helplessness. Much against her will she had gone with her mother to a foreign clinic where Jocelyn had intended to commit assisted suicide. The experience had been so scarring, frightening and unpleasant that Jocelyn had fled home and continued with her life, physically deteriorating but able to get enjoyment out of the smallest things. At first, Penny, an unmarried barrister, had moved back home to be her carer but she had found it upsetting and difficult, so she had returned to her flat, struggling with work and having psychiatric help and medication for depression, unable to face even calling on Jocelyn briefly. There had been a succession of carers, some good, some poor, none lasting. After spells in hospital and in a private home, Jocelyn's condition had deteriorated so far that Cat felt justified in admitting her to the hospice.

Now she was in the terminal stages of her illness, tube-fed, paralysed, breathing with help, only able to speak a little before becoming exhausted. But serene, accepting and – cheerful? Yes. It sounded so unlikely, Cat thought, closing the door quietly behind her. But true.

Jocelyn Forbes opened her eyes, eyes that were fading, growing paler. What had been sapphire was now rinsed-out blue-grey. But there was a light in them still, and she smiled through the oxygen mask. Cat went over to her bed. The eyes did the talking now. The eyes said, 'Please take this thing off my face.' Cat did so, and quickly replaced it with two thin tubes that went into her nose and connected via them to the oxygen supply.

Jocelyn smiled. She could move the fingers of both hands, but not raise an arm. She could turn her head a little to the left but not to the right. Her neck was supported in a collar, which made sleeping uncomfortable. She did not complain. Every time she had seen Cat after her return from what she always referred to as 'the death place' she had said she had been given back her life, or given a new life, had been reborn or even resurrected, that everything she saw and heard and smelled and sensed was as if for the first time. Colours were brighter, sounds clearer, the air sweeter and fresher, music and voices more melodic. She had been overwhelmed by it, before being plunged into a period of darkness and guilt.

61

'I'm not religious,' she had said to Cat, 'I didn't believe in God before and I don't believe in God now. This didn't do anything to change my mind. I know some people want to end their lives for good reasons and I think they have a right to, so why do I feel guilty? Because I've no right to have this delight in life given back to me, have I? In spite of the illness, and what the end will be, I wake every morning with such joy in every single thing. I don't deserve it.'

'Do we all get what we deserve and not what we don't? I'm a believer and you are not but it often seems so random – like the good and the bad being chopped up into pieces and thrown out of a window. They just fall where they fall . . .'

'It rains on the just and on the unjust, you mean. So which am I?'

Her condition had deteriorated over the past week. Now, as Cat took her wrist to feel the weak, uneven pulse and saw that breathing had become a great strain, she doubted if she would live much longer, and was glad it was so. Her quality of life was almost at zero.

Jocelyn smiled her lopsided smile and Cat wiped the dribble from the side of her mouth.

'Thank you,' she mouthed. No sound came, just the hiss of breath.

'I'm glad I could get here. Have they told you how much snow there's been? Lafferton is at a standstill.'

The smile again. It lit her face, even though the muscles of her mouth could barely move now.

For the next half-hour Cat stayed, and it took all of that for Jocelyn Forbes to try and say what she wanted to say. But by Cat's questioning, repeating and suggesting, while Jocelyn tried again and again, they came to an understanding. It was simple and not unexpected. She did not want to be kept alive with tubes, or to be resuscitated, or to be given antibiotics if she contracted pneumonia. She knew that she was close to death and she was ready to die. She also knew that Penny would not be there. She had not seen her daughter for almost two months.

Outside, someone was shovelling snow, someone else

laughing. The tyres of a car spun round. Jocelyn dozed, woke to the noise, smiled at Cat. Dozed again.

Cat would stay as long as she could before starting on the general work of the day because this was why she did the job. Over recent years there had been a major push for 'hospice at home' – terminally ill patients looked after by palliative care nurses, away from both hospital and hospice. Sometimes, it was the perfect answer but Cat was concerned that the chief reason for pressure on patients to die at home was financial. Often, because of a shortage of trained nurses, difficulty over pain and symptom relief, and even more because of unsuitable home circumstances, she was sure that dying there was not the right option. Better a good death in a hospice than a distressing one at home. But there were great pressures on doctors not to refer patients to a hospice unless it was unavoidable and that made Imogen House's very existence look uncertain. How would people like Jocelyn Forbes fare then? They would be sent into a general hospital, and the whole palliative care movement itself would start to be undermined.

The rest of the morning was unusually busy, with other arrangements being made for patients who could not get in because of the weather, relatives stranded on their way to visit, which left those who were longing to see them disappointed and distressed. And inevitably some staff had also found it impossible to get in to work.

Cat was trying to adjust a syringe pump with which one of the junior nurses was having trouble, when her pager bleeped. She ignored it. The syringe failed again and she decided to give up on it and get a replacement. As she went out into the corridor, Lois was waiting.

'I've had Hannah on the phone. I think you'd better come. I'll get someone else to sort that out.'

Cat ran.

'Mum, Molly hasn't got up yet. I've given Felix some cereal. What shall I do next?'

'Have you been up to her room and knocked on the door?'

'Loads of times. She didn't answer.'

'Did you go in?'

'No, because you always say Molly's room is her room and –'

'I know, but this is different Hanny. Take the handset with you and go upstairs. Bang on the door again, and if she doesn't answer, go in . . . and then tell me what's happening.'

'She often sleeps in but I thought I ought to ask.'

'You did the right thing. Don't worry though, because sometimes she takes tablets if she can't sleep and they make her woozy.'

She could hear Hannah's breathing into the receiver and her footsteps up the stairs. From below came the sound of the television, fading as she climbed higher.

'I'm here.'

'Right, bang hard first.'

The banging started, stopped, started again.

'She isn't answering.'

'OK, in you go. If she's sound asleep try and wake her – but gently, don't yell in her ear or anything.'

'The curtains are still drawn but it's really light because of the snow. She's turned the other way in the bed.'

'Put your hand on her shoulder and shake her gently, and say her name as you do. Just go on doing that until she stirs. The tablets make her sleep quite deeply.'

She waited. Heard Hannah's steps. Hannah's voice, saying Molly's name quietly. Then more loudly.

'Mummy?'

'Has she moved yet?'

'No. Mummy, I think she's dead.'

Seven

'Oh, wow!'

They had walked through the belt of pine trees, their footsteps making almost no sound on the grassy-sandy ground. No one else was about and there had only been three other cars parked down the long avenue that led from the road. They had stepped onto the last section of boardwalk and then clambered down the uneven steps cut out of the bank, which were treacherous with ice. And then, they were on the beach.

'Wow!' Sam said again as they stood looking ahead to the faint gleaming line of sea far away, to the silver rivulets of frozen water criss-crossing the flat sand, and to the snow, a couple of inches deep and extending seventy or eighty yards out, until it thinned away to nothing. The huge sky was pale silver blue, arching over them and over the sea, the sand, the shoreline. There was no wind at all so that apart from the plaintive mewling and calling of seabirds it was utterly quiet. They stepped down onto the snow.

'The sand is *frozen*,' Sam said. Then he went a few yards on and bent down beside one of the saltwater pools. 'And the seawater is frozen. Wow!'

Simon looked at his watch, as smothered with dials as the control panel of an aircraft, as Cat had said when he'd bought it the previous year. Among the dials was a temperature gauge, showing minus one.

'Come on . . .' Sam began to run.

Simon followed more slowly, looking up at the sky as a skein of geese went honking over, arrowing their way inland. To the right, two dog walkers stood watching their black Labradors chase one another, the wild barks coming sharply across the flat open space. Another walker came in sight, terriers giddy with delight, kicking up sand and glittering arcs of icy water that caught the brilliant sunlight.

Sam was far out now, his scarlet woollen hat marking where he was running towards the tide's edge.

They had been in Norfolk for three days, had another four to come and Sam was like the gleeful child he had once been, shedding his adolescence and the mild sullenness and sloth that went with it as he walked beside Simon for miles, read and listened to bands via his headphones while Simon drew seabirds and church towers, apparently perfectly happy. They had rented a cottage just off the marshes, which in winter were quiet, the streets of the little villages empty except for twitchers and dog walkers. Simon had promised for too long to take his nephew away so that they could have some time together. There had been plans for climbing in Wales, walking over the Brecon Beacons, visiting the Scottish island where he had enjoyed a month's leave, but one thing or another, usually police work, had got in the way. This Norfolk week, Sam's half-term, had been arranged at the last minute. The snow had come as they had headed east. They ate in pubs, or Simon shopped for local fish and cooked it with great panfuls of chips, and Sam was easy company. The one thing he did not do much was talk. Simon, used to being by himself on holiday and when walking or out with his sketchbook, was untroubled by this but his sister had hinted strongly that the week away would be helpful in getting Sam to tell his troubles, and perhaps talk about his father. It was almost four years since Chris Deerbon's death. Felix was too young to remember and Hannah had cried all of her emotions out, but Sam had barely reacted and would never answer questions about his feelings.

Now, looking at him bounding and leaping at the far shoreline, Simon saw a boy full of energy and simple *joie de vivre*. Did it matter whether he talked about himself or not? Simon was sure

66

that Sam would not share his feelings. He was not like his mother, nor the kind of open, cheerful character his father had been. Sam was like him.

He waved to his nephew. The plan was to head round the three miles to Wells and enjoy hot chocolate and buns in the cafe there, before returning to the cottage, but as Sam started to jump over the pools on his way back, Simon's mobile rang.

'Where are you? I've been trying to reach you . . .'

Rachel. Rachel, whom he loved as he had never loved a woman before. Rachel, who was loving in return, and generous, understanding of both his job and his personality. Rachel, who struggled with her conscience, married as she was to a man in the late stages of a debilitating illness but who had given his tacit blessing to her relationship with Simon. Rachel, who was beautiful, troubled, loyal. Rachel, whose calls he had been avoiding since coming here.

'Hi, sweetheart. Sorry – this is a black area for phone signals.'

'Can you hear me OK now?'

'Yes, I'm on Holkham Beach and it seems to be fine but if we get cut off suddenly you'll know why . . .'

'I just wanted to hear you. I wasn't sure where you were.'

'I've brought Sam up here for half-term . . . good for us both. Sorry, I should have let you know but it was all arranged at the last minute.'

'You never have to apologise to me.'

'No. No, I know that. You're . . .'

He felt ashamed of himself – something else new to him in his relationships with women. Rachel never demanded, never blamed. She accepted him as he was, loved him for that. Yet still he sometimes felt a desperate need to dodge, to run, to shut her out.

'Is everything all right – are you?'

'Fine, now I know you are.'

'And . . .?'

'The same. It's no life, Simon. He . . . yesterday I went into the room and he didn't hear me and he was crying. Not loudly. Not so I could hear. He was just quietly crying. I can't describe . . .'

'Listen, I'm coming back on Friday. I'll ring you when I'm home. Come there. You can, can't you?'

He heard a faint sound, then silence, as the phone signal went.

'Hey, it's fantastic out there, the sea's so thin . . .'

Simon laughed in spite of himself.

'Thin? The sea is thin?'

'Shallow then, but you know . . . it's so far out and the edge . . . no, I was right first time. It's thin.'

'Great description. You look frozen, Sam, your face has gone blue round the edges.'

Sam thumped his arm, and they turned to walk towards the headland. Close to the bank the snow was thick, and the ground slippery, so they moved out to the sand which was firm and clear.

'I could so live here,' Sam said, whirring his arms round, 'right here and never go back. Can we do that?'

'I wish. But we'll come again, no problem. Glad you like it.'

'Love it.'

'Know the feeling. I get fed up with being landlocked.'

'Move then. Move up here. I could come as well.'

'Job, Sam.'

'They have police in Norfolk.'

'Yes. Not necessarily ones likely to move over and make room for a new DCS.'

'You don't know that. How do you know till you ask?'

'True. There's other stuff, though.'

'Like what?'

Ahead, a spaniel raced towards a flock of geese, feeding on a stretch of marshy grass, and the geese rose as one, making a racket that gave Simon an excuse not to reply. After the geese had left and they had walked round the spit of land into the next bay, Sam said, 'I'd leave like a shot.'

'What – home, friends, all that?'

'Yup.'

'Right. Why?'

'Just stuff.'

'Always is.'

'You still on with Rachel?'

Simon missed a step. Caught up. Did not look at him.

'It's OK, I won't say anything. I don't.'

'Fine. It's just that – people don't know.'

'Ha.' Sam gave him a sharp look. 'You'd be surprised. Or maybe you wouldn't.'

'You been listening at keyholes?'

'Shut up.'

'Sorry. No, I know you wouldn't.'

'Nothing to listen to anyway. Mum doesn't say anything – only I did just happen to hear her and Judith talking, that's all. Then I saw you.'

'Where?'

'Went to someone's house and his dad was driving me back. Saw your car.'

'Sam . . .'

'Yeah, I know about it, her husband being ill, all that. Hey, look – hello!'

A Border terrier had come running up and dropped a ball at Sam's feet, before standing back and waiting, making little yaps of demand. Sam threw the ball far and fast. 'Wow, look at that.' The terrier went across the sand like a greyhound, splashing through pools and retrieving the ball.

'I miss Wookie,' Sam said. 'He'd have had a great week.'

'Next time, we bring him then.'

The dog came back with the ball, dropped it and looked at Sam. 'He's laughing,' Sam said. 'Look at that.'

Yes. A laughing dog. A laughing boy, throwing the blue ball away again. In the distance, some people were shouting, waving, trying to get the dog back.

Stuff, Simon thought. What 'stuff'? What would make him sure he could leave Lafferton at the click of his fingers, and be happy?

Stuff.

There was always stuff.

They were tucked into a sofa in the Wells Beach Cafe with two mugs of chocolate and a pile of hot buttered toast when Simon had a surge of anxiety about Rachel. He should have told her he was coming away. He should . . .

But it was Sam's mobile which rang next. When it did so, his face closed up so tightly it almost snapped. He looked at the screen, then got up quickly. 'No signal. Shan't be long.' He disappeared like a shadow through the door and out of sight.

Simon finished his hot chocolate. Sam. Stuff. Something was – well, what? He didn't know. Something. That was all.

The door opened on three people and one Border terrier, blue ball in its mouth, followed by Sam, who asked for more chocolate, then moved to the opposite sofa and bent over to make a long fuss of the dog. It was some time before he could be parted from it and when he was he scooted out of the door ahead of Simon, managing not to meet his eye. He bought two more drinks and slices of cherry cake. He would read the paper and wait. Hassling Sam would be counterproductive. The call would be from one of his friends – fourteen was the age when innocent phone calls suddenly became intensely private.

A second later he banged in through the door, face screwed up in panic.

'I just . . . I was just talking to . . .' He stood trying to get his breath.

'Hold on, calm down –'

Sam waved at him furiously, took several more quick breaths. 'I just stopped talking to Jake and it rang again and it was Mum, she tried you but she . . . and Molly . . . Molly . . . she's gone to hospital, but the roads are so bad down there, Mum said, they might not get there in time . . .'

'Sit down, Sam. Now, tell me slowly. What's happened?'

Eight

Harry answered the phone. It was gone eight, the boys were in bed, flat out after playing in the snow since the early morning. There was a smell of bacon coming from the kitchen and Harry had a bottle of lager in his hand. Things couldn't get better, he thought, picking up. Things could not get better. Funny that.

'Harry?'

'Hello, Rosemary. How are you?'

Rosemary didn't answer to the usual description of 'the wife's mother'. She never interfered, was always good-humoured and had her own life. She had welcomed Harry from the start, and never breathed a word of criticism. Harry would not have gone so far as to say that he loved Rosemary Poole but he had no problem with her at all.

'Karen's cooking supper – can she ring you back?'

'No, just give her a message . . .'

'Have you been OK in this weather? I meant to ring you only I know you've got the neighbours.'

'Oh yes, Geoff Payne has been wonderful, got a gang together, cleared everybody's front. No, I had a letter . . . post didn't get through until after two and then what with everything . . . only I've got one. One of those sheltered bungalows. You know – Duchess of Cornwall Close.'

'The new ones?'

'That's it. I've been allocated one. It was in the letter.'

Rosemary had been on the waiting list for sheltered

accommodation for three years, long before she needed it – she was only seventy-six now – but she had diabetes and the previous year a hip replacement operation had been unsuccessful. She was struggling to cope in the old three-bedroomed family house which had a big garden and was too far out of Lafferton.

'Now that's a bit of good news. When do you get the key?'

'Two weeks. The thing is, Harry . . .'

'You need help with moving. I'm working all hours but we'll sort something.'

'It's brand new. I can't get over it. Never moved into a brand-new house, Harry, I'm over the moon.'

He had a thin moustache, like kids draw on faces with a biro. He never took his eyes off me. Staring, staring. I hated him. But who else had I got?

'You're nobody. This is no-man's-land, here. You're not the person you were any longer and you're not the person you're going to be either. It's my job to graft that new person onto you until the graft takes and it's part of you – no, not part of you, that's wrong. You. It's you. Do you follow?'

I couldn't sleep for it. I'd get up and look out of the window onto that bloody square where they did their drill and I'd try not to think about it because it was the future and the future scared the shit out of me. What he said. The stuff he made me repeat after him. Scared me.

So I stood and looked out at the empty square and I thought about the past. I felt good then and they couldn't take that out of my head even if they took it in every other way. The past was mine and it'd always be there, to make me feel good.

Nine

Nights were best. Days, he mostly slept. People walked their dogs along the towpath past his shack and annoyed him, them chatting and the dogs barking, and when the kids went by on bikes the tyres made a screechy sound and that annoyed him too. Nights were best.

He generally went out, even in the rain. Didn't mind the rain. The snow he hadn't liked at all, it went over his shoes and soaked his trouser ends and once he got a few yards it was too deep anyway, so he stayed in. Got his stove going, got some soup on. Thought a lot.

But before the snow, it had been very good. Cold but good. He'd been walking for a bit, watching, listening, waiting, and then it had happened, right where he was. That had been a good bit of luck, the car reversing fast, the man and the woman on the corner nearly getting run over, then the crash of the shop window as they backed in. He'd felt his heart thump. He could have told the coppers everything because he'd seen everything, but they didn't want to know. It annoyed him. A lot of things annoyed him. He'd heard what one of them said – 'Get Parks out of here.' What for? He hadn't done anything and he had evidence. Nobody else had seen what he'd seen, which was all of it. Nobody else. He saw a lot of things at night that nobody else saw. He could have told the coppers plenty. But why would he? 'Get Parks out of here.' They'd no respect.

The snow had stopped and was starting to melt a bit, but he

wasn't going out unless he had to and he didn't have to yet. He'd got plenty of tins, he'd got tea. He was all right. By the time he had the feeling he had to go out at night or his head would burst, the snow would have gone.

He turned over the blanket and did the same with the old eiderdown, which had a rip in the top and stuffing coming out. He turned his pillow over as well. That was the bed made. The curtains at the windows were thick wool, made out of ancient coats strung together. They helped warm the room.

There was an upstairs room in the shack. Two rooms. But he hadn't been upstairs for fifteen years.

He took off his jacket, kept his trousers and jersey on. Got into bed again.

A siren sounded along the main road. Then it was quiet. Snow made everything quiet. It was just before noon.

Nobby Parks slept.

Ten

'Stay with us, Molly . . . stay with us. You all right there, Doc?'

Cat was cramped up beside the stretcher in the air ambulance, holding Molly's hand and watching the paramedic adjust the leads that were attached to her, recording everything, showing the faintest of pulses, the blood pressure so low it did not seem possible the girl could be alive. Her face was chalky and looked oddly flat beneath the oxygen mask, as if the features were sinking back into her head.

'Any idea how many she's taken?'

Cat shook her head. Molly had been prescribed antidepressants, tranquillisers and beta blockers by her GP. Cat had found two empty foil packs, one with a few tablets left, but she did not know how many there had been for Molly to take in the first place.

The helicopter began to descend. Out of the window, Cat could see nothing but white fields, tipped at a sick-making angle. Air ambulance pilots were skilled and experienced and she was not afraid, just queasy.

'Landing in two minutes. How's she doing?'

'Be glad to get there,' the paramedic said into his mouthpiece. Meaning, get a move on, we're losing her.

Cat agreed.

She had rung Hallam House before leaving the hospice but there had been no reply. She had left a message, then tried as many other people as she could think of, but either nobody answered or else her friends were marooned by the snow.

'I can look after Felix. We'll be fine. I know what not to do and you *have* to go in the ambulance with Molly.'

Cat had looked into her daughter's face. Hannah's expression was assured, serious.

Could she? How irresponsible would it be to leave her in charge of a five-year-old, when she had no idea how long it would be before she could get back?

'No,' she said. 'I know you're twelve and I know you're sensible, Hanny, but anything could happen.'

'Such as what? I won't cook anything, I won't answer the door, I won't –'

'Anything might happen.'

'You have to go with Molly. What if she wakes up and doesn't know what's happening or where she is? That'd be so scary. Listen . . .'

The helicopter had clattered over the house before coming down into the pony field where the snow had drifted high up against the barn, leaving patches of grass just visible.

Dear God, what should I do? Tell me what to do.

The answer came with the sound of an engine and Judith, driven in a neighbour's Land Rover.

'One minute.'

Cat had her hand over Molly's. She could still feel a thready pulse but in spite of the thermal blanket over her, the girl was cold.

Judith sat at the kitchen table with a mug of coffee and her laptop. Hannah was about to go into Cat's study and onto the computer.

'Han, I don't mind playing Internet Scrabble – I rather like it. I just don't see the point when we're under the same roof and there's a Scrabble board in the cupboard.'

'Nobody plays it with a board any more, the letters slip all over the place. I really thought Molly was dead.'

'I know, darling. It was frightening, but you did the right thing.'

'You can die quite a long time after you've taken an overdose. If it's paracetamol. I mean, like, days and days after. It makes your liver fail.'

'I know, but that wasn't what she took. Are you sure you don't want a drink of anything?'

'I might get some water in a minute. Everybody should drink plenty of water. You should. Coffee is full of caffeine, it can dehydrate you and it makes your heart race.'

It was difficult to extricate oneself from this sort of conversation with the health-obsessed Hannah. The phone came to her rescue.

'She's gone into intensive care. I didn't think we'd make it this far.'

'I can stay as long as I'm needed, you just decide as you think best.'

'What about Dad?'

There was a very slight pause before Judith said, 'I'll let him know.'

Cat was not too preoccupied to notice the pause, and the edge to her stepmother's voice.

I sometimes wonder what would happen if I said my old name. Not by accident. Said it, told someone. I had enough warnings about how you slip up, get caught off guard. Man comes to the door with a parcel. 'Name?' and before you know it, you've told him.

Eleven

There was still work to be done on the sheltered bungalows in Duchess of Cornwall Close and the maisonettes were nowhere near ready. The snow had delayed them for another three days and if it had been up to Nick and Piotr there would have been no turning up on day four either. Just after nine, the building manager had been on the phone to them both. Just before ten, they were on site, by which time Matt Williams was sitting on a window ledge drinking tea, having been at work since eight and well ahead with the wiring.

'I hate the bastard. I fuckin' hate him. What'd he have to come in for?'

Piotr shrugged. 'I guess the snow is going pretty quick.'

'Wouldn't be surprised if he hadn't fuckin' slept here, make sure he was on time. I fuckin' hate him.'

'So shut up with your fuckin' everything.'

Matt did not look up from his *Daily Mirror*.

The three of them had worked together for several weeks without exchanging more than a dozen words a day, mainly because of Nick.

'I just don't like him. Work with him if I have to but I don't have to like the bugger as well.'

'He's OK, this Matt, what's your trouble with him?'

To Piotr, dislike of a fellow human being who had done you no harm, without any reason forthcoming, was wrong. Matt said little, but worked hard.

The previous week, Nick had asked Piotr to have a pint at the end of the day and pointedly not invited Matt.

'Rude, I think, Nicko, you maybe ask him another day.'

'I fuckin' won't, I don't like him.'

'Wish you give me good reason.'

'He's shifty.'

'What is shifty?'

'Don't trust him.'

'How you don't?'

'Take it from me.'

'He maybe likes only to be with himself.'

'Maybe.'

Matt was on his hands and knees working on the wiring for a double power point. The room was full of light from the sun reflected off the snow but it was very cold.

Nick made a gesture with his foot towards Matt's backside. If he hadn't been so bloody keen to get back to work they could have had another day off. At least.

'There's a minimum temperature you're allowed to work.'

'For offices,' Matt said, not looking up.

'Course it's not only for offices. Why would it be only for offices?'

'Otherwise it would be for farmers ploughing fields and men on trawlers and roofers and scaffolders and gardeners and –'

'All right, all right. It's still fuckin' freezing.'

'Work harder then.'

Piotr was a tall, broad-shouldered man but it took all his strength to separate them. By the time he had, Nick had a bloody nose and a cut above his eye. Matt had tripped and fallen, got up again and charged back into the fight like a bull.

'You stop this, stupid bastards, quit. You quit, OK?'

Piotr looked Matt full in the face. Matt stared him out, angry, dangerous, fists still clenched.

Nick was trying to stop his nose bleeding by pressing it on his overall sleeve. Piotr handed him a paint rag but the blood went on dripping.

'Go get snow and push it onto your nose, it will work, like an ice pack. Maybe you also, Matt.'

81

Matt's cheekbone was flaring dark red. He shook his head and turned away, went back to the power point. He said nothing. He didn't need to – the set of his back was enough. Piotr got Nick to the door, and rolled some snow into a small heap in his palm. Splashes of blood stained the snow on the ground but the cold pack worked after a moment.

'He's fuckin' dangerous, he'd have bloody killed me, half a chance.'

'No. But maybe you better not kick him again in the arse, OK?'

'Bastard.'

'OK, now, back in, back to work. Better we all just work.'

They were meant to go on until four when the light began to fade but it was so cold that they left just after three. Matt walked out by himself. Nick and Piotr went in Nick's van. It was below freezing again but with the snow thawing all day, the roads were easier.

'Pint?'

'Cup of tea. Too soon for drink.'

'Get on.'

But Nick parked on a patch of waste ground near the Cypriot cafe.

'Face OK?'

'I could have him for this,' Nick said, feeling his nose.

'Stupid, you started it, you kicked him in the arse.'

'I hate him.'

'Yes, you say so over and over again. OK, you hate him. Still stupid to kick him in the arse.'

'He got a wife?'

'How do I know that? He never talks.'

'Won't have. He'd never get it together.'

'He looks OK, he's big strong man. Has to have.'

'Says his dad might have one of the bungalows.'

'Well, OK.' Piotr's mouth was stuffed full of doughnut. He washed it down with the last of his tea and went to get two more mugs.

Nick fingered his face, knowing he'd been stupid, knowing he'd have a great bruise the next morning, knowing what she'd

82

say, knowing his own temper. Stupid. There were men to walk away from and Matt was one of them. He hadn't been able to stop himself.

'Cheer up.' Piotr banged down his mug of tea. 'Maybe he finish the electrics tomorrow so we won't work with him any more days. Nice though.'

'What?'

'Those places. If his dad get one, good luck. Nice places if you're old.'

Some days, I wake up laughing. I even wake in the middle of the night laughing, but then I always did.

I wake up laughing because I think where I am and then I think where I might have been. And I was there for seven months, so I know what it's like, and I fully expected to be back there for a whole lot longer.

So I wake up where I am and I start laughing. Just laughing. With my life. How it is now. How it's turned out.

Twelve

She was coming up from very deep down, where it had been lightless and sunless and soundless. She had been there for a long time. Years? Yes, it must have been years. Then strange sounds began, faint pulsing, watery and regular, like the sound of a baby's heartbeat in the womb heard through the fetal monitor. There was still no light but the intense blackness had begun to shrivel to grey at the edges, curling inwards and sucking in the dark. She had been lying heavy and inert at the bottom of the black soundlessness for those years. Now, she was being pulled slowly up and her body felt lighter. The greyness was solid, then opaque, then misty.

Someone pulled the plugs out of her ears, abruptly releasing her, and she surfaced.

'Molly.' The back of her left hand felt something warm covering it and the warmth moved.

She had opened her eyes, but when she did so, what she saw was so terrifying she tried to will herself back down into the blackness and soundlessness again. She saw a white sheet on a bed, the end of a bed rail, a white wall, and a figure out of focus, standing at the bottom of the bed. Something at the top of the figure was shining and she knew that it was a bald head, the bald head of a man, the man who had tried to kill her in the room with the white-covered bed. She had no recollection of him, his name or why he wanted her to die, but she knew that if she opened her eyes again he would be there but that she would see him more clearly and when she saw him he would look at her directly and she would know his name.

'Molly . . .'

The warmth moved slightly against her hand and there was a little pressure. She liked the voice. The voice made her feel safe.

'Molly, can you hear me? I thought I saw you open your eyes. Can you do that again?'

The hand smoothed the back of her own hand. She knew the voice and that it was not a man's voice, and a name belonging to the voice was floating about just ahead of her, bobbing like a balloon on a string, but just too far away for her to touch it and pull it in so that she would know the name.

'I'll keep talking to you. I can stay a bit longer. I came to see you this morning and I told you this so perhaps you did hear. If you can't open your eyes, just squeeze my hand. If you can remember what happened to you, squeeze my hand. Can you squeeze my hand now? You needn't try and squeeze hard. Just hold mine a bit more tightly.'

She knew that she could, but the trouble was if she squeezed this person's hand to show that she had heard her and understood her, what might happen then? Who else might touch her? The man with the shining head might press his hand on hers, might . . .

Molly heard her own voice, crying out but not saying words. Just crying out.

'It's all right. You're in hospital and I'm here with you, Molly. You're fine.'

Without knowing that she was going to do it, Molly opened her eyes and at once they focused not on the man with the shining head, not on her own hand, not on the white covers, but on a face she knew.

'Cat . . .' she said.

'She's going to be all right. No brain damage, her lungs are clear. Once they come round and there's no organ failure, then it's very fast forward.'

Cat knew the tone of voice and every nuance of expression because she used them herself. Confidence, an almost casual assumption that there would be full recovery, not even the caveat that 'providing this or that does not occur'. Molly was still young enough to go from death's door to fit and well within a short space of time.

'Physically, anyway.' The registrar waved his hand as he turned away and went off down the corridor.

Molly's father, mother and brother had arrived. For the first time in many hours, Cat was free.

In the League of Friends café she bought a cheese and tomato baguette, crisps, a bar of chocolate, tea, suddenly ravenous with the hunger that accompanies relief.

Physically, he had said. That was his area. He left the rest to other medics. Molly was seeing a counsellor but Cat was doubtful if it was helping her enough – or why would she have overdosed to the extent she nearly died? She was almost a qualified doctor. She knew what she was doing. Clearly she needed more intensive psychiatric help and Cat would try and make sure she got it. Molly was not merely a lodger, she had become part of the Deerbon family. They loved her. Cat owed it to her to do more than get her good professional care. The trauma she had suffered at the hands of Leo Fison would live in her head forever and certainly she would not be able to return and take her medical finals until she had her reactions more under control. But even if she passed her exams, would she ever be able to cope as a doctor? Cat finished her tea. She was angry at a man who could so disregard his fellow human beings and their feelings. He would have killed Molly, she had no doubt, but he had vanished. No one had seen him, he had left no tracks.

'You'll get him,' Cat had said confidently to her brother.

'Maybe.'

'But he's a dangerous man.'

'There are plenty of dangerous men on the Wanted records of every police force in the world and lots of them are never caught.'

'Don't let Molly hear you say that. She has to feel she's safe.'

'I know.' Simon did know but he doubted if Fison would risk showing his face within a hundred miles of Lafferton again. He just could not give Molly a cast-iron assurance about it.

*   *   *

At Imogen House, Jocelyn Forbes was in a coma, with the breathing tube in place again. Cat looked at her charts. Perhaps she would slip peacefully from sleep into death with the ease they always tried to ensure for patients. She looked calm.

'Good, you're here.' Cathy Loughran, the Staff Nurse, came in, looking agitated. 'I'm going to blow a gasket if that daughter of hers doesn't get her act together and come in while there's breath left in her mother's body.'

'Perhaps she's in court, she's a barrister –'

'I know what she is. I've spoken to her . . . she's not well, she's had a breakdown, she's trying to come to terms with her mother's illness, she's . . .'

Cat led her gently outside into the corridor, though it was unlikely that Jocelyn could hear them.

'I'll phone her.'

'Good luck then. Maybe you'll have more patience.'

'Come on, Cathy, you're one of the most patient women I know.'

'Not with the likes of Penny Forbes I'm not.'

The phone rang seven times before it was answered by a machine. Cat left a brief message, waited ten minutes and then rang again. The answerphone. She left no message, merely redialled, and redialled, until, at the fifth attempt, she got Jocelyn's daughter, by which time she was as annoyed as Cathy but, also like Cathy, well able to conceal the fact.

'I'm sorry, I have a major case to prepare. I'm back at work tomorrow and in court for the rest of the week.' She sounded crisp and professional. And hard. But Cat knew a front when one was put up before her.

'I understand. I know Sister Loughran rang you but I thought I should do so as well as I'm the medical officer for the hospice and I've been looking after your mother for some time. I was her GP, as I think you know.'

Silence.

'She's is in the final stages and I'm concerned that if you don't see her you may regret it very much.'

'I will come and see her.'

'When?'

'Look, I don't think you understand what it's like and I certainly don't think you know what an ordeal I went through with her on that terrible journey to the clinic . . .'

Cat took a deep breath. 'I do know, I promise you. It was horrible for you both and I can guess what a toll it took on you as the one who had to be responsible for everything. It was a very loyal and loving thing to do. I'm not surprised you've had such a reaction. Is there anything I can do to help you? If you feel it would help to come and talk to me I'm more than happy . . .'

'My own doctor hasn't been very supportive, to be honest. I have sleep problems, I have flashbacks, I have panic attacks.'

'Your GP should be able to refer you to a counsellor.'

'I don't think I could face that, going over and over it and then delving back into my childhood, stirring up all sorts of memories. I just need something to calm me down. I have to be in control when I'm in court, I can't look ragged with lack of sleep. Is there anything you can prescribe for me?'

'I'm afraid not, but . . . would you feel able to talk to me? I can make sure I'm free when you come to see your mother.'

Penny Forbes sighed deeply. 'I don't know if I can face that yet.'

'Talking to me?' No, she thought, of course that isn't what you mean, you selfish, self-regarding, self-absorbed cow.

'No. I meant my mother.' There was a catch in her voice.

'You really don't have much time.'

It's winter. I had to wait, wait, wait. Bloody cold, day and night, and it's night I like. Once the clocks go forward you've lost a big bit of the night. I've been thinking back. Spring was best. It was warm. I used to love that. Wait for it. Warm nights, walking back home. Big moon. Huge moon.

I love the moon. Moon nights are best.

Big moons.

Thirteen

'I can't get over it, I just can't. I knew it would be nice but I didn't think it would be like this. Look . . . look at the fridge!'

Harry laughed. 'It's only a fridge like your old fridge.'

'No, it's not, it's got a much bigger freezer box.'

Rosemary opened a cupboard door, then another. Went to the sink.

'What's this?'

'Waste disposal.'

'What does it do?'

'Munches up your potato peelings and all that. Turns them into a slurry.'

'Looks as if it could turn your fingers into a slurry as well.'

'It could. You be careful.'

'Let's go back into the sitting room.'

There was a pair of double doors onto the patio, which faced west. There was a raised step for pots. A small shed. A gate to the bin area.

'I'll get a bird table. One with a seed feeder. And a bird bath.'

'Nice outdoor table and chairs. Tell you what, Rosemary, let me buy you those . . . house-warming. Let me know what sort you like. You can have breakfast out here, anything, it's pretty sheltered. Not overlooked either.' He climbed on a couple of slabs to look over the fence. 'Not overlooked. But you're not far from next door either.'

'Wonder who I'll get. We share a front path. Hope we get on.'

Harry put his arm round her. 'You get on with anybody and everybody, Rosemary. Never known anyone so friendly.'

It was true. One of the best things about her.

'The electrics aren't finished by the look of things. I'll keep an eye on that, and they haven't done a second coat on the paintwork.'

'I'm not moving in for another three weeks, Harry. Nobody's moved in.'

'They'll sign them all off together. Wonder if the flats are done?'

'I'm relieved I haven't been given one of those.'

'What's wrong with a flat? Call it an apartment – see the difference?'

'There isn't any – and I don't care what it's called, I couldn't live in one.'

'Good job you won't have to then. This is going to suit you very nicely.'

On the other side of Lafferton, Gordon Dyer was spending another day clearing out cupboards. Kitchen cupboards, bathroom cupboard, cupboard above the wardrobe, cupboards in the sitting-room wall unit, and then there were the shelves, and then there was the shed. He sat down. It was cold in the kitchen but the gas had gone up sky-high and even in this snow he didn't put the heaters on until seven and went to bed at nine, unless there was something he wanted to watch, when he kept it low, put on another jumper and sat with the old car rug over him. Greta had thrown the rug out a dozen times, and he'd always managed to sneak it back again. When she went, he had it cleaned and then spread it on the sofa. She'd have hated that. But then, Greta would have hated a lot of things he'd changed. Hated the kitchen table being on the other side and the bed against the wrong wall and the shower he'd had put in and the wallpaper up the stairs and the blue three-piece suite. She'd left him six thousand pounds, though where she'd got it from heaven knew – probably been squirrelling it away for years. He'd gone out and bought all the new stuff for the house and still had just over three thousand left.

He looked at the electric-blue sofa. She'd have hated it.

What she would have said about a move to the sheltered bungalow he could guess only too well. 'Poky place.' 'What would I want to be among all old people for?' 'Call that a garden?' 'Why'd they have to name it after royalty? I can't do with royalty.'

Gordon was happy to have his new home named after anyone or anything. He was pleased with it. He needed far less space, he needed neighbours, he needed someone listening out, he needed a new start. Why not? He might even meet somebody. He and Greta had never been more than accommodated. He wondered if seventy-eight was too old to find a woman who might be more. Love even.

He wondered what it might be like.

Twelve bungalows. One block of four maisonettes and a warden's flat. But Duchess of Cornwall Close still wasn't quite finished.

'Typical,' Elinor Sanders said, having to spend the night with her sister Muriel while her furniture went into the depot.

'Stop complaining. You're lucky to have a place. Not that I know why you bothered coming away from Newcastle.'

'Nothing left for me in Newcastle. Newcastle's a young person's place, all those students, all those out on a Friday night. Nothing for anyone my age.'

'Never heard anything so daft. I suppose you want a sherry.'

'Not fussed.'

'Well, do you or not?'

'Nothing left there at all.'

'I don't know what there is for you in Lafferton either.'

Elinor looked at the twin sister she had fought with since trying to elbow her out of the shared womb. 'And you, my only surviving flesh and blood.'

Muriel snorted.

The sherry brought their animosity to a head. They quarrelled over Elinor's gloating that at least she had had a husband and spent the evening in silence.

'She'll be gone in the morning,' Muriel reassured herself as she got into bed, 'they'll get the heating sorted tomorrow, surely to God.'

They did. By four o'clock Elinor was surrounded by her own chairs and tables in 12 Duchess of Cornwall Close, and at seven, Muriel was drinking her sherry alone.

It's better, Elinor thought, even though the bungalow was so silent, the street outside a traffic-free cul-de-sac, and only a couple of other houses occupied. 'It's better we live near one another and I won't miss Newcastle.'

But that night, lying in a bedroom as yet without curtains and quiet as the grave, she did.

Two doors away, Ray Hartwell had been asleep since nine. Ray had not wanted to move. They were starting to demolish the other houses in the street and he had sat tight. The landlady had bribed him and then upped the bribe. The landlady had tried to get the council involved but they were not prepared to move someone physically and told her to negotiate. She had upped the bribe a last time, offering him far more than he was worth, and then, recognising a final offer when he saw one, Ray had agreed to move if the council gave him somewhere new in a decent area of town and on a subsidised rent. Duchess of Cornwall Close was entirely allocated and with a waiting list. Ray had threatened to occupy his house while they tore down the walls around him. He had suggested arson and made sure he was seen carrying a petrol can. The offer of a maisonette came the following day. Ray did not like maisonettes or flats, so he stuck out for a bungalow. A few more days of building small bonfires, prowling round them with a box of firelighters, and he was given the keys to number 8 as the builders left. Number 8 was supposed to have been the warden's.

A leaflet had come through the door, a welcome letter from the warden and a note about activities and facilities that would be available before long.

Ray threw it in the plastic carrier bag he used for a bin. Activities and facilities did not interest him and he could do without the welcome letter. The front-door key had been his welcome.

Ray lay on his back and snored and a faint wash of snores

94

even reached Elinor Sanders two doors away and ruffled her sleep so that she turned over and back and murmured quietly, but did not wake. She had gone to bed in the knowledge that if she wanted to sleep in she could, though her conscience would not have let her stay in bed beyond eight thirty.

Ray would wake at five and get up at ten minutes past, as he had done for sixty years. He made black tea with four spoons of sugar and sat at the window drinking it, looking out. He would do the same in Duchess of Cornwall Close, staying at his window for an hour or more.

Ray liked to think he missed nothing.

How long does it take to stop dreaming about the old life? I walk those streets not these streets. I see the people who live there not here. They call me by my own name. This name isn't my own name and never will be, even though I went through all their tripwire tests until they were satisfied. How do you stop being the person you were since the day you were born? You're born all over again with this new name, new past, new place, new house, new life, but your memories aren't new, are they?

Anyway, I like those memories. I liked that life. I like to think about what happened. Everything. I like to walk those streets in my dreams not these streets. I like to lie in bed before I drop off and go back there. Go back. Be me. Remember everything.

Keeeps me warm at night.

Fourteen

Quiet. A strange, muffled quietness. A cool moonlight coming through the window and silvering the opposite wall.

Elinor Sanders had slept a little, woken, slept a little less. Switched on the light and switched it off again. Then sat up suddenly, afraid of the silence and the odd light. It was bitterly cold. She was used to cold, used to living in the North-East after all, but the walls of the new bungalow felt raw-cold, without having had any heating to penetrate the bricks and settle there. The bed was deep and soft and she was warm inside it, but the air outside chilled her face and one arm which had been outside the covers.

She got up and went to the window. The paving stones on the paths were pale as bone. The air was brilliantly clear, the moon full. Cold.

She went into the kitchen. Colder. Looked out of the window again, waiting for the kettle to boil. There was a light in one of the other houses. Someone else not able to sleep. Would it be all right here? The North-East was very friendly – too friendly, sometimes, but you were never ignored, never left to rot, never without someone you could call on, or call out to. Would that be true here? 'The South?' they'd said, wondering at her state of mind. They weren't friendly in the South. They kept themselves to themselves and nobody just popped in.

The light went out. The moon had gone behind heavy clouds. She drank her tea. She should get a cat. If cats were allowed.

Dogs were not, she knew that, there were notices up already, little wooden signs in the grass. A cat could be the best company and no trouble at all.

She sat for some time in the soft silence but then, as she went back to bed, something caught her eye. It was snowing again, great fat flakes like goose feathers spinning slowly down. Elinor stood looking at them and some memory of childhood came back to her, of their father holding them both up at the window to see the snow falling, she with his right arm round her, Muriel with his left, trying to make him put Elinor down, trying to get all his attention.

That's how it always was.

She watched the snow falling until her eyes crossed with following the flakes and trying to see where exactly each one lay on the ground. By the time she had climbed into bed the grass was already covered in a soft eiderdown.

She went to sleep, snow flakes twirling and turning behind her eyes, warmer.

Happier.

It was after eight when she woke, unusually late. She lay in bed, enjoying the warmth and the sense of rest after a poor night. She might get her tea and bring it back here with the new *Woman & Home* she had not yet looked at in the flurry of moving. Why not? What else was there to do? Muriel boasted of being up at seven in all seasons and weathers, but when she was up, what did she do? Clean the house that was already so clean it was in danger of being rubbed away. And when did she ever have tea with a friend, read a book, window-shop, go on an outing, take a proper holiday, play cards? It was clean, clean, clean.

Elinor got up and put on her dressing gown. She would fetch tea, toast, the magazine and the new book of needlepoint she'd treated herself to for her birthday, and get back to bed to relax, a word Muriel did not understand.

It had obviously gone on snowing for some hours, though now it had stopped and the sky was blue and cloudless. The lawn and the paths were pillowed in snow.

Beautiful, it seemed to her. Beautiful, and untouched.

But not untouched. Footprints, clear and deeply trodden, came diagonally across from the corner where the paths met, to her bungalow.

Just footprints.

Fifteen

'Can you drop me in town?'

'Of course I can't, Sam, what are you thinking? How would that would go down at home? You've been away for a week.'

Sam hunched into his seat and did not reply. He had spent much of the journey from Norfolk sending and receiving text messages. Once, a call had come through but he had said, 'Text, I told you,' and clicked off. Otherwise, he had said little. They had stopped for lunch, and again in mid-afternoon at a service station which doubled as a shopping arcade, and Simon bought some groceries. Sam sat over a Coke and a banana, alternately texting and watching the people coming in and out through the swing doors, as if he were expecting to see someone.

The mobile signal in Norfolk had never been good, so perhaps he was catching up with his friends now. Simon remembered his own adolescence, albeit without the text facility, when he had closed the door before taking a phone call at home, though the call had usually been about nothing much. Cat had monopolised the phone every evening, so much so that their father banned its use except within strict time limits. The age of fourteen had caught up with Sam. His old talkativeness had died to long silences and occasional grunts, though he had been better on their week away than he was at home. They had talked about plenty of things, including police work, music of all kinds, Sam's future, cricket, seabirds, books and films. Chris had not been mentioned. It seemed to be the only no-go area, one of which Simon was keenly aware.

Brown earth showed through the snow in the fields of the Midlands but by the time they headed towards the M5 it had scarcely thawed at all and towards late afternoon a freezing fog descended, slowing them down to a crawl.

'Ring your mum, will you? Tell her we'll be later than I thought.'

'She won't worry.'

'All the same . . .'

Sam sighed and started to text.

'Can't you call her?'

'She picks up texts OK.'

'I know. Just thought she might appreciate a voice.'

'I hate talking on the phone.'

Simon focused on the fog warning signs and the queue of traffic ahead. He knew what Sam meant. He spent a lot of his working day talking on the phone. When he was off duty he liked the silence of his flat, sometimes music, and messages left so that he could reply when he felt like it – often by text.

The only person he always wanted to talk to, always wanted to hear, was Rachel.

Rachel. He felt delight that she was no more than fifty miles away and that surely, surely, he would see her, tonight even, certainly tomorrow.

The traffic queue shunted on for a couple of dozen yards, then stopped again. Sam had his iPod on. He listened to a strange mixture of sound and words – *Just William* and *Sherlock Holmes* audiobooks, classical trumpet and oboe music, obscure new rock bands. And bagpipes. He had his head back, eyes closed. Simon glanced at him. His face in repose was still a child's face just overshadowed by that of the young man to come. It was like watching a new creature emerge from a chrysalis, seeing the nephew he had known since he was ten minutes old change as he inched towards adulthood. Would he ever have his own children? He was happy to share his sister's three, engage with them as much as he liked, while always able to leave. He could not imagine being in the thick of what he saw as the general mayhem of family life. If he and Rachel . . .

They had never let themselves touch on the subject, because

101

of her situation, because of Kenneth, because they did not dare venture into such dangerous territory.

The traffic began to crawl again. Outside, freezing fog, darkness, snow on the fields and piled high along the verges where the ploughs had been through.

He glanced at Sam again. His face was innocent and expressionless in sleep. He did not stir when Simon's phone rang.

'Hi. We're jammed on the motorway. Should have been back an hour ago but the traffic's solid.'

'OK. I'm still at Imogen House, and there's been another snowfall today. The main roads are fine but it's bad around us. How's Sam?'

'Asleep.'

'I've missed him. I didn't think I'd miss him so much.'

'He's missed you but he'd die rather than say so. We've had a great week. Any news?'

'Sort of. Hannah is in the last three for this film part . . . It's ridiculous, I shouldn't want something so shallow and frivolous for my twelve-year-old daughter and I want it so much I can't focus on anything else.'

'She'll get it. And you'll focus.'

'Bit worried about Dad and Judith. Storm clouds banking up there.'

'Oh God . . . he just can't help it, can he?'

'I know. I'm treading on eggshells though. Can't say anything.'

'Listen, we're moving again.'

'There's plenty of food in. Stay the night?'

'Let's see. God, I forgot – what about Molly?'

'Discharged home with her parents and recovered – physically at least.'

'That says it all. We're moving properly now. See you in a bit.'

Cat put the phone down and finished her tea. The staff-room was empty and she was glad of it, as they all sometimes were when a break was badly needed. She had done some slow breathing, looking out at the darkening sky and the snow. Now that her son and brother were on their way home and Molly was safely off with her family, she could relax at least one part of herself, the part that was always tense when this or that person was away or travelling. There remained the semi-anxiety, semi-excitement about Hannah – but Cat had a feeling that she would get the film part, even though she tried to keep it out of her mind. When it came to Richard and Judith she veered between hope and despair and that was harder to forget, it flowed deep down and even through her dreams, like underground water, it clouded her waking and troubled her at random moments.

'Cat . . .?'

She got up, knowing at once where she was needed.

'I think you should try her daughter again.'

'Would you mind doing it? Not sure I've the patience.'

'Not sure I have,' Cathy said. 'But let me practise.'

Whatever response Cathy got from Penny, Cat saw as she went into Jocelyn Forbes's room, was now irrelevant. Jocelyn lay, her right hand on the cover, palm upwards, as if waiting for someone to put theirs into it, eyes closed, face already changing as death took over. Cat took hold of the hand, utterly unresponsive as it was, and pressed it.

The silence in the room was absolute and like a balm, a healing silence. She had known it so often, this strange sense of being 'at the still point of the turning world', and never ceased to be overcome by it. Death, she thought. Death, how little we know. How often and how surely you come at the perfect moment and make things right and how little we trust to that. Even Chris, she realised now. Everything that had been wrong was put right, even though her world had split open from end to end and forever.

She sat beside Jocelyn Forbes, hand still on hers, remembering, understanding. Saying goodbye.

The door opened quietly. Cat looked at Cathy, who shook her head.

But half an hour later, Penny Forbes burst through the doors, dishevelled and out of control, upsetting a woman and two teenage children who were waiting to see Cat after the death

103

of a beloved husband and father. They were quiet, stunned, pale, anxious, needing tenderness and gentle answers to unanswerable questions. Penny gave no sign of being aware of them as she stood wailing, demanding to see her mother, demanding to know why she had not been told that Jocelyn was about to die so that she could have been with her, demanding to make a complaint, demanding, demanding . . . The family huddled together, looking at her out of shocked and tear-stained faces, the mother trying to distract her son and daughter from the scene being played out a yard or so away, looking desperately at Lois, the receptionist, willing her to make Penny disappear.

It was the ever-capable Cathy who fielded her, led her to the family room, listened to her rage, brought her coffee and tissues, sat beside her.

'I want to see Dr Deerbon, she's the one who's answerable for this, she's the one who has to explain.'

'Dr Deerbon will be with you as soon as she can. She's seeing a bereaved family.'

'I'm bereaved, and I've had a lot to go through these last months, she knows that. And I've been unwell, I've had to take a lot of time off work as a result of the strain of it all. I think Dr Deerbon owes it to me to see me before other people. I could have seen my mother before she died, I could have talked to her, and we had a lot of unfinished business. I had her and now I've no one.'

Staff Nurse Cathy Loughran knew all there was to know about Penny Forbes in relation to her mother, but said nothing, nodded sympathetically, sat patiently. She was used to every sort of family reaction, even to people coming to blows – used to genuine grief, mock grief, grief which ran deep and did not show, showy grief which ran shallow. Penny had hidden away, frightened of a final encounter with her mother, self-absorbed, not wanting to face the truth. Now she had retreated into her own world and erected a ring of defences around herself. The inevitable had happened – Jocelyn had died without her daughter saying goodbye and resolving any tensions and differences they might have had. Guilt would run riot.

* * *

104

Cat stayed longer with the bereaved family than she might have done, letting each one of them have time to speak about what they felt, knowing how irreplaceable these moments were and how they would value them for the rest of their lives. They left the building in a sad, close group, clinging to one another for comfort, looking back several times to where they had left the one person they wanted to be able to take with them and to the place which had meant everything and could no longer do so. People had strong feelings towards the hospice in which those they loved had died, wanting to stay, to come back and help out, to continue being a part of what they could not bear to abandon.

Cat had watched from the doorway until their car turned out into the road, after which she took a deep breath, sent up a prayer for strength and patience with a woman who was, in truth, one more of the bereaved in need of compassion.

Penny Forbes was angry with herself and directed that anger onto Cat, who could take it but who still had to bite her tongue when accused of keeping the woman away from her mother. She let her rant for some time, saying nothing herself and then suggested that she might go to see Jocelyn now. She had been moved into the hospice chapel of rest, which some staff preferred to call 'the viewing room'. Cat led Penny in. It was a place of comfort, a place where suffering was at an end and the dead person was safe from fear and at rest, whatever beliefs or unbeliefs were held. Cat never failed to gain consolation and strength from being in the chapel with the dead, always felt herself to be in the immediate presence of God. Few, if any, left unmoved.

Penny grabbed Cat's arm and dug her nails into it, pulling her back. 'I can't. I can't face it.'

'It's entirely up to you. But you should see her. You need to make your peace with her, Penny.'

'What? What do you mean by that?'

'And you need to say goodbye. If you don't you'll regret it for the rest of your life.'

Penny had turned away and buried her face in a handkerchief. Cat felt her patience fraying to breaking point.

'I'll come with you.'

'I don't want to see her like that.'

'But not long ago you were going to watch her kill herself in a Swiss clinic. This is going to be easier.'

'I must have been mad.'

'No, you were being loving and supportive.'

'I've never seen a dead body. A human one.'

'This is your mother, Penny – not "a dead body". She looks peaceful and she looks younger.'

It was several more minutes before Penny shuffled reluctantly in behind Cat. The door swung slowly to and closed with barely a sound.

Jocelyn did indeed look peaceful and younger, her face less lined now and her features relaxed and gentle. Cat went over and put her hand on the dead one. Cool. Very different from the last time. But Jocelyn's hand, nonetheless.

One second and there was a blessed silence. The next, there was a sound that made Cat step back as if in self-defence. Penny had put her head back and let out a terrible noise from the back of her throat, a noise between a roar and a wail that echoed round the small room. It seemed that Jocelyn lay as still as she did out of a sort of defiance, eyes closed against it.

The door opened and Cat made a small gesture to the member of staff who had been passing, to indicate that she was all right, but then she took Penny by the arm and led her out of the chapel.

Sixteen

It was lovely. You got out of bed just after midnight. Had a pot of tea. Made a big fat doorstep sandwich of cheese and pickle and sardines. Bag of crisps. Bar of KitKat.

Then into your coat, your hat and your boots. Big boots. Then you went out.

And there was no one. The snow had covered the towpath and the banks of the canal. Over the bridge it was piled three inches. Down the steps. Hold onto the rail, mind.

Then you were down on the other side and up the street and there was no one. A car on the main road then not another for ages.

Nobby smiled, crunching the snow. Sweet as a nut. Lovely. He pushed his boot down into it. Stood still. Pushed the other boot down. Stood looking round. The sky was clear, the stars like the bright heads of pins in a velvet pincushion.

They had names, and he knew some of them but not which name belonged to which.

He walked slowly. No one about. Empty world. Half a mile. A mile. Into the town. Along the road past the hill which was like one of the Alps in a picture.

Untouched snow. He laughed as he sent it flying, kicking it in all directions. Then he fell over and rolled in it. Got up before his clothes were too wet and walked on and laughed now and again because the snow made him happy. Snow and night. Night and snow.

No one about. No one to see Nobby. That was all right. Then a dog saw him. Ran away. He got near town. Lights on. A car or two. A cat. Snow. But it was messed up here where people had trampled it on the pavements. He hated them. How could they make snow into such a dirty mush? They should respect it.

Yes.

Respect.

He said it aloud.

'Respect!'

A police car went slowly round the town square so he dodged into a shop doorway. They'd stop and ask him, where was he going, what was he doing, why was he in town at this time, get in, Nobby, we'll take you home, you're better off out of this cold, aren't you? What did they know?

He waited till they were well away. It was cold but all right in the doorway and he liked the smell of the night air, sharp and clean. He couldn't see why people said they hated snow. Snow was good. Snow was a beauty if you walked in it, though it messed up the roads for cars. But cars messed up everything, messed up the quiet and the emptiness. Mucked the snow.

After a bit it got too cold just standing so he went down the narrow lane towards the cathedral and stood marvelling at the snow there, great white billows of it, curvy and soft, over the grass, over the stones, on the paths. Holy snow. He wouldn't walk on holy snow.

Nobody about. Nothing. Taxi rank had two cabs. Empty ones.

Then there was somebody, walking quickly, softly down towards him, hands in pockets, collar up, head down. Nobby stopped. You never knew. He pressed himself into the wall on his left. The man walked on. Didn't pause in his stride. Then he was up the slope and round the corner into the darkness. Not glancing back. Never saw Nobby Parks.

It was like school lessons. They wrote down a chunk of stuff about where I'd come from, my family, where I was born, where I went to school, all that. All made up. I couldn't get my head round it. I said that was daft, anybody'd find out I hadn't lived in that street and been to that school, especially now, with what you can get on the computer. They said I had lived in that house, been to those schools. I said I hadn't. They said, You have now. It's all in there. Someone checks those school registers, there you'll be. That street. There you'll be.

'So, what about Lynne then?'

'You don't know any Lynne.'

'My wife. Lynne Keyes.'

'You're divorced.'

'No, I'm not.'

'Yes, you are. You're divorced. Now. It's all been done, all legal. Alan Frederick Keyes had a wife, Lynne Margaret Keyes. They're divorced.'

That's what they do.

This stuff they put under my nose. House I'd lived in, schools, even people in my class. Best friends = Jim Little. Peter Wainwright. Larry Urmston. Their addresses. Names of their brothers and sisters. Birthdays even.

That's another thing. My birthday.

'When's your birthday?'

'Twenty-second of March.'

'That's Alan Keyes's birthday. When's yours?'

'Fifteenth of July . . .'

'Think again.'

'Twentieth of . . . July.'

'OK. You have to snap it back. Nobody hesitates about answering when their birthday is. When's your birthday?'

'Twentieth of July.'

'Good.'

Seventeen

'I can't talk about it here. It makes me feel even more guilty.'

They were the only ones in the Italian restaurant apart from a solitary businessman eating with an iPad propped in front of him. The roads were still difficult. Simon and Rachel had walked from Cathedral Close. How the businessman had arrived they had already asked themselves in whispers.

They had eaten hot langoustines with lemon mayonnaise. Spaghetti alla vongole was on its way. The bottle of house red was already three-quarters empty.

Simon put his hand over Rachel's. He had not wanted to ask about her husband but it never seemed right to ignore the subject altogether.

Rachel smiled. 'I'm so pleased you had a good week. You needed that.'

'Sam did too. I'd broken my promise to him too often. I just wish it had been us. Or that it could be us soon anyway. Can we ever get right away together?'

Her eyes clouded with anxiety and Simon wished he could take the burden of guilt away from her, knew he could not. Ken was no better, not much worse. And so it went on.

The waiter topped up their glasses. The spaghetti came steaming in its bowls.

'I love you.'

She looked down quickly. Picked up her fork. 'Yes.'

'I don't want it to go on and on like this.'

She ate.

'Rachel?'

'Don't. Leave it. I know, I know, but what else can I do? You know how it is.'

'Yes, I know how it is. I'm sorry.'

And then he glanced up and saw two figures he recognised pass the window, and the door of the restaurant opened on his father and stepmother.

'Darling!' Judith first, warm, loving, coming quickly over to kiss him on the cheek. To look across at Rachel. She knew about Rachel.

Richard, looking buttoned, shook Rachel's hand, put his fleetingly on his son's arm.

'Good time with Sam?'

'Terrific. He loved it – snow and all.'

'It's been absolutely awful here – we decided we'd risk it in my car or we'd go stir-crazy. It's all right for those within walking distance of course.'

'Judith, come and join us,' Rachel said.

'No, we have our own table reserved, we won't intrude.'

'Don't be ridiculous, Dad – at least have a drink with us.'

'No, you're halfway through your dinner.' He gave Judith a sharp look. Simon watched. Usually, she would have ignored it, joined them, as he had suggested, for a glass of wine, before retreating. This time, she simply nodded and followed him to their table at the other end of the restaurant.

'You didn't tell me you'd met Judith.'

'No. I didn't, did I?'

He frowned. 'How?'

'We both go to Emma's book group. So does your sister.'

'Why didn't you say?'

'Oh, one reason and another.'

'What reason and another?'

'*This* reason,' Rachel said calmly. 'You see? Because I knew you would make some sort of fuss about it, and really, there is no reason why I shouldn't go to a book group with members of your family, is there?'

'There's every reason.'

'We don't talk about you, Si. We never have. Not once.'

'That puts me in my place . . .'

Rachel smiled. He pushed back his white-blond hair from where it had flopped, as ever, over his forehead, a gesture she had grown to understand. He made it when his hair annoyed him, but also when he felt caught out or embarrassed. As now.

The waiter came to take their bowls away and offer the dessert menu.

Simon waved it away. Rachel put out her hand to take it. 'Thank you,' she said, still smiling her open and beautiful smile. Then she put her hand on Simon's. 'Listen, I'm enjoying my evening. I'd like a pudding. And coffee. And you should take a deep breath and stop sulking. And forget your father and step-mother.'

He looked at her.

She was teasing him. Smiling.

He relaxed suddenly.

'Better?' Rachel said.

'I'm sorry.'

'No need. No need for any of it actually.' She kept her hand over his as the waiter hovered. 'We'd both like the raspberries and Chantilly cream, please. And two black coffees, one decaf, one strong.'

She turned back to Simon. He saw in that moment that she loved him absolutely and that whatever happened she would go on loving him. He understood her, and he knew, too, that he had no excuse at all for not looking after her, protecting her, being loyal to her. And loving her in the same way.

He snatched a glance over his shoulder. There was something about the way Richard and Judith sat, a little apart, carefully not touching, the slight distance between them more than the sum of its parts. She was looking down, he was staring straight ahead in the way Simon recognised so well. He could imagine his father's expression, haughty, proud, detached, giving away nothing. But polite. Ever and meticulously polite.

Rachel raised an eyebrow slightly. He shook his head.

A single large white bowl of raspberries was set down in front of them. Two smaller bowls. Another, of Chantilly cream. The waiter brought a bottle of raspberry liqueur and poured some over the fruit.

'I love her,' Simon said now. 'And if my father loses her, I swear I will kill him.'

Rachel looked at him gravely, her violet eyes clouded. 'No,' she said, 'no, you won't and please never say that sort of thing again. You of all people.'

For a moment he was angry. No one spoke to him like that except his sister, the only person he would take it from, though his mother had sometimes been critical, as had Judith once or twice. But their tone was different. Rachel spoke in the way Cat did, almost as if he were Sam's age and behaving childishly. He looked at her across the table. Her eyes were steady on his, as she ate her pudding quite calmly.

And then he smiled. 'Yes,' he said. 'You're right. Of course you're right.'

'It's so easy. "I will kill him", "I wish she were dead", "I hope I don't live to see it". So easy.'

'And then something happens.'

'Even if it doesn't. Once . . .' She held her spoon very still and did not look up. 'Once . . . it had been a really awful day . . . in all sorts of ways but mainly . . . oh, Kenneth's illness and . . . and I wished he would die. I didn't say it but I thought it very clearly. "I wish you'd hurry up and die." And I've remembered it and felt terrible about it ever since and whenever something happens, whenever he deteriorates or . . . the thing is, you never forget what you wish and you never stop feeling guilty and . . . and when eventually it does happen . . .'

On their way out, Simon looked towards Richard and Judith's table but they were turned away and he did not want the awkwardness of going over to say goodnight.

'They'll be fine,' Rachel said, taking his hand. 'People who come out to have a quiet dinner together in this weather are not at loggerheads. Trust me.'

The pavement was treacherous and the gutter hidden beneath inches of frozen snow. She let him lead her down through the icy cobbles, under the east arch and into the close, empty, white and ghostly under the moon.

'Not even a cat's paw print.' Rachel looked across the stretches of untouched snow. There had been another light fall and the air smelled of cold, metallic and clean.

They stopped. Rachel had a fur-trimmed hood that outlined her face in soft whiteness. Simon held his breath, looking at her.

'No,' she said. 'Things are better left unsaid.'

'I can't –'

'For now anyway.'

She smiled. Her expression was open and happy. She had learned the trick of setting the Kenneth part of her life aside. She would return to it again tomorrow. That was the only way she could divide herself between Ken and Simon without ruining both. Simon had learned to help her do it.

'Come on,' he said. 'A fire and a glass of Laphroaig.'

She bent, made a snowball, and threw it at him. They ran, laughing, towards the house in which his flat at the top was an eyrie and a refuge.

Nobby watched them, from his hiding place in the shadow of the cathedral. The stone gave off the cold but he would not move away until they were out of sight. He heard the echo of their laughter across the blue-white snow. Silly laughter.

He waited another few minutes before slipping out of the shadows and round the side, into the lane. Shadows here too. High walls. Icy. Be careful, Nobby, he said. You don't want to go having an accident and getting taken to hospital and having to answer a lot of questions. You mind your feet.

There was no one else about until he reached the top of the lane. Then there was someone. Just one person, like him, walking and not as careful as he was, so once and then again he slipped and almost fell. Nobby kept back. He didn't want to see anyone else's accident either, have to stop and help and answer questions there as well.

Stay back. The other one reached the square and turned the corner. When Nobby caught up, he was gone. Nobody. A single taxi waiting at the rank. Then a man and a woman getting in. Not the same man.

Nobby kept to the shadows of the shops and the pub and the bus shelter, slipping in and out. Not a bad night, and it wasn't over yet.

Eighteen

A long wail of distress. Then another.

Harry Fletcher opened the door of the boys' bedroom on the third, by which time Bradley was sitting up and leaning over his bunk. Harry got him to the bathroom in the nick of time.

'Daaaad . . .'

'Hang on.' Harry grabbed a flannel, wet it and wiped his son's face. 'Better?'

'No . . .' Bradley bent his head abruptly over the toilet bowl again.

'What's happening?' Karen came into the bathroom, half asleep.

'Muuuum . . .'

'Throwing up,' Harry said. He could cope with it. Sick. Nappies. Toilet upsets. All the stuff that seemed to accompany having kids. He mopped up, changed pyjamas, got a bowl for beside the bed. Looked at his son's pale pinched little face with sympathy. He remembered being sick as a kid and how it had frightened him. He didn't want his own being afraid of anything.

Outside, the snow fell again, covering the pavements and the paths and the gardens. Covering up footprints and paw prints and tyre marks. Covering every trace.

Karen's mother had been due to move into her new bungalow the previous day but with the bad weather it was thought best to postpone until a thaw.

In the morning, Bradley was candle-coloured and weak in the

117

aftermath of his sickness, Harvey had complained of tummy pains. They would be puking puppies, and Karen would be stuck in with them all day. He couldn't stop work for sick lads. Couldn't afford to catch anything.

He got into the van with a sigh of relief, feeling like someone escaping the prison cell. He loved his sons but money was scarce and he needed the work. He loved them more than he'd admit to anyone. He'd had no idea what he'd feel about having kids, hadn't dared to look ahead, had been worried by the whole business. But the minute he saw them, he'd known. He'd do anything for them and he'd kill the person who ever wronged them. Simple as that.

Duchess of Cornwall Close was nice enough but it looked a bit raw and bleak with snow all round, no greenery, none of the bits and pieces people put on their window ledges, no doormats or pots or notices about junk mail. But a white van, bigger than his own, was parked up. And the front door was ajar.

Rosemary's was on the far side. Bit close to the neighbour on the left, Harry thought, but it had a patch of lawn and some fencing to the right. The gardens here backed onto a path and a line of trees. They wouldn't hear much noise from the road.

He went up to the front door and pushed it further open. 'Who's there?'

A man emerged from the kitchen.

'Didn't know anyone was still working in here, thought it was all done.'

'Checking the electrics. Who's asking?'

Harry stood his ground. 'Family,' he said.

'What family?'

'Of the new tenant in here. Doing a bit of checking myself.'

'Right.'

'You worked on all of these places?'

'Most. They're not bad. Went up a bit fast, some shoddy workmanship, but they're not bad.'

'Which is the warden's house?'

'Now you're asking. Was going to be the bottom maisonette in the block.'

'Was?'

'Not any longer. No warden after all. No money for a warden.'

'You're kidding? That's diabolical!'

'Tell me about it.'

'What are these old people meant to do if they have a problem, they have a fire, or they can't make the heating work, or they get taken ill? Anything could happen.'

'Yeah, well, I don't make the rules.'

'That's absolutely not on. I don't like the idea of her being here on her own, no warden, nothing.'

'Your mother?'

'In-law. Good for her age but that's beside the bloody point.'

The electrician had gone back into the kitchen. Harry went into the sitting room. Bleak, with nothing in bar the carpet. It looked cold and felt cold. He went round, checking each room. Doors and windows, fastenings, locks, taps. The electrics were off. Bit of slapdash paintwork on the cupboards in the kitchen. He opened the window and closed it. It fitted badly. The door needed a draught excluder strip.

'I'm done. You want me to let you out or what? I'm over to the flats now.'

Harry watched the sparks shut the front door and double-lock it, then walk off without another word.

When Harry passed between the bungalows he saw that the residents could be neighbourly but not too close, talk across the paths from their front doors but be secluded in their back gardens and patios, where the fences were higher. They were well designed, so that they would all get a decent amount of sun in the afternoon and evening, mainly on the gardens – the front rooms might be a bit dark but, in his experience, kitchens and gardens were what people would prefer to have bright and warm. The bedrooms were either at the back or the side, well placed for quietness. The heating system was communal, the roofs had solar panels, the walls had been decently insulated. The storage space could have been better but who wanted to bring a load of clutter forward into old age?

He went back to his van and rang Karen to report. Her mother was going to enjoy herself here, she was going to be comfortable, warm, peaceful, safe, with plenty of neighbours nearby. The only fly in the ointment was that there would be no warden, as they'd been promised.

'I'm going to jot down a list – few odd things need finishing off. The usual workmen rushing to get done and on to the next, screws missing here and there, paintwork not properly coated underneath shelves and inside doors . . . but on the whole . . .'

When he'd gone through everything, he asked how Bradley was.

'It's more Harvey now, he's been sick three times and he won't get off the toilet.'

Harry said he was late to look at a boiler breakdown on the other side of the town and cut her off before she could go into any more detail.

Forgetting who you were. Remembering who you are. It's hard. You wake up in the night for months after, sweating because it's all gone, everything — names, places, the way to your old house, the way to your new one.

Only then you remember something else. Why. And then you laugh. You have to laugh.

Nineteen

'Where were you?' Cat said as she walked round the kitchen putting shopping away. The thaw had set in and the supermarket home delivery had reached them. She had made it to Emma's book group the previous evening, but Judith had not, which was surprising as she had been one of the first and most enthusiastic members, had never missed a meeting, and the book they had discussed was her choice.

'Things cropped up, you know how it is.'

Cat took the hint and did not pursue the subject. But things did not just 'crop up' to keep Judith from the book group.

'What are we reading next?'

'*Wide Sargasso Sea* . . . I've got a spare copy somewhere if you need it.'

'I'm pretty sure there's one here, thanks. I have read it, but years ago.'

Cat bent to put cheese into the fridge, the phone to her ear.

'By the way, we went to the Italian for supper last week, the night before it thawed. Pretty hairy journey into town mind.'

'Worth it though. It's a comfort place, that restaurant.'

'I needed a bit of comfort. Simon was there.'

'Well, it's his local. On his own?'

'No, with Rachel.'

'Aha.'

'Good thing?'

Cat sighed, heaving cat food tins up onto the shelf. 'For him, yes.'

'But . . .'

'Do you know, I just can't worry about Simon and women any more. I've had so many years of it, I've picked up so many pieces – not his usually – I've decided to stay out of it. He's a grown-up for heaven's sake. No, hang on . . . maybe that's going a bit far.'

'I have a theory. Serrailler men never grow up. I know they seem to manage to hold down quite grown-up jobs, but they themselves are fatally underdeveloped.'

'Wonder if mine will inherit that. Sam sometimes seems to be going backwards. He had quite a lot of sense when he was nine.'

'When does Hannah hear about this film part?'

'Final choice on Thursday. It's down to two of them and to say nerves are frayed would be the year's understatement.'

'Do you think she'll get it?'

'I know she wants it. We'll see. But listen, Judith –'

'Darling, I must go, something on the stove . . . Talk later and ring the minute you hear anything.'

There was nothing on the stove, Cat was certain. Judith had not wanted their conversation to veer back in her own direction, nor had she been prepared to answer questions. 'Something's up' – that had been Chris's catchphrase, and he usually had good antennae for what, but even Chris wouldn't have been able to get over the barrier Judith seemed to have erected recently. Hannah fell in through the door, arms full of homework bag and sports kit, expression alert and anxious.

'Have you heard anything?'

'No, and we won't until Thursday – you know that. Do you want cheese on toast or eggy bread?'

'Marmite.' The bags fell in a heap on the kitchen floor.

'Han . . .'

'OK, OK, sorry, but I'm so wound up I think I might go ping.'

Cat laughed. 'It's no good saying try and forget it because you can't but at least try and practise diversion tactics. Such as what's for homework?'

'English essay but I've got three days.'

'Nothing else?'

'Read the first three chapters of *Jewish Feasts and Festivals* and be ready to discuss.'

'Interesting.'

'Yes, did you know . . .' She hitched herself onto the worktop counter stool, ate a slice of toast and Marmite until her mouth was stuffed full, then began to explain how Passover was celebrated. Usually, Cat would have prompted her to swallow first. Now she said nothing. Hannah was indeed liable to 'go ping'. Cat looked at her daughter, a Serrailler in features but not in colouring, whereas Sam was as blond as Simon and Felix was the carbon copy of his father, chunky, dark-haired, square-faced.

Hannah was on the cusp of adolescence, grown tall, slender and long-necked. It was possible to see what she would look like as an adult. Interesting, Cat thought, trying to be dispassionate, she will be interesting and intelligent, but with every emotion and passing thought visible on her face, every joy and sorrow chasing one another like clouds across a bare hill. Her desperation to get the film part was obvious and painful. Don't let her be disappointed, Cat thought, as she had thought so often in the last couple of weeks. Please let her have this or she will be beyond devastated. Was she praying then? Not exactly. She always had the sense that prayers ought to be about serious matters, not trivialities, so she would pray with and for patients in Imogen House every day, but hesitated to ask for anything for herself. Was asking this for Hannah trivial?

Not to Hannah.

She sent up a quick prayer, a proper one this time, as the car bringing Sam home pulled up outside.

124

Twenty

'Looks half finished,' Muriel said, opening a couple of cupboard doors and shutting them, then inspecting the join in the worktop. 'See, the underside of this, it's ragged, never been stuck down properly.'

'Seems all right to me.'

'That doesn't surprise me, you've never paid attention to detail.'

'What's that supposed to mean? You say some very odd things.'

'Is that all you've got?'

'It's a very nice sherry.'

'No, I mean those Twiglet things. Far too salty and I have to watch my blood pressure. I'm surprised you don't, being the same as me.'

'Yes, well, so far as I'm aware my blood pressure is what it should be. Let's go into the sitting room.' Elinor carried out the tray with glasses, sherry bottle and bowl of Twiglets.

'That dresser looks too big in here.'

'Muriel, please . . .' Elinor set the tray down and turned to her twin. She was on the verge of tears. The move into her new bungalow had been exhausting. The snow had thawed so rapidly that the gutters could not cope and had overflowed, the double glazing was faulty and had steamed up between the panes so that it was impossible to see out of any window apart from the bedroom, the central heating had broken down twice, the

125

electricity was playing up and some of her furniture was too bulky to come through the front door. At present it was in the removal firm's stores, awaiting her decision. The dresser had been manoeuvred in with millimetres to spare and Muriel was right, it looked too big in the room.

'Mu, I think we should make a pact –'

'Don't call me Mu. I hate Mu. *Nelly.*'

Elinor sighed. They were six years old again. They were always six years old, competitive, argumentative, jealous, angry. But she was determined to make one last effort. And it would be the last. She had come to live here in order to spend whatever years she had left closer to Muriel, and to try and be reconciled once and for all. She had even talked to a counsellor about it and learned what they had called some 'strategies'.

'Muriel, sit down and have this sherry. I want us to talk.'

'Sounds ominous.'

'No it isn't, it's just sense. Cheers.'

Muriel lifted her glass a fraction and sipped. 'It isn't poisoned' was on the tip of Elinor's tongue but she bit the words back. That was what would have to stop, that quick sarcastic or hurtful retort, one of them always trying to get a rise out of the other. She said as much now. Muriel looked at her over the top of her glass and looked away again. Said nothing.

'It's daft, all these years, quarrel, quarrel, quarrel, we're sisters for heaven's sake. Twins. What could be closer than that? People would give a lot to have someone as close in old age.'

'Not so old.'

'Muriel, I am the same age as you and, whatever you want to think, we are in our old age.'

'I should know, I'm four minutes older than you.'

'Does that really matter? You've tried to use that to patronise me and put me down and lord it over me all our lives. Four minutes. It has to stop. I want it to. Why do you think I've made this move? Come all this way?'

'You've never said. Seems odd, if you want to know. All your friends being up there.'

'I've precious few left, I've told you that. I think we're very lucky to have one another.'

126

'I've friends. A lot of friends.'

'I'm very pleased to hear it. And I hope to make my own here. We don't have to live in one another's pockets.'

'I should hope not.'

'Just be friends, if we can't be closer than that.'

Muriel looked into her empty sherry glass, not actually commenting on how small it was. Elinor got up and refilled it without a word. Her own was barely touched.

'Maybe we should put it on a bit of a formal basis,' she said. 'Make a plan. Say, you come to lunch here one day a week, I come to you another.'

'I might be doing something.'

'Well, then we change it of course.'

'Make an appointment to see your sister?'

'You don't have to sound like that. And of course you'd be welcome to come any time, drop in when you like. Oh, Mu, don't always start arguing, it makes me tired.'

'I wonder how friendly you'll actually find the people here. It's not the North.'

'I know that. I shall make an effort though. You have to make the effort.'

'Of course, I've known most of the people round me for thirty years. Or I did. There's been changes. Always are. I still know quite a few but we don't just drop in without notice. That's what you'll find different.'

'You needn't worry, Mu. I'll never drop in on you without notice.'

They sat in silence then, sipping their medium sherries, looking out of the window at the bare branches of the tree on the other side of the fence.

'You'll stay and have a bit to eat with me?' Elinor said eventually.

'No, I've got a lasagne to finish up from yesterday, it won't keep.'

'Chuck it out then, what's a bit of heated-up leftover lasagne?'

'Money. I don't know about you of course but I have to watch every penny.'

*　*　*

Elinor let her go. Nothing had changed, and nothing had been agreed and there was no truce between them, nor ever likely to be, she thought, taking out cheese and eggs from the fridge to make an omelette. There were lamb chops. She had planned those if Muriel had stayed but the heart had gone out of her to bother with them tonight, or to bother with anything else much. She could see what was on television, she could read, she could sew up the hems of her new bedroom curtains, which trailed onto the floor. She put away the sherry bottle and washed the glasses.

The bell rang.

The electricity had cut out twice that day, but come back on again before long.

'It shouldn't go off at all,' the electrician said, when Elinor let him in. 'I take a pride in my wiring.' She was unsure where the switchboard and fuses were but he knew. 'I ought to,' he said, opening the cupboard.

'Is there anything I can get for you, Mr . . .?'

'Matt. No thanks. If I drank all the tea and coffee I was offered . . . Right, let's have a look-see.' He shone a powerful torch.

Elinor hesitated, then went back into the sitting room. She switched on the table lamp, which promptly went out again with a small flash.

'Gotcha!' Matt said from the cupboard.

Twenty minutes later, the electricity was sorted to his satisfaction and he left to check two other bungalows.

'I never expected this sort of attention, you know,' Elinor said, watching him walk down the path on his way to number 1. 'You still working at this time to make sure we're properly fixed.'

Matt nodded, not looking round.

Twenty-one

Muriel sat in front of the television, which was showing a documentary about families who had emigrated to Australia, a tray of supper on her lap – the warmed-up lasagne and two slices of bread and butter. She had barely eaten any of it. The television was talking to itself.

She was angry, angry with Elinor and angry with herself. She had not intended to let her sister get the upper hand. But somehow Elinor contrived it. She did not try to win arguments, as she had when they were young, nor did she try to gain by possessing some item Muriel hadn't got or having more money left over at the end of the week. In the past, Elinor had gained the moral high ground simply by being what she was and Muriel was not – a wife. Marriage had been Elinor's triumph. She had never gloated about it. There had been no need. The very fact of Bill's existence and of her own changed name had been enough.

Since he had died things had evened up, but now Elinor had discovered a new way of seeming superior to Muriel. She had become sweet, forgiving and sisterly. She had moved four hundred miles, from the place where she had lived all her married life, to be near her twin, so that they could spend their last years trying, as she had put it, 'to mend bridges'. So far as Muriel was concerned, there had never been any bridges, so they couldn't very well be mended.

She had come away from the bungalow in Duchess of

Cornwall Close feeling wrong-footed yet again. Elinor had been reasonable, affectionate, resisting the slightest disagreement. Muriel was cross with herself because she had intended to turn the other cheek, to admire the bungalow and approve of the new life, to sound pleased about everything and envious of what would clearly be a friendly and neighbourly community. Instead, she had not bitten her tongue, she had retorted, been sarcastic, pointed out all the pitfalls and shortcomings of the place.

Since early childhood they had disliked and been jealous of one another and that was now inextricably part of their deepest nature. None of which was her fault. Elinor had brought it all about. Elinor gave her the rope, playing it out eagerly until Muriel hanged herself. Perhaps it had been a game when they were children. It was no game now.

She sat in the dark, her food uneaten.

She should ring. They were too old for all this, Elinor was right, it was too wearing. She should ring or even get out her small car and drive back to her sister's house. Apologise? No, of course not. What did she have to apologise for? But just arrive, stay for five minutes, say something warm, something welcoming, something Elinor would immediately interpret as a gesture of remorse.

Why did she feel so strongly that she ought to do this? She had nothing to feel bad about. They just didn't get on. Plenty of sisters didn't get on. Plenty of fathers and sons, mothers and daughters, brothers, aunts and nieces. It was the way of things. Blood might be thicker than water but that very fact probably made matters worse.

Family. Muriel got up and switched on the light, carried her tray into the kitchen. She had often thought the entire concept of 'family' overrated.

She made a cup of coffee and went back to the television, which was now showing a drama about MI5. Muriel was fascinated by spies. She wished she could have been born a generation earlier and worked at Bletchley Park.

In Duchess of Cornwall Close, the lights flickered two or three times. Elinor went to the window but, so far as she could see,

130

other people had electricity and there was a blue glow from the television at number 1, opposite. Her lights went out. So whatever the man had done hadn't solved the problem, and it was gone eight, he wouldn't be about now.

The doorbell made her start but as it rang the lights came on again.

'I thought you might find a torch handy, I've got a spare.'

It was Rosemary Poole. Nice-looking woman, Elinor thought, tall, well-styled hair, seemed too young to be living here.

'Come in, come in. Have your lights been playing up?'

'On–off, on–off, it's going to give me a migraine if it goes on.'

'Are you sure about the torch? That's very kind of you.'

'I'm quite sure. It may be all right now, but if you need to get up in the night and they're not working . . .'

'I was just making myself a cup of coffee, can I tempt you? Or tea?'

'That's very nice, I will. A weak coffee would be nice.'

Two hours later each woman knew a good deal about the other – past lives, husbands, jobs, changes.

Elinor talked a lot about Muriel and felt both relieved and disloyal. Rosemary Poole was a good listener. 'I only had a brother,' she said, 'eight years older, so I never really knew him. He was married and away by the time I remember much. I longed for a sister.'

Elinor shook her head. Took the coffee cups away. The lights went on and off. On again. Stayed on.

'Did that electrician call on you earlier?' she asked Rosemary. 'He was supposed to have found the problem and sorted it out but clearly he failed.'

'I didn't let him in actually.'

'Oh.'

'I suggested he come back in the morning. He didn't have any sort of card or badge and of course I didn't recognise him. He could have been anybody.'

'Well, I let him in here and he seemed all right. Faffed around with the wiring and the fuses and so on. Still . . . now you say that, I probably shouldn't have.'

131

Rosemary got up. 'Take no notice, it's my son-in-law Harry talking. He makes a fuss about that sort of thing. He's very good, keeps an eye out for me, but I tell him, I've got all my faculties and I've lived a long time. I don't need a nanny.'

'Perhaps I'll see you tomorrow.'

'Come over to mine. My daughter baked me a cake and I can't eat it all myself. About eleven?'

'I'd like that. Thank you, Rosemary. And for the torch.'

Elinor watched the light go bobbing down the path and across to number 1, and did not close the door until her new friend was safely inside.

She knew that she would feel uneasy until she rang Muriel. The fact that she had had such an unexpectedly pleasant evening with Rosemary Poole made her conscience raw about the hostile atmosphere that had surrounded her parting with her sister.

She rang but the answerphone picked up.

'Mu? It's me. I'm sorry, you've obviously gone to bed. I just wanted to have a word – I don't like it when we seem to part on such bad terms. So – if any of the ill feeling was my fault, I'm sorry. Let's try again. I'll give you a ring sometime tomorrow. I've had a nice evening with a neighbour who popped in so I hope you'll meet her too. All right, talk tomorrow, sis. Night-night.'

Rosemary Poole rang her daughter. A grandson answered.

'Is that Bradley?'

'No.'

'Hello, Harvey. Isn't it time you were in bed, sweetheart?'

'Yeah. Here's my mummy.'

'Hi, Mum. Everything all right?'

'Everything's fine, I've had a really pleasant evening getting to know one of my neighbours – Elinor Sanders. We found we had such a lot to talk about, quite a few things in common. I'm going to be very happy here, Karen. Oh, and the electrician is coming round, will you tell Harry? I'm going to get him back tomorrow. Is Harry there?'

'No, it's one of his snooker nights out. You make sure that electrician does come back, Mum, I don't want you having a fall. Proper lighting is very important.'

'Yes, thank you, dear, I do know that.'

'Sorry. Listen, I've got to go, they're both in the bathroom with the taps on. I'll talk to you tomorrow, might try and pop over after work.'

'Only if you've the time, Karen. Don't you worry about me. I'm very comfortable. You see to those two terrors now.'

'Night, Mum.'

'Goodnight, dear, big hug for the boys and Harry.'

I'm a lucky woman, Rosemary thought, as she put the phone down. It had just struck her as she was speaking to Karen. Lucky to have her and a son-in-law and grandsons she loved, lucky to be near them but not too near, lucky to have this nice brand-new bungalow with one friend made and the prospect of plenty more.

Lucky.

She went cheerfully in search of the *Radio Times* to pick her programmes for the next few days.

Excited. I haven't been excited for all this time. No ups, no downs. No probs. Thought it was all sewn up, to be honest. I mean, who'd be stupid enough to rock this lifeboat I'm in? Got lucky, that's all, but when you get as lucky as that, you keep your fingers crossed and don't walk under ladders. Who'd have expected luck like mine? At least, that's what it seemed like. Luck.

In the depot, where they were brainwashing me – because that's what it was – they were all buttoned up and proper, not allowed to let out what they were really thinking, but they'd give me a look and I knew what it meant. I knew what they really thought. That I was guilty as hell. I'd done all of it. Just got lucky. Well, they were right, weren't they?

They said, 'None of this is going to be down to luck, it's down to learning, remembering, watching yourself, not slipping up, always being on your guard, never being able to relax. It'll get easier, mind. In five years a lot of it will come easy. Someone asks your name, you'll give them the new one, someone asks where you were born and when, you'll parrot it off because the old place and date have gone from your mind. It'll feel odd on your birthday – the one you have now. The day'll go by and nobody'll mention it because there'll be nothing to mention. But suppose you get married in the future –'

'Hang on, I'm married already.'

'No, you're not, you're divorced.'

'So . . . you're telling me I can get married again?'

'Nothing to stop you.'

134

'What about the papers, all the forms you have to sign? It's all legal stuff. They'll be wrong, won't they?'

'No. The forms will be correct in every detail. New name, date of birth, place, occupation, all of it.'

'But it wouldn't be legal.'

'It will be legal, take my word for it.'

'Passport?'

'Passport.'

'Driving licence?'

'Everything. Every last bit of paper. All legal. You'll be legal.'

'So if I get married . . .'

'You get married.'

'What do I tell her? She – whoever she is – she'll have a right to know who I am, won't she?'

'She'll know who you are.'

'Not the real me, she won't.'

He'd sighed and leaned forwards across the table. 'It will be the real you. The old you won't exist any more.'

'She could find stuff out.'

'No, she couldn't, because there'll be nothing to find.'

'How do you mean, nothing to find?'

'Wherever she looks – this woman you might marry who you haven't yet met – wherever she looks, if she does, she'll draw a blank. Hospital records, schools, register of electors, bank, credit cards . . . you name it. She won't find anything because there'll be nothing there. There was stuff there – it was all there once. Not any more. It's gone. Thin air. That person you called yourself – that person you were . . . he doesn't exist any more. Do you get it yet?'

The police officer had clicked his fingers.

Gone.

He didn't exist. There was no trace left of him.

But he was sitting here. Breathing. Drinking a cup of tea out of a plastic beaker. Hand on the table in front of him. His own hand. The same hand he'd always had.

'I'm still me. This is my flesh and blood.'

'It is,' the officer said, closing his file. 'And then again, it isn't.'

Kept me awake that one did.

Still does sometimes.

Twenty-two

Simon put a mug of tea carefully down on the bedside table. Rachel was asleep, head turned away from him, one arm flung out. He touched her hair.

'It's seven o'clock.'

She stirred slightly but did not wake.

'Rachel . . .'

No response.

They had enjoyed three days together, the rest of his leave after Norfolk. They had spent most of it in the flat, Rachel cooking, listening to music, reading, watching Simon sort his new drawings. Plus a night in the hotel where he had first taken her to dinner. It had been a time out of time, they had seen no one else.

When he returned this evening, she would be gone. Kenneth returned from his respite care today and Rachel was adamant that once he was home he deserved her presence and full attention. Kenneth knew about their affair. He was an honourable man. He loved Rachel, enough to free her, so long as she did not leave him. How long his illness would drag on, no one knew. Years? Possibly, though Rachel did not seem to think so. It was not something they discussed. For now, Simon was content but he knew he would not always be so. And Rachel? How did she really feel about dividing her life and betraying her husband? There was no chink in the face she presented to the world, but he was under no illusions. It would wear her away. Ultimately, if nothing changed, it would destroy her.

He put on his jacket. Phone in his inner pocket. Keys from the small silver dish his mother had given him when he had made Inspector. He paused and looked down. Rachel breathed gently, peacefully, arm still flung out.

Simon bent and kissed her cheek. Then he scribbled a note and put it next to the mug of cooling tea. *Love you x.*

Driving to the station for the first time in almost a fortnight, he anticipated what he might have missed, speculated on the papers that would be piled on his desk, the email load on his computer. He knew there had been a ram raid, just before the snow had more or less blocked off the town centre, that two school kids of fifteen had been caught red-handed trying in a hopelessly inexpert way to hold up a post office, and that there had been a flasher out and about in the back gardens of the Dulcie estate. Other than that, the weather had deterred a lot of criminals and the force had been busy on emergency traffic duties.

There would be the usual welcome, the sarcastic jokes about Norfolk, the wry comments about everything running a lot more smoothly than when he was at work . . .

Other than wishing Rachel could be in the flat when he returned that night, Simon wanted nothing more than to be back in harness. He had loved his time with Sam, he felt refreshed and energetic. He swung the car into his space and ran up the stairs, into one of the DCs running down.

'Morning.'

'Guv.' The man shot past Serrailler barely glancing at him.

'Everything OK?'

The DC paused. 'Nasty one.' He ran on.

Along the corridor, DS Ben Vanek was heading out of Simon's own room. 'There you are, guv. About to ring you.'

'What's up?'

'A death. Came in half an hour ago. Incident room's being set up.'

The DCS's room looked bare, clean and tidy, but there was a neat stack of files on the desk and his coffee machine was already filled up – his ever-efficient secretary, Polly, welcoming him back.

'Fill me in.'

'Duchess of Cornwall Close, the new sheltered housing . . . lady aged eighty, only just moved in, tied to a chair in her bedroom with electrical flex, and strangled.'

'Who's on the scene?'

'Patrol were first, Steph – sorry, DS Mead – and DC Dotman are there now, forensics and pathologist on the way.'

'Where's the DI?'

'Ah, you don't know – he had an RTA . . . very smashed up, still in intensive care at BG.'

'Who's acting?'

'No one. You were coming back so –'

'Right, consider yourself Acting DI for now. I'll clear it with the Chief later.'

'Guv . . .' Ben flushed pink.

'Right, I'm over there. What else is going on?'

'Ram raid on the post office in Burley Road. The owner was on scene and they beat him up, lots of stuff taken, mainly booze and fags, bit of money, plus a load of chocolate Easter eggs.'

'Wankers. Is the man conscious?'

'Yep. Nasty head wound and a broken wrist but nothing life-threatening.'

'OK, I'm leaving that to you.'

Serrailler was back on the road a minute and a half later.

Duchess of Cornwall Close was stacking up with police vehicles, and crime-scene tape had already marked out number 12, its front path, the whole of the grassed area around it and the bungalows on either side. Everyone was stopped at the tape to give names and details to the uniform on duty. A pressman and his photographer, sticking out a mile from everyone else, were turned back but the tape was lifted for Serrailler. He nodded at the pathologist who was coming in behind him.

'Good holiday, Simon? Sun and sea?'

'Thanks. North Norfolk. Snow and sea.'

'Good God, man, you could have got that staying at home. Morning, Sergeant.'

Nick de Silva's voice boomed out cheerfully as they entered the bungalow among the forensics in white coveralls, but as they walked through into the small bedroom, he fell silent. Among so many of his gung-ho, sometimes ghoulish pathologist colleagues, Nick was well known for his care once in the presence of the dead. 'This is a corpse,' Serrailler had heard him say one time to a lecture hall full of police and students. 'This is a victim, and unless it is proved otherwise, it is an innocent victim. But whether innocent or guilty, it is the body of a fellow human being. Treat such bodies as you would treat one of your own loved ones and as you would wish to be treated yourself.'

Now, he looked at Simon and sighed. Forensics evaporated to take advantage of a break.

The chair was in front of a mirrored dressing table. Serrailler saw the reflections – Nick's, his own. The woman's.

'He put her there so she could watch.'

Nick nodded. He leaned forward, touching nothing, and looked closely at the woman's neck. The piece of electrical flex was wound round it three times and pulled tight and the loose ends had been tied to the chair back with several knots.

'Reef knots,' Simon said. 'Unusual?'

Nick shrugged. 'Statistically, probably not significant but you'll obviously check.'

She wore a pink fleece nightdress which was rucked up to her knees. Her feet were bare. Her head hung forwards, eyes bulging.

Simon left the pathologist to his job and went slowly round the bedroom. New paintwork, new wallpaper, new carpet. Wardrobe with a few clothes on hangers, boxes full of more clothes below. Nothing had been disturbed so far as he could see. Bedside table. Lamp. Pack of tissues. Glasses beside their open case. Nail-clippers. Pack of prescription tablets for arthritis with a few already removed. Neat. Everything was neat.

In the kitchen, crockery and cutlery were in drawers and cupboards. A few things in the draining rack. Tea towel folded over the rail. Lino tiles were spotless.

DS Steph Mead, aka Mrs Ben Vanek, was in the hall.

'Guv, the front door was on a chain and a security bolt. Not touched. Entrance was by the sitting-room window which also has a bolt but it hadn't been dropped down. I wonder if she'd forgotten. Seems unlikely.'

'Maybe not. Hadn't she recently moved in?'

'Day before yesterday.'

'Then she might not have got the hang of all the security fastenings.'

'I'll get a check on whoever fitted them and how they were left. She wouldn't have had a window open in this weather.'

'What do we know about her?'

'Mrs Elinor Sanders, aged eighty, widow, moved down from Newcastle where she'd lived for fifty years. Apparently she has a relative in Lafferton but we haven't an address yet.'

'When forensics have finished look through everything to find one – that's urgent.'

'Guv.'

'Neighbours?'

'Only four have moved in so far. We've spoken to all of them briefly. The lady at number 1 saw her last night – had a coffee together. She's extremely upset.'

'Questioned?'

'I didn't want to go in too hard yet, guv, I don't think she could cope.'

'Get the doc in to her now, we've got to have everything she can tell us asap.'

'Man in number 8's a bit of a curtain twitcher, knows all about Mrs Sanders moving in. Knows about everything.'

'Odd – men aren't usually interested but he might prove useful. Let's hope he's an insomniac.' He went into the front room. The curtains were still drawn but he lifted a corner carefully and looked out. Two men were taking a short cut across the grass towards the bungalow opposite.

'How the hell did they get under the wire – bloody *Gazette*. We'll have the TV vans and the men with furry mikes here any minute.'

He shot out of the front door, yelling across. 'Get off there, you should bloody well know better, this is a crime scene, yes, Baxter, you, and if I catch you lifting a finger to any of these door bells I'll have you in for trespass. You know the rules, press conference later, now bugger off.'

His voice was less angry than his words. One of the reporters raised an arm in acknowledgement. Two minutes later, they were driving off. Simon phoned the station press officer to organise a conference for noon, then went back into the bungalow.

Nick de Silva was peering at the flex round the dead woman's neck, touching it lightly with his gloved finger. He straightened up as Serrailler came in.

'She died somewhere between midnight and five this morning – I'll know more when I get her in. Strangulation, obviously. No evidence of sexual assault, no other injuries visible . . . there are some faint bruises coming out on her hands. She might have tried to hold him off, but she couldn't put up much of a fight – she's old and she isn't a very big woman, and there's marked osteoarthritis in the hands and finger joints. Her grip wouldn't be strong. The boys and girls will be back in here once we've moved her but at a glance he was very clean and tidy indeed. Knew what he was about. No mess, no obvious traces. He'll have worn gloves, possibly left his shoes outside . . . doesn't look like any sort of burglary – she'd left a couple of rings there on the dressing table. Hasn't touched them. Rest of the place?'

Simon shook his head.

'No, this is just killing for killing's sake. Poor woman.' Nick touched his finger gently to her cheek, his face tender. 'She can go now. Sooner I have her on the table the better.'

Steph Mead stood aside as the pathologist went out. 'Forensics say they're doing the kitchen next.'

'What about the neighbour?'

'Daughter's on her way, GP says he can't call till after morning surgery, doesn't do many house visits, can she be taken in there?'

Simon exploded. 'Tell him no, she's in no fit state, she needs a medical check before we can question her and we have to start that within the next hour. Kick his arse.'

Steph made a face and went out as Simon's phone rang.

'Simon, I presume you're SIO on this murder? Brief me please.'

'Morning, ma'am.'

The Chief Constable had been on sick leave for several months and there had been rumours that she would move from there seamlessly into retirement. She had not and once back she seemed to have doubled her old energy and focus, was up to

141

speed with every detail in every corner of her force and had dished out timely warnings to any slackers and coasters. Simon got on well with her, partly because he genuinely liked and respected her, partly because he had worked hard to do so.

'I wonder if you should hold off a press conference until this neighbour has seen a doctor and been cleared to talk to you?'

Paula Devenish was a stickler for protocol and under everyday circumstances would never presume to give instructions to an SIO, but Serrailler knew well enough that a suggestion with a question mark at the end from the CC should be treated as an order.

'Agreed. I'm trying to get the doctor here, but he isn't being very cooperative.'

'Go and fetch him. Don't give him an option.'

'I can't arrest him, ma'am.'

'Of course you can't. You won't need to.'

Twenty-three

The reluctant GP had arrived in a patrol car, spent two minutes taking Rosemary Poole's blood pressure and pulse, written a prescription for diazepam and been driven back. Harry Fletcher had been working out at Starly but dropped everything and was in the kitchen making tea and taking mugs out to every member of the force. Rosemary had a cup untouched beside her. Karen was sitting up close.

'How do you feel now, Mum?'

Rosemary shook her head. She was weaving her fingers together in her lap.

'You ought to eat something.' Harry came in from the kitchen. 'Just a biscuit. Or a square or two of chocolate. Have you got any? Shall I pop down the road and get some?'

Rosemary shook her head again, her fingers moving ceaselessly. Harry went back to the kettle.

'Mrs Poole, I'm DS Steph Mead. I know this is very hard and I do understand what a terrible shock you've had. But now the doctor says you're up to it, I need to ask you a few questions. We have to find who did this dreadful thing and you may have seen or heard something, anything – that could be vital to us.'

Rosemary shook her head to and fro several times. Karen took her hand and held it tightly.

'I know. I wish I could leave you quietly for the rest of the day to try and recover and I promise I'll keep my questions to

143

the absolute minimum and then leave you with your family. But I have to do this now. Do you understand?'

Some minutes passed in silence. Then Rosemary gave a slight sigh and looked up.

'Yes, I do. I'll do my best. I owe it to her. She was a very nice woman.'

'Mum, listen –'

'I said I'd do it. I will do it. Then I'd like the police to go.'

'Of course.'

Harry appeared in the doorway again. 'Anyone want tea? Coffee?'

Karen glared at him but he didn't move.

It took an hour. What Elinor and Rosemary had eaten and drunk, where they had sat, exactly what time they had parted. After that, Rosemary recounted in full detail her own movements in watching television, making a last drink and getting ready for bed. She spoke clearly but with long pauses, she wept, she occasionally gripped her daughter's hand. But she was brave and determined.

'I owe it to her. She was nice. I thought we were going to be good friends and neighbours.'

'Have you any idea, roughly, when you went to sleep, Mrs Poole? Did you maybe glance at the clock as you switched off your lamp?'

'I always do. It was twenty past eleven.'

'Did you go to sleep at once or did you lie thinking for a while?'

'I lay feeling very happy that I'd met Elinor Sanders. I think she was happy too. She'd moved a long way, you know – Newcastle. It isn't easy.'

'How long do you think you lay awake, Mrs Poole? Minutes? Half an hour?'

'No, no, not as long as that. I drop off quite quickly.'

'Ten minutes?'

'It wouldn't be more.'

'And did you wake during the night at any time?'

'It was cold last night . . . well, it's been bitter, hasn't it? The heating had been playing up so it was probably the cold that woke me.'

144

'What time was that?'

'Ten past two. I put on the light, you see. I went to fetch an extra blanket but I couldn't find it . . . a lot of things are still packed. So I just refilled my hot-water bottle.'

'Did you look out of the window? The kitchen window or your bedroom?'

'Yes, I did. I just looked round the corner of my curtains. I wanted to see if it was snowing again.'

Rosemary closed her eyes and her head nodded forwards for a moment.

'Leave it there, Sergeant, she's had enough. She's exhausted.' Harry Fletcher had been standing in the doorway but now he came into the room and put his hand on his mother-in-law's shoulder. She opened her eyes and looked at the hand, then up into his face.

'Harry.'

'You shouldn't have to put up with this any longer, I was just saying. You've told them everything.'

'Mr Fletcher, I'm sorry, but I do have more things to ask so I'd be grateful if you wouldn't interfere. Perhaps Mrs Poole could do with a cup of tea?'

Rosemary shook her head. 'It's all right, Harry. Go and make a pot of tea.'

She had little more to add. She had slept quite well, woken once more and gone to the bathroom, but returned to bed without looking out of any window and slept again at once. In the morning, she had woken a bit later than usual.

'But the heating was working again so the place was nice and warm. It had been playing up a bit, you know, like the electrics and the plumbing. That electrician came round, as he promised.'

'How many times has he called on you?'

'The first time I didn't let him in. Elinor let him in, but I didn't. I don't know why. He was all right. The second time he told me how much pride he took in his work. I believed him too, he was determined to get it right.'

'How long did he stay with you, Rosemary?'

She closed her eyes again. Replaying the scene, doorbell

145

ringing, putting on her slippers, the man standing there again. Not smiling.

'Funny that,' she said suddenly. 'He never smiles.'

'The electrician?'

'He's a perfectly nice fellow, very polite. Just never smiles. He didn't stop long – ten minutes maybe? Checked the fuses and things in the cupboard, all over again.'

'When he left this house did you see him go to Mrs Sanders's bungalow?'

'No, I closed the door, it was very cold, you know.'

'I've nearly finished but will you just take a minute to think very carefully? Did you hear anything in the night? Any sounds at all, usual sort of sounds, a car maybe? Or anything unusual? Did you hear any doors banging, a window being tapped . . . footsteps? You said you woke twice and went to the bathroom once. Are you quite certain you didn't see anything – anything at all?'

'Tea,' Harry said, coming in with the tray and setting it down with a bang on the table beside Rosemary's chair.

Steph Mead shook her head, looking all the time very carefully at Rosemary Poole.

She had leaned her head back and closed her eyes.

'You're worn out, you don't have to put up with any more of this,' Harry said, and turned to the DS angrily, 'Can't you see how she's feeling? If she's taken ill I'll be blaming you. It's time you left.'

Steph Mead hesitated, half inclined to lay down the law, send him out of the room with an order not to come back. But he was right about his mother-in-law. She had gone ash-pale, and looked completely drained. Steph stood up.

'We'll come back later.'

'Try not to,' Harry said.

There's a moment you say 'No'. You mean it as well. No. Then a moment you say 'No' but you don't mean it. Not long, then the moment when it's 'Yes'.

Nothing like that moment.

Until the next, when you're on your way.

Until the next, when you're there.

Until the next, when they hear something and then they see you and then they realise you're there. Then it's all the moments after . . .

Twenty-four

Serrailler needed to think slowly and deeply, with a notebook and pen, and he thought best if he was out of the office. It was too early for the pub and the Cypriot deli would be packed. He got a large takeaway coffee and drove out to the Hill. The sun was out and he sat on the lee side with his back to the Wern Stone. It was sheltered and almost warm, though he turned up the collar of his waxed jacket.

He could never have said that he enjoyed working on a murder – who could? He had a vivid picture in the front of his mind, of the elderly lady sitting in her own bedroom chair, flex tight round her neck, facing her own image in death, as she may well have been made to face it in her last moments of life. She would have seen her killer standing behind her. In death, the most unique, private, intimate moment of everyone's existence, others stood behind her and looked into the same mirror, seeing their own images behind hers – the uniforms who had been called to her body, the forensics, the pathologist. He himself.

But the worse the case the stronger his determination and the keener his focus, and even though the word 'enjoy' had no place, Simon found this part by far the most interesting – the thinking through, the search for parallels, motives, method, the careful piecing together of every detail which might help him towards such a murderer by letting the man gradually into his mind. What kind of a person did this? What was his background, his past, his state of mind, his usual daily life, his work, his family?

And then what triggered such hideous, calculating violence? This was no killing in a rush of anger, or in self-defence; this was a careful, methodically planned killing of a particular kind, for a particular reason.

He made notes about everything he had observed at the crime scene, sketched the layout of the bungalow, then of the new close, then mapped out the area surrounding it – main roads, side roads, trees, bushes, shrubs, hedges, ditches, grass verges. He marked his map of Lafferton in red and green felt tips, circling, underlining.

He sipped his coffee, thinking differently now, not about the place but about people, real people, killers he had known through his police career. As he remembered them he listed their names, crossing many out almost immediately because their murders had been a part of robberies gone wrong, family feuds, domestic violence, city-centre punch-ups, revenge against cops – careless, messy killings, unpremeditated, done by stupid people who had left their crime scenes cluttered with evidence, or handed themselves in, or been caught within minutes. There were too many of them, and though he had a very good memory, inevitably some had been forgotten because they were open-and-shut cases and, so far as murders went, uninteresting.

It was the others he went over in detail now. The sun was warm on his face, there was no one on the Hill, he could dive down into the past and recover faces, conversations, physical details, and link them to the present, as well as to what he had learned in his profiler's training, a course which had been intense and absorbing, and which he had updated a couple of times in the last few years.

'Think yourself into his mind. You are him. Be him now. Think like him, fear what he fears, boast to yourself like he does, plan it all out in the same way. Build up the resentments and the obsession, going back years. Forget everything else. This occupies your every waking thought and your dreams as well.'

He finished his coffee and got up. A black Labrador bounded round the corner, snuffling at Serrailler's jacket, the owner in pursuit. A fire engine went along the perimeter road, sirens blaring. The peace and quiet on the Hill had been good while it lasted.

* * *

149

Fifteen minutes later he was back in the station, had moved the press conference back to four o'clock and called the team into the incident room. The whiteboard already had photographs of the dead woman, the exterior and interiors of her bungalow, and of the whole Close, and a list of residents, with a red tick beside those who had been interviewed.

'Take a good look at this.' Serrailler pointed to the photograph of Elinor Sanders, facing her own dead image in the dressing-table mirror. 'Look hard. Because this is what should motivate you for the next however many hours and days, working round the clock if we have to. It should be in front of you when you're asking questions, handing out leaflets, doing door to door, measuring out how many paces between here and there . . . whatever routine bit of the job. This is Elinor Sanders. This is a lady who was starting a new life, in a new sheltered housing complex where she ought to have felt totally safe and secure, a lady who was sleeping peacefully in her own bed, after having made her first local friend, the neighbour who lives opposite. And who died like this. She was wakened by an intruder, dragged out of her bed, pushed down into the chair in front of her mirror, and then strangled with a piece of electrical flex. As she was forced to watch. Imagine that for a moment. Forced to watch yourself being murdered. That would rank as a war crime. So what does it rank as here and now in an ordinary peacetime city?

'Let me give you an idea about the sort of person who did this. Cunning. Stealthy – walked between the houses and broke into Mrs Sanders's bungalow in the middle of the night without being heard or seen – so far as we know up to now anyway. He's planned this. He planned a murder. Not a burglary. Nothing was taken. Her purse, with over fifty pounds in it, was in her handbag; there was a small jewellery case on the chest which was untouched – nothing of huge value but quite enough to make it worth stealing by an opportunist thief. Forensics found no prints at all, so, unsurprisingly, he wore gloves. He no doubt carried the flex with which she was strangled – she isn't very likely to have had that lying about or stored in a cupboard. Motive? We don't know but it wasn't sexual in the usual sense – the path. found no evidence. She had just moved hundreds of miles, from Newcastle, to be closer to her twin so she didn't know anyone locally – other than the neighbour she met yesterday. Her death isn't likely to be related to some sort of long-standing quarrel. No, this bears all the hallmarks of our worst nightmare – the mad but clever, ruthless killer, who murders for sick reasons of his own. Is this the first time? We're obviously trawling HOLMES and details are out there with every other force. This sort of murder is rarely a one-off. But every killer starts somewhere so this could easily be a first. Which implies the first of – how many? Several? Two? The guy who did it is happy at this moment. He did it and he got whatever weird kick he was hoping to get. He's going over and over the night in his mind. He hasn't forgotten a single detail – they never do. He gloats over them. Chances are he took photographs. Like that one up there. Chances are he has an identical picture and maybe others up on his wall, and that he's gazing at them, getting more kicks that way. This is a dangerous killer and we have to get him. We will get him. But it is the sort of case that is likely to be solved in the course of some painstaking, routine, repetitive police work.'

'Unless he makes a mistake.'

'The chance discovery, yes. But we're not dealing with someone careless and stupid here. He will anticipate every last little thing. People like him don't make many mistakes, though sometimes luck goes against them, no matter how careful their planning. We need that luck. But I think we've got time on our side because he won't do this again in a hurry. He has weeks to enjoy feasting on this murder. He'll squeeze the orange dry before he starts getting restless and planning his next. That planning takes time as well. He won't be in a hurry. That's where we have a head start.'

'How long are we talking, guv?'

'No idea – but I'm pretty sure not days. So let's use the time we've been given. Right . . . house to house within this area . . .'

He drew a red marker pen round Duchess of Cornwall Close and then a second ring within a two-mile radius. 'We're liaising with Newcastle – it might be necessary for someone to go up there but not at the moment. The key to this murder is likely to

151

be not "who?" as in Elinor Sanders but "who" as in an elderly lady. I think the only reason she was killed was her age. And witnesses – if there were any it was one of the neighbours and we're going to talk to them again and again and again, and I don't need to remind you how carefully that has to be handled.'

'What about random people out on the road – whatever route he took in his car, he's going to be noticed, isn't he? At two or three in the morning?'

'Is he? Surprising number of people drive about at night and we've no idea what sort of vehicle we're looking for. But I'll ask for the usual info at the press conf. He isn't going to be driving anything that would draw attention to himself of course – no home-sprayed fuchsia-pink Mini Cooper, it'll be a carefully maintained two-a-penny Focus in silver grey without any "I've been to the Safari Park" stickers or other paraphernalia. He wants to blend in, look anonymous. I repeat, he's clever and careful and his attention to detail will be second to none. Don't underestimate him. Right, off you go – and take another close look at that photo as you leave. Elinor Sanders. She's why we're doing this job. We owe her.'

Twenty-five

The St Michael's Singers were rehearsing Bach's *St John Passion* for Easter and Cat had come in late, slipping into her place to a glare from the conductor. She had then come in late twice when singing, to a sharp nudge from her neighbouring soprano.

'Stressed?' Mel McAllister asked as they nudged their way through the throng to the bar of the Cross Keys later.

'Sorry, sorry . . . I should have been up to speed and I wasn't. I need an evening with the score and a CD.'

'Thought your days were calmer now you're not a GP. Dry white wine?'

'Small one, yes please – but it's my turn.'

'Oh, turn, schturn. You grab a table . . .'

Cat did, the last one, in the far corner near the toilet door, with the wobbly chair leg. She pretended not to see the choir-master waving to summon her over.

'End of a bad week?' Mel set down their drinks.

'And it's only Thursday. I was called in to a finance committee meeting this morning. The moment I walked in I knew. When Sir John was chair he always tried to give you the good news first, put a brave face on . . . not Gerald Hanbury. Face like a hangman.'

'That would figure.'

Gerald Hanbury had taken over as chair of the Imogen House Board of Trustees the previous autumn, when he had retired as a High Court judge, but as he was not a man who understood the meaning of the word 'retire' he had filled a number of high-profile public and charitable roles within weeks. He was a steady pair of hands, sharp, focused and dedicated, but he was also a man at ease with bad news and there had been a look on his face that Cat had thought almost greedy when she had walked into the room.

She had walked out of it forty minutes later not only shocked and distressed but angry – angry that she had been kept out of the loop until matters were decided, sidelined as if she were the man who delivered the supplies twice a week.

John Lowther would never have behaved in that way. He would have consulted, discussed, asked for advice, counselled – even if the decision had been the same in the end.

During the last year of his chairmanship the financial position of the hospice had become so bad that a four-bedded ward had been closed and, a few months later, two further beds had gone. Things had apparently improved, and the day centre had taken up at least some of the slack. But although the centre cost less to run than the beds and although they had a loyal and active body of friends and supporters, the whole place drained money and the recession had hit hard.

The decision had been taken, apparently irrevocably, to turn Imogen House into a day-care hospice only. The remaining wards would be closed within the next three months and the area absorbed into treatment and consultation rooms for people to attend as outpatients.

'But my aunt went to a day-care-only hospice for almost a year and it was great, she saw the doctors, got treatment, and there was a social life to it as well – had her hair done every week right to the end and that did her a power of good. It isn't all bad, surely? Not as if they're closing it altogether.'

'I know. I'm in a bit of a minority on the subject of day-care-only.' Cat finished half her wine at once. 'Pros and cons, but my view is that we need both. There really is no substitute for inpatient care for a lot of people. The latest thing is hospice at home – it's being bigged up as great for the patients but the real reason is financial. As ever. I know a lot of professionals disagree with me so maybe my feelings are based on resentment at being kept out of the decision until it was made. I always liked doing home visits and I'd get some of that back of course.'

'And you'll still be the boss, won't you?'

'In theory, but it will mean far fewer hours. It's a downgrade, whatever good spin they put on it – which they will.'

'So – what will you do?'

Cat shook her head. 'Too soon to know. Lots of thinking.'

'Another drink?'

'No, thanks, I've got to get home. Hannah was due to hear about this film part today but they've delayed. No text from her, so I suppose that means more waiting. Poor child needs it to be resolved one way or the other. By the way, did you hear the rumour about what we're singing after Easter?'

'I hope it isn't Bach again – not that I don't love Bach . . .'

'No, Hans Werner Henze.' Cat pulled her scarf round her neck and smiled sweetly. 'But as I said – it could be just a rumour.'

As usual, she had parked outside Simon's building in Cathedral Close. His car was not there – she knew he was heading up the murder inquiry and likely to be working round the clock so she sent him a quick cheering text. Her phone beeped almost at once, so she'd hit him at a lucky moment. But the text was from Judith who was in charge at the farmhouse, as usual on Cat's choir night.

Are you on your way?

Cat rang her at once. 'What's wrong?'

'I thought I'd better prepare you. Hannah didn't get the part – they rang half an hour ago. Unfortunately she was still up, so things are a bit fraught.'

'Oh Lord, poor Hanny. I'm just leaving now.'

'That isn't quite all, but I'll fill you in when you get home. Hannah doesn't know.'

'Know what? Honestly, I don't want any more bad news this week.'

'The trouble is, in one way this is great news.'

'But?'

'There's Felix, I'd better go. See you soon, darling, drive safely.'

155

She started the car just as her phone rang again.

'Si? How's it going?'

'Grim. You?'

'Don't ask. Nightmare week and it's not over yet. Lunch on Sunday?'

Simon groaned. 'Love to – can you just expect me if you see me? It may have gone quieter by then, we're in the middle of all the immediate stuff, but if I know this sort of case we'll be into needles and haystacks pretty soon.'

'No ideas then?'

'Plenty of those. It's suspects I need . . . Gotta go . . . love to the rabble. By the way, has Judith said anything to you about her and Dad?'

'No, but then I've hardly seen her. She's staying over tonight so maybe . . . You?'

'No idea, but something's up.'

Cat opened the front door onto total silence. Wookie rushed to her giving tiny yelps of pleasure, but then returned to the sofa and his place curled up beside the cat Mephisto, from whom he was now inseparable. Cat found no one else downstairs, but heard a faint murmur from Felix's room. She went up very quietly.

'". . . in case the Tiger should come to tea another day,"' Judith's low, slow, gentle reading-you-to-sleep voice said. '"But he never did."'

Deep silence. Cat pushed the door. Judith was lying on Felix's bed, the book she had just finished reading beside her, the little boy tucked into the crook of her arm, but then he stirred, flopped over onto his side and gave a deep sigh.

'That's unusual,' Cat said in the kitchen.

'Yes, but there's been a certain amount of upset and he woke up, came down, wouldn't go back, then couldn't sleep . . . it's taken four readings of *The Tiger Who Came to Tea*. I tried a move to *The Gruffalo* but for some reason that's out of favour. Right – lasagne in the bottom oven, and salad in the fridge. Hannah wouldn't eat anything, Sam had a bit. I thought I'd wait for you.'

'Can you open this bottle of red? I'd better go up to Hannah.'

'She's asleep . . . the sort of deep sleep into which you escape when life has become unbearable. Not getting the part was bad but then Sam came home.' Judith sat down at the kitchen table and closed her eyes.

'You look exhausted. Here, drink this, and tell me.'

Judith reached for the glass. 'Sam came home. The film people had been into his school, a few weeks ago –'

'He didn't say anything.'

'No. They didn't do any auditions or see anyone in particular. He said they just "hung about the place watching". They went onto the sports field, into the recreation ground, some classes . . . nobody was told much about who they were or why they were there so Sam said everyone thought they were school inspectors. One of his friends said he'd been told they were there to assess the teachers not the pupils.'

Cat had put the food into the top oven. Now, she sat down with her own wine.

'But they were film people?'

'Film spies, as Sam put it. By the way, the other girl didn't get the *Christmas Carol* role either. Apparently they're starting again. Meanwhile, they want about twenty boys for *Lord of the Flies* and they found a good few of them at St Michael's.'

'Including Sam? Really? He's not a natural actor. Still, being in a crowd isn't exactly acting. How does he feel about it?'

'Cock-a-hoop. And he isn't one in the crowd, he would be one of the leads and the Head told Sam today they hope to talk to you this week.'

'Sam? In a film? They're taking the piss.'

'Apparently not.'

Cat took a long drink. 'And he came home crowing that he was going to be the lead, while Hannah came home . . .'

'Precisely.'

'Wonderful. God, I should have been here, I shouldn't have gone to choir.'

'How do you work that one out? You're hardly out every night and I think I'm perfectly able to hold the coats by now. But poor Hannah really does mind very much.'

157

'While Sam won't give a toss.'

'He's not playing it like that. In fact, I gave him an earful and sent him up to bed early, he was winding her up so much. And I don't think I have ever had to do that before.'

'Forget everything.' That's what they said. 'Forget everything.'

So I did.

Almost.

But I didn't forget how it feels. All these years, I remembered. But then again, I thought maybe I didn't. Not actually remember. Not really.

I remembered all right.

Remembered pretty well.

Know that now.

Still, I've got my little reminders. Just in case.

They never knew about those. Nobody's ever known.

My little reminders.

And now there's another one.

Happy with that.

Happy.

Twenty-six

'I've booked.'

'Simon . . .'

'It's an anniversary. I'm no good at them but this is different . . . Rachel?'

He knew what the silence was about and it was not because she didn't want to have the dinner, didn't want to be with him, didn't want to remember. It was Kenneth. Always.

'He had an awful attack last night – I had to give him oxygen, he was in such a panic.'

'How is he today?'

'Better. He's slept a lot. And much better this aftenoon – he's had something to eat and he's watching the Test match. God bless satellite television or he wouldn't have half the pleasure he can still get.'

'And we're winning.'

'Are we? Oh yes, he said something about that.'

'Perhaps you can get the carer who likes cricket to come and sit with him.'

'Tim. I can try.'

'Otherwise, when do we see each other, how do we see each other?'

'How's the inquiry?'

'A long progression of detail, most of which will turn out to be insignificant and irrelevant and one iota of which will be vital.'

'So can you get away for an evening?'

'Yup. I'm always on the phone, but you know . . . I'm not worried. I wouldn't risk it if I was.'

'Our anniversary . . . I remember sitting on that sofa and shaking so much the ice in my glass chinked.'

'Green sofa.'

'Yes.'

Green velvet sofa. The picture of it, of Rachel sitting there, of her face as she turned towards him. It wasn't a question of remembering, because he never forgot.

He had never been in love with any woman for this length of time, though he had been linked to Diana for longer. But linked was not love. Even Freya Graffham . . .

He stopped himself. About Freya he would never know.

'Shall I pick you up?'

'Of course not. Simon, I have to see if I can organise this first.'

'But you want to?'

'Yes,' she said.

Simon felt wretched after he had put down the phone. Why couldn't anything be straightforward? Why had he never met someone, fallen in love with them, married, settled down, had a family, in the usual uncomplicated way? He walked along the corridor to the CID room feeling sorry for himself.

It was late. The team were at computers, trawling through data, trying to find matches for this, links with that, to marry the forensic detail of X with Y. It was thankless and they all knew there would be days, weeks of it. But he was confident. The murder had been some sort of signal, sent out by a man with a grudge, almost certainly not a personal one, against elderly women. This was not an opportunist. This was a psychopath. A sicko, as they all said. He had left no prints, not the tiniest fragment of his clothing or cell of his person. He knew the score. Knew just how careful he had to be.

And, somewhere, he was now gloating, going over the night in his mind, loving every detail, squeezing the last pip of satisfaction out of what he remembered seeing, hearing, touching.

It was the hardest sort of murderer to pin down, the sort with whom Serrailler had always felt an odd personal connection, as if this was between the two of them.

'Nobody work beyond midnight. This is going to be slow and relentless so don't blow all your energy now. Go home, switch off, eat, play Scrabble.'

'*Scrabble*, sir?'

'Euphemism,' Simon said.

Twenty-seven

'Mum, you can't stay here by yourself. I'll be worried out of my mind.'

'I'll be perfectly all right. Of course I will. You heard what the policewoman said – they'll be keeping a close eye on us.'

'Yes, and what does that mean? Swanning past in a patrol car twice a night instead of once.'

'It'll be more than that, I'm sure it will.'

'You've had a terrible shock.'

'I have. But I'm better now. And I think I should stay because I owe it to her – to Elinor.'

'How do you make that out?'

Rosemary shook her head.

'And a couple of other people have moved out – I overheard –'

'Yes, well, that's up to them, but you can't live your life running away.'

'Well, if you're determined, why don't I come and stay with you for a few nights?'

'No thank you, Karen.'

'Mum . . .'

'Your place is with Harry and the boys. I've got a phone, the police have given us all a special number, and you're not far away for goodness' sake. I don't want to talk about it any more. Now, I'd like to go into the town, maybe have a sandwich lunch? I need to buy some more hooks from Frobisher's – can you see where these curtains are sagging? I thought at the time I hadn't got enough.'

'Do you feel up to that?'

'Of course I feel up to it. Cheer us both up. You don't have to fetch the boys until half three, you can drop me back here just before.'

Karen still hesitated. Harry had said before going off on a job that she should leave the decision to her mother. 'She's not a child, she's perfectly capable of deciding what she thinks is best for her. She knows if she wants to stop here for a night or so she'll be welcome, but personally I think she's best facing it right away. It'll be much harder if she leaves it. Only don't tell her that, let her make up her own mind.'

She looked at her mother. It was still on her face – horror, disbelief, sadness. The flesh seemed to have sunk down and there was a deadness in her eyes. Karen wanted simply to pick her up and carry her home, settle her on the sofa in front of the fire, with a cup of tea and a magazine, shelter her from the rest of life. She felt as if their roles had been suddenly reversed and Rosemary was the child now.

Her mother stood up. 'I'll go and powder my nose and get my coat. Then we can be off. All right, Karen?'

'If you're really sure?'

'I am.'

Twenty-eight

Sometimes he just wandered, but tonight he knew which way he'd go. He couldn't keep away. He had no feelings about any of it, just curiosity and a sort of disbelief. A woman had been in bed, safe as houses, fast asleep. Dead of night. Next thing, someone had got in, dragged her out of her bed, put her in a chair and strangled her.

Not in a story, not on the telly or at the pictures, not in a magazine. In Lafferton. His own place. On his beat.

Nobby shook his head.

He'd found a leather jerkin in a skip, together with a thick fleece and a wooden bench. He left the bench in a ditch to pick up on the way back but the leather jerkin was practically new and he could wear the fleece and then put the jerkin over it. Warm as toast. Not that he worried about the cold. Summer bothered him a whole lot more. Plus it was light till nine or half past in summer, not so easy to hide.

He slipped alongside the hedge and through it onto the path. Quiet. Cold. Starry sky. He liked skies. He tried to work out the star names. He could do the Bear. But then there was so much stuff in the way now, satellites and that, confusing you.

Quiet. Cold.

He went along the path to the back where the fence began. Couldn't climb that, no chance.

Quiet. Cold.

He walked a bit further then between the houses. A shadow. No one. No lights. No cars. Not even a cat racing in front of him. But there was the red-and-white tape all round the one bungalow and a couple of lamps on, big moon-faced battery jobs.

Nobby stopped very still.

There'd be a copper on duty.

He inched his way round until he had a good view of the garden, the path, the front door, the windows. No, no copper. Just the tape. Probably done with the place by now, crawled all over it, got everything. What else was there? No point a copper standing there all night.

And then a light was shining right into his eyes.

'Stand there, don't move.'

He wasn't moving.

A shout. 'Here.' Feet pounding towards them.

'I said, don't move.'

Hands on him, bending his arm behind his back.

'Hey, you –'

'Save it. Now walk.'

Nobby walked because he had no choice. He said nothing because what was there to say? He'd been stopped and questioned enough times. They just didn't like him, though a few were all right, gave him a lift home, told him to mind himself, sometimes even bought him a cup of tea from the van. Once, they'd bought him fish and chips. But, usually they saw him, didn't like him being where he was, pulled him in, told him off, sent him home.

So he wasn't bothered.

They opened the patrol-car door and pushed his head down, as if he didn't know the form.

'All right . . .' Nobby said.

But they said nothing. One drove. The other sat.

'Where are we going? I don't live this way.'

'You'll have a chance to say all that.'

'All what?'

'Details.'

166

'What details?'

But they shot through the empty streets at a hundred miles an hour and he got no answer.

'Out you get.'

Hand on him again.

'What am I at the police station for?'

'Stand there.'

Nobby stood. They weren't any of the cops he knew.

The desk sergeant was a hundred feet tall.

'What've we got?'

'Brought in for questioning. Loitering in Duchess of Cornwall Close. You'll need to get someone down.'

'Name?'

'Have I been arrested?'

'You have not. Brought in for questioning, you heard the constable. Name?'

'Nobby.'

'Full and proper name?'

'Norman Parks.'

'Address?'

'By the canal.'

'Don't mess me about please.'

'The shack by the canal.'

'And the postman calls there, does he?'

'I don't get post.'

'Postcode then?'

'No.'

They got no further because of the noise made by two half-naked young men brought in, handcuffed, fighting, shouting, singing, swearing.

'All right, Mr Parks. Someone'll be down in a bit. Room 3.'

'Can I have a cup of tea?'

The PC didn't answer, just stood by the door. Nobby sat at the scabby metal table and looked at the scratch marks. Room 3 smelled of something.

He had no real idea why he was here but maybe it was to do

with where they'd picked him up, in which case he didn't blame them and he could see it hadn't been the best idea he'd ever had. Going there, hanging about. So, no, he didn't blame them. He'd sit here and wait, someone'd come and ask questions, he'd answer and then with luck they'd take him home.

Twenty-nine

'Right, anything?'

The team looked tired and low-spirited.

'One lead – sort of. Patrol brought in Norman Parks – Nobby Parks, lives in a glorified shed down by the canal, near the old warehouses. Bit of a weirdo. Patrol found him skulking around the sheltered bungalows, near to number 12, just after midnight. Got nothing out of him at all. Seen nothing, heard nothing, no idea why he was where he was. Says he just likes being about at night.'

'Wasn't he a witness to the ram raid couple of weeks back? Obviously likes hanging about at night.'

'Nobby Parks has been hanging about Lafferton at night for years,' Serrailler said. 'Harmless loner, one sandwich short of a picnic. He shouldn't have been up at the sheltered housing but he wouldn't have been able to resist. Nobby wouldn't kill anyone. No motive, no history of violence. Just a pity he wasn't hanging about there the night before, he might have seen something important, but don't waste any more time on Nobby Parks. Joanne?'

'Guv. We've interviewed all the workmen who were finishing off at the Duchess of Cornwall Close bungalows in the past three weeks. None of any interest except the electrician, Matt Williams.'

'Yes, odd this. Have we found out if the electricity was actually faulty? Did he have a bona fide reason for going back to the bungalows, and Elinor Sanders's in particular?'

'Been checked. It's true there was a general power blip which tripped everyone's electricity. Williams went to three houses, checked everything, apparently found the fault which our boys have confirmed. But they couldn't understand why he went back again to number 12. Nothing particular there and it wasn't the source of the outage – that was number 1. Fault in the original installation . . . the full report's in the file.'

'And why was he working so late? What do we know about Williams? What's he have to say for himself?'

'We haven't got hold of him yet.'

'Why the hell not?'

'Hasn't turned up for work since the night Elinor Sanders was killed, no reply at his flat and his phone is off. Been trying all day.'

'Car?'

'Van – all kosher, insured and so on, but it wasn't at the house and no one's seen it. The number's out there.'

'CCTV on the bypass and the motorway service stations? When was he last seen?'

'Bloke who lives in the flat below says he didn't hear Williams come home that night, and apparently he usually gets back around six or so, unless he goes to the pub. His local's the Garter's Arms and they haven't seen him for a couple of nights, maybe more.'

'Done a runner then. Anything on file?'

'No. He's self-employed like a lot of them but the building contractors have his details, payslips, bank and so on and that's all in order – he's worked for them on and off the last three years. Before that he was employed by a Bevham firm, Bickerstaff's – they're checking. They have to dig out past employment details and their office is one down today but we're pushing.'

'Married? Previous addresses?'

'Not married so far as we've found.'

'Get round to his place again. Keep ringing the phone. Check vehicle reports. If he isn't back by tomorrow afternoon we'll get a warrant to search his rooms. I want to know where he's worked before the Bevham firm, going back as far as we can, and any serious violent crimes while he was in those areas, particularly attacks on elderly women, robberies, assaults . . . nice bit of delving.

'OK, forensics – not a thing, crime scene clean as a whistle . . . no prints, no hairs, fibres, skin cells, blood, saliva . . . This is Mr Disembodied.'

Thirty

'I need a few details, Mrs Stewart. Your name and address please? It's only for our files, don't worry.'

'Hilary Stewart, 30 Cumberland Avenue.'

And so on, through date of birth and the rest, while she twisted her fingers together and bit her lip and then told herself to stop, because she was behaving as if she had done something wrong, and she'd done absolutely nothing wrong, not a thing.

But the policewoman was pleasant-faced, though not pretty, had neat hair, nice jacket. But bitten-down fingernails. You can get stuff for that, Hilary wanted to say. Tastes disgusting but it works.

'Thank you, Mrs Stewart, that's all. Now, tell me what I can do for you?'

'This may seem rude, but can I ask how long you've been been here – at this police station?'

'Two and a half years. Why?'

'Then you won't know. I'll have to tell you. It's my sister . . . Lynne, Lynne Keyes. Have you heard of Alan Keyes?'

'Nooo . . . no, I can't say I have.'

Hilary sighed. 'Right. I'd better start right back then.'

It didn't take long and everything she said was noted quickly down.

'I'm sorry,' the DC said when she'd finished. 'So is your sister Lynne living with you now?'

'No, she's in a grotty bedsit. But I've sorted it with my husband that she can – she should come and stay with us. They didn't use to get on that well but it was a lot better after Alan was off the scene. Once we knew Alan wasn't ever coming back we all felt . . . well, relieved for a start. He's a nasty piece of work, Miss . . . Mrs . . .'

'Rose is fine.'

'Rose. Right. Thanks. The thing is, read it all up in the newspapers and you'll see. He killed those three old people as sure as I'm sitting here, everybody knew it, your lot knew it, the lawyers knew it . . . we knew it. Nobody was more sure of anything, it was cut and dried, he was going down for life. And then there was something wrong with some bit of evidence . . . some mix-up, someone forgetting what they'd seen – all rubbish, none of it was very important, we knew he was guilty. And then he wasn't.'

'You mean he was found not guilty?'

'It was – what do they call it? – a travesty, a travesty of justice if ever anybody saw one. Only it happened, that was that, and he just vanished. Nobody ever saw him again.'

'I'll have to look all this up and check with my boss obviously. I don't know anything about it, and to be honest I've never had to deal with this sort of case before. Someone being given a new identity is very unusual. It would have been for his own protection, given that the acquittal was so controversial.'

'If he'd have shown his face, he'd have been torn apart. He wouldn't have walked away alive.'

'Which is why he was whisked off.'

'How do they do it?'

'I'm afraid it's something I can't tell you much about, Hilary. One thing I am pretty sure about is that no one – not you or anyone in your family – will be able to make any sort of contact with Mr Keyes. Of course he won't be called Alan Keyes now. He probably won't look the same as he did either.'

'What, you mean glasses and a big black beard?'

'Bit obvious.'

'They were divorced, him and Lynne. She didn't ask for that, though I know she'd have got round to it sooner or later – she just got a letter telling her it would happen and then not long after she got the decree thing through the post. So she isn't his wife now but she was his wife for thirteen years and I just think it's human decency to let him know. Not that Alan knows what human decency is himself. But it is.'

'Hilary, have the doctors given you any idea how long Lynne has to live?'

'They hedge their bets, don't they? But I managed to get something out of one . . . he said he thought a month or so . . . not more than three, probably a bit less. That was what made me decide I had to find a way of letting Alan know.'

'Did Lynne agree?'

'I haven't told her. I haven't told anybody. I thought I'd find out how the land lay and get some advice from the police first. She wouldn't want to see him though, I'm dead sure of that.'

'She wouldn't be able to see him. Now, let me get you some tea.'

'Coffee would be nice, thanks. Milk, one sugar.'

'I'll be back as soon as I can, when I've had a word with the DCI. You won't want to spend much time with our coffee.'

Rose was not long. The reply was brief and conclusive. There could be no contact on either side and no further information would be given.

'So that's it then?'

'I'm afraid so.'

'Right . . . Goodbye then.'

She was about to go through the doors of the station, but turned round on an impulse, and hugged the policewoman. She had no idea why. But she was full of emotions which bubbled up and spilled over, so that her eyes filled with tears, for her sister's miserable marriage and lonely years since, her illness, the fact that she would die soon, and for herself, because a nail of guilt had gone into her one night ten years earlier, and was still painfully there and could never be removed. The tears were of anger and frustration too, and grief for the women Keyes had murdered, and their families who had never been able to come to terms with any of it and more so because of his acquittal. It

174

was ten years ago and it was yesterday and today, and it would be tomorrow.

The only person she did not shed a tear for was Alan Keyes. Or whoever he was now.

Thirty-one

Matt Williams was recognised at a builders' merchant's in Plymouth. Forty minutes later, a car was on its way to pick him up. By seven o'clock, he was in Interview Room 1 at Lafferton Police HQ.

'Present, Acting DI Ben Vanek, DC Frank Gilmore, Matthew Kevin Williams and Mr Iain Ferguson, Duty Solicitor. For the benefit of the tape, will you please give your full name?'

'Matthew Kevin Williams, and the first thing I need to say is I've been brought here against my will.'

'All right, you'll get your chance to protest, but for now, you'll answer some questions please.'

'I haven't been arrested.'

'No, you haven't.'

'Or charged with anything.'

'No.'

'So if I want to get up and walk out of here you can't stop me.'

'No, I can't.'

Matt stood up and pushed his chair back.

'Sit down please.'

'I'm not under arrest, I can go. You said. So I'm going.'

'Listen, if you stay here and answer all my questions, so that I'm happy to let you go, that's in your best interests, Mr Williams. Because if you go now, I can tell you, your action will be saying something about yourself and you'll become the subject of even

176

closer police interest than you are now. In fact, you'll be back in here before you know it.'

'You'd have to charge me.'

'We'd think of something, don't fret. I think the Plymouth officer said he'd noticed the tax disc wasn't correctly displayed on your van.'

'Nothing wrong with my tax disc. Nothing wrong with my van.'

'Glad to hear it.'

'So I'm out of here.'

'And you put up a bit of a push and shove with him when he asked you to go with him from the store. Made his arm ache. He said.'

'Now listen –'

'Just sit down, answer the questions, get it over with, we can all go home.'

'I've got nothing to hide.'

'Then you've got nothing to fear, have you?'

Matt Williams glanced at the solicitor. The solicitor nodded to the surface of the table.

'OK, get on with it.'

'Good. Right decision there, Mr Williams. Now, I have some questions to ask you about the day before yesterday, 28 February. You were working at Duchess of Cornwall Close, is that right?'

'Yes. Been working there for weeks. It's new-build bungalows.'

'Have you been working alone or with a team?'

'Plenty of other tradesmen. Well, obviously.'

'Other electricians?'

'Two. But I work on my own, I'm not with a firm.'

'So sometimes you'd be working on the electrics by yourself in a house, or a flat, other times you might be there with – what? Another electrician? A carpenter? Tiler?'

'Could be anyone. Chippies. Ps and Ds.'

'Did you get on all right with them?'

Matt Williams shrugged. 'Some.'

'But not all?'

'Same every time. I can't stand the skivers . . . sit about drinking tea and reading the racing pages half the day then have

a mad rush for the last couple of hours. I can't stand the ones
who want to talk all the time either. Or the ones with loud
radios.'

'Seem to be a lot of people you can't stand then.'

'Some.'

'What about Nick Flint and Piotr Sikorski?'

'What about them?'

'You've worked with them?'

'Yes.'

'You get on with them? Or can't you stand them?'

'They're all right.'

'But you picked a fight with Flint and you were so violent
Mr Sikorski had to intervene and separate you, try and calm
you down.'

'I don't pick fights.'

'So what happened?'

'Nothing much. Bit of a disagreement, that's all.'

'What was the disagreement about?'

Matt shrugged.

'Are you married?'

Matt looked up in surprise. 'I was once.'

'But not now? What happened to Mrs Williams?'

'What's that got to do with all this?'

'Answer the question.'

'Divorced.'

'Do you have a mother?'

Silence. Then, 'No.'

'Father? Uncles and aunts?'

'I've a brother in New Zealand.'

'So both parents have passed away?'

'They're dead, if that's what you mean.'

'How long ago?'

'Good few years.'

'What – five, ten?'

'Mother died when I was seven. Dad when I was twelve. If
it's any business of yours.'

'It might be. So who brought you and your brother up? What's
his name by the way, your brother?'

'Gran did.'

'Your brother's name?'

'Mark.'

'And how was it? Your grandmother bringing you up?'

'How do you think?'

'I don't. I'd like you to tell me.'

'She looked after us. Fed us and clipped us round the ear and sent us to school. Did what she had to.'

'Did you love her?'

Matt shrugged.

'Did she love you?'

'She did the right thing by us.'

'So you don't bear her a grudge?'

Matt Williams looked at him. Ben Vanek could not fathom the look.

'How long have you been an electrician, Matt?'

'Why?'

'How long?'

'I'm a bloody good electrician.'

'Did you do an apprenticeship?'

'I'm properly trained and fully qualified.'

'For how long?'

'Long enough. Ten, twelve years. I can't remember exactly.'

'What did you do before that?'

Matt opened his mouth and shut it again.

'Something different. You're, what, forty-three . . . so you didn't start out as an electrician.'

'No. Car mechanic.'

'What made you change?'

Shrug.

Ben Vanek leaned across the table. 'You see, what I'm wondering is this. If you're a fully qualified electrician, been one for ten or twelve years, how come you made such a muck of the electrics at the sheltered bungalows?'

'I did no such thing.'

'So why were there power failures?'

'Nothing to do with my wiring. I traced it all back to a faulty lamp.'

179

'What lamp?'

'In her bungalow. Mrs Sanders, the one who got bumped off, poor old lady.'

'So is that why you went back there at eight o'clock in the evening?'

'No. I went there earlier because someone rang me about the power outage. I went round the other places that had people moved in and I couldn't find anything, then I went to hers, and it was her lamp.'

'Which lamp exactly?'

'In her sitting room. Wiring was all wrong. She switched it on and blew the whole power circuit.'

'And all the rest of the power in the other houses?'

'You've got it. Yes.'

'Seems a bit odd, that. Didn't it seem odd to you?'

'Why would it? Happens every day.'

'One small lamp of – how many watts, hundred?'

'Sixty.'

'Sixty watts can bring down the electricity in an entire row of houses?'

'It was lethal, that lamp. Time bomb. Whoever wired that up wants shooting.'

'Right. So you sorted it out all right?'

'I did. When I left it was working fine. Everywhere.'

'So why did you go back?'

Matt looked down at his hands.

'Did Mrs Sanders or someone else from the close call you back? Had something else gone wrong with the electrics?'

'I couldn't stop fretting about it. That lamp was dangerous, I told you. She could have electrocuted herself.'

'And it was all right?'

'It was fine.'

'Let me go through these visits to Mrs Sanders's bungalow. Where did you go? Hall, kitchen?'

'I went everywhere. To the fuse box first – it's in the passage, same as in all of them. But then everywhere.'

'Sitting room?'

'Yes.'

'Mrs Sanders's bedroom?'

'Yes. I checked everything everywhere, I just said.'

'So by the time you'd been round you had a pretty good idea of the layout of Mrs Sanders's bungalow?'

'I had that anyway, didn't I? I mean, I'd worked on them and basically they're all the same.'

'So you didn't have to go back that evening to fix in your mind how to break into Mrs Sanders's bedroom?'

'Hang on – what are you talking about? I didn't break in. When I went in that evening, it was through the front door and she let me in. What are you suggesting?'

'Where do you keep your tools, Matt?'

'In the van. There's some in the shed behind the house I live in, but everyday stuff I use all the time is in the van. Why? Anyway, for the bungalows, they supplied all the stuff.'

'So you didn't use anything of your own there?'

'I did use some of my own tools. Always do. But this was a subcontract job so it was just the tools.'

'Who supplied the electrical flex?'

'They did.'

'Where is it kept?'

Matt's face went ash-pale. 'Now listen . . . listen . . .'

'I'm listening.'

'If you think . . . She was strangled with electrical flex, wasn't she? Now listen –'

'Sit down.'

Matt was standing, leaning across the table, his face scarlet with rage now, one fist up in front of Ben Vanek's face. Ben did not flinch.

'I said, *sit down.*'

A pause.

'You touch me, you so much as put one finger on me, and I'll have you in a cell quicker than you can say ten thousand volts. This isn't going down too well, Matt.'

The room seemed to crackle with tension. But then Matt Williams slumped in the chair, the anger and defensiveness out of him like a gas.

'I want a drink.'

Ben poured him some water, and handed the plastic cup over.

'That all you've got?'

'That's all.'

Matt glared at the cup.

'Why did you go back to Mrs Sanders's bungalow, Matt?'

'I told you.'

'You know, I'm not sure I really buy this. You tell me you're a great electrician, take a pride in your work and so forth, but not only do you race round there when someone reports a fault – fair enough, I suppose, things do happen – but when you've sorted it, you then worry enough to go all the way back to double-check that one bungalow. You said the power going out was down to a faulty lamp in Mrs Sanders's sitting room?'

'Yes.'

'You're absolutely sure about that?'

'Yes, I bloody am, I told you – I'm a good electrician.'

'So . . . you mended it, you checked everything, no one reported any further problems. Why did you go back?'

'I didn't want them all to be without power in the night, did I? If they had, whose fault would that have been? Who'd have been off the case? There are far too many freelance sparks as it is. You're only as good as your last job.'

'So you didn't go back in order to kill Mrs Sanders? Perhaps you didn't leave her bungalow at all. Perhaps you stayed in there? Made yourself comfortable. Hid yourself even.'

'Where the fuck would anyone hide in those rabbit hutches?'

'You tell me, Matt.'

Matt shook his head.

'Did you walk in through the door? Did you ring the bell in the middle of the night? Or did you break in through her bedroom window?'

'Fuck off. I'm not having any of this.'

'You see, the odd thing was that no one actually broke in through the front door or the kitchen door or through a window. Someone had actually left the bedroom window unlocked so it wasn't secure and the arm was loose. It only took a bit of fiddling and pushing to open – no need for any noisy glass-breaking.

182

Mrs Sanders didn't bother to check properly. She obviously felt safe. But she wasn't safe, was she? Because you'd played about with the window and when you came back in the middle of the night, by which time she was in her bed and asleep, you –'

This time, Ben was ready for Matt Williams as he lunged, kicking over his chair. Both officers were on their feet trying to pin him face down, arms behind his back. The solicitor was standing too, but poised to run, not to pitch in and help.

'Ring the bell,' Vanek shouted. Williams was as strong as a bull.

When two uniforms burst in, it took the four of them to handcuff him.

'Matthew Williams, I am arresting you on the charge of murdering Elinor Sanders, on 28 February 2012. You do not have to say anything . . .'

Williams went on bellowing, long after he had been put into a cell.

Thirty-two

'Who's that?'

Sam glanced up from the sheet he was cutting out of a magazine. 'MYOB.'

Hannah leaned over his shoulder. '"Damian Lewis". Who's Damian Lewis?'

'He's about the most famous actor on television right now.'

'Well, I've never heard of him.'

'Shows what you know. Ever heard of Dominic West then?'

'No.'

'Benedict Cumberbatch?'

'You just made that up.'

'Ha.'

'Who are they then?'

'I said. Famous actors.'

'They can't all be the most famous actor on television.'

'No. Duh.'

Hannah turned away.

'You're crying.'

'I am so not crying.'

Sam jumped up, grabbed her arm and spun her round to face him. 'Ha. So what's that on your face – dishwater?'

She bent her head and bit him on the hand. Sam yelped.

'You little weasel.'

'Shut up, shut up . . .'

'Look, you made tooth marks.'

'Teeth marks. Yes and I'm glad and I hope it bleeds and you get HIV.'

Sam snorted.

'Or tetanus.'

'Well it would be something pretty evil if I caught it from you.'

Hannah grabbed the magazine on the table and ran out of the room with Sam after her. In the hall, both of them crashed into Felix who was on his way to find them. His wail of fright as he hit the ground had Cat flying out of her study. 'What in heaven's name is going on here? Sam, what were you playing at?'

She dusted Felix down and inspected the knee he was rubbing. It was turning red and had a small scratch. 'All right, I'll put some cream on that, sweetheart. Sam?'

'Look at that . . .' Sam held out his bitten hand. 'That little bitch did it. And now she's stealing my magazine.'

'Sam!'

Hannah was already halfway up the stairs. Seconds later, her bedroom door slammed.

'Sam, come here.'

'I'm doing something.'

'I'm not interested. All right, Felix, sit still, I'm only putting a dab of cream on, you're fine.'

'And a Bob.'

'Yes and a Bob.'

'Baby.'

'Sam, I don't know what any of this is about but it has nothing to do with Felix. How did he come to be on the floor with you two on top of him?'

'Hannah's fault.'

'I doubt that. There.'

Cat pressed a Bob the Builder plaster onto Felix's scratch and lifted him down from the worktop beside the sink. He inspected his injury closely, beamed, and wandered off to the den.

'Right, sit down, and tell me exactly what was going on and why you were speaking to Hannah in that way. I won't have it, Sam. What happened?'

'Nothing. She's only sulking.'

'No, she is disappointed and upset and are you really surprised?'

'And jealous.'

'Of course she's jealous. Think about it. She was hoping – no, she was pretty much expecting – to get a part in a film. She didn't get it, so she was gutted . . . and this is what she loves doing, what she's good at. But what's worse is you, into whose head the words film and acting had never entered, who didn't ask for any of it, just swan into a much bigger role in a much bigger film. She could even cope with that, eventually, but not if you gloat and lord it over her. Which is what you've been doing for over a week, and you should be ashamed of yourself. You aren't four, Sam, but you're behaving like a spoilt brat.'

'She's the spoilt brat, if you ask me.'

'I'm not asking you. I don't want to hear one more word from you to Hannah on this subject. And if I do, or if Hannah tells me that you've started up again –'

'You'll do what?' Sam sighed.

'I'll contact the film company and tell them you can't take part. That's all. Now go and get on with your homework.'

'You wouldn't do that.'

'Try me.'

Sam attempted to stare her out and, failing, slouched away upstairs.

Which child to see first? Cat was about to check that Felix was happy constructing another tower block with his Bob the Builder Site Kit, then go to Hannah, when she had one of her increasingly rare moments of feeling alone. The life of a single parent was far worse for most other women, without adequate housing, money, family, friendships, but the lonely responsibility was the same. She had support, enjoyed her work. Then came evenings like this one and she struggled to know which way to turn, and longed for the presence of just one other adult. Any other adult.

She checked on Felix, who barely looked up from his massive fibreboard building site, made herself a coffee and rang her brother.

'Serrailler.'

'Hi, you in the middle of something?'

'Sorry, didn't check it was you. How's stuff?'

'How long have you got?'

'Ah . . . not all that long actually.'

'The case?'

'No, I'm off tonight. It's looking good.'

'You've got him?'

'Think so. Problem of lack of evidence but we'll find it. So, I'm in a small towel, having had a shower, and I was just choosing a shirt.'

'Aha. Date then.'

'Yes and I'm running a bit late . . . You all right?'

'Fine,' Cat said. 'Just wanted a catch-up but we can do that another time. Supper tomorrow night?'

'Great. Thanks. Can we have roast chicken?'

'Sure. And maybe you can have a word with Sam at some point.'

'See? Knew there was something. What's the new Daniel Radcliffe done now?'

'You may jest, but it's gone to his head in a really unpleasant way.'

'OK, I'll have a word.'

'Thanks, bro. Have a great evening. Love to Rachel.'

She thought about Rachel as she finished her coffee. Felix was singing 'Can We Fix It?' happily in the den. Upstairs was silent. Even Hannah's Radio 1 didn't seem to be playing.

Occasionally, Cat worried about Rachel, because she was so vulnerable and because of Simon's track record with women. She wondered if he had ever seriously loved any of them and then checked herself – yes, he had loved Freya Graffham, she was pretty sure. And Rachel? Yes. He had not talked very much about her, but when he had there was a seriousness in his voice, a depth of emotion he had rarely displayed before. He was sensitive to her situation and to how difficult it was for her to split her time and her loyalties between him and her invalid husband. Kenneth might have accepted her relationship with Simon but, even so, guilt would be there, and anxiety, worry about the future. Kenneth was in the late stages of Parkinson's but that did not mean he was going to die any time soon. They had snatched hours and the occasional weekend. They would have this evening and tonight. And then? Besides, she wondered if Rachel understood just how committed he was to his work, how much it took up not only of his time but of his mental, physical and emotional energies and commitment.

She sighed, putting her mug in the dishwasher. She loved her brother completely, but sometimes she saw a time ahead when he was still the bachelor uncle, still playing the field, in his sixties and heading for retirement. And then what?

'I think I'll be put to bed now,' Felix said, coming in.

'I see – is the builder's work over for the day then?'

'Yes, but tomorrow, we are doing a demolition job so I need a lot of sleep.'

He was the only one of her children who had ever voluntarily suggested that it was bedtime and he did so often. At the top of the stairs, he glanced round at her and she caught a flash of her brother's looks on his five-year-old face, the same slow half-smile. 'I wish Molly would come back.'

'She will, but not quite yet.'

'Does her mummy still need to have her?'

'Yes. And she needs to have her mummy.'

'She sent me a particular crane I needed for the job so I love her.'

Cat laughed. 'I know. But you love her anyway, even without the particular crane.'

She watched him strip off his shirt and jersey as he went into the bathroom, putting them neatly together on the chair. He was the easiest of her children in every respect, by a country mile.

Twenty minutes later, he had fallen asleep in the middle of *Horrid Henry*. Cat switched off his light, went across the landing and listened. A slight sound from Sam's room – probably a page turning. Sam read more books than anyone she knew apart from Judith. She decided she wasn't yet ready to have things out with him. That would almost certainly involve a full-scale row and she needed to prepare herself carefully for what she would say, to minimise the damage it might do to them both.

Let Sam stew.

'Hanny?'

Silence.

'Can I come in?'

Silence. Then a muffled voice.

Hannah was sitting up on the bed, fully dressed but with her duvet pulled up around her, and her diary open on her knees.

'I don't want to talk about it any more and don't tell me I have to be loving and forgiving because no way.'

Cat sat down and put out her hand. Hannah ignored it.

'Don't take it out on me, Han.'

'He's mean and I hate him. He didn't even want to be in a film, he doesn't even do drama, so what's fair about that?'

'Nothing.'

'And don't say sometimes life is unfair because I'm not listening.'

Cat wondered what there was that she could say to help and decided probably nothing at all. Hannah was right – it was unfair, life often was, and Sam had indeed been mean. She hadn't got the part in the film after longing for it so much; he had a bigger part in a bigger film he hadn't so much as tried for. What was there to be said about any of it?

'I just wish I could do something to help. I wish I could make it up to you.'

'Well, you can't and buying me stuff won't work so don't bother.'

'Han . . .'

Hannah flung herself across Cat suddenly, her arms tightening round her, and sobbed and sobbed, and Cat saw that it was the only thing she could do and all Hannah wanted, even if it did not and could not change what had happened, or the unfairness of it all.

I'm laughing. That's all. I heard it and I started to laugh. Not aloud. Inside. It all happens inside. Laughing like that, to myself, cracking up to myself inside, with a normal face, it has to be the best thing.

I always used to smile afterwards. I couldn't keep the grin off my face. I had to be careful with that one.

But laughing, I can do that inside and no one will ever know.

So tonight, I laughed until I had a pain in my belly.

Laughed and laughed and laughed.

Because what could be funnier? I ask you. 'Police today issued a statement . . . Police have charged . . . Police have charged . . . in connection with . . . Police have charged . . .

I'm in bits. I really am.

In bits.

Laughing.

Thirty-three

'There's a tuna pie in the fridge for your supper, and cheese if you want to grate it on top, and the boys have got fish fingers –'

'Karen . . .'

'– and don't forget to stand over Harvey while he brushes his teeth or he won't.'

'Karen . . . have I looked after my sons for a night before? Have I?'

'Well, yes, only—'

'Or fed them, and fed myself, and watered that bloody plant . . . just go.'

'Right. I've rung Mum and she sounded all right.'

'She'll be fine, they've arrested someone, stop worrying.'

'Does that mean there won't be any police up there now?'

'I'd think so. If they've got him why would they waste resources – public money and all that?'

'Just for peace of mind, I suppose. Listen, if she rings you –'

'She won't, she'll ring you. She knows you're going to Topsham, doesn't she?'

'Oh yes, I've got a bagful of stuff from her for Shona and the baby. Just think . . . Mum's a great-granny!'

'You'll get caught up in traffic if you don't move. And watch the roads, they forecast black ice in the morning . . . Look, 'I'll ring your mother first thing.'

'That'd be kind, love, she'll appreciate it. She's very fond of you.'

Harry laughed. 'Yes, well . . .'

'No, she is. Right . . . thanks.' She leaned over and kissed him.

Harry pointed at the door.

'I'm gone,' Karen said.

Harry turned on the television, but the arrest of the electrician Matt Williams was yesterday's news and there was only a brief report that Williams had been remanded by Lafferton Magistrates until a later date, bail having been refused.

Harry marked up a couple of programmes and a film he wanted to watch later, then turned over to Sky Sports.

'Dad . . . can we go and see Nana?'

'No.'

'I want to see her.'

'Bradley, it's freezing cold out there, I'm not getting you and Harvey into the car and driving over now. You can see her tomorrow.'

'Can I ring her then? I really, really want to tell her about my double gold.'

'That's a better idea. She'll be chuffed. Does Harv want to speak to her as well?'

'Dunno.'

'Then go up and ask him!'

Bradley shot off.

'Rosemary, it's me. Just checking up on you, making sure you haven't got a party going on.'

'Hello, Harry. Nobody feels much like having a party round here yet. Still, very good news and very clever of the police force, wasn't it?'

'Too right. You'll sleep a lot easier. Have you been out?'

'I have. Mr Dyer walked with me round to the shops on the main road. He lives at number 6. We both wanted a few bits and bobs and it felt safer on the pavements, they never cleared them properly, you know, they're still quite treacherous.'

'I know, so you be careful. If you need anything getting and the weather hasn't improved give us a shout.'

'You're a good fellow. Has Karen gone?'

'Yes, all excited with a bagful of bootees. She'll be back tomorrow afternoon. Listen, there's someone else here who's overexcited. I've got to let Bradley have the phone now, he wants to tell you something. You take care now, Rosemary.'

Bradley snatched the receiver and promptly dropped it. Harry could hear his mother-in-law's voice chattering away on the floor. He went to put the tea on.

He checked up on her again around ten o'clock.

'Is everything all right, Harry?'

'It is. Boys sound asleep and I'm just about to start watching the footie so I thought I'd make sure you were safe and sound first.'

'Have you heard from Karen?'

'Yes, got there safely. Is there anything you need? Are the police out there?'

'No, I don't think so, but then I haven't been outside to look, not in this weather. Anyway, I'm warm and comfortable and off to bed soon.'

'Have you got a hot-water bottle?'

'You're as bad as Karen. Yes, I have, and a hot drink and my book. Thank you for ringing though, Harry, I do appreciate it.'

'I know you do. Night-night, Rosemary. Sleep tight.'

'Goodnight, dear. God bless.'

She settled herself in bed with one of the three paperbacks she had still not read since getting them for Christmas. She had always used the library too but it was a bit far from here. When the community hall and sitting room were built, as they'd been promised and seen on the plans, maybe a library could be started in a small way for the residents here. She had plenty of books, others might have discards, relatives could bring some, and though it might be more of a swap system on a couple of shelves than a proper library it would serve. She kept a notepad and pen on her bedside table and she started to make a list of the sort of books people here might enjoy. Crime. Romance (nothing dirty). Anthologies. Classics. She began to put down names too. P. D. James, Joanna Trollope, Katie Fforde, Ruth Rendell, Penelope Lively, Victoria Hislop . . .

She was well into her stride, remembering books she'd loved, wondering if this or that novel was out of print, adding 'Miss

Read' hastily, then 'Nancy Mitford' and 'Denis Lehane' – one of her own favourites but possibly a bit too raw for some.

Rosemary's stomach for crime fiction was surprisingly strong, though she found the dark Scandinavians a bit hard to take.

She was enjoying herself, and had just jotted down Daphne du Maurier when she heard a sound. Inside? No, outside. A cat? One had tried to sneak into her kitchen and resented being thrown out. Rosemary was allergic to cat fur and did not want to have days of sneezing and reddened eyes.

Then she heard something louder. Her heart jumped into her throat like a goldfish leaping out of a bowl, and then beat so loudly she could hear the blood pulsing in her ears.

Again. A little louder. Nearer. She thought someone must surely be trying to get in through the bedroom window, which was how . . .

No. The window was secure and the sound was coming not from there, but from the front hall. The front door.

She sat up in bed, clutching at the top sheet, not knowing if she should cry out or stay silent, get up or stay still.

She did not have many seconds in which she was still free to decide.

You can never be sure. You need to know that. You have to hammer it into your skull. You can never relax, never believe you're safe, never drop your guard.

Have to be careful. So careful. Have to go over everything and get rid if there's even a shadow of a doubt. Because if . . .

No. Doesn't bear thinking about.

Better to be sure.

Absolutely sure.

Better to be on the safe side.

Only thing is, I hate being in a rush. That way you make a stupid mistake, you slip up because you're in a panic, and I've never been in a panic, me, never once.

Not in a panic now.

But time's not exactly on my side, is it?

Thirty-four

Just before eight the next morning, when the Fletcher boys were fighting on the stairs, the phone rang.

'Harvey?'

'Stop it. Stop IT. Mum, Bradley's kicking my shin, he's –'

'Listen, Harvey, listen to me. Get your dad, now, it's really important.'

There was something in his mother's voice.

'Dad? Mum says it's really important.'

'For heaven's sake, I'm frying bacon, watching the toast . . . Go and get dressed, you two. Now.'

Harry took the phone.

'Listen, I've been trying to get Mum for the last half-hour and she isn't answering.'

'It's only just eight and it's Saturday, stop fretting.'

'She's always up by seven, you know that, often much earlier. There's just no reply and I'm really worried.'

Harry sighed. 'She could be in the bath.'

'Not all this time. Harry, will you go over there, love?'

'But I've got the lads, the breakfast's on, I'm not feeling great either . . . Tell you what, you get yourself sorted out, I'll keep ringing her, and if I haven't had an answer by nine, I'll go over, take the boys.'

'That's too long, Harry. She might have had a fall and be lying there, she might –'

'Half eight then. Just let me get breakfast down them and I'll go.'

'Or call the police . . .'

'You can't call the police every time an old lady doesn't answer her phone, Kaz.'

'But because of where she is –'

'You're forgetting something. They've got the bugger. He's behind bars.'

Karen sighed. 'I suppose. Yes.'

'You're getting yourself worked up. Still, she ought to be up and about by now. I'll go. But if you get hold of her in the next quarter of an hour, or she rings you, do me a favour and call me, Karen. I don't want a wild goose chase with both boys, in this weather. We've got freezing fog here. What time will you be back?'

'I'll have lunch with Elaine and then set off.'

'Don't leave it too late – if it comes down like this again it'll be nasty driving. You look out for yourself.'

'I will, sweetheart. Ring me straight away if anything's wrong up at Mum's.'

'What do you take me for? I'm as concerned about Rosemary as you are.'

'I know. I'll be fine once I hear she's all right.'

Harry shouted the boys down to breakfast. 'And make it snappy. We've got to go and check on your gran. No messing.'

As they tumbled downstairs, he picked up the phone and dialled Rosemary's number. It rang and rang and rang.

Thirty-five

'Rachel . . .'

'Mmmm.' She stirred, then turned and pulled the duvet back over her.

Simon kissed her forehead. 'Breakfast will be here in ten minutes.'

A brief pause and then she sat up. 'What . . .?'

He laughed. 'You remember? We decided a large breakfast in bed would be the thing.'

'It's not that long since we ate a fantastic dinner.'

The hotel had recently been awarded a Michelin star and it showed, not in pretentiousness but in fresh, carefully prepared dishes, full of intense flavours, and in presentation that in itself was like a work of art, yet without any over-embellishment. They had drunk Veuve Clicquot and a fine bottle of Pomerol, and come to the luxurious room with its vast bed and deep mattress and pillows in a haze of happiness. Rachel had looked at the room-service menu and they had ordered breakfast.

Simon leapt out of bed, and went to run a scalding shower. One of them had to be ready for the waiters.

When they arrived, two young men carrying the silver trays at shoulder level, they set up a table by the window, where the room overlooked the hotel's park that sloped up to a crown of trees. The grass was frosted white, the sky brittle blue.

'Oh my God, Simon . . .' Rachel gazed at the breakfast, when the waiters had departed with silent and respectful smiles. 'I don't eat breakfast.'

'Nor do I. All the more reason and you look beautiful.'

She did. She was. Hair pulled loosely back in a band, skin creamy-pale. He looked into her eyes. Their violet had been darker last night, in artificial light. Now, they were amethyst-bright.

She stared at the breakfast, the silver pots of coffee and milk, the freshly squeezed orange juice in its crystal jug, the basket of warm croissants and chocolatines, the racks of toast, the butter set over a cooler of water, the plates of peeled and sliced fruit, melon, kiwi, pineapple . . .

'Honey, strawberry jam, fig jam, marmalade, lemon marmalade . . .' Rachel said wonderingly. 'It's like the picnic in *The Wind in the Willows.*'

'No porridge . . . You forgot to ask for porridge, with cream and brown sugar.'

'Simon!'

He held out her chair, opened her napkin and set it on her lap. Kissed her. Sat down opposite. The smell of the hot coffee as he poured it was so rich he closed his eyes to savour it. To savour this, now.

His mobile rang.

The station number was on the phone display.

He looked at Rachel.

'Please answer it.'

'It's work. No.'

'It'll just ring until you do.'

'Not if I switch it off.'

Of course he did not. He had never failed to reply to a call from work, wherever he had been, whatever the time or the day. They had the roster. They didn't ring him on his day off with a report of a stolen bicycle.

'Serrailler.'

'Morning, guv. Sorry, but you're going to have to come in.'

'What?'

'Another one. The sheltered housing. Mrs Rosemary Poole, number 1 Duchess of Cornwall Close. Exactly the same MO, every detail.'

'How did we find out?'

'The lady's son-in-law called us. His wife had been ringing her without getting an answer, so he tried and when he got no reply he went over there. Had to take his two kids, he was in charge overnight while his wife was away.'

'They didn't . . .'

'No, he left them in the car. They didn't see anything but he was in a pretty bad state . . . they're all here at the station now. Car's fetching the mother, she's in no fit state to drive.'

'On my way.'

Simon stood holding the phone, staring out at the frozen park. 'Fuck,' he said. 'Fuck, fuck and fuck again. Sorry, Rachel, I'm –'

'For heaven's sake . . . what's happened?'

He told her as he was getting dressed. The breakfast table stood, laden with untouched food and drink, beside the window.

'Eat,' he said, slipping on his shoes, 'enjoy it, eat for me as well. I'm so sorry.'

'Simon, it's your job. I'm fine.'

She put her hand to his face and kissed him. 'Now, go.'

She watched him stride quickly away down the hotel corridor.

The scene at Duchess of Cornwall Close was depressingly familiar. Vans. Forensics. Red-and-white tape. Uniform guarding the door. Only the bungalow was different.

'Guv.'

He went straight into the bedroom. Same. Same horrible scene all over again. Rosemary Poole had been placed – presumably forced down – into a wicker chair in front of her dressing-table mirror. The same electrical cord was pulled tightly into a knot round her neck. She was wearing her nightdress but her feet were bare. The bed was as it must have been when she got or was pulled out of it. A blue china mug of milk, skin formed on the surface, stood next to an Ian Rankin paperback. A pair of reading glasses was on the floor. And some nail-clippers. Nothing seemed to have been disturbed, nothing taken. Killing for killing's sake.

The pathologist came in as Serrailler was looking at the

200

woman's image in the mirror, the hideously distorted face, blue throat, bulging eyes.

'Simon.'

'Nick.'

Nick de Silva sighed. 'You've got to get this monster.'

'Thought we had.'

'Do we know who she is?'

'Yes. Nice woman. Friend of the previous victim, she was very shaken up about it.'

The pathologist was looking closely at her neck, touching nothing yet.

'He knows what he's doing. But what's this sadism all about, Simon? Setting them to stare at their own dead faces?'

'Is that what he does? Or does he strangle them while they're watching?'

'No. Or, I don't think so. That would be difficult even for a strong man, unless he half does it, then puts them in the chair when they're no longer able to resist. Difficult to fight a man off when you're also fighting for your breath.' Nick lifted the woman's hands one by one and examined each finger, each nail. 'No sign of skin under the nails which would mean she'd scratched at him . . . but it could be too small for the naked eye to see. We'll find that out.' He looked at her bare feet. 'Bet it's the same as the other one: she'd recently cut her toenails.'

'Time of death?'

'Maybe a bit earlier than the previous one. She's been dead for nine or ten hours, at a guess.'

'Around midnight then. I'll leave you to it. Anything else you spot before you get her in, let me know, will you? On her, around her . . . anything that sorts this one from the last.'

'Will do. But this isn't a copycat, Simon. This is the same guy, and he's an expert.'

Serrailler saw the car from the top of the road, before he reached the police station. By the time he had parked, the Chief Constable was in the building and her driver was reversing into a convenient space.

Despite the fact that he got on well with Paula Devenish, he knew what was coming. The Chief took no prisoners.

Ben Vanek was coming down the stairs and made a sympathetic face, jerking his thumb towards the CID room. Simon nodded. 'You OK?'

'I'm off to an arrest. Patrol in Bevham pulled over a black 4 x 4 with bull bars, for having a broken tail light – and a load of gear in the back taken in a ram raid last night. Result.'

Simon headed on up the stairs. Hesitated. Go on into the CID room, or wait until the Chief came to his office?

No. Get stuck in there. He turned down the corridor.

The CID room was full. People were at their desks, faces at computer screens, ears to phones. The Chief was walking round, keeping a low profile, having a word here and there, not interfering or holding up the work. Waiting for him then.

'Morning, ma'am. Sorry, I didn't realise you were coming in or I'd have driven straight here.'

'From?'

'Duchess of Cornwall Close. I'll do a brief in about half an hour.'

'I'll come in on that, but can we have a word first?'

His secretary had the coffee ready, cups not mugs, milk hot, biscuits chocolate. Polly had things done before Simon had thought of them.

Paula Devenish sat down and drank half the cup of coffee before she spoke.

'Simon, I did come in to have a quick word about all of this but there's something else before we get to the murders. Don't look alarmed, you're my best DCS, this isn't a dressing-down.'

'I've jumped to some over-hasty conclusions, I know that.'

'This sort of case puts immense pressure on the SIO, I know only too well . . . the pressure to be seen to be acting, succeeding, making an arrest, putting an end to it all. But I'll come to that . . . Listen, you'll hear about this tomorrow but I'm telling you and a couple of other people in advance – I'm retiring.'

It was the last thing Serrailler had expected. The Chief had been very ill the previous year and on sick leave for several months but she had returned in great heart, full of energy and

202

new initiatives. Any of them would have said she was certain to go on in the job until she reached the age limit. She had six years before that.

'I'm not going to explain why at the moment, but I hope you'll come and have a drink and I'll tell you more about it.'

'Are you staying in the police?'

'No. If I were I'd be staying on here – I've got the perfect job.'

'I take it as a compliment that you've told me before it's official.'

'You can take it as that – you might also think of another reason.'

But he had no idea.

'I think you should apply.' She held up her hand. 'I would dearly like you to be my successor, though of course I won't have any influence. But let's stop right here because you've a briefing to take.' She finished her coffee and stood up.

Serrailler had got his head together by the time they walked in but the others in the room were immediately on edge when they saw the Chief. She was very much liked and respected but they were always ready to feel defensive if she became closely involved with a particular job.

Knowing that, she sat at the back.

Simon pointed to the whiteboard and a blown-up photograph of the sheltered housing complex. The two bungalows in which the women had been murdered were outlined in red. Beside them were their photographs – the one of Elinor Sanders taken some ten years before, that of Rosemary Poole just a few weeks ago, with her grandsons at Christmas.

There was also the ID photo of Matt Williams.

Serrailler pointed to it, then took it down. 'That was our prime suspect, Matthew Williams, electrician. He has been released from our custody without a stain on his character.'

'And he's kicking up a hell of a stink,' Joanne said. 'Official complaint, compensation, the lot.'

'It'll get him nowhere. Yes, the evidence was circumstantial but there was quite a pile of it – there was every reason to arrest and charge him and I'd do the same again. But of course a second murder, in the same area and with exactly the same MO, was committed while Williams was our guest.'

'Unless he committed the first murder and this is a copycat.'

'Very unlikely. We haven't made public some key details about the murder of Elinor Sanders. We've told the press that she was a strangled with flex. But we haven't told anyone that she was placed on a chair in front of a mirror. That information is strictly under wraps and has been from the beginning. No one has access to it apart from us and the pathologist and forensics. Rosemary Poole was treated to exactly the same ritual – whatever that means. But the two women were almost one hundred per cent certainly killed by the same man and that man was not Matthew Williams.'

'Guv, not sure if you know this but a patrol picked up Nobby Parks again late last night, hanging about in the area of the sheltered houses. That's the second time. He was brought in for questioning but there was no reason to hold him.'

Serrailler sighed. 'I wish Nobby Parks would go on holiday somewhere warm for a month or two. He's getting in our way. Someone go down there, give him a talking-to, have a look around. But he's not a killer. However, no doubt you're thinking I shouldn't sound quite so confident because I got it wrong on one count. I said the profile of a killer like this would indicate that there'd be a lapse of time before he struck again. That's because he plans very carefully and meticulously and also because he will want to savour every detail of what he's done, go over it, picture it, for quite a long time. He can live off it. Talking of pictures, he could very well have taken photographs of his victims after death – now we're in the age of digital nobody has to take their little roll of film to be developed at a chemist's shop so a killer is much more likely to take the small risk of photographing the scene. But I was wrong. He killed again almost immediately. This may mean that he was afraid of something – of having been seen perhaps. If there's the faintest doubt in his mind about anything, he has to be sure. Perhaps he thought he saw Mrs Poole's curtain shift slightly, when he was leaving Elinor Sanders's bungalow after murdering her. Had she seen him and might she be able to identify him?

'A pattern is beginning to emerge. This is a man who kills old people, probably only old women. He is cunning and he plans carefully. He probably cases out the scene and watches the movements of his victims for some time before making any move. Who is likely to do that? Anyone lurking about for a while, just watching, is going to attract suspicion, but plenty of people had legitimate access to these houses – workmen, in the main. One good reason why we arrested Williams. Removal men. The same firm has moved in no fewer than three of the new occupants of these places – including Mrs Poole. I want details of all their men, backgrounds, criminal checks, the lot, and of every workman who was on the Duchess of Cornwall Close since the building started.'

'Sorry to bring you back to Nobby Parks, guv, but he's now been stopped twice for hanging around at night, and he's known to wander the town regularly. We can't just discount him.'

'No. But Nobby Parks isn't mentally capable of planning and carrying out this sort of murder even once, let alone twice. He scarcely bothers to hide himself – hence he's always being picked up. He's known to taxi drivers and late-night bar staff going home, as well as the boys on the food bus that looks out for the prostitutes and the rough sleepers down near the printworks and the canal. Still, I'm not ruling him out, you're right. If we haven't got his prints on file we'll have those too. Though as the crime scenes have been near enough sterile, they aren't going to be much use. Nobby wouldn't have a clue how to make a crime scene as clean as these were. Now, family interviews – Mrs Sanders's twin sister ought to be seen again, plus both Karen Fletcher, Rosemary Poole's daughter, and her husband Harry, but we won't get anything there. We're looking for a psychopath, a cold-blooded murderer who kills for reasons inside his own twisted mind. Two murders do not a serial killer make, the usual definition is three or more, but two murders whose MO is virtu- ally identical and the red light is flashing. He'll do it again. So I want permanent but discreet police presence at the sheltered housing complex all day and all night from now on, doubling up on street patrols in any part of the town where there's a concentration of older people – and generally an increased night-time presence. The public will have the wind well and truly up now, and justifiably.

'Don and Clare, you need to get up to Newcastle, go to where Elinor Sanders used to live, talk to neighbours and so on, find out anything at all about who she knew, visitors, anything that might make her vulnerable to attack. It's a long shot but we have to do this now. When her twin sister is interviewed again, delve into any links there might have been between her and Rosemary Poole, past or recent. It's not something we looked at before but it should be checked out now.

'OK, that's it. I've a press conference at two. I'll be covering the second murder, an update on the first and the release of Matthew Williams. And remember, details of these crimes, especially any mention of the way the victims were placed in front of mirrors – none of that leaves this room. Right. Thanks, all. Let's step this up some gears.'

Simon went to the door, expecting more close questioning from the Chief. But Paula Devenish had gone.

Thirty-six

'Any chance of you both coming over for lunch on Sunday?'
Cat asked.

Judith hesitated for some time. Then, 'Darling, I think maybe
not.'

'Si's coming – at least if he gets off he is.'

'I just think perhaps we won't. Do you mind?'

Something was wrong. Judith sounded closed off and she was
one of the most open people Cat knew.

'No, of course not. But could you and I have a coffee or
something? It's just that I want to talk through something –'

'Hannah?'

'No, for once. She's miserable, but she's accepted it and I've
threatened Sam with the pains of hell if he's nasty to her again.
No, it's me – job and plans and so on.'

'I can come round after your lunch. Have to take some charity
shop stuff in and to the chiropodist but I can be with you around
two.'

It was ten past when Judith's car turned into the drive. Watching
her through the window, Cat thought she looked older, thinner
– not that she had ever been fat – and had a sadness in her face
that had never been there before. Obviously, things were awry
between her and Richard and, just as obviously, Judith was
keeping quiet about it.

'I brought Hannah a CD of Justin Bieber – a pound from the

charity shop – plus a nice copy of *Lord of the Flies* for Sam, all of 50p. He ought to read it, since he's going to star.'

'Hardly – one of the boys, not the main boy. But thanks, and the Bieber is spot on. Let's have coffee in the sitting room, the sun's on that side.'

She followed Judith after a few minutes, carrying the tray. 'I feel guilty about this room. We hardly ever use it now – we live in the kitchen and the den, or else I'm working in my study.'

Judith sat down by the window. The garden was bare; the field beyond, with the white pony grazing in its winter rug, sunlit but bleak. But the sitting room was warm and retained a calmness Cat tried to keep up, because it was free of the children and their clutter, and her own work files and papers. It was a room with books, the piano, pictures and the hi-fi system, but no television.

Cat wanted to make Judith talk to her. She sat holding her coffee mug between her hands, looking out of the window at the aluminium sky. But Judith said nothing.

'You know Gerald Hanbury has taken the financial bull by the horns,' Cat said to break the silence. 'Imogen House is a day-care hospice from the beginning of next month and my hours have been halved. So I have to do something else. It's not the money – things are all right because of Chris's life insurance which I invested and that backs us up. But I'm at a crossroads, Judith, and I feel I might get stuck there.'

'I was thinking about that only yesterday, oddly enough, but I didn't like to barge in and ask you.'

'Oh, never worry about that. Advice and suggestions welcome. I wondered what Dad would say actually.'

'He'd tell you to make your own decision.'

'True.'

'You're done with general practice?'

'Yes, I am. It's changed, even more since I left it, and there's so much I dislike about the arrangement of it now. I could do locums but they're so badly paid that you end up working for peanuts after tax and I'd rather volunteer for something. Besides, locums are very unsatisfying. You never get to know your patients, you almost never get anything interesting because those people wait to see their own doctors – they just bring locums the sore throats. So . . .'

'Have you enjoyed the hospice work? Has it been fulfilling?'

'Very. That's why I'm gutted. I know day care fills an important need and I'll carry on, even if only for two and a half days. If they can afford that.'

Judith poured herself more coffee and sat silent for a moment. Then she said, 'I think you have such a good brain and such a really deep interest in palliative care that maybe you ought to do something a bit more academic. You found studying again gave you a lot of satisfaction, though I know it was partly a means to the job. But would you think of doing a PhD? You could spread it out over time, as you're working and still have the children.'

'What would I do though? It's a big jump to a doctorate and I don't have a particular subject in mind.'

'You'd find one. Go to the Cicely Saunders Institute, talk to them, read – think about what's happened at the hospice. It will evolve. If you know you can afford it, go for it.'

'I would still need to keep the day job. We're not actually rich.'

'No, but the pressure isn't so great. Sensible Chris.'

Cat felt the tears well up. Yes. He had been. He was. She remembered refusing to discuss things like life insurance policies and investments for the future, burying her own head in the sand, living for the day. But sensible made Chris sound dull and he had never been dull for a moment of his life.

'I hate people saying "it's what they would have wanted", when what they really mean is "it's what I want". But Chris would approve. He'd be proud of you, you know that.'

'Yes. I think he would. Besides . . . well, what you just said. It is what I want. I don't see anything wrong with that, Judith, do you?'

They finished their coffee, went into the kitchen, talked briefly about the tensions between Sam and Hannah and Simon's case. Judith left, hugging Cat hard, in a way that she took as meaning, 'Please, don't ask me.'

She did not.

Thirty-seven

'Shall we bring him in, guv?'

Serrailler sighed. Nobby Parks was becoming more than a thorn in his side. He had been seen by patrols twice the previous night. The first time he was in the city centre and had been taken home. An hour later, he was spotted walking slowly down the main road away from the area of the sheltered houses. This time, he had refused to get into the car and, before the uniforms could stop him, had run, fast and over a fence, into the darkness of some scrubland near the disused railway line. The patrol had given up the chase as pointless.

Simon went along to the CID room, where the atmosphere was one of heads into computer screens or down on files, and the usual badinage was subdued. Murders did that.

'Nobby Parks,' he said.

There was a massed groan.

'I know. But someone, go down to his place, give it the once-over, give him a talking-to. He's not our man but he's got to stop this hanging round at night.'

'Unless he happens to see something, guv. Can't we look on him as an unpaid extra pair of eyes?'

'You have a point. Here's another. If our killer's going to strike again, he's probably not going to go to D of C Close. Too many patrols. But if he does, even if he only starts sussing one of the places out, and if Nobby is around and if he sees Nobby, then Nobby is immediately in danger. This lunatic won't want to kill him, it doesn't fit his pattern and he hates stepping outside his own self-imposed frame, but he might have to shut him up. So – go down there and if necessary explain that to him. Frighten him a bit, within limits. We've got to keep him off the streets at night.'

Thirty-eight

Jake thumped Sam on the shoulder. The news was out. It had been under wraps, as they said, secret, he'd been sworn practically on the Bible. But the previous day, he'd had a morning's exeat to attend the film press conference in London, and today, it was all over the papers, and Sam was ten feet tall.

When he'd walked into class that morning, they'd cheered. Nice. He'd had that happen once before, after scoring the winning goal for the county junior hockey team and securing the trophy. But that had been different somehow.

'It's well cool. When do you start?'

'Not yet. Spring, I think.'

'You get to bunk off to a film set for months and months?'

'No, I get to go for days and maybe a week on and off and I get to do extra prep, I get extra time to make sure I don't fall behind. Yawn, yawn.'

'Right. Still, being on a film set, being the star . . . got to be good.'

'Not the star. That's Piggy.'

'Still. You'll get stopped in the street and girls will scream at you.'

Sam shoved Jake until he tripped off the kerb. A passing van blasted its horn.

'Bloody hell, Sambo.'

Sam laughed.

'Hey, will you still be at nets and trials? That's the same time.'

'Dunno. Not that bothered.'

'You so are, you could be captain this year. Nat Perkins hasn't a prayer.'

'Cricket's all right, only I think I've had it really. Not sure I'd be bothering even without the film stuff.'

Jake looked at him closely. 'You better not mean it.'

Sam lifted his arm in a vague half-wave, as he crossed the road to the bus station.

Jake watched him. Worried. Only half believing.

If this was what being in a film did even before it had started, he wasn't happy.

The bus dropped Sam at the corner. He had a couple of hundred yards' walk to the farmhouse, which he could see as he alighted. He'd been allowed to go to and from school on his own for the past year, so long as he had no late sports. If there was anything out of routine, Cat or sometimes Judith picked him up, or he got a lift from a friend's parent. At the beginning Cat had stood on the doorstep waiting for the sound of the bus, once or twice even coming halfway down the road towards him, but after Sam had protested loudly and pointedly walked two paces behind her until they got to the house, she had stayed indoors. After that she had let him get soaked or frozen or up to his knees in snow, always overcome with anxiety and guilt, never admitting to either.

Tonight, it was dry but the temperature was near freezing. He scooted up the lane and in via the paddock gate, then stopped. There was a light on in the pony's stable. The little grey pony was only ridden by Felix now, walked round the paddock on the leading rein. Hannah had grown out of him and lost interest, Sam had never ridden. But Peanuts was part of the family, and would be kept for the rest of his life.

Wookie came hurtling towards him from the stable, yelping and leaping the usual noisy welcome. Sam followed him into the stable, expecting to find his mother, filling the hay net or defrosting the tap yet again. Instead, Hannah was there alone, standing beside the pony with her face buried in his neck.

'Ha, crybaby.'

213

She jumped but then bent her head again, saying something darkly into the hairy coat.

'You still sulking?'

'Go away.'

'You've forgotten something.'

'What?'

'It goes, "Go away, I hate you".'

'Yes, well.'

Sam dropped his bag and sat down on the rickety stool. 'Got the first week's filming schedule.'

Silence.

'On a day, off a day, on half a day, then –'

'Shut up.'

'Then we go on location, after the studio week. An island somewhere. Do you know who the adults are being played by?'

'I don't want to know . . . I just want to know why you're being so horrible to me. Why are you?'

'Because I like winding you up. That little key sticking out of your back . . .'

Hannah patted the grey pony, picked up the empty bucket and went out, ignoring her brother completely. Sam stuck two fingers in his mouth and whistled.

Hannah turned, her face pale and brilliant in the light over the stable door. 'What?'

'You dare say anything.'

'About what?'

'You know. "Muuuummmmy, Sam's being meeeeeean . . ."'

He expected her to scream, burst into tears, even hit out at him, but she just turned and walked quietly away towards the farmhouse, leaving Sam smouldering with pent-up frustration in the stable. He kicked the wooden half-door hard. If it had not been so cold, he might have stayed there.

Cat came out of her study as Hannah appeared, white-faced and miserable, but when she asked what was wrong, Hannah shrugged. 'It's freezing out there.'

'Has Peanuts got his rug on?'

'Yes. Can I do my homework in here?'

Usually Hannah worked in her room, occasionally in the den.

214

'Yes, but I'm going to start supper.'

'That's OK.'

The side door banged and then Sam's bag hit the hall floor. He passed the kitchen on his way upstairs, whistling softly, but Cat called to him. He stopped.

'Homework?'

'Natch.'

'Supper in an hour.'

'Isn't it always?'

'I beg your pardon?'

'Sorry.'

'Everything all right?'

'Yup. Can I go now?'

Hannah started to get the books out of her bag and organise them on the table as soon as the conversation with Sam was over. Cat felt uneasy and anxious, fully aware of the permanent atmosphere of tension and conflict between the two of them, of Sam's bullying moods and Hannah's unhappiness, uncertain as to how best to handle it. Hannah was easier – plenty of attention, affection and a listening ear when required seemed to smooth most things over. But the abrupt change in Sam, from easy-going, good-natured boy to ill-tempered, rude adolescent required different skills. She was not sure she had them. Chris would have known, at least in part, how to cope with Sam, Simon had the knack. But Chris was dead and Simon absorbed either in work or in Rachel.

She could ask Judith, who was extremely good with both Hannah and Sam, but right now was not the time to enlist Judith in family problems. Cat guessed she had enough of her own.

She chopped up vegetables for a stir-fry, sliced chicken breast and put it on to cook, took jars and bottles from the cupboard, all the time attuned to Hannah, who was writing, underlining neatly, turning a page here and there, but somehow taut as a wire.

'Please show me what to do. Please help me to get all this right,' Cat said silently. She wished the film companies had never come near Lafferton. The quarrels and jealousies had started there, Hannah's disappointment and unhappiness, Sam's cockiness and jaunty attitude.

215

There was a sudden burst of crying from upstairs, then rapid footsteps. Then quiet. Felix had been unwell the previous day, and she had kept him off school today. He had a slight fever and had gone to sleep early, happy to be tucked up with a story tape, but when he felt ill he often had bad dreams.

She went upstairs. Sam was lying beside Felix on his bed, arm around him, singing him his Bob the Builder song. Felix's eyes were closed, his body relaxed back into sleep.

Cat crept out. But she was, as so often, baffled by this other side of Sam, his tenderness and gentleness with his small brother, the way he took endless trouble to play with him, comfort him, read to him, take his side in any upset.

He was a different boy from the one who teased Hannah so sadistically. Two boys. Which was the real Sam?

Both.

Neither.

She went downstairs and opened a bottle of wine.

I think about it a lot. The reasons. The old reasons and the new reasons, because they're not the same. The old reasons were Alan's reasons, and to be perfectly honest with you, they all boiled down to one. Fun. Call that pleasure, enjoyment, satisfaction, whatever. It was fun. But Alan doesn't exist, does he? I exist. I'm still me. But I'm not him. I'm this new person. So my reasons are different. Some of them anyway.

At first I thought I started doing it again for fun. Just like him. Well, that's a bit of it. I get a kick out of it. I get a buzz. So, yes – fun.

But there's something else. I don't know who I was. I know who I am. I've no real problem with that now, not after ten years. I know who I am. I don't ever forget, give the wrong name, fill in a form with some of the old details. But I've begun to lose touch with who I was and I can't cope with it. I can't go back, ever, and any case, who is this person who would be going back? Not him. He doesn't exist any more.

I can't go back and I need to feel like him again, just sometimes. Like who I was. Like Alan Keyes. Like who I AM. And the only way I can think of is to start the killings again. I feel better because I've found a way of getting back in touch. It's like going to one of those mediums and finding someone you were really close to and who'd died. Only they hadn't died altogether.

Apparently.

Alan Keyes is dead. But when I went into that first bungalow, I met him. And that was when I got a great wave of relief. Because if he still existed, I still exist. The person who is really me. Was really me. Shit.

I've worked out the difference now and why who I am can never be real. Not really, truly, completely real. And the reason is simple really, once you work it out.

It's because Alan Keyes was born. He had a real flesh-and-blood mother who gave birth to him, and a real flesh-and-blood father. He was born. OK, so all that stuff has been rubbed out now. You won't find his birth details on any register or on any certificate or even in any hospital records. But he was born. And I know it. I can be sure of it in my bones and beneath my skin.

But this other guy, this person I am now, he was never born. He was made up. Like a person in a story. He was invented by someone, doing their job in an office. All his details were invented. You'll find him if you know where to look. You'll find out where he was born, when, who his parents were, where they were living. It's all there.

Only thing is, it's all lies. He was never born. I was born. Alan Keyes was born. Well, of course we were born. That's the only way you get into the world, isn't it?

Only no. It isn't.

Apparently.

It started to do my head in so badly that I got afraid none of it would stay there, afraid that I'd let something out.

The only way I knew to sort myself out was do something that would remind me of who I really was, who I used to be, who I am. Jesus. Which is it? All of them.

But when I walked into her bedroom, when I felt the flex in my hand, it was OK after all.

I said, 'Hello, Alan.'

And then it was OK.

Thirty-nine

Saturday. Half past six. Minus two. Hard little spits of hail. Serrailler was refilling his coffee mug, searching the biscuit tin in case the bottom of it would yield one last chocolate digestive. The harsh fluorescent strips made his office seem even bleaker, but at least it was warm. He could work with his jacket off.

He had a computer screen full of murder, none of it apparently relevant in the slightest to the killings in Lafferton. But just in case, just in case . . . a circle had been drawn around a twenty-mile radius of the sheltered housing complex and another, inner circle, of ten miles. Killers, more often than not, struck within this distance of their home territory, for a variety of reasons, most practical, a few psychological.

He set the coffee mug down and picked up his phone. He had barely spoken to Rachel since he had left her with the sumptuous hotel breakfast, though a couple of texts had indicated that she knew that the job came first, felt no resentment, bore no grudge. And the breakfast had been delicious.

He hoped she could talk to him. She would be in, keeping Kenneth company, making sure he was warm and as well as he could be in this weather, setting up an audio tape for him, preparing supper.

'Guv?'

'Come in, Steph. What's up?'

'Went to see Nobby Parks. God, what a place. How does he survive there? He's got an ancient paraffin stove that stinks to high heaven, smokes like a tar factory – it's lethal. And his shack is piled with the junk of ages.'

'I know. He picks up stuff from skips and tips – might come in useful, he says. He'll bury himself in it one of these days. So, I hope you read him the riot act about hanging about at night?'

'Started to. But while I was talking to him, Kevin was nosying around. Found a reel of electrical flex hidden underneath a pile of old pillows.'

'Oh hell.'

'Yup.'

'Sit down a minute. What's your take on this, Steph – your honest take? If it had been anybody else, I'd have had you go back there and bring him in.'

'And I wouldn't have waited for you to send us, guv. Only . . .'

'Only this is Nobby Parks we're talking about. Did the flex match?'

'Yes. Green and yellow for live. Nice half-full roll, the sort used by professional electricians, bought wholesale.'

'The same then. What did he say?'

'Said he got it off of a skip up at the sheltereds. Got a nice set of plastering tools and a lot of firewood as well. And some rolls of wallpaper. Want to see?'

'He has an old cart he sometimes takes and fills it up with junk – and with useful stuff as well. So?'

'Nobby Parks isn't a killer, guv. I'd swear on it.'

'So would I. I have.'

'And it's a reel of very commonly used electric flex.'

'Did you bag it and bring it?'

'Yes. He was quite happy about that so long as he got it back – alternatively, he said I could have it to keep for a fiver.'

'Get it to forensics first thing Monday. It's not worth an over-time call. Nothing else down there?'

'No. Well . . . he's got an ancient TV set up running off the mains. He knows all about the murders.'

'That's an offence and it's another bloody life-threatener. We'll have to take the TV off him.'

'Guv.'

'On Monday. Let him have his weekend of interesting and

enriching programmes before we confiscate it and he gets fined and can't pay and it goes to court . . . Bloody hell.'

'I'm off from eight until Tuesday. We're going to London to see *We Will Rock You.*'

'All right for some . . . Go on, rock off, Sergeant.'

Steph closed the door, laughing.

But were they right to laugh about it and leave it? Nobby Parks, dippy old Nobby, one sandwich short, not the sharpest tool in, one brick less than a load.

One half-reel of electrical flex, yellow and green, for live.

One nutter.

Simon wrote a long, careful list on his pad, mainly of one or two words. Underlined here, an asterisk there.

Nobby Parks.

Two elderly women.

Both strangled with new electrical flex.

Yellow and green, for live.

The phone rang.

'Guv? How're you doin'?'

Hearing the voice of his former sergeant, Nathan Coates, gave him a big lift. Nathan had left the Lafferton force several years earlier, for Yorkshire and to rise to DI status. Simon heard from him far less than he would have liked, saw him rarely, but when the two of them spoke, the years between meant nothing. Simon could picture Nathan's hair, sticking up like the bristles on a yard broom, and his cheerful-ugly face, which Cat had said always looked as if he'd fallen flat on a pavement from a great height. Nathan, ever-chirpy, ever-optimistic, ever-energetic, sometimes needing a restraining hand, a bit of steadying. But he was a fine copper, with the right instincts, the right priorities. Yorkshire had been lucky to get him, and they valued him accordingly.

'DI Coates! How are you? Where are you? In this neck of the woods? God, I hope so, I could do with cheering up.'

'Sorry, guv, up here. Oh, and – erm, I don't take kindly to being down-ranked.'

'To being . . .? Bloody hell, Nathan, you're never a DCI? They wouldn't be mad enough.'

'Oi.'

'That's fantastic news. Well done. You see – it's the early training that counts.'

'So I always say. Is this OK for a minute or three or are you out somewhere?'

'You're kidding. In the office, and I'll be here till late. You've heard why, no doubt.'

'That's what I'm ringing you about. I might have stumbled on something useful for you. If it is, and you need any more inside info, I can always come down.'

'Tell me.'

'One of our old DSs, chap called Roy Pickens – been here forever, retires later this year . . . well, he came into my office. He'd seen about your murders in the paper, and it rang a bell with him but he couldn't think why, not straight away. So he dug about and then he found a reference and the case came back to him. A few years before I came up here, there was three murders on this patch, all of them of old ladies. They were linked by all sorts of stuff, but there's a confidential file which has a detail only a few who were on the cases ever knew about. It never came up in the trial, was never made public. They was scared of copycats, and the info was restricted.'

'Which often means eight people were officially in the know and about eight hundred actually did know.'

'Yeah, right, but I think it was tighter than that. Maybe twenty? None of whom talked, beyond these walls, as it were. So it's still confidential, still pretty secret.'

'What's it to do with?'

'Specifically, the killer's MO and common to all three murders. So if it doesn't relate to yours, I've wasted a call, except it's always good to speak to you.'

'Right. Tell.'

'We need to talk on the secure line though. I know it's ten years ago for us but it's current for you.'

'I'll call you back.'

Three minutes later, both on the safe line, Nathan said, 'Our murderer strangled his victims with electrical flex. That's public. What isn't is that he set them in a chair, either before or after he killed them – that's never been completely settled – in front of a mirror – twice it was a dressing-table mirror, once a mirror hanging on the inside of a wardrobe door. So they were confronting their own dead bodies, if you get me. Maybe they had to watch themselves being strangled. And that never came out, not ever, not at the trial or in the press.'

Simon whistled.

'Does any of it ring a bell, guv?'

'It rings several. You said "the trial" – so what happened?'

'Right. Big scandal. He was acquitted – on a technical, and a witness being confused and going back on her statement when the defence ran rings round her. I've been reading it all up.'

'Who was he?'

'Local to the town. Man of thirty-two, self-employed builder called Alan Keyes. And he walked.'

'Where did he walk to? I'm amazed he lived to tell the tale.'

'They didn't even let him out onto the steps of the court. He was spirited away, for his own protection. No one knows where, but he must have left the town. Could have gone anywhere. No idea about that, I'm afraid.'

'Can you get me forensics, fingerprints and so on?'

'Yup. First thing Monday morning.'

'Try harder.'

'You want me to pull a favour? I'm not in forensics' good books right now, for reasons we won't go into, involving a total fuck-up. But I'll give it a go.'

'Good man. This is the first bit of light at the end of a black tunnel. One thing – do you know if there have been similar cases in any other part of the country, between your murders and now?'

'No. And I've got no one I can set on to it, we're flat out at the moment with terrorist stuff. I hate terrorist stuff.'

'Come back to Lafferton. We don't get any of that here. How's the family?'

'Great. Josh is in year two, Luke's in nursery, Adam's waving his legs in the air. Em's looking to go back to work part-time next year. If we don't have number four.'

'Bloody hell.'

'Em wants a girl.'

'Yes, and you know what would happen.'

'Too right I do. All right, guv, I'll go and grovel to the foren-sics' duty officer.'

'I owe you.'

'Nah, you're all right. But I'll have a pint off you next time we meet.'

Simon looked at his desk for a moment, then switched off his computer and the lights and left, feeling more cheerful than he had for days, partly because any time he spoke to Nathan Coates he was cheered, but mainly because of the info Nathan had brought to him.

He had planned to go home, have a bath, a whisky, a casserole Cat had given him, and early bed with a Patrick O'Brian novel – he had never been able to get into them, but Judith had persuaded him to try again.

He started the car. The windscreen was already iced over, and while he waited for it to clear, he thought he might call in to Hallam House on the way. Cat was sure things were awry between Judith and his father, and though he wasn't interested in cross-questioning, he was concerned. Having had a rocky start with his own feelings about his father's remarriage, he now recognised that she had been the best thing to happen in Richard's life for years. He dialled to ask if he could drop in for a drink, but the number was engaged. He would just go. If it wasn't convenient, he'd leave again, no problem.

The streets were almost empty. A few people were going into cafés and bars, huddled together, hoods up, scarves wrapped round their faces against the bitter wind.

The traffic lights at the corner of the town square went red as he approached them. He stopped, cursing mildly, and glanced left.

He was not immediately sure of what he saw but then he was quite certain and his heart lurched.

She was standing alone in a doorway. She had a small backpack at her feet, a navy-blue parka with a hood pulled up. No scarf. No gloves. Jeans. Wellington boots. The street light caught the side of her face, which was anxious, pinched and unhappy.

Simon pulled the car to the kerb and jumped out and as she saw him he could tell that she was about to get out of the doorway and run.

'Hannah, what in God's name are you doing here? Where's Mum? Where's . . . Oh, Hannah, darling girl, it's OK. It's all OK now. Get in the car. You're frozen, you're shaking. Hey . . .'

He sat holding her as tightly as he could, feeling her thin body shake and shake, and her sobs mix with the trembling, her tears damp on the front of his jacket as she clung to him. He released her gently, pulled the seat belt round her and held her hand.

'Hanny, listen. I'm going to ring your mum, then we're going home. I don't want you to talk, you don't have to tell me anything. I've turned the heater to full blast, you'll get warm. All right?'

Hannah nodded, still crying, her face paper-white. She was beyond talking.

'Hi. Me. Listen, it's all right. I've got her.'

'What are you talking about? Got who? Where are you?'

'On the way to you now. *Hannah*. I've got Hannah.'

'What do you mean, you've got Hannah? Hannah's at Lucy Gold's staying over.'

'Hannah's here in the car, with me. It's all right. Ten minutes?'

'Simon . . .'

But he had clicked off and accelerated fast out of the town.

Forty

'I want to leave here, and when I do, I never want to hear the name of the place again.'

'Karen, listen, sweetheart . . . I understand where you're coming from, I totally understand, but you're not thinking straight. Course you're not. And who'd blame you? I don't. Bloody hell, of course I don't.'

Harry sat on the sofa beside his wife. It was three thirty in the morning and she had been up for an hour, the sleeping pill she'd been prescribed having had no effect. He'd made her tea, got her to eat a couple of biscuits, sat and listened to everything over again. Now this.

'When they let us – when we can . . .' She had to stop, as she choked on her own tears. He held her hand and waited patiently. 'When we can have the funeral, after that . . . I don't care where we go, Harry, but we can, you can work anywhere.'

'Well, up to a point, Kaz, but it's hard enough to pick up work here, where people know me. I'd have to start all over again somewhere else and just at the moment it ain't easy.'

'You'll do it. You're good. We should go somewhere where there's building going on. I don't mind where it is, honestly, you can choose . . . Scotland, the Isle of Man, Cornwall –'

'Now that would be a daft place to go. More unemployment in Cornwall than just about anywhere.'

'London.'

'Couldn't afford to live in London, sweetheart, no matter how

226

much work I got. Home Counties might be better – Surrey, Sussex –'

'Sussex, yes. Yes, we could live by the sea. Hastings or Brighton or somewhere. That would be good for the boys. Let's try and do that, Harry.'

He picked up the teapot but she shook her head.

'Thing is, Karen – if we did, if we went somewhere else, would it be any better for you? Because – I don't mean to be cruel here – but what's happened has happened and you can never forget it, never get away from it. Wherever you go it'll be inside your head. Running away never solved very much, you'd just take it with you – all this stuff with your mum, everything that happened.'

'I wouldn't want to forget Mum, not for a second.'

'Of course you wouldn't and nor would I. I was very fond of Rosemary, it's cut me up every which way.'

'She loved you. She was so relieved when you came along, after some of the people I'd gone out with . . .'

'Neither of us is going to forget anything, but I don't see how moving away from here will help any of us.'

'So you're saying we can't? Never, ever?'

Harry sighed. 'No, I'm not saying that. If it's what you want I'll do it, I'll do anything to try and make you feel better, Kaz. It was just a bit of a heads-up, that's all. I'm looking out for you. Now listen, it's four o'clock. I'll get the boys up and off, I've a quiet morning before I start on these flat renovations, but we need our sleep. You need it most. Come on.'

He put out his hand to Karen and she took it and got up wearily. Harry put his arms round her.

'It's in my head all the time. These questions keep popping up and I can't answer them . . . What was it like for her? What did she think? How terrified was she, did she try and fight him off, how much did it hurt her, did she take long to –'

'Stop it, love. Just turn your mind away from all of that. Think of the boys, think of their futures, think what you have to be for them.'

'I do.' Karen went up the stairs one slow step after the other, as if her body were a lead weight she had to haul.

In bed, in the dark, she leaned against him. 'Harry? Promise me you'll think hard about it – moving. Promise we can at least look into it?'

Harry tucked her into his side and stroked her arm.

'I do,' he said. 'I do promise you, Kaz. I promise you anything you want.'

A few moments later, he felt her body relax, as she slept.

Forty-one

'Guv? Got a massive file. I'll bring it down myself. Set off at crack tomorrow morning, be with you by twelve.'

'You can't do that on a Sunday, that's your day with the family.'

'Em don't mind, I asked her – not if it's for you. And she's meeting up with her best friend . . . she's got twin boys same age as Josh – it'll be bedlam. Shall I come to the station?'

'Certainly not. I'll buy you lunch and that pint. Let's go to the Oak at Up Starly.'

'Ah, happy days. That'll bring back a few memories.'

'I'll be there from twelve thirty – if you're earlier give me a bell. I'll book us in for their famous Sunday roast.'

They arrived together in the pub car park. Nathan handed over a thick file and an envelope containing a CD before they went inside, to pints of the Oak's local bitter, Starly Brewery's Old Man of Wern, and roast beef cut from the joint.

Looking at his former sergeant across the table, Simon saw small changes in him, a greater air of authority to go with his DCI rank. But, in general, Nathan was still Nathan, cheerful, optimistic, open-faced and sparky.

They went through family and police talk until the cheeseboard and two more pints were on the table, when Simon pointed to the file beside him.

'I appreciate this, Nathan – not just the file but you bringing it down. I need every thread of inquiry for the team to follow up, but there's been precious little once we let our single suspect go. You know, I'd have put money on him being our man and going down for life.'

'Interesting that. You've got one bloke who did three murders, sure as God made little apples, got arrested, got charged – and got acquitted. And you might've had another bloke who didn't do two murders, got arrested, got charged, got convicted. Wrong both times. And that don't happen too often.'

Simon shook his head. 'We'd never have got the CPS to agree about Williams – plenty of evidence and all of it circumstantial. It'd never have stuck. So, tell me about this one.'

Nathan filled him in about Alan Keyes, with more detail than he had gone into on the phone the previous night.

'He was guilty as hell, you've only got to read it. Told you about my old sergeant – he remembers it all now. Said there was an outcry like you've never known – whole county was in an uproar. Couldn't believe it. He'll have gone somewhere miles away, for sure. There was relatives and friends and neighbours of three dead women swearing vengeance – someone would have had him. They smuggled him off somewhere for his own safety. That's the last anyone knew. Anyway, wherever he went, his MO was all his own. There was the same style of electric flex every time – yellow and green.'

'For live . . .'

'Yup. And there was the planting them in front of the mirrors. Sick that is. I mean, yeah, it's all sick. And something else . . .'

'Right. And with ours too. But you first.'

'He cut their toenails with clippers. All of them. Left the clippers behind, but always wiped clean as clean, not a trace of a print anywhere.'

'But he took the nail clippings with him. No trace, not a fragment, on the carpets, in the bins . . . anywhere.'

Nathan had a large chunk of Wensleydale cheese raised to his mouth. Now, he lowered it back to his plate. 'Gawd almighty.'

'It's got to be the same,' Serrailler said.

'Too right it has.'

Simon downed the rest of his beer. Then he remembered what the case had erased from his mind.

'Give me a bit of advice, Nathan?'

'You're jokin' – learned all I know from you.'

'Until you went up north and forgot it again. Listen . . . goes no further, not even to Em, all right?'

Nathan nodded, his mouth full of cheese. This was a man Serrailler knew he could trust with his life, let alone with any confidential info he gave him.

'The Chief's retiring.'

Nathan raised his eyebrows.

'This autumn. And she suggested I apply.'

'Go on.' His voice was cautious.

'So . . . I want to know if you think I should.'

'You don't need me.'

'I'm asking you. I value your opinion and you know me as well as anyone.'

'Right. Well then, first off, do you want it? *Really* want it. If your heart jumped and you thought "job of my dreams" – go for it. Nice though, getting asked like that.'

'It's not in her gift . . . she was just suggesting she'd approve.'

'Come on, more than that, guv.'

'I wish you'd stop calling me guv.'

'Can't. She means you'd be the best at it, best successor she could want, all that.'

'Yes. Very flattering.'

'Chief's not an oiler. No need to be.'

'That's true.'

'So?'

Simon leaned back. The dining room was full but they were in a quiet corner and he saw no one he recognised, and certainly no one from the station. He could talk freely, as ever, to Nathan.

'I just don't know. When she said it, that did happen – I did think, "Crikey! Wow, yes please." For a second or two. But then this case took it clean out of my head and it stayed there – until just now actually. I hadn't given it another thought. But relaxing over this – it came back to me. You know me, Nathan. You know this nick. You know this force pretty well – it hasn't changed

231

much since you went, not essentially. You know what the job is all about.'

Nathan looked at him. 'Yeah, I do know you, I reckon. I know you and the job. And I know pretty well what a Chief's for. So I'll tell you. Don't touch it. Come on, guv, you're not an admin, big-picture, strategy copper. You're a hands-on, off-beam tec. Always have been – DCI, DCS, whatever, you're the same. You get your hands dirty, you don't pull rank, 'cept when arses need kickin'. You don't break the rules but you don't treat them with kid gloves. You get results. You lead a great team on a case. Nobody better. Chief Constable? Not saying you couldn't do it. Course you could do it. But you'd 'ate it. You'd 'ate it from day one and there'd be no going back into CID and your old desk. Right, I've said it.'

Forty-two

Serrailler's phone rang on the way in to the station. He listened. Exploded.

'Right, I've had enough. I'm going to talk to him. Not you, not anyone else from CID or uniform, I'm going. Get this sorted. Anything else?'

'Matt Williams, guv. Seen today's papers?'

Simon groaned.

'Can't get a job any more cos one of the guys he worked with on the bungalows had a bit of an argument with him, hates his guts, told a reporter Matt was a psycho, bit of a weird one, blah-blah. The media blew it up, had a photo of him looking like someone out of a locked ward. Press office are doing their nut. He's demanding compensation.'

'Of course he is. And how many millions is a subcontract sparks worth? Leave it to the press office, they're good at their job, and he's on a hiding to nothing anyway – we had every reason to arrest and charge him. It's one more damn thing getting in the way, but not worth worrying about. Right, if anyone wants to know where I am, you've no idea.'

'The Chief's already asked.'

'You've still no idea.'

The DS sighed. 'Guv.'

The temperature was still only hovering around zero but the sky was cloudless, a bright sparkling blue. Lafferton looked as if it had been rinsed clean, the cathedral tower standing out in 3D against the clear sky. Simon parked his car at the top of Metal Street and walked down towards the canal, which ran darkly gleaming beside the towpath. There had been talk for years of clearing up the old warehouses down here and, once, a start had been made, when the Old Ribbon Factory was converted into expensive apartments. But the developer had run out of money, there were engineering problems to do with the site, the conservationists and the Friends of the Canal had organised themselves vigorously and, finally, they had begun to clear downstream for a proposed future reopening of the waterway to canal boats. The old warehouses and sheds stayed as they were, some collapsing in on themselves gently as the weather worked on their fabric, others still in fair condition.

Simon went over the bridge and along the towpath. The willows had been pollarded the previous year and looked bald and stumpy but the whole area served as a lung to the town. The field beyond had a couple of gypsy horses grazing, with an old trailer full of hay nearby. Two women were walking briskly across, their dogs racing and running in circles.

He had meant to come down here and draw the old warehouses before it was too late. Which it would be one of these days when there was money about. Councils liked tidying up. He would come when it was warmer.

Nobby Parks's shack was fifty yards ahead. There was no sign of life but as he got nearer Simon could smell the faint fumes of paraffin from his ancient stove. The door was made of flimsy wooden fencing and there was a broken padlock hanging from the handle. Nobby wasn't troubled by the idea of intruders.

He banged on the door, then on the wood panel beside it. Silence. He banged again and there was a muttering and swearing from inside. Serrailler pushed open the door and the paraffin fumes came at him more strongly.

'You'll set fire to yourself one of these days, Nobby.'

His eyes grew used to the dimness and he made out the rickety table, bench, wicker chair, and the bed in the corner, piled high with blankets, quilts and old sweaters. Nobby was struggling out of it, wearing another of the sweaters, with long johns and a cap.

'Morning,' Simon said. 'Sorry it's early for you. Got a kettle and some tea bags?'

'All right, all right. Give me a chance. What you doing down here? Thought you was too high and mighty to come bothering innocent members of the public.'

But his tone was not unfriendly. Simon went back more than fifteen years with Nobby Parks, from his first days in the force as a DC.

He looked around. The place was more crammed with junk than ever, inside and out, stuff Nobby took from skips and tips and bins, ditches and waste ground. Never from people.

'For heaven's sake, what do you want with a bag of old golf balls?'

'Come in handy. Never know.'

'And all these roof tiles?'

'Could sell those. Old tiles fetch a bob or two.'

'Not when they're broken they don't. OK, well, just don't go climbing on church roofs nicking lead or I'll have you.'

The tin kettle whistled sulkily on the stove. Nobby got down two mugs and rinsed them in a bucket of water, found tea bags from a tin. The milk was out on the window ledge.

'Don't need any fridges, see? Butter as well. Bacon. Bit of cheese. All lives out there.'

'What do you do when it's hot?'

'Suffer. Help yourself. Got no sugar, sorry about that.'

'I don't take it. Thanks, Nobby.'

'This is about the other business, isn't it? Them poor women.'

'It is.'

'You got no need to take me into your station again, there's nothing else I can say. Said everything.'

'Where did you get that reel of electrical flex, Nobby?'

'Skip at the back of the bungalows. It was a disgrace what they threw out when they'd done – enough paint to do a lot of walls, enough wood to make a few window frames. Look – nails, screws, cabling. All just thrown out and wasted. Do you blame me?'

'No, I don't, and if you can get a bob or two for it I'm not looking. It's not that and you know it, Nobby.'

'You don't want me out at night. Only I've been out at night for years. You know that. I like it at night. You see this, you see that. You get the run of the place.'

'That's all right, Nobby – and you were in the right place at the right time when you saw that ram raid in the Lanes.'

'Ah, you see . . .'

'I don't want to stop you doing what you want. I'm not bothered where you go when, and it's your problem if the patrols pick you up.'

'Always shoving me in their car and giving me a lift home, think they're doing me a favour.'

'They're doing it for your own good, Nobby. At the moment, you're in our way and every time you go out there at night, especially up near the sheltered housing, you're even more in our way and you're having us suspect you of things I know you'd never do. But if you're seen hanging about there at two in the morning when a woman was murdered a few yards away what do you expect us to think? What do you expect to happen?'

Nobby drained his mug of tea and reached for another tea bag, then for his tobacco and Rizla papers on the table. He showed them to Simon.

'No thanks. Never fancied them.'

'Don't know what you're missing.'

He bent his head and started the neat, finicky business of laying the strands of tobacco along the paper. Simon looked around again. Did a double take, then got up.

'What?' Nobby said.

'Get this off a skip as well?' Simon reached for a mobile on top of a pile of old magazines.

'Picked it up in the gutter.'

'Work, does it?'

'Never tried. Takes pictures though. I was playing around with it and something went flash bang wallop. Took a picture of them shelves there. They come out all right.'

Simon scrolled down, working out the way the unfamiliar mobile worked quickly enough, scrolling down through the digital pictures Nobby had taken, which turned out to be bits of wall, stretches of icy grass, an upside-down tree, the back end of a cat, a parked car, a run of fencing. They were mainly taken after dark and either vivid in the flash or too dim.

He went on scrolling. Pictures of women shopping in the Lanes. Women loading car boots with groceries at the supermarket. Random men, walking. More dark shots. And then a bungalow. Another. A doorway. Dark. Dark. A van. A car, too out of focus.

Elinor Sanders, walking up the path of her bungalow. A removal van outside it. Her open front door. The bungalow lit by a flash, curtains drawn.

'I'm going to have to take this in, Nobby.'

'What for? You won't find anything indecent on there, I don't do indecent.'

'I know. You took quite a few pics up at Duchess of Cornwall Close, though. We might find something useful on those.'

'Help yourself, only I want it back.'

'You'll get it back but I can't promise when.'

'And I want a receipt.' He lit his cigarette.

Simon did not carry evidence bags these days but he poked about until he found a couple of plastic food bags on a shelf. They seemed unused, though they'd probably be contaminated with something or other, like everything in Nobby's shack.

'Thanks, Nobby. Thanks for the tea. And remember what I said. Keep out of our hair for a bit.'

'You're all right, Mr Serrailler. Sure you don't want to try a roll-up?'

'Dead sure. And you watch lighted matches and cigs in this tinderbox. Don't want you carried out with your lungs full of smoke.'

'How long have I lived here? How long have I smoked these?'

'Too long. Cheers, Nobby.'

'And don't send those twelve-year-olds in their panda cars down here again neither.'

'Behave yourself and I won't.'

At first, when I woke up I used to be confused, just for a second or two. Who am I? I couldn't work it out. I'm not him any more? No. I'm him then. Right. Never going to be him again. Right. It got better. I never do it now. I didn't. I do. Shit.

I've started again. And I'm glad I have because I realised that I didn't want to lose touch with him. Because that meant losing touch with me. The born one. Not the invented one.

When I look in the mirror now, though, I'm not surprised any more. Not surprised I've got a shaved head, not surprised it's contacts not glasses. Always hated wearing glasses so that's been a good thing. Not surprised by the moustache.

The contact lenses are brown. Ordinary, muddy sort of brown. Whereas Alan Keyes's eyes are blue.

Surprising how quickly it didn't matter what I looked like. Funny that. It's what's inside my head. That's where it was harder. But I thought I'd got it. Well, I had. I could reel off all the new stuff. Turned out I'm a good learner. That's why I could do the plumbing course. And I could tell you 'my' schoolmates and neighbours and names of my sister's kids. The sister I haven't got. I mean, I have. But I haven't.

In the end, though, I missed him and I wanted him back. I wanted to be him again, and it was never going to happen and that was what started doing my head in.

Then it came to me. What I had to do.

And it worked. When I walked out that night, quietly up the hill and into that dark little street, when I went up to her bungalow, as

238

soon as I did all that, I knew it had worked. I was him. I hadn't lost who I was after all.

I'm still him.

And I can be him again any time I want. I know what I have to do.

Only thing was, I never meant it to happen again so fast. I never wanted to do that second one. What sort of monster do you think I am?

But I was worrying that she'd seen something, seen me, even a glimpse, even in the dark, even across the grass, so I had to do it. I'd no choice, had I? Just in case.

Maybe she didn't see me. Maybe I imagined it.

But I couldn't take that risk, could I?

Forty-three

'Ah, Cat. Do come in.'

Judge Gerald Hanbury lived in one of Lafferton's oldest houses, tucked away behind a high wall near the cathedral. Few people knew a house was there at all. A plain door in the wall had a single bell with an electronic eye beside it, let into the brick. Cat had rung and there had been a slight sound. She pushed the wooden door and it opened.

Ahead was a handsome Queen Anne mansion at the end of a gravel path, with two rectangles of perfect lawn on either side of it. The house was in Pevsner. 'One of the finest examples of this style of perfectly proportioned town house in the country. Fault cannot be found with its design or its execution.'

Gerald Hanbury had been a High Court judge until the previous year, a man much respected for his coolness, his intelligence, balance and fairness, and feared for the way he came down on anyone not entirely respectful of the traditions and solemnities of the law. He was generous to counsel, never bullied juniors, was never patronising to witnesses and never tolerant of careless policemen. But there was a touch of distance, an austereness about him, which kept some people at arm's length. They mistook it for disapproval and severity but Cat had soon discovered that neither was the case. John Lowther had been a very different chair of trustees of Imogen House, much warmer, but he had lacked the necessary degree of ruthlessness when required to take unpopular decisions. Lowther had resigned because he felt guilty that he had introduced Leo Fison as head of a new fund-raising sub-committee, though he had been supported by the entire body of Trustees, not one of whom had laid a speck of blame on him later, for Fison or what he had done. But John Lowther was a man of conscience and he had decided his own position was untenable.

Hanbury was altogether steelier and Cat had felt great distress over the decision to close Imogen House to inpatients. She had also felt downgraded and devalued, in spite of reassurances.

Now, Hanbury had asked her to have a drink, talk to him. She liked him, in spite of it all, and she knew that he had precious little alternative to the draconian measures he had had to take. If he had not moved fast, the financial situation had been bad enough to have precipitated complete closure.

Judge Hanbury had been widowed as a relatively young man and his wife had left him with two small sons. He had brought them up himself, lovingly but in a slightly austere way, and married again much later in life, a formidable fellow judge in her fifties, previously single. Judge Nancy Cutler was the scourge of incompetent barristers, muddled witnesses and any form of disorder in her court, but famous for her generosity to women defendants and plaintiffs, especially those treated harshly by police or press, and in particular those brave enough to stand up against rapists and brutal partners.

Cat had met her a couple of times at formal occasions. She and Hanbury made an elegant and distinguished couple.

It was Nancy who opened the door now.

I am a confident woman, Cat thought. Yes, on the whole that is true. I have a good medical degree, I have been a practising hospital doctor and GP, I am clinical director of a hospice, I have three children, I run a house, I have been up against a number of terrible situations and come through. I dress quite well, I take care with my appearance. But faced with this sort of woman, my self-confidence drains out through the soles of my feet and I stand here feeling a mess, stumbling over my words, more or less as I might if I were up before this woman on a charge.

'Dr Deerbon, how nice to see you.'

She was tall with a good figure but was not over-thin. Her hair was held up in a chignon with two combs, her make-up

241

was discreet but applied as if by a professional. She wore a taupe dress and jacket which had not been bought on the high street. And her smile was warm and genuine. Why had she waited until her fifties to marry? Career? Presumably.

But there was, Cat thought, a shadow of something about her face, an anxiety or a wariness. Then it was gone, and she was leading Cat into the surprisingly informal and homely sitting room, where a large ginger cat sat on a linen-covered sofa and opened its topaz eyes briefly and haughtily before recurling itself back to sleep.

'My husband's just taking a phone call. Can I get you a gin, a Martini, a glass of wine?'

Cat asked for wine. A bottle of chilled Sancerre appeared with the judge who came in briskly, apologising, and then, like many men who have no small talk, embarking on the reason Cat had come, the subject of the hospice.

'I know how much you've put into Imogen House,' he said, after the glasses were filled, 'and I know how you prized the excellence of our inpatient wards. But it's only because we've taken this big step that we can survive. None of which helps you, I know. You've lost half a job, you don't altogether approve of the day-care-only model – and you deserve an apology.'

He had an imposing presence and he still spoke as if he had the full attention of a court. His voice was strong, measured and with the slightest hint of Edinburgh Scots. He wore a pale yellow cashmere sweater over a dark blue open-necked shirt, with dark blue cord trousers. A touch of the dandy, Cat thought.

'Tell me what you feel now. Tell me if you think you can work happily in the new set-up, eventually at least.'

Cat told him. Nancy Cutler had gone out, but returned now and sat quietly listening and looking at Cat with complete attention. Her Honour Judge Cutler. And after an hour and two large glasses of wine, Cat felt that everything she had said had been taken on board and understood. She had the full confidence of the chair of trustees, which meant the whole board, and Hanbury had suggested she take some days out to visit other day-care hospices, to study how they worked in practice and see if

Lafferton could not only learn from them but bring something new and some real improvements to the model.

'We would pay,' he said, 'that goes without saying. These would be legitimate expenses – visits like that can only boost our profile, and I think they'd be of real interest to you.'

'I agree. But I wouldn't want my expenses. They'd be small and in our present precarious situation it would be wrong. Thank you for the suggestion though. I'll start making some arrangements.'

He also approved of her plan to do a PhD.

'When I retire,' Nancy said, to a short laugh from her husband, 'I'm going to forget all about the law and take another degree altogether.'

'What in?'

'Medieval palaeography. I want to spend days and days with eleventh-century manuscripts.'

That follows, Cat thought as she left. A structured, disciplined study in which detail mattered, and also a rather rarefied one, completely detached from everyday life.

They were a compatible pair, complementing one another, and who doubtless enjoyed enriching and mainly intellectual conversations at dinner. There was obviously friendliness and affection between them and they seemed completely in tune. But love?

It was seven forty. Silke, the sweet German au pair she now shared with another family, was at the farmhouse, getting supper and doing bedtime with Felix. Since Molly left, Silke had become a reliable alternative.

Cat had parked in front of Simon's building and walked round to the Hanburys'. Now, as she bent her head against the biting wind that was whipping down Cathedral Close, she saw that the lights were on in his flat. His car was parked next to her own but there was no other, which probably meant no Rachel, though she sent him a text all the same.

In? Am outside but no prob if busy.

Reply came back *In. Cooking. Come up.*

*   *   *

243

'I've been living off bananas and cheese sarnies for too long. Sick of it.'

Cat looked into the heavy pan full of beef, vegetables, thick gravy, watched him pour a glass of red wine into it and stir it round. Her brother's cooking was spasmodic, consisted of about four dishes, was never based on any recipe and never failed.

'Stay?'

'Love to. I'll text Silke.'

'Good, because I need to talk to you.'

They sat at one end of the long elm table, with candles and a bottle of burgundy, and thick fresh bread to dip into the casserole. Opposite Cat on the white wall, lit carefully in the way Simon always planned his picture lighting, was the drawing of their mother he had done just before she died. It was in a distressed heavy gold frame which might have drowned out the pencil and charcoal lines but somehow did nothing of the sort. Every time she saw it, Cat was hit both by its beauty and by the way he had caught Meriel's warmth, the generosity of heart that had always been coupled with a slight austerity of expression. It also caught her innate toughness of character.

'Leave that to me in your will?'

Simon smiled. 'I wouldn't let it go anywhere else.' He cut the crusty bread and handed a slice to her on the point of the knife. 'Hannah,' he said. 'Have you talked to her?'

Cat put her fork down, a faint nausea rising together with the memory of the night she had learned where her daughter had been found and what might have happened to her if she had not been.

'The thing is, I'd talk to her but I think that now the dust has settled maybe it ought to come from someone else. What you've said will have been mixed up with all your own emotion about it. What I might say would be some of the same, and also like "Uncle Simon the copper, boring on". She still might not take me quite seriously enough.'

'Who else is there? I wouldn't want to ask Judith or Dad at the moment . . .'

Simon shook his head and poured another glass of wine. Cat put her hand over her own glass.

'Steph,' he said, 'Ben Vanek's wife. If I took Hannah into the station and got Steph to sit with her in one of the interview rooms we use for sensitive cases – meaning, there's a sofa and a pot plant – it would really get home. Steph's good, she'd hit the right note, make her understand what could have happened and stress how serious it could have been. But she wouldn't terrify her or make her feel as if she was some sort of young offender.'

'God, poor Hanny.'

'I know. But it might have been much poorer Hanny. I still can't believe I was the one to drive by and that I actually turned my head and saw her. I could just as easily have roared off on the green light.'

Cat shivered. Since Hannah had run away she had shivered involuntarily quite often, even woke in the night shivering.

'I'll fix it up and you can bring her in – maybe one afternoon after school?'

'All right. Thanks. One thing though . . . the best person to try and get Sam to see the error of his ways really is you. I can't get through to him, Si, and I sometimes just don't recognise him. I can put up with him being grouchy and monosyllabic, and I know how to snap him out of it, usually anyway. But he is being downright vile to Hannah. That's the reason she left that night. God, think about it. A twelve-year-old doesn't want to come back home but stands in the middle of town on her own on a bitterly cold night, frightened and distressed, because her fourteen-year-old brother is bullying her so badly. I feel as if I'm living out one of those awful stories in the tabloids when social services get brought in.'

'Something's going on and it's not just adolescence. It can't be.'

'So find out what it is. And bring him up short, Si. This mustn't ever happen again.'

'The problem is I'm not sure when. The best thing would be if the weekend stays quiet. I can just drop in casually and take him out for an hour or so.'

'He's got a match on Saturday afternoon and it's an away so he won't be back till after seven.'

'Sunday morning then, all other things being equal.'

245

'Right . . . How's Rachel?'

Her brother looked up, and at once she saw his expression blank as he pulled down the old, invisible portcullis.

'Fine.'

'I guess the job doesn't give you much time with her either at the moment.'

'No. Want some more of this?'

Cat shook her head. 'I'll have to get back after a quick coffee. Silke doesn't stay overnight.'

Simon got up. Cat removed the plates. The coffee was made. They sat on the white sofa in his beautiful long sitting room, perfectly amicably, yet a hundred miles apart.

'Have you got any further forward with these killings?'

'A bit. Got some files to go through here.' He pointed to the pile on the table.

'It's looking as if we just might have a breakthrough, which God knows we need.'

Cat finished her coffee. 'I'll leave you to it.'

Five minutes later she was driving out of the close. Rachel's name had not been mentioned again.

Forty-four

After Cat had gone Simon cleared the table, poured himself another black coffee and opened the large file Nathan had brought. He also opened his laptop and slid in the CD.

He knew what was coming but, in general, a detective is well used to seeing unpleasant sights, and he went through the photos carefully, examining each one in detail.

The images of three elderly women, dead in Yorkshire, could have come from the crime scenes at Duchess of Cornwall Close. The way the bodies, all of them wearing nightdresses, one a woollen cardigan on top, had been posed sitting in front of mirrors, the way they had been strangled, the yellow-and-green electrical flex . . . the women were different, but everything else was startlingly the same. He clicked through more photographs, close-ups, pictures of beds, doors, windows, wardrobes, dressing tables, mirrors, then of the women's faces, necks, hands. And feet. Bare feet with freshly clipped toenails. He looked quickly through exterior shots of a complex of sheltered flats and bungalows, older than those in Lafferton but not dissimilar in layout or type.

The file contained the pathologist's reports, SOCO reports, details of forensic analyses, dustings for prints. Then came the details of the trail that had led to Alan Keyes being arrested and charged – the result of a lucky break. Keyes had been caught on CCTV cutting through the town centre and had come just within range of the cameras at a bank, at three in the morning, after the last murder. No one else was about. The cameras captured only one or two random cars and a stray dog. CCTV on every building in the city centre, on the nights of the other murders, had been examined but he had obviously been careful to steer clear of them. His image was fuzzy but they had done their best with it and the press had gone to town. Soon after the lunchtime news, the calls had started to come in. Alan Frederick Keyes had been arrested that day.

At two in the morning Simon was reading the accounts of the trial in disbelief. The evidence against Keyes was solid. The press had had him hung, drawn and quartered well in advance.

And he had been acquitted.

After the full transcript of the trial, and the judge's final remarks, the file came to an abrupt end. Someone had pencilled 'Case closed' on the last page. That was that.

Serrailler went to bed puzzled but buoyant. Find Alan Frederick Keyes and he'd find his own killer.

The following morning when he arrived in his office at eight o'clock, the photographs taken from Nobby Parks's phone had been downloaded and sorted and were in a file on Simon's computer. Forensics had eliminated a few obvious non-starters – blanks, flashes of brilliant light and nothing else, close-ups of brick walls, pictures of the road surface, a set of bus tyres and a patch of grass. These were in a side file.

He got his first coffee of the day and started on those they had signalled as worth further attention, though even of these at least half seemed to him of little use or relevance. But the others – maybe fifteen shots – he saved in a new file, to look at more closely. He also copied the whole team in on them.

Three looked of certain interest. The first was a shot of Rosemary Poole in the entrance to her bungalow, looking out, but with her hand on the door as if she was about to close it. The light was poor, the shot obviously taken late in the afternoon. He enlarged it by 200 per cent. It went completely out of focus. 150 per cent . . . not much better. At 75 per cent he could see Mrs Poole's face more clearly. She looked as if she had been saying something to a person just ahead. Perhaps she was greeting them, perhaps saying goodbye.

The next was the rear of a white van with the number plate, all but the last digit, clearly visible.

The third was of the grass outside the bungalows, frosted over but also struck by a shaft of thin wintry sunlight. A shadow – no, not a full shadow, maybe half or two-thirds of one – lay across the grass. It was almost certainly the shadow of a person, but he could not tell much more.

At nine fifteen, Simon had the whole team in the CID room. The photos were up on the screen.

'Keep looking at them,' Simon said. 'Get the images in your head. Nobby Parks was hanging around the D of C houses at all hours, usually after dark. He took these pics at random – he was playing with his toy without a clue how to use it. But there'll be something on these . . . some detail, some link . . . it won't hit you in the face – if it did you'd have got it. But there'll be something.'

He filled them in on the files Nathan had brought down. 'The case is out there – HOLMES, court proceedings, national and local papers. Won't take you more than an hour to bring your-selves completely up to speed with Alan Frederick Keyes and the Yorkshire murders which are blow-by-blow the exact same as ours here. Only difference, there were three elderly victims up there, we only have two and let's make sure it stays that way. I want everything you can find about this man Keyes – everything in Yorkshire, before and after the murders and the trial, but more importantly since then. That's ten years. Search our force's database – all the forensics, CRIMIN, every sort of local and area record. I want to know where he's living, what he's doing. This is now our number-one suspect. I want him found. I want him brought in. When he's here, I want him grilled until his ears smoke. But we've got to catch him first. Local records, electoral register, council tax lists, register of marriages . . . Link anything you find with the info I've given you from the file. It's on your computer now, code name 'BarleyMow'. Keep it there. If you strike gold and find any sort of photograph, bring it to me. But I don't just want his picture. I want him.'

Forty-five

London. He would never want to live here again but for an occasional day there was nothing to beat it and he always returned home feeling reinvented, ready to raise the stakes, challenge himself all over again, both in work and as an artist. Why it had this effect of a quick inhalation of pure oxygen Serrailler could never quite suss out but it hadn't failed him and he knew it wouldn't fail him now. He stopped his cab at the top of the Mall. It was cold but the sun was bright. There had been a state visit a few days previously and the flags were still out. He walked down the wide paths, past St James's Palace, past Clarence House, and turned to climb the steps into Carlton House Terrace when there was the sound of massed hooves coming at a spanking pace up the Mall towards him. The Household Cavalry, jingling and sparkling, plumes swaying, went past to the occasional tourist's camera and wave, lifting his heart. As a small boy he had longed to be one of those guardsmen looking resplendent on their way to Buckingham Palace, or escorting the Queen's state coach or carriage. He remembered with a smile holding a silver-painted wooden sword, riding the arm of the sofa throughout Trooping the Colour.

He was meeting Joel Winslow, now a professor, at his club. Winslow had been his lecturer on the two profiling courses he had taken, and had even tried, without success, to persuade Simon to divert his career that way. They had forged a bond and Simon had gone to him for an opinion about peculiar or difficult cases once or twice before. Winslow would not be proud of him for making such a basic error after the murder of Elinor Sanders.

'Always bear the alternative in mind,' he said now, as they sat in the bar before going in to lunch. 'This isn't an exact science, Simon. I seem to remember trying to impress that on you.'

'You did. I'm doing more than kick myself.'

'Don't bother. In general, you were right. Your man was more than likely to wait a few weeks or even much longer before he killed a second time. Your only mistake was in upgrading a "likely" to a "definite" and calling off the patrols.'

'I didn't call them off. I halved them – and some.'

They were sitting at the end of the bar, a comfortable room adjacent to the entrance hall. Serrailler had been to this club a few times and enjoyed the excellent food and the handsome rooms, some small and intimate, others vast, formal and rather intimidating, with high ceilings and huge portraits on the walls. The dining room was wood-panelled with tables well separated, so that private conversations were perfectly possible. He wouldn't like to belong to one of these places, though his father loved it, but he could enjoy the surroundings and also be amused by the people. Club members out of central casting, he thought, as two entered the bar now. Pinstripes, stiff collars, plum-coloured faces.

'From what you've told me, it's pretty clear that the second killing was out of necessity rather than choice.'

'He got the wind up.'

'The old lady saw him or heard him, or else he thought she had. He couldn't take the risk. But he still killed in the same meticulously organised way, he was very much in control. No panic, no mistakes, even if he was in a hurry. He's a cool customer, this one. Anything else you can tell me?'

Over their excellent, entirely traditional lunch – potted shrimps, rare beef from the trolley, cheese, a bottle of the house claret – Simon went over the killings again, stressing the trademarks and telling him the confidential secrets that had been kept from the press and the public.

251

'Give me a portrait of your killer,' Joel said, 'see if I agree.'

'Psychopath. Sadist. Ritualist.'

Joel nodded, his mouth full of Yorkshire pudding and gravy. 'Loner.'

'Not necessarily. Loner inside himself certainly – but he could live a perfectly ordinary life otherwise. He won't want to draw attention to himself in the normal course of things. He can blend in.'

Simon described Nobby Parks but after only a few sentences Joel shook his head.

'This man is highly organised, neat and tidy, folds his clothes. And he isn't so stupid as to wander about the area in which he operates, at night, being seen, having patrol cars take him home. Rule him out – well, the usual 99 per cent anyway. You always leave a crack to let yourself back in, but I put money on it not being this Nobby Parks.'

'Grudge against old women.'

'Possibly, yes. Had an elderly female relative who treated him badly when he was a child. He could have been brought up by her – a grandmother, an older aunt. He hated her, and more than likely, that was because she humiliated him. He's getting his own back for that – he's humiliating his victims. Making them sit in front of a mirror, cutting their toenails. I wonder if he was made to do that for this old relative when he was a boy?'

'Or she could have cut his, and he felt ashamed or embarrassed.'

'So this would be a way of getting his own back.'

'What sort of age?'

'More difficult. Somewhere between thirty and fifty? He's still physically strong and he's fit.'

'You don't have to be that strong to kill an eighty-year-old woman. Could "he" be a "she"?'

'Possibly.'

'But if this is a twisted sort of vengeance on the old woman relative, why does he – or she – need to go on killing? Isn't one enough? He's had his revenge.'

'It's satisfying – the first time, he felt a terrific high. So far as he was concerned, he'd got his own back, even if it wasn't

252

actually on the same woman. But after a while, it started eating into him again. And, he'd enjoyed it. That's the other key. He likes killing. He likes the way he does it. He likes to humiliate.'

The cheeseboard was not over-elaborate. A half-truckle of Cheddar. Stilton. A creamy white Cheshire. Nothing foreign, nothing runny. Classic, Simon thought, as a slice of Cheddar was laid reverently on his plate. The celery was in a proper celery jar. There were no other embellishments.

'And he keeps trophies. They usually do. Sometimes they cut a lock of hair. Quite a few sadistic killers of younger women, prostitutes and so on, have been known to take pubic hair. In this case it might be nail clippings. He may collect newspaper reports of his murders and when the police get something wrong he'll gloat. Or he could keep it all on a computer. If he lives with someone, wife or girl or boyfriend, that's easier to conceal. He knows his way round. Round the police system, round houses, especially this sort. Round the town. This is night-time but there's always somebody about – a late taxi, a police patrol, someone walking home from a late shift or a club, someone taking a dog for a last pee – so he won't march prominently down the main roads, he'll take short cuts and alleyways and know his way round back gardens and across rough ground.'

'Local then.'

'Oh yes.'

Simon had not mentioned the Alan Keyes case files to Joel and, on the spur of the moment, decided to keep them to himself for the time being.

They drank coffee sitting on the sort of library armchairs in which old men fell asleep. One or two were already doing so, newspapers sliding gently onto their laps. The coffee was the only thing with which he could find fault. It was filter, it was bitter, and it was not hot enough.

Time he got back home.

'Anything else you want to run past me, call,' Joel said as they parted on the flight of marble steps that led to the door.

'It helps to see the picture a bit more clearly. Thank you.'

'You need to catch him sooner rather than later. You're the

DCS, I don't want to teach my grandmother to suck eggs, but he'll do it again, Simon.'

They parted and Simon walked down Piccadilly to his gallery off Albermarle Street. It was some time since his last exhibition and he had a conversation about plans for the next, probably in May of the following year. He looked round the current show of paintings which were not greatly to his taste, went down Burlington Arcade and bought Rachel a violet cashmere shawl and Cat a box of her favourite dark chocolate gingers, before heading for the train. As it pulled out, the late-afternoon sky was dark and a drizzle had set in. He had had the best of the London day.

He sat in a quiet carriage with his iPad, and in the light of what Joel had said, he sent an email to the team urging them on, stressing that the killer could strike again, and another asking for an all-night uniform guard at the sheltered houses and extra patrol cars in the area. There were two men and two women in residence now, but the rest of Duchess of Cornwall Close was still empty, although every bungalow was spoken for. Understandably, people were reluctant to move in until the killer was caught and, understandably, the council was also putting pressure on CID.

Simon closed the screen down and was about to open the paper when someone tapped him on the shoulder.

'Say if you would rather not be seen with me.' The Chief Constable, in her London suit and with a laptop bag, had been looking for a better seat. 'I mean it, Simon.'

'Don't be silly.' He indicated the one opposite to him.

'Not going to talk work, or anything else much, I've got a load of stuff to read. I have been wondering if you've thought over what I said the other day though.'

The job. He had not thought about it once since asking Nathan for his opinion.

'I have. It's not for me. I need to be hands-on – but you knew that already.'

Paula Devenish looked at him steadily. 'Yes. I'm not surprised, though I wish you felt otherwise.'

'No you don't. Nor does the force. It needs a very different sort of person. Actually, it's got what it needs already. You're not going to change your mind?'

She shook her head. 'We all hate change,' she said, opening her laptop. 'But we also need the shake-up we get along with it.'

They did not speak again until the train was drawing into Bevham Station, where the Chief's car had just pulled up at the forecourt entrance. Simon's was stowed away in the multi-storey opposite.

He appreciated the fact that she had not harangued him about the murders, though she would be as concerned as he was to make progress. She had not taken advantage of having him trapped in a seat opposite her. She delegated. She trusted. She knew when to leave someone to get on with their job.

He was going to miss her.

Forty-six

None of the team spoke in answer to Serrailler's question. He looked around, puzzled.

'What's going on here?'

After a second, Ben said, 'I think it means just that, guv. There's nothing going on. Nobody's found a single thing. We've all come up against a sort of hole in the ground.'

'Into which this Alan Keyes fell.'

They all piped up.

'Nothing in the electoral rolls, nothing in any of the civil registers . . . he hasn't married, had children or died.'

'Nothing in employment records.'

'I've been onto every employer large and small. No one's taken on a builder of that name, permanent or temp, in the last ten years.'

'What's the radius?'

'Employment – fifty miles of here, guv.'

'But civil registers, guv – we're talking nationwide. I've done a full trawl.'

'Prisons? Mental institutions?'

Heads were shaken.

'Like I said – he's dropped down a big black hole, guv. It's like he just ceased to exist.'

Simon stood up and banged his hand on the table. 'That's it. Got it.'

'No death records.'

'There won't be. Alan Keyes dropped down said black hole. They drew a line under his name and rubbed out everything there ever was about him since birth. Including birth.'

'What, new ID job?'

Simon nodded. 'It's crystal.'

He went to the front of the room, then paced back again, working it out as he spoke to the team.

'This is a man who pretty certainly committed three murders. But he was acquitted. The jury found him not guilty and the judge had no option but to let him go. He was rearrested on a trumped-up charge – "assaulting a police officer". Come on! He got into a very minor tussle with a PC who was trying to stop him leaving the court by the front entrance. For his own safety. It's clear from the files that if Keyes had appeared in public that day, or any other, he'd have been torn limb from limb. So they gave him a new identity. He was spirited off somewhere – either another nick or a safe house. These are often army bases. And he was trained until his new ID was engraved on his mind and heart. He had no further contact with any family or friends or neighbours. Gone. Rent and mortgage records, bank accounts, NI . . . you name it, it no longer exists in his name. Every record has vanished from public access. It's all in a file somewhere, locked onto some computer under a code name. Nobody has access except a couple of people, under high security.

'Keyes is someone else now. He's learned to be that someone. He's been taught to forget his old self and everything about his former life and start again. By now, ask him where he went to school or the name of his mother's sister and back the right answer will come, automatically. The new answer. Gradually, he's merged into everyday life in a new place, a long way from the old one. His appearance has changed too – and of course he's ten years older. If he had a beard, it's gone; if he had perfect eyesight, now he wears specs with clear glass. Everything's new. But deep down inside, he's the same man he always was. Of course he is. They can't transplant a personality – yet. And what defined Alan Keyes, in the end, was his desire to murder, and murder not just anyone, but old women. He likes to set them in front of a mirror. He likes to clip their toenails. These

257

particular pieces of info were never made public. Everything else is on record, in the news reports and so on. So this isn't a copycat – besides, ten years is stretching it a bit for a copycat. So we're looking for Alan Keyes before he kills again, but as Alan Keyes no longer exists – he has changed into God knows who – therein lies our problem.'

'His fingerprints won't have changed. Or his DNA. Can't do anything about those.'

'That's true, but his prints and dental records and notes on his blood group as *Keyes* – all those things will have vanished when he vanished.'

'But they're still on file – however well hidden in the bowels of somewhere or other, however protected. And given we've every reason to believe the two killers are one and the same person, presumably we can get access easily enough.'

'Have you ever been involved with a new ID, guv?'

'No, I haven't. Unsurprisingly. They're very rare. Has anyone here come up against one?'

Steph said, 'I was on a case just after I joined CID – Liverpool. Woman murdered her two babies just after birth. She wasn't judged to be insane and she served a prison sentence but not a long one because there were still doubts about her mental state even after the psych report. She was given a new ID. Rumour had it she went abroad – maybe Canada. No one knew of course and we got a lecture about gossip and rumour. But I wasn't that close to it.'

No one else had personal knowledge.

'Right,' Simon said. 'Get home. No point in doing a late night at this stage. I'm going to see the Chief – getting access to Alan Keyes's secure file is a job for her. She'll make the application, I'll get the files. Thanks, guys. I know it's been frustrating coming up against a blank wall with every direction you've turned this last couple of days. But in fact, taken as one, the blank walls have been very informative.'

Forty-seven

'Get in!' Serrailler shouted.

The ball sneaked fast and at an acute angle, so that the keeper barely had the chance to see that it was coming at all before it hit the back of the net. Two seconds after it did so the final whistle blew.

Sam's teammates surrounded him, clapping him on the back and hi-fiving him.

Simon did a thumbs up as his nephew caught his eye.

'What are you doing here?'

'Your mum asked me to pick you up – she's got an emergency. I was in time to see the last ten minutes or so. Glad I did. Fantastic goal, Sambo.'

'Why aren't you at work? I thought you were twenty-four-seven on the OBMs.'

'The what?'

'Old biddy murders. Or have you arrested the wrong man again?'

Simon opened the boot and Sam slung his hockey gear inside.

'I'll be back at the station once I've taken you home, and I'm working late, so I'm going to grab a meal now. Steeleye's in the Lanes serves all day. You up for that?'

Sam sighed. 'What's all this about, as if I didn't know? Hanny Fanny been telling tales?'

'Do you want me to take you to eat or do you want to walk home, with your kit, from the crossroads? Your call.'

'OK.' Sam shrugged.

'Thanks, or no thanks. That's the least I'll settle for.'

'Thanks.'

Simon nodded.

The brasserie was quiet and they got a table in the window. The shops in the Lanes had closed but the windows were lit, and plenty of people used this as a short cut to the car parks. The table had tea lights under small glass domes, and the food was decent. If he had not had a sulky and grunting nephew for a companion, Simon would have looked forward to enjoying his rib-eye steak, chips and salad.

Sam had the house speciality – called a stereo-burger, which came in two buns, laid side by side. He had eaten his way stolidly and silently through half of it, plus a lot of chips, before Simon said, 'Right, Sam. Spill.'

Sam looked up blankly.

'I thought I knew you pretty well. I had you down as bright and thoughtful. You work hard, you were fantastic to your mother when your dad died, you were the one person who helped get her through all that at the time. You've always had your quarrels with Hannah because that's what happens between brothers and sisters. Your mother used to get up my nose, I can tell you. Still does occasionally.'

Sam set down his burger. 'Look, cut to it. I know what you're going to say, right?'

'What am I going to say?'

'My fault she ran away, my fault if she'd got herself abducted or raped or something, my fault she's snivelling all day and night, my fault she didn't get the part in her fucking film.'

'That's enough!'

'Sorry.'

'You should be. Swear blue if you trap your finger in a door frame. That's what it's for, not for casually slagging off your sister. All right, you've acknowledged some of it. Yes, it was your fault Hannah ran away and you're bloody lucky none of the rest happened.'

'So's she.'

'It is not your fault that she didn't get the film part. Any more than you did something particularly wonderful to get yours. Happened. Didn't. Luck and bad luck all round I'd say, wouldn't you? Winding her up about it, crowing about your success – I suppose that's normal and I'm not saying I wouldn't have indulged in a bit of boasting myself. But this has gone way beyond winding her up, Sam.

'You've been unkind and cruel and vicious, you've sneered and jeered and made her feel small. Rubbing it in doesn't even begin to cover it. What's that all about? Look at me. No, I said look. Now answer me. You can tell me anything. It won't go any further. This conversation isn't going back to your mother or anyone else. Anyone. You hear me? So what's it about? Do you hate Hannah so much?'

Sam pushed a chip round his plate, head bent. He was going to be good-looking, Simon thought. His adult features were already beginning to take shape. He was also going to be tall. But on the cusp of growing up, something was churning him up inside that he wasn't able to articulate or deal with other than by bullying his sister – and for all Simon knew, bullying other people too, smaller boys, younger boys, fat boys, boys with problems or glasses or acne.

'When people start behaving like you've been behaving, Sam, there is always a reason. But a reason is not an excuse. You haven't been brought up on some council estate where your dad beat your mum and it was everyone for themselves and nobody ever taught you right from wrong. You didn't grow up learning to thieve and hit out and torment kittens. Those people have reasons why they behave as they do but reasons are still not excuses. You know what I do. I see people who beat up and knife and shoot and threaten and abuse others. I see them every day. And they all started somewhere – being vile to their siblings and younger kids at school, then joining street gangs and bigging themselves up by carrying knives and doing drugs and, eventually, landing up with us, then in court, then in a young offenders, then in prison. And once they're started on that road they almost never get off it.'

'You trying to scare me or what?'

'No. I don't think I need to. I'm trying to make you see things as they really are, though. And where they can lead. I'm trying to get you to look at yourself. Then pack it in. Now. Pack in hurting Hannah, pack in treating her so horribly that she actually ran away from home rather than stay there with you around. She's twelve years old, Sam. And she walked out into the freezing cold night, caught a bus into town and hung about with some half-baked plan – or maybe without any plan. I happened to see her. I don't need to go into what might have been the outcome if someone else had got there first. Do I?'

Sam's head was still bent.

'Look at me.'

Eventually, Sam did. His eyes were brimming, his face contorted in the effort to stop himself from crying at all costs. Simon understood completely.

'Fine,' he said. 'I'm having a coffee. They do great hot chocolate brownies with ice cream. Do you want one? Yes, I have an amazing ability to tell when people do.'

He turned to look for their waitress and give his nephew a chance to wipe his eyes and take hold of himself.

'Last word on this, Sambo, and then I'm done. Please say you're sorry. To your mum, to Hannah. I don't know how you'll choose to do that – leave it to you. But do it. And mean it.'

The brownie and his own espresso came.

'Right. I'm always here. I'm always available to you, to listen, to talk, to help out if I can. We get along, we had that great week in Norfolk. I want us to go climbing next time. I'd like to take you up to the island too. You're good company and you don't rabbit on.'

Sam smiled slightly.

'But wherever, whenever, I'm here. Got that?'

After a moment, Sam nodded. 'Got it.'

Forty-eight

The thaw had set in the previous day and the canal towpath was thick with mud, in which pools of dark water were concealed as a trap for the unwary. The unwary included Gus Norwald, who had not thought to put on boots or even heavy shoes and whose feet were now soaking. But if he got what he was determined to get it would be worth it. Anything would be worth it.

Local papers were dying, one of the old guard on the *Gazette* had said to him gloomily the previous day, just as he had said it on the day before that, and the previous week and at any time he could get someone to be bored to death by his sermon on the end of everything, in the Royal Ensign on the corner by the paper's offices. Soon, the *BG* would go weekly. After that, it would go online only, and who wanted to bother with a local paper like the *Bevham Gazette* online? Not even the classified would survive.

Which was why Gus Norwald, looking to number one, was constantly in search of the story he could pitch to one of the nationals. He had had two good ones already this year, picked up by the *Mail* and *The Times*. With luck, this might be his third. He'd had a tip from a mate in the police. He knew what he could make of this one.

The towpath got muddier, and the canal was high. All around Lafferton streams and brooks were filling and cascading down into the canal and the river from the hills. If it started to rain as well, as they had forecast, Lafferton would be in for another flood.

By the time he saw Nobby Parks's shack, Gus was chilled and wet and the black smoke coming from the tin chimney was actually a cheering sight.

It took several attempts at knocking and banging before there was any response from inside, and when Nobby did come to the door, he was in two thick sweaters, his cap and a pair of greying long johns.

'Morning, Nobby.'

The two knew one another. Nobby had given Gus a tip-off here and there, though only one had ever amounted to anything. He'd also given him a racing tip or two, both of which had come in. Gus wondered if Nobby had a sack of gold hidden underneath his frowsty mattress.

'Not sorry to see you. Feel like company. You want a roll-up?'

'No thanks. I'd like a cuppa though.'

Nobby shifted a stack of old telephone directories from the only chair other than his own, sacred wicker one. Gus flipped through them.

'These are from the 1960s and 70s.'

'I know that. I can read, don't think I can't.'

'What do you do with them?'

'Might come in useful.'

'Some day.'

'That's right.' Nobby dropped two tea bags into mugs, one of which was from the coronation of 1953, the other commemorating Lafferton 4th Cub Pack Jubilee, 1988.

'You ever buy anything, Nobby?'

'Not if I can help it. No shortage of free mugs if you know where to look. Builders' yards, construction sites . . . they move on, dump their mugs and their tea-bag tins. Shocking waste.'

'Not while you're around to field them.'

Nobby laughed. 'Glad it's you,' he said. 'Could tell you a thing or two about these murders.'

Gus put his mug down. 'Now listen . . . if you've seen or heard anything on your night prowling, you have to go to the cops, Nobby. Cops first. You know that.'

'I know that, I know that. Only they got to me first. They're always harassing me, stopping me when I'm walking about doing no one any harm, bringing me back here. Only last time they had me in the station. Wrongful arrest. I could go to the papers, I said, destroying my good name. Good character. Whatever you call it.'

'Are you really telling me they arrested you? And charged you?'

'Obstructing the police in the course of . . . Let me go though. Had to. Nothing on me. But anyone might have seen me get taken in there, get brought out. It's my reputation.'

'Sue them.' Gus meant it as a joke but that was not how Nobby took it.

'You think I could? I reckon I've got a case. You want to write about it then?'

'I doubt you could sue. I don't know – have to check. You could try asking for compensation, say it's meant you can't sleep properly, had to see the doctor.'

'I haven't seen a doctor for thirty-six years. Wouldn't go near them. And hospitals – forget it. Go in a hospital you come out with worse than you started. Or dead. You want one of these?'

The packet of Bourbon creams was almost full. 'Picked them up in the car park behind the Tesco. Dropped off a trolley so they're a bit broken. But they're all right.'

They sat and munched for a moment. Gus looked at Nobby. Nobby looked suddenly sly.

'I had a personal visit here,' he said. 'From the police.'

'Well, I'd keep that quiet.'

'No, no. This was the Chief Super. Mr Serrailler. Known Mr Serrailler since he was a plod. Well . . . near enough.'

'The DCS came here to see you? Get on.'

'Oh yes. Wanted to ask for my help.'

Gus went still. Nobby's stories grew stories on them but he wasn't a liar.

'Wants me to keep my eyes and ears open when I'm out and about. They don't have enough cops, you see, money being money, so they want my help. Sort of undercover.'

'Right.'

'You can smirk. There's plenty I see and hear. I'm quiet as a cat, me.'

265

'So the idea is, you hang about and tell them if you see anything suspicious?'

'Not anything. I'm not doing their dirty for them looking for girls and rutters and reporting kids having a joint. Just to do with these murders. I'm up there a lot, round the sheltereds. I could see anything . . . cars, people slipping down alleyways. I've already been a great help to them. Mr Serrailler told me as much. Said it could provide vital evidence.'

'What could?'

'Mobile phone,' Nobby said.

'You've got a mobile?' Gus just stopped himself from saying 'but you don't know anyone to ring'.

'I have. Or I had. He took it.'

'Serrailler?'

'Said it could prove very helpful.'

'Yeah, you told me. I don't see how. Who's been ringing you then?'

'Nobody. Nor me ringing them. Don't have no use for it. But I took a lot of photos, see? And they could have anything on them.' He took down his tobacco tin and Rizlas.

'Vital evidence.'

Forty-nine

Serrailler arrived at the mortuary of Bevham General just after ten. He parked up, beside de Silva's ancient Citroën DS, which in his police view was unroadworthy but which presumably must have passed its tests. Beautiful car though, he thought, touching the long sloping bonnet. He loved classic cars but he needed one that had every sort of latest aid to driving and safety, not one that would let him down at the roadside. But after this case, he decided now, time to look for something a bit more fun.

Nick de Silva was in the middle of an autopsy on an RTA victim and began pointing out various interesting spinal fractures. Simon was hardened but felt no wish to spend too long looking closely at the body of a human being which was now barely recognisable as such. He wandered off into the waiting area, got a coffee from the machine and leafed through back copies of *Modern Pathology* until Nick came through, gown untied, face mask down.

'I know you've sent in your report but I'm going to nag you about something . . . try and pin you down.'

'I'm pretty careful never to let that happen.' Nick brought his own coffee to the standard-issue foam-filled hospital sofa, model name 'Uncomfortable'. 'But you can always try. This is our strangulations?'

'Is there any way you can say if the women were strangled first, then put down in the chairs in front of the mirror, or whether they were placed there, under duress, then strangled?'

'No. No way I can tell. There's just a chance your forensics might though.' He was silent for a moment, thinking. 'Both of them were fairly close to the mirrors, as I remember.'

'About where any woman would sit if they were doing their hair.'

'Well, if that's near enough, and they were not dead when they were placed there, then they could have exhaled sharply enough for saliva to have gone out from the mouth on the breath, and been sprayed very finely on the mirror, or even on the dressing-table surface. If it's there, your guys can find it – should have found it by now actually. Have you had forensics' full reports yet?'

'Yes. Nothing on either of the mirrors.'

'Get them to go over the surfaces again. Dressing table, drawers, glass. Kick arse. Forensics aren't what they were; not since they stopped being done in-house. Next thing, they'll be privatising us. I've got to get back.'

'How long before you decide your RTA victim is dead?'

'Oh, I've done that one – I've got two more from the same crash now. The bypass pile-up.'

'Shit, yes. I've clearly been too tied up in CID trivia.'

Half a dozen emails and messages had come through to his mobile but the signal on this side of the hospital was too weak to pick anything up. Simon walked round to the busy front entrance, the usual main highway of ambulances, patients in wheelchairs, paramedics, nurses and lost visitors. He would go to the League of Friends café, get a sandwich and another coffee, call that lunch, and answer his messages before he headed back. But then, down the long corridor, he saw Rachel, unmistakable to him even though he only glimpsed her back.

When he caught her up in a few strides and touched her arm, she spun round with shock.

'Darling? What's happened?'

She was pale and looked stricken with anxiety and confusion, almost uncertain even where she was or who he was.

She leaned against him with relief, but then pulled back. 'No.'

He understood. 'I'm going to get coffee – come with me.'

'I . . . I couldn't drink anything . . .'

'Just sit with me then.' He guided her gently forwards, his hand firm on her shoulder. The place was as busy as usual, but as usual, too, someone was always just leaving and they got a table.

'It's been the worst twelve hours of my life. Kenneth woke up hardly able to breathe and the oxygen didn't seem to help him. The doctor came out – he's pretty good, though I know it's what we pay for, and he rang for an ambulance within a minute. He's in intensive care – it's pneumonia and he's very ill but I came out because they were intubating him and it's terrible to watch.'

'They don't want you to watch – it's a tricky procedure.'

'I was just wandering round wondering where to go or what I should do. I was going to get a paper or something but . . . I couldn't even find my way to the shop.'

'Do they know how to reach you?'

She looked appalled.

'Right. I'll take you back.'

He took her to the bank of lifts and put her into one for the intensive care floor. He did not touch her, just watched the doors close. Rachel could not look at him.

Fifty

There was a message from the press officer to call her, but as her lines were busy Serrailler drove back to the station and went down to her office instead.

'Thought you might have been on my tail never mind me on yours,' she said.

'When do I get time to read newspapers? I look to you.'

'Download the apps onto your iPad.'

'Still wouldn't have time. Besides, I'm old-fashioned, I like the nice crackle of newspaper between my hands.'

'I bet you like the nice feel of a hardback book as well.'

'Don't start me.'

'Yes, well, I wouldn't read half the books I do, and I read a lot –'

'– if you didn't have a Kindle. Heard it all from my sister. Right, what've you got?'

'You're going to love this.'

The daily papers were all on a big table. Anything of particular interest Simon could mark and it would be on his computer in electronic version within seconds. The *Daily Mail* was on top of the pile, opened at a large photograph of Nobby Parks.

'Police use me as their spy,' says man living in rubbish dump. 'They're even relying on photos from mobile phone I found, for "vital evidence".'

The interview with Nobby was colourful, rich in elaborate detail about his shack and its contents, outraged in tone, and implying that the Lafferton force was so cash-strapped it had to borrow Nobby's phone, disregarding the fact that they knew it was stolen, and so undermanned and incompetent that they had to use him as an undercover night-time investigator. Simon imagined only too well what fun Nobby had had enriching the story of his own visit to the shack. How much had they paid him? Fifty? A fiver more like.

Actually, more like zilch, except for a pack of his tobacco.

'Fun, isn't it? What do you want me to do?'

'I'm assuming they've rung to get a comment.'

'Phones haven't stopped. That and "When can Lafferton's old people sleep safe in their beds?"'

'Do nothing. I'm not available for comment. This is all rubbish except the phone stuff and I was well within my rights to take that.'

'He's popped in as well, by the way.'

'Nobby? What, asking when's he taking delivery of his Queen's Police Medal?'

'When's he getting a receipt for his mobile phone.'

'Shit. I'll do one and get someone round with it or that'll be in the papers.'

'It already is.'

Fifty-one

Simon shut his door and asked for no calls. He then sat down and reread the summary of the files Nathan had supplied, including every detail of the Yorkshire murders, and of the last day of Alan Keyes's trial, until he was doubly sure. Then he picked up the phone to the National Fingerprint Board. He was not going to delegate any of this.

He gave Keyes's full name, age and last-known address, and asked for a fingerprint check.

In a small anonymous-looking office some distance from both Lafferton and the NFB, an alert flashed up on one particular computer. The message, that Lafferton Police had put in a query about the prints of 'Alan Frederick Keyes', came through to one particular officer, who logged it in a file, code-named 'Jogging Sparrow', only accessible by two passwords, known only to the same officer.

The message came back to Serrailler. 'No matches.'

Keyes had been removed from the system. He no longer existed. He had a new identity.

Apart from Keyes himself, only one organisation knew what that identity was.

Simon made another phone call. It was answered by a woman. She gave no name, only said, 'Floor Five.'

When he repeated his details and enquiry, he was transferred. An anonymous voice said, 'Forty-four.'

'This is DCS Simon Serrailler of Lafferton Police. I am SIO on a murder inquiry, two separate incidents, two victims. The MO indicates close similarities with murders committed in Yorkshire in 2001. Alan Frederick Keyes was arrested and charged but acquitted on trial. I've reason to suppose that Keyes now has a new police ID and this is a formal request for information about that.'

'Forty-four' – whoever he was – had not interrupted Simon, nor given his name. Now he said, 'Let me have your details again, please.'

Serrailler gave him his full name, rank and number, contact details. 'Can I stress the urgency of this? We've got two dead women. I don't want any more, as I'm sure you'll appreciate.'

'Everything is logged. Someone will get back to you.'

The man in the small anonymous-looking office closed down the file he had been working on and opened a new one, as a sub-file to 'Jogging Sparrow', and reported the call in detail. He then closed the file, and put through an internal request on the closed network for a check on Serrailler, and a second, for full info, via HOLMES, on the Lafferton murders. Both were headed 'Priority'.

He then accessed 'Jogging Sparrow' and began to read up details of the three Yorkshire murders. By the time the HOLMES report came through, he had the full picture in his head. He then read the details about the ongoing Lafferton cases.

He accessed 'Jogging Sparrow' again, after inputting the two passwords, and immediately being given two new ones, for use the next time, via the computer.

It was like opening a box within a box within a box, each with a different key. A lot of people would have found the process, and the information in the file, beyond exciting. But police officers who worked in this section were not easily excited. That was one of the reasons they were picked and why the work suited them.

The screen opened up for the third time. In front of him were the full details of a man who had once been Alan Frederick Keyes. This was his new biography, details of his invented past, parents, birth date and place, his national insurance number, passport and driving licence, his school examinations record, dental and medical info – whatever anyone could ever want to know.

The officer read it all through carefully again, memorising what he needed. On a separate sub-file were details of the 'contact' originally in charge of Keyes. That member of CID had retired. Keyes had been assigned to a new police 'contact', whose details were on the next page. They had not changed for the last four years.

The officer wrote down a name and a mobile number, closed and locked the file. The next time he logged on, he would enter the new passwords, for one-time-only use.

He filled in a further report, on a closed file, and sent it through to his boss. Then he switched off his computer and locked the system, closed and locked his office door, and went down to the canteen.

Fifty-two

He'd been a night man for as many years as he could remember, starting when he was a miner on shifts. Always preferred the nights. When the pit closed and he eventually got another job it was as a nightwatchman. So he thought it must be in his nature. Maybe he'd been born at night? He never knew his mother after the age of five, so he couldn't ask, but he had a feeling. Everything seemed to fit him at night, everything seemed to work better. He could hear more keenly, see further, and he had a sense of things happening, round the corner, on the other side of a wall or a patch of shrub.

The man from the paper had dropped a copy off at the shack, and Nobby had read what had been written. It included a nice bit about him at nights. 'Nobby Parks likes to look out for other people,' it said, 'especially when they're sound asleep. He keeps an eye open. Many a burglar has been deterred, noticing Nobby wandering down the street at two in the morning. And when there was a late-night ram raid on a jeweller's in Lafferton's small exclusive shopping area, the Lanes, Nobby was around. "I was handy," he says, "I saw what happened and gave them some useful bits of information."'

He had folded the paper up carefully and put it not among the piles of others but in the top drawer of the old sideboard, where he kept essentials – his reading glasses, his out-of-date passport, his pension book. A photo of himself in pit gear, coming off the very last shift the day it closed for good. The collar and lead from a dog he'd once had.

Now, he had been twice round the perimeter of the Hill, gone in and out of the maze of streets called the Apostles, down the Lanes once or twice. He'd stood in the square watching the last taxi driver give up and set off for home, pressed back into a doorway when a group of drunken lads started a punch-up and the police sirens came wailing down. It was milder now, the sky cloudy but there was no rain and the towpath and verges were drying up a bit. He went down to what he called the Jesus Bus, by the printworks, got hot chocolate and a slice of cake, and had a chat to the lads, who knew better than to try and preach to him. Anyway, he'd told them he was a fully paid-up Christian who didn't hold with church. After that, they'd given up.

It was gone three when he finally made his way home. He was pleasantly tired. He'd have a brew, a roll-up and the last couple of chocolate Bourbons before getting into bed like a mouse into a deep nest, and sleeping the sleep of the just.

No one about. He didn't need any sort of torch or light to show his way. He knew every inch of this towpath. He heard a rat plop into the canal water, just under the bridge, saw a car go over, lights sweeping across the arch of bricks and away.

A hundred yards to home. He might read the article in the paper again before he went to sleep.

Fifty yards. The old lean-to against the warehouses was in deep shadow. The door was loose on its hinge and in a wind swung and creaked so much that sometimes Nobby had to get up and shut it and hold the broken padlock with a piece of stick. But tonight, it was still. The canal water was like glass. The air was moist and heavy.

The lean-to door was open but he didn't look closely enough to see a shadow within the shadows, or sense the slight flicker of movement.

He pushed open the shack door and went in. He switched on his torch and went to the paraffin stove. Lit it. Lit the paraffin lamp. Put the torch back on the shelf, his coat and boots by the door. Then he made a brew. Rolled a cigarette, and sat back in the wicker chair, enjoying the peace and quiet.

For a moment, something seemed wrong. Something was slightly different. He looked round. But the shadows of the lamp didn't reach the corners of the shack and he couldn't see anything unusual near to hand.

He sat thinking. Pleased with himself. Pleased with events.

It was another roll-up and twenty minutes before he got up, went outside to the dense patch of weeds and peed into them.

It had begun to drizzle a little.

He looked round but the cloud cover was too heavy for him to see anything. Even the movement of shadow on shadow over by the old lean-to.

He went back inside, latched the door, half undressed, into his long johns, jumper, socks. Got into his nest of bedding and old coats, turned on his side and pulled them up almost over his head.

Slept.

Fifteen minutes later, the darkness, silence and stillness were disturbed by a single figure, moving swiftly. A small flicker. A flare. A carefully aimed lob. The flaming ball of material hit the wooden shack roof, swift as a falling star. Seconds later, the whole place was an inferno. The shadows were broken again for a split second as someone ran, along the towpath, under the bridge, across the waste ground and away.

Nobby Parks's shack blazed like a tinderbox throwing flames high into the night sky.

Stupid. Stupid. Fucking stupid. You never do that. You know it and you always knew it. You plan, you work it out, for weeks, months maybe, and that's part of the whole thing. Part of the pleasure. You never let a single thing happen without a plan and you have backups to your plan, and you have an abort to your plan.

Bad enough having one fuck-up. You could have waited. You weren't sure she'd seen you, but you panicked. You never, ever panicked before. The reason it went wrong before was down to bad luck. Simple. Not you making a mistake, not the cops being clever. Bad luck.

But now?

This is not what you do. Not part of the game at all. Shit, what kind of a bloke would torch an old dosser's shack with him in it, out of panic?

He didn't deserve that. Even if he had seen something. Heard something. Knew something.

Yes, but if he had. If he did.

You can't take that chance.

And how else was I supposed to shut him up? Tell me that.

Fifty-three

'What are we reading this time? I'm so behind.'

'*The Great Gatsby*.'

'Yes, I remember now. I read it donkey's years ago, but I haven't had a chance to read it again. I'd better not come.'

'Judith! You missed last time. It's in the bookshop tonight as well. Emma gets agitated if people miss. She's having a tough time keeping an independent bookshop open . . . come on. You can just listen and if you start now you can get a couple of chapters under your belt.'

I have got to get to the bottom of this, Cat thought, putting the phone down. Something is wrong, I have no idea what, but Judith is not herself and she won't talk to me.

Her stepmother had made one excuse after another for not coming to the book group, to Sam's matches, Hannah's play, lunch with Cat at Steeleye's. Enough.

She sat at the kitchen table reading the paper over her coffee, a fifteen-minute break before going back to her desk and working through more papers, trying to firm up some of her ideas for the PhD. She had taken Wookie for a long walk and the house was quiet apart from the distant churning of the washing machine.

But she could not get Judith out of her mind, and if it was not Judith, Sam and Hannah probed their way in. Simon had told her briefly about his conversation with Sam and indicated that he thought things would now improve. Certainly Sam was behaving better, was less inclined to sneer at Hannah, grunt at Cat and slouch off to his room rather than give any help. Hannah was still wary, and tried not to be on her own in a room with him.

It was not the ideal setting in which family life could thrive.

But Molly had emailed a couple of days before to say that she was coming down to see the medical school about taking her finals or possibly repeating her last year altogether. She asked if she could stay a night or two at the farmhouse.

Cat was delighted. Molly sounded steadier and more optimistic in her email. If she had made enough improvement, there was no doubt in Cat's mind that she ought to finish her qualifications and it would be good to have her about the house again. But she knew how careful the med school would be. PTSD did not vanish in a hurry. They had to be sure that Molly could cope, for their sake but most of all for her own.

Wookie pattered after her into the study and turned round and round on his bed, which was in a patch of winter sunlight, before finally settling into a satisfactory nest and looking at Cat with one eye. After a moment, sensing in some way that he was there, Mephisto strolled through the door and climbed in beside the terrier. There was barely room and the cat overlapped the bed with his huge fluffy tail and forepaws, but his head rested on Wookie, without any protest from the dog. Both slept.

Silke came at half past six. At ten to seven, Cat phoned Judith.

'Are you ready? We can both park outside Si's and walk through if you like.'

There was a pause. 'Darling, I can't – my car seems to have something wrong with it.'

'What sort of thing?'

'Making a sort of – grinding noise. I don't want to risk being stranded.'

'Use Dad's.'

'Heavens, you know what he's like about anyone else driving his precious car. No, I'll –'

'Right.' Cat said. She clicked off.

Twenty minutes later she was driving up to Hallam House. She waited a moment.

The lights were on in the back rooms and one on the upstairs landing but the kitchen was in darkness.

She did not get out of her car, just hooted loudly. Nothing. Hooted again.

A light went on in the hall but no one came to the door.

Cat rang Judith on the mobile.

'Hello? Oh . . .'

'I'm outside,' Cat said. 'Waiting.'

'Oh Lord, you shouldn't . . . you're going to have to go on without me, I can't –'

'I am staying put here until you come out, wearing your coat and carrying your copy of *The Great Gatsby*.'

She sat back and put on the radio, to hear the beginning of *Front Row*. They were into the third item, about an Eric Ravilious exhibition, before Judith came out of the front door. She had on her coat, carried her bag, and had a scarf pulled up round her neck and covering her chin.

'Dentist . . . root canal. I daren't let the cold air onto it.'

The air was much milder after the weeks of sub-zero. Cat looked at Judith carefully for a moment, then set off. They talked about her PhD on the way, the options, the areas of particular interest she had narrowed down to, how long it was going to take her and what it might lead to at the end of it all.

'You're looking forward to it, aren't you?'

'Yes. Nervous though. A PhD is a big step from a short course. What happened to your thoughts on doing an Open University degree by the way?'

'That's all they are. Thoughts. I don't think I could do it.'

'Why not? People of ninety do degrees.'

'Nothing to do with age. Just commitment. And your father isn't keen.'

'Now that doesn't sound like you.'

There was a difficult silence. Cat had deliberately arrived early for just this eventuality. They were in the centre of town now, but she pulled up in an empty side street and switched off the engine.

Judith looked out of the window.

'If you want to talk and not go to the book group you know that's absolutely fine. We can go and get something to eat or –'

'No.'

'I'm concerned. You know I am.'

'It's all fine, darling. We'd better get a move on.'

There were ten members of the book group but they rarely had a full house. Tonight, eight sat round the front of Emma's bookshop. The idea was that although the Lanes were quiet at night, people still went through, and the bar on the corner and the brasserie were open until eleven, so lights on and a group sitting talking in the shop full of books attracted attention.

Emma provided coffee, others brought cakes and biscuits, and they all put money into a communal pot to buy wine. Cat always looked forward to the group evenings, and until the last few months, so had Judith. Tonight, she sat at the back, on a chair behind two others, her scarf still round half her face. Someone asked if she was all right, and sympathy was universal at her murmured 'Dentist. Root canal.'

It was Emma's turn to introduce the book and she held up her copy to get their attention.

Cat listened, but every so often took a covert glance at her stepmother. The discussion began but Judith did not say anything. They had some pleasantly fiery disagreements, the usual people took the floor and wouldn't give it up, the usual others said little. In five minutes they would break and whoever's turn it was would go out to the kitchen to organise the refreshments.

A slight movement caught the corner of Cat's eye and she looked at Judith. The scarf had slipped. The right-hand side of her face, around her cheekbone, was badly bruised and flared red, and there was also a livid patch on her jaw.

Cat looked away but not before Judith had realised. She flushed, and pulled the scarf back up.

Cat sat through the rest of the evening on autopilot, drinking a glass of wine too quickly, then a cup of sweet black coffee, eating nothing, her heart racing. She could not look at Judith again, did not say a word about the book, nor even take in the rest of the conversation.

'I think that's it, then. What a great discussion. Cat, you're hostess next month, your turn to choose our book. What are we going to read?'

She hadn't the faintest idea, not given it a second's thought. Now, she looked quickly round the shelves.

'*The Magic Toyshop*. Angela Carter,' she said, seeing a new edition displayed on the table.

People said this or that – they had read Carter, they hadn't, they admired her, they weren't sure.

Cat took Judith's arm as they went out into the street.

'I'll get a taxi home, no need for you to bother coming out all that way.'

Cat said nothing at all, merely walked down through the narrow streets to Cathedral Close and her car, parked at the top. Simon's own car was absent, his lights not on.

Judith sighed. 'The pressure he must be under.'

'I know. But he has the coolest head of anyone I know. He never lets it get to him, just works harder.'

'Did you hear about the fire? That poor man, burned to death – it must have gone up like a tinderbox. They say he had a paraffin stove and lamp – dreadfully dangerous things. You really should have let me get a taxi, darling.'

Cat said nothing, simply drove out through the archway and hit the road home. She switched on the car radio to a Bach cello recital. It was like a balm as she drove through the darkness, praying that she would get it right, say the things she had to say and not upset her stepmother.

They turned off the bypass.

'Wrong way.'

'I know,' Cat said. 'I'm taking you back to the farmhouse.'

'No, please, I have to get home . . . your father . . .' Quietly, turning her head away to look out of the window and away from Cat's sight, Judith began to cry.

The children were all in bed though Sam's light was still on. Silke left in her battered Mini.

Cat got out a bottle of wine and held it up.

'Or would you rather have a whisky? Yes. So would I. Let's go in the sitting room.'

Judith did not argue now. The spirit of protest and keeping up appearances seemed to have gone out of her.

'Let me take a quick look at your face.'

'It's fine.'

'Maybe.'

Cat saw harsh bruising, inflamed skin, a contusion down Judith's right jaw but nothing worse. 'What have you put on it?'

'Cold water.'

'Painkillers?'

'Yes. All the usual. It's not sore now.'

Cat poured two stiff whiskies, splashed in the minimum of water. She was still giving herself time, still shocked and uncertain exactly how she should handle it, what she should and should not say. Inside, she felt a great tumble of emotions.

Judith's eyes were red, the skin beneath them hollowed out and dark. She had taken two large swigs of her whisky. Cat poured another measure.

'How long has this been happening?'

'You mustn't think this is . . . I'm not a beaten-up wife, you know.' She made a slight attempt at a laugh.

'Excuse me, that is exactly what you are. I've seen enough of them. Once or a hundred times, it makes no difference and you know it, Judith. My father – Christ, I can't believe this . . .'

But in fact I can, Cat realised, I'm horrified to discover that I can believe it only too well.

It was an appalling thing to acknowledge that her own father was capable of hitting his wife. Had he done the same to Meriel? To her own mother?

'How long has this been going on? You have to talk to me, Judith. It's serious and you know it is. You haven't spoken to anyone, have you? You've pretended and covered up, it's all been in silence behind the closed front door and the drawn curtain. It always is.'

'No, darling, that's ridiculous . . . it isn't like that at all.

284

I'm not one of those poor beaten-up women with brutal husbands.'

'Yes, Judith. Yes, you are. The fact that he is a highly respected physician and pillar of the Freemasons, living in a handsome detached country house, makes not one iota of difference. He is your husband and he hits you. How often? Every week? Every day?'

'Goodness no. Of course not. It was a stupid argument about nothing, Richard had had too much to drink, I was irritable with him – oh, you know how these things flare up.'

'No. I know people quarrel and have silly arguments about something trivial and don't speak for a few hours. I've done all that myself, heaven knows. Most married people have. But most married people don't have husbands who escalate the quarrel to the point where they lash out, physically. You're trying to pretend this is a one-off. I don't believe you. When did it start?'

'I know I can be an annoying person to live with –'

'Don't you dare claim this is your fault! Dear God, who are you trying to protect? Tell me when it started. You seemed so happy, it all looked so right from where we were standing.'

'But we were. It was. It still is. In a way.' Judith finished her drink but put her hand up to refuse any more. 'I love Richard. Loved. I don't know now. It takes a lot of accepting – that the person you love and married is someone else, at least part of the time. I always knew he had another side – I've seen how he is with Simon often enough. I knew he could be sarcastic, cold. He isn't someone who shows warm feelings easily but he has them. He loves me, loves you and of course he adores the children. He actually does love Simon. It's because he loves him that he gets so angry.'

'Rage and disapproval aren't the most usual ways of showing love. Nor is hitting your wife.'

'I know,' Judith said so quietly Cat could barely hear her.

They were both silent, Judith tracing her finger along the pattern in the cushion, Cat thinking furiously. The last thing she wanted to do was behave as if she were in her surgery with a traumatised patient, distancing and detaching herself from

285

what she had just been told, which was tempting because she felt so shocked and bruised.

She got up, went to sit beside Judith and put her arms round her.

'Listen, we'll sort this out. I'm on your side and I'll do whatever you need me to. I understand why you didn't tell me or anyone else. I'm glad you have now because this is where it stops. It won't happen again, Judith, it can't. Stay here tonight, and for however long you need.'

'No, of course I can't do that, I have to go back now, it's late, Richard will wonder what's happened.'

'Let him. You can't go home.'

'I'm not leaving him, if that's what you're thinking. And please don't say anything to anyone else about this. Swear to me.'

'Why? What good will it do pretending it hasn't happened?'

Judith got up. 'I'll ring for a cab.' She made for the door.

'Stay tonight,' Cat said. 'It's something you've done often enough before at short notice. If you really care about what Dad thinks, I'll call him.'

'Of course I care what he thinks. What do you take me for?'

'A woman who has been subject to domestic violence.'

Judith turned to her. Her face was flushed and angry. 'I am going to ring for a taxi. I wish I hadn't told you . . . no, wait a minute – I take that back, because I didn't tell you anything, did I? You insisted on drawing conclusions based on an accident I had.'

'Ah yes. You walked into a door.'

'How dare you!'

'Judith . . .'

But she was in the hall, picking up the phone and looking down the pad where the taxi numbers were written.

'It will be about twenty minutes.'

'Please come and have another drink while we wait then, if you really won't stay tonight. I can't bear this.'

They went back into the sitting room. Cat had a small Scotch and a lot of water, Judith the reverse.

'I don't want us to be like this. I won't let you go until you tell me that whatever happened or happens you and I are never going to quarrel. Not about anything.'

'Not ever never, as Felix says.'

'Yes, that.'

'You didn't promise not to talk to anyone else about this, Cat.'

'I don't often make promises. Promises are dangerous things.'

'Meaning you will, you'll pick up the phone to Simon the minute I leave here.'

'That is not what I mean and not what I'm going to do.'

'I don't want us to talk about this again.'

Cat looked at her without speaking. There was nothing she could say, not now – not until she had thought a lot and got her head round everything, when she was calmer.

There was the sound of a car, then a horn hooting.

Cat went to the door, cursing the laziness of drivers who would not bother to get out and ring the bell.

She put her arms round her stepmother and held her tightly, kissed her on both cheeks, and then, because she could not stop herself, touched her forefinger gently to the bruises.

Judith turned away and went out to the taxi. She did not glance back.

Fifty-four

'Serrailler.'

'Are you DCS Simon Serrailler, Lafferton Police?'

'Yes, I am.'

'I'm calling regarding your enquiry.'

'And not before time. It's two days since you said someone would get back to me and I'm in the middle of an investigation into two murders.'

'Your enquiry was about an Alan Frederick Keyes?'

'Do have any idea what could happen in two days? Yes, of course you do. Now, what can you give me?'

'We can neither confirm nor deny that we have knowledge of an Alan Frederick Keyes. That's all.'

'Hang on a minute. I'm pretty certain your department gave Keyes a new ID ten years ago, for his own protection as a result of his being acquitted on three –'

'I'll just repeat, Superintendent. I can neither confirm nor deny that we have any knowledge of an Alan Frederick Keyes.'

'What are you, a bloody robot? Listen –'

'That's all I've got for you.'

The line went dead. Simon swore vividly.

Half an hour later in a small meeting room on Floor Five, three men sat at a table. Two had laptops open in front of them, one had nothing.

'"Jogging Sparrow." Are we on song?'

The others nodded.

'Right. Alan Frederick Keyes was given a new ID in 2002. Code name: Jogging Sparrow. As Keyes, mid-brown straight hair, light blue eyes, clean-shaven. As "Jogging Sparrow", shaven head, dark brown contact lenses, moustache. General appearance as Keyes, tidy, grey trousers, shirt, jacket or zip-up anorak, leather shoes. General appearance as JS, always jeans, T-shirts, sometimes fleeces, trainers. Scruffy but not dirty. Slight Yorkshire accent but Keyes only arrived in the county at the age of seventeen, so not pronounced. Birthplace Mansfield but moved about a lot until he left home and took himself north. JS, birthplace Rotherham. All early records based in Rotherham. Alan Keyes worked as a general builder with a range of skills, set up his own small building firm doing subcontracting. Married to Lynne Dodley, 1989. No children. Parents both dead, and Keyes lost contact with them as a teenager. Jogging Sparrow lived in Leeds. Last known address for which we had contact, 226a Pinder Road, Leeds.'

The man with nothing on the desk in front of him said, '". . . *for which we had contact*"?'

'Yes. His liaison officer with us was DS Paul Merriman, known to JS as Paul Q. Merriman retired six years after we placed JS.'

'Who took over?'

The officer looked anxious. 'Officially, DC Lester Hodges.'

'"*Officially*"?'

'It looks as if DS Merriman was the last person from us to be in touch with JS, sir. After that . . . well, JS disappeared off the radar.'

'Did a runner, you mean?'

'Apparently.'

'So we don't know anything. *Apparently*.'

'No, sir.'

'He sank without trace four years ago. How much effort was put into trying to find this man?'

'It looks as if some enquiries were made in the early days . . .'

'Which led nowhere.'

'It looks that way, sir.'

'Was JS red-flagged on the system?'

'Yes, sir.'

'From the beginning?'

'Yes, sir.'

The man, who outranked both the others in the room by several degrees, was silent for a moment, finger-tapping the table and looking down. The other two did not look at one another.

'Right. We need some damage limitation. Here's what we do.'

Fifty-five

'This,' Serrailler said, pointing to a large blow-up image on the wall, 'is a photograph taken in 2002 of Alan Frederick Keyes. It was used extensively in the press at the time of his trial and is regarded as an extremely good likeness. You'll each get a copy emailed over. Now, heads up . . . these are half a dozen images done by the identikit team. Take a good look. They are of what Keyes may look like now, given that he has aged ten years – he's now early forties – but also given that his appearance would have been changed when he got his new ID. These will be emailed too, and you can print them off. They're going to patrols but they are not on public noticeboards or available to the press, so keep them confidential. We've no idea which, if any, he now looks like and of course he could have changed his appearance in small ways several times. So he may have grown a beard, then shaved it off, for example, or had a close-cut beard and grown it longer. You know the sort of thing. I want you to memorise these so far as you can and you need to be able to call all of them up, plus the original of Keyes, on your phone at a second's notice. You may need to check very quickly and surreptitiously.

'The man who was Alan Frederick Keyes has a new name but we've no idea what that is. Special Op won't play ball. He is known to have relocated and I'm pretty certain he came onto our patch some time ago but I've no hard info about it. Needle in a haystack – yup. But Lafferton isn't the biggest haystack in the world and we have to pull it apart. So let's hope for some luck. Off you go and get these faces imprinted on your memory. Thanks, guys.'

He went back to his office, and sent a text to Rachel. He had sent one earlier, and two the previous day. She was not answering her phone but he had a reply the previous night. *K still v ill. Am at BG most of the time. So hard to watch him. Difficult 2 be in touch with you. R x.*'

All he could do was send loving messages, reassure her that she could ring him any time. Hope. But he felt deceitful that his hope was twisted by his own longing for Rachel to be free and his conscience bit him every time he contacted her.

He went out, to get a decent coffee, fresh air, some exercise, and to go around the town for an hour with his eyes open. He went to the brasserie in the Lanes and got a seat in the window, with the paper and a large espresso. This was the part of the job he had enjoyed as a junior – hanging about, watching, scrutinising faces, the way people walked, the routes they took, learning the routine of a place. You went out with something in mind and perhaps saw nothing, or perhaps by chance hit upon something quite different, and sometimes you even got the information or the person you'd gone out looking for. He remembered one beautiful summer afternoon when he'd been with the Met, and after a weary morning processing a car-theft gang, had gone out to sit at a pub table on a Soho pavement and drink a bottle of lager. He remembered everything about the five minutes after he had sat down. He had turned his face to the sun and closed his eyes for a moment. When he opened them, a couple of men had come to sit at the next table. Both had worn lightweight summer suits and sunglasses. They were drinking vodkas with ice. And with a twist in his gut Simon had recognised them as two major players in a violent drug-running and fraud gang, who had been in the sights of half the CID of London since a raid months earlier, during which both had escaped. He had turned sideways, taken a sip of his lager, and sent an urgent text on his phone. Then he had gone on apparently reading the paper and drinking. The men had been absorbed in conversation, taking no notice of the street

292

scene, the passers-by, or other people who were now filling up the tables.

A large posse of uniform, plus added CID presence, had come out of the pub door and from a side alley as if someone had waved a wand. The men had been surrounded and handcuffed before they knew what was happening. By the time anyone else had clocked the incident, it was over. Simon had stayed where he was, quietly finished his lager and ordered another.

He had no such luck today. He read the paper, drank two coffees and then went out to walk about the town, until rain and a bitter wind whipping down the side streets drove him back to the station.

No one else in the team had any luck either. It was scarcely surprising. Uniform patrols might have success but when you did not know exactly what the wanted person really looked like, the odds were too long. It would be luck or nothing. He went back to an afternoon of dull admin.

At the same time, a man in a navy parka identical to dozens of other navy parkas about the town that day drove towards the centre of Lafferton. He had mid-brown hair, an unmemorable face, and an elderly silver-grey Ford Focus. He went slowly in and out of the streets and inadvertently down a one-way route and had to reverse out of it. As he did so he managed to run over the kerb, shaving by a cyclist with little to spare.

'Shit.'

'Excuse me.'

The PC was tapping on his window with the usual, neutral expression.

'Good afternoon, sir. I wonder if you realise that you had a bit of a close shave just now.'

'I do apologise. My satnav took me down this street, not recognising it as a one-way, bloody thing, and then of course I had to reverse and it's very narrow.'

'Best to rely on the evidence of your own eyes and use satnav as a backup in a town centre situation, sir. Now you're pulled up, may I see your driving licence?'

The man produced it out of a black wallet.

293

'Thank you, sir. Any other ID on you at this time?'

He had a snooker club ID card with his photograph, and a couple of bank cards, plus the paper section of his licence. The constable took his time over scrutinising them, then checked the car's tax disc and registration with the central database. The reply came back within seconds.

'Thank you very much, sir. Everything in order. Just make sure you pay full attention to street signage in the future. You staying with us long?'

'Not sure yet. Possibly tonight.'

'Right, well, safe journey. On your way.'

As the Focus drew up at the next traffic light, the man's mobile phone beeped for a text. He pulled into a garage forecourt.

What the fuck are you doing getting caught by a plod?

He swore and deleted, then drove on towards an area of new housing, built, it seemed, on the design of a complicated crop circle. He had set his satnav for the postcode that contained Duchess of Cornwall Close. He saw it ahead, glanced and then accelerated past. Red-and-white crime-scene tape was still hanging limply outside one of the houses.

He spent the rest of the day alternately driving about without any apparent aim, and parking and walking up and down residential streets, looking about him in a rather vague and bored way.

He left the town just after the evening was drawing in and headed ten miles for an anonymous, functional motel by a service station. He checked in, went to his room, showered, changed, sent a couple of texts, and then went down, with his iPad, to the bar. He ate a burger and chips supper, and did not leave the motel until after breakfast the following morning.

His movements were monitored and recorded on the fifth floor of the building in which he worked.

After he checked out just after eight the next morning he drove around until he found a piece of waste ground behind a disused warehouse, where he unlocked the car boot, took two number plates from a canvas bag, removed the existing ones and exchanged the tax disc on the windscreen for another. He then locked the boot and drove off, once again in the direction of Lafferton.

During the afternoon, he approached the sheltered housing complex and turned into the street adjacent to Duchess of Cornwall Close. The area was deserted. Lights were on in two of the bungalows; a car showing a disability badge was parked in a designated space. The man reversed out of sight of a street light and opened his door. As he did so, a police car emerged from the shadows in which it had been concealed and stopped beside him. Two patrolmen leapt out.

'Afternoon, sir. We meet again.'

Shit. Shit, shit, shit. What kind of luck was this, to be pulled up by the same copper twice?

'Can I ask what you're doing here? Going to visit someone in the Close or what?'

Copper number two stood in front of him, arms folded, daring him to run, while his old friend, copper number one, walked round the car quickly, then held his torch to the number plate.

Thirty seconds later, the man was inside the patrol car.

'Right, let's have an explanation, sir, and try to make it a good one. I catch you driving somewhat carelessly in the town centre yesterday. Number plates and disc all come up fine, matching your ID. I let you go with a caution about road safety. Thought no more about it. Now I find you parking out of the way in the immediate area of a crime scene – which is why you were stopped. Routine at the moment for every car that parks in the vicinity. Only to find your number plate doesn't match the one you had on this car yesterday. Nor does the disc. Seems the same car. You're the same driver. So what's going on?'

Copper number one got back into the driver's seat.

'Checks out. Checks with the name, the ID, the road fund licence, car itself.'

Shit. Shit, shit, shit, shit.

His mobile beeped for a text.

'I need to pick this up.'

'If you don't mind, sir . . .'

But he had the screen open. *Abort. Abort. Abort. We'll deal.*

'My boss,' the man said. 'He's about to contact you.'

'Oh yes? Now why would that be?'

'Confirmation of my bona fides. Explanation.'

The two cops exchanged a glance. Then the radio went live.

'Base to 108. Driver of car licence number OYO 04 JOH to be released without further questioning. Confirm action taken.'

There was a slight pause.

'There you go. My boss's seen to it. Sorry about all this,' the man said. 'No one's fault.'

Though he knew it was his. His fault for driving carelessly, his fault for getting too close to the crime scene without taking permanent police presence into the reckoning. His fault.

Shit.

'Out you get then.'

He got out of the patrol car. 'Cheers,' he said.

Neither of the coppers spoke. They just watched as he walked to his car, started it and drove away.

Shit.

Another text.

Get your arse back here now.

His car left Lafferton, going surprisingly fast for a 1.2 Focus, in the direction of the motorway to London.

I could have been an actor, the guy said once. He watched me put on the new sort of clothes. He followed me for half a day, just walking around, going into a shop, a post office, a pub. I could have been an actor if I'd thought. I'd have quite liked that. I'd got my walk a bit different, to go with the new clothes, held myself different, I'd never once looked uncomfortable, I'd looked as if it were – well, normal. Normal.

I knew that. None of it ever bothered me.

Only what was inside here, in my head, that bothered me. At first I thought it had all gone, didn't cause me to lose any sleep, but then little things began to niggle. Only not often. I'd wake up and think, 'Fuck, who am I?' Voting. I'd always voted Labour. Never thought twice. Now I was supposed to be a right-wing Tory, veering towards BNP. But in my head, I couldn't do it. I could never think like that. The voting ballot's secret so that was all right, I voted how I always had. But in my head . . .

Sometimes the whole thing did my head in so much I had to go to bed. I got migraines. I'd never had anything like that. The only head-ache I might have had was the usual if I'd a bit of a hangover, which wasn't often as I've never liked drinking to excess.

But I got really blinding headaches, with zigzags in front of my eyes and flashing lights and being sick as a dog. I got them more and more often. In the end I had to go to a doc, and he asked me how long I'd been getting them and when I said not too long, he was surprised. Said people usually started getting them as teenagers. Asked what triggered them, if I could think of anything – usually something you eat, he said, like chocolate, that's common, or red wine, but could be lots of other stuff. I said I hadn't noticed anything.

He gave me some tablets and they helped a lot. Didn't stop the headaches coming but they made a big difference when they did.

But I knew they'd never go altogether until my head was sorted out. Who I was. Who I really was. The one that had been born, or the one that hadn't.

The days when the migraine headaches were really blinding, when I could hardly see, I took double the tablets, and when they began to work, I started going out at night again, like the old days. His days. The first time, that woman Elinor Sanders, I sat on a wall behind some bushes and when the pain quietened down to just a blurred feeling, I went in.

And straight away, as soon as I'd finished, I felt something like a shotgun going off inside my head and it cleared. The migraine might never have happened. It was like a boil bursting.

But why didn't that ever happen before? Why didn't he get migraine headaches? The one that was born, I mean? Keyes. Go on, say the name. Alan Keyes. Why didn't he?

Because his head wasn't split in two. Because he knew who he was. Well, of course he did. Why wouldn't he?

It was only after they took him away from me and made me forget all about him, when they wouldn't let me stay in touch. That's when they started up.

And there's one other thing. I don't know why. If I knew once, then I can't remember, but I wonder now if I ever did know, if they ever actually said. Why? Why did he have to disappear, as if he'd never been born, and why did this new one have to take over?

It's like things you read, or see on films, about people being possessed by aliens or evil spirits against their will. They can't do anything about it. They stop being themselves. They're someone different. It goes back a long way. Jekyll and Hyde, all that.

In the end it drives you mad.

Fifty-six

Olive Tredwell had had her name down for one of the new sheltered bungalows since the day her grandson had shown her the notice about them in the paper. She was ninety, she lived in a house with too many stairs, and although she hadn't had a day's illness in forty years, her sight was failing. The old neighbours had all died or moved away and the bigger houses had become flats. The streets were more down at heel than they had been, and it was not altogether safe at night.

She had spent six months getting rid of the accumulations of her long life, throwing away, giving away, taking to the charity shops. Her grandson had even made her several hundred pounds by selling things on eBay, things which she had not realised were of any value at all.

She had got him to drive her up to Duchess of Cornwall Close every week to watch the progress of the buildings. They were put together nicely, Anthony had said, and he would know, being in the building trade.

She had had the letter saying she had been allocated one of the bungalows, then another giving her the number – 4. She had got rid of some more furniture and Anthony had gone with her to a huge superstore on the edge of Bevham, where she had spent most of her eBay money on new items. It was very different from the old post-war dark wood stuff and Anthony had been startled that she had wanted it, thinking her eyesight was even worse than she pretended.

'Nan, it's very Scandinavian – you know, Swedish and that. Pale wood and checked covers. Do you think –'

'I like it. Don't you?'

'I do, but – well, it's not really . . .'

'. . . for someone of my generation. You'd be surprised. It isn't even very expensive, not for all new.'

'You do have to get someone to put the chest of drawers and things together – everything comes flat-pack.'

'That's all right, isn't it? You can do that.'

Anthony wondered how much time he would have to give up to his grandmother after she'd moved. He hoped perhaps less. On the other hand she was ninety. The sheltered housing was a real plus. He'd dreaded having to come and live with her, if she refused to move and her health failed, but now he'd be able to carry on living in his flat in Bevham and come over to see her – just not so often, not be tied to it. It was all systems go.

And then the first murder happened, followed so quickly by the second.

'Well, that's that,' Olive said. 'I'll just have to have the new furniture in here – not that it'll look so well.'

'Listen, Nan, I agree with you there's no way you can move there yet, not for now, I wouldn't think of letting you –'

'I wouldn't think of letting myself.'

'But once the police have caught him, which they will any minute now, and all the dust has settled, then you can go.'

'What difference would it make if they catch him or not?'

'Well, obviously –'

'The place is tainted. It's got the mark of the devil on it. Nobody in their right mind would dream of going there to live after what's happened, they'll have to tear the whole lot down and start again somewhere else. That's what they do. Remember Fred West? Remember Christie? Their houses were torn down and they didn't even build new ones on the space, they left them like air. That's what they'll do here. Those bungalows will be haunted until they do and you don't think royalty would want their name associated, do you?'

There had been no point in arguing with her about it.

The new Scandinavian furniture had arrived. New blue-and-white gingham curtains came as well, held by wooden rings on wooden poles, not by plastic clips on plastic rails, plus a lot of cheerful sunshine-yellow china and a bright red rug for the hall.

The remarkable thing was that now the old stuff had gone and the rooms were done, Olive was certain she could see better.

'It's made the world of difference,' she said to her grandson on the phone, the day everything was finished. 'What with that and the new light for the porch and the locks you got me. I don't really know now why I ever thought of moving.'

She pottered about the brighter kitchen, making hot milk in one of the sunshine-yellow mugs, pleased with everything, her eyes picking out detail she hadn't been aware of for a long time. This house had suited her for fifty-nine years. It had needed freshening up, that was all. It would see her out. If anyone moved into the sheltered bungalows now, they were fools.

But they never would, she thought, switching out the lights in the sitting room and hall, and struggling with the new lock on the front door, before going carefully up the steep stairs, carrying her drink in the sunshine-yellow mug.

She was a light sleeper and she put earplugs in because of the late-night and early-morning traffic noise, so she did not hear the sound of the back door being tried. But she had bolted the back door. The windows were well secured because of the locks Anthony himself had fitted.

Breaking in by smashing windows was a mug's game, for kids and amateur burglars. He had never broken a window, never would.

He had two others in mind if this one was tricky. That had always been the secret. If complicated locks and bolts and alarms were all in place, leave it.

He tried the front door, on the off chance. It was unlocked. He shook his head in disbelief. He went in, closing the door softly behind him.

Even without her earplugs, Olive would probably not have heard a sound.

301

She was deeply asleep when the stairs creaked, and creaked again, and the loose floorboard on the landing outside her room bumped slightly.

She remained deeply asleep, even when the door of her bedroom opened, and only woke, startled and bewildered, when the light went on.

Fifty-seven

The Chief Constable heard him out without interrupting. She knew Serrailler well and she had seen him in many moods but never as angry as now. They had gone to Chalford Road together, to the house in which Olive Tredwell had been murdered, and where her body was still upright in the new white-painted chair with its bright blue cotton cover, in front of a large oak cheval mirror. The electrical flex was still tied tightly round her neck, knotted on the left-hand side, as all the others had been. She wore a long floral nightgown. Her feet were bare, the toenails freshly clipped.

When he had walked in and seen her, Simon had wanted to weep, with frustration, anger, grief, and with a terrible feeling of guilt. But he had shaken himself within seconds. The other emotions he accepted, but if anyone other than the killer was guilty, it was not him.

'I'll have the skin ripped off their bloody backs.'

'Simon . . .'

'I mean it, ma'am.'

The pathologist had been and gone and forensics had finished the first part of the job. They heard voices now, then the tread of footsteps on the stairs. The bump of a loose floorboard.

The men with the body bag and the stretcher.

'Ma'am . . .'

'It's fine, get on with your job, guys. We're out of here.'

At the front door, the Chief said, 'Press conference?'

'Yes but the bare minimum for now. They're asking even more awkward questions, unsurprisingly, and an army of TV and radio vans are outside. I can deal with the press, but those bastards at Special Ops will hide behind their walls of secrecy. They think they're not answerable to anybody.'

'They're not, in the normal course of events, they're a law unto themselves, most of the time for good reason, but this is precisely why they can't make mistakes. Nobody's going to cut them any slack, Simon.'

'Cut who any slack? Nobody knows they exist. Punch them and it's like punching a hole in a cloud.'

'Forget revenge for now. Find this man before we have a fourth murder.'

'Fifth,' Simon said wearily. 'You're forgetting Nobby Parks.'

'You're sure about that? A different MO, though it definitely wasn't an accident.'

'Of course it wasn't. Nobby had to be shut up. He'd been talking to the press about the mobile-phone pictures. He might have seen and heard anything on his night walkabouts. That's what the killer was afraid of.'

'Did he see anything? Is there anything on the photos?'

Simon shook his head. 'That's the sad part. Not a thing. And I doubt if Nobby knew anything either, he was just enjoying his hour in the sun, poor bugger.'

Paula Devenish walked a few paces away from her waiting car so that they were not overheard.

'My resignation's gone in. Have you thought any more about it or is this all getting in your line of vision?'

'No. My line of vision is clear. As I said when we met on the train, I'm grateful for your vote of confidence but it's not for me.'

Simon watched her car speed off before going to his own and heading back to the station, seething with anger and more than ready to do battle. His mobile rang as he was taking the bypass fast so he had to ignore it. As he entered the building, Polly was coming down.

'Looking for you. Priority call two or three minutes ago. They wouldn't speak to me, but they'll ring back at ten fifteen.'

It was ten fourteen. Simon got to his office, closed the door and hung up his jacket.

The phone rang.

'DCS Serrailler?'

The voice was familiar by now.

'Can I have a name?'

'Floor Five. Your current situation has been under close consideration this morning. As you are aware, we can't answer questions, we cannot confirm or deny anything, or make comments on names or cases. But in view of the most recent incident we're prepared to pass on one piece of information.'

'Now listen –'

'As I say we cannot comment or answer questions, so if you would just listen to me, Superintendent.'

Simon realised that this was to be as near as they would come to some sort of climbdown and face-saving exercise, though neither would ever be admitted. He also knew that whatever they were about to give him would be all.

'Go on.'

'I can tell you that we retrained the man you named as a plumber.'

'From what? What was his original trade?'

'No further information and I can neither confirm nor deny anything else.'

A climb-down. Jesus, what a way to work. Asking questions was a detective's default setting, but these guys worked strictly on a need-to-know basis. They asked no questions and answered none, they lived in little numbered boxes, among the anonymous, those with code names, and those going only by a number. Their cases were filed under computer-generated passwords and they had personal control over only a severely limited corner of a jigsaw, the rest of the pieces being under the control of many others, none of whom they necessarily knew. It would drive him mad, just as terrorist and code work would drive him mad, though surveillance and undercover operations had always got his blood flowing faster.

He pulled out a sheet of paper and a pen, and after thinking hard for a few minutes about what he had been told, began to draw out a plan of action, writing furiously.

Then he called the whole team for a meeting in an hour's time.

'Olive Tredwell,' he said, pointing to the usual hideous pictures. 'Same MO, same clean crime scene – no prints, no blood, no semen. But forensics have the mirror and they're examining it for any trace of saliva. They have it as top priority. But they found nothing at the other crime scenes. Nothing on the mirrors or the surfaces.'

'Guv?'

'Yes, Steph?'

'Mrs Tredwell's place is nowhere near the sheltered housing.'

Someone else jumped in at once. 'But who'd risk going up there now we've got the patrols?'

'True. I just thought – well, it's completely on the other side of town, and her street isn't entirely full of older people, it's got all ages.'

'Which could mean he's started walking about, looking, keeping watch. Not so easy, but nor is it difficult to find old people living alone. Most streets have them.'

'I think this is a copycat.'

Simon shook his head. 'Remember, we haven't released details about the MO. Nothing about putting the bodies in front of a mirror has got into the media and it won't, nothing about the toenail clipping. This isn't a copycat. Now, heads up. I know it's frustrating, I know you feel got at, you feel demoralised, you feel he's running rings round us. He has done that but he won't be doing it for much longer. He's getting cocky now – and once that happens, he'll make a mistake. Cockiness always leads to errors. They start thinking they're invincible. They believe that they *cannot* be caught.

'More important. I have a bit of inside info. I know we're looking for Alan Keyes. I don't know the name he's using, or whether he's changed his appearance, but he's working as a plumber.'

'So we need to find a plumber?'

'Exactly. OK, entrapment is the name of the game and let's hope to God it works. Can any of you come up with a likely venue?

A small industrial area maybe with individual workshops, a disused repair garage. We'll be setting up a backstreet builders' base, with a couple of vans, workshop, carpentry and brick stuff . . . plastering . . . all the supplies will be there but not in huge quantities. Crummy office at the back – you know the sort of place.'

'Girlie calendars from 2001 and no tea mug without a crack in it.'

'You've got it.'

'Are we trying to find this place and get the owner to vacate?'

'Too risky. We're setting the whole thing up ourselves. In Lafferton, doesn't matter too much where so long as it's tucked away.'

'Waterloo Terrace.'

'Nelson Street,' someone else said.

'Right,' a DC said. 'I did an op round there last year, had to hang about for days, got to know it like the back of. It's the old working end of Lafferton, terraces, two-up two-down.'

'Got you,' Serrailler said.

'Run-down. Some of the houses are boarded up, some have dossers, some students. One or two of the old locals left but they've pretty much died off. There's a couple of pubs, bookie, two corner shops. Disused church. But halfway down Nelson Street there was a repair garage, with a yard. Got wooden gates, padlocked but kids broke the padlocks. Got an office, outside lav, sort of waiting area for people collecting cars. Could make a small builders' yard.'

'Get on to it, find out who owns it, we want to rent it, by the month. Any To Let signs?'

'Been a For Sale one for yonks. Garage must have closed five or six years ago, maybe more.'

'OK, you get on with that asap, Barry. Next up, small ads. I want them on cards in all the corner shops and newsagent windows you can find. Then in the free papers – wherever you see "Kittens for Sale" and "TV Aerials. Good Rates. Reliable." Get them ready to go up but don't roll them out until the yard's set up. Nice excuse to requisition some new felt tips from stationery. Off you go, won't take long, but I want to see what you've done.'

One by one the team picked up on their jobs. Simon pulled in three uniforms for overtime work, playing the roles of extras round the yard.

The most difficult to assign was the builder who owned the yard and was doing the advertising. Getting him to look the part was not as hard as having him sound it.

But by the end of the afternoon, he had his team, and the DC had come back with a deal done easily on the empty garage. They were in business. The text of a small ad printed out was on his desk, and two cards beside it.

PLUMBER WANTED. Must be fully qualified and experienced in variety of installation/repair/emergency work, including CH. Gas-fitting cert. and own vehicle a plus. Plenty of long-term contract work for right applicant. Top pay for top man..

Hendry's Builders, 44 Nelson Street, Lafferton. Phone 222848 for appt.

Simon ticked approval and asked for twenty handwritten copies.

He was about to leave, and drive round there for a recce, then go to Rachel's, hoping that she might be back from the hospital, when he had a call from forensics. They had found a minute amount of saliva on the mirror in Olive Tredwell's bedroom. If the DNA was recoverable and matched hers, it meant that she had been strangled after she had been placed in the chair. She had watched it happen. They were running final tests and would know definitively tomorrow.

Fifty-eight

Even Sam was on the doorstep to greet Molly. She had spent the day at Bevham General, seeing her tutors, and come over to spend the night at the farmhouse. She looked older, thinner, and her face had changed subtly. The old Molly had been plump, still half childlike in her soft round features, but now her bone structure showed. She would never be a beauty but she was pretty, with an interesting, thoughtful face. Felix wrapped his arms around her, and every bit of news spilled out of the other two as they went in, Sam carrying her bag.

She had driven herself there. 'I don't think I'll ever cycle like I used to,' she said to Cat, as they went upstairs to her old room. 'I know nothing that happened had anything to do with cycling, but it seems to have attached itself to that. I'd be terrified.'

'But apart from that, how are you?'

'Good,' Molly said firmly. 'I feel steady now. I've learned to cope with flashbacks, I know what to do if I have a panic attack, but I'm not having many now. I've had a lot of help from the psychologist – I never realised the half of what they do. Oh God, it's lovely to be back here, Cat . . . it's just the same but something's different.'

'We've painted the walls. New bedcover. Better lamps.'

'It's still home though.'

Cat sat on the edge of the bed. 'So, what did they say?'

'I'm repeating my final year and taking the exams after that. No worries. The prof said the experience might prove very useful even if it doesn't seem so at the moment. Empathy with patients being the buzz phrase – I'll understand about PTSD better than most . . . She asked if I had thought of going into psych. I hadn't, but she suggested I give it some thought. I don't know though . . .'

'No, and you won't yet. Listen, you don't have to – there's no pressure and I'd totally understand if you wanted to be at the hospital for the year instead – but if you wanted it this room is yours and you'd be more than welcome. Think about it.'

But Molly had already flung her arms around Cat.

'I was going to ask but then I thought probably you wouldn't need me, or want anyone or . . . well, anything might have changed. Yes, please!'

'That calls for a celebration bottle then. I'll go and open one. Take your time, have a bath, come down when you feel like it. I'll keep the marauders at bay.'

'No, don't, I want to see them. There's a lot to catch up on. I know you told me about the hospice . . . how's everything else? Simon married yet?'

'Oh ha ha.'

'And how are Judith and Richard? I heard at first but not for a bit now.'

'Fine,' Cat said, going out. 'Busy. But fine.'

Hannah was coming up the stairs as she went down, bursting with things to tell Molly, ask Molly, complain about or boast about or share in confidence with Molly. She left them to it.

Simon finally left the office at nine that evening. Rachel was not answering her phone, which meant she was at the hospital, but he drove round past the house anyway. Her car was not there. Lights were out.

He had stopped for fuel and bought a bunch of flowers on the forecourt, but now he looked at them on the passenger seat and saw that they were dismal and looked cheap. He scribbled a note on a torn-out page from his diary and put it through the letter box instead.

Thinking about you. Ring when you can S. x.

He dropped the flowers in a bin on the way home.

Fifty-nine

Olive Tredwell's son had written to the Chief making a formal complaint against the police and Serrailler in particular. Muriel Atkinson had telephoned several times in distress to ask why the killer of her twin sister had not been caught and why others had been allowed to die in the same terrible way. Simon was about to have a team meeting for an update on the builders' yard set-up, when a call was put through to him from Rosemary Poole's daughter.

'I keep reading this and that in the paper, I keep seeing your face on the television and you're being all full of sympathy for the bereaved families, but we don't get told anything, we're fobbed off with "ongoing investigations" and what we can guess from the TV. It isn't good enough. I've got two little boys here asking questions I can't answer, wanting to know what happened to their Gran, and what am I to say? I don't think you understand.'

'Mrs Fletcher, I assure you absolutely that I do. And you were right to ring me. I can't promise that I can tell you everything because some things have to remain confidential to us – if they got out they could hinder our progress.'

'You're saying you've made progress? Seems like the exact opposite to me.'

'I know it does. As I say, I can't tell you everything but you're right to pick me up on my failure to keep you and the other relatives informed and hear what you have to say. I'm going to ask all the bereaved families to come here and meet me, and ask whatever you like – and I promise you I'll do my very best to address all your concerns.'

'You sound like a politician.'

'God help me, I hope not. We'll arrange a time suitable to everyone and meet you all here. Perhaps we can even organise it for late this afternoon, if that isn't too short notice.'

'Make it for two in the morning. I'll be there.'

'Someone will ring you later and give you a time.'

'The TV people won't be there, will they?'

'They will not. This will be a closed and private meeting, you have my word.'

'To be honest, I thought I'd be wasting my time – I never expected to get to speak to you, thought I'd be fobbed off with someone or other. So I'm grateful.'

The meeting was held in the conference room at six o'clock and the press officer and Polly had set it out with the chairs in an informal half-circle, with a table of tea, coffee and biscuits, places in front for Serrailler and the Chief. No one else. There was no desk, no microphone, no reporting, no interruptions.

Simon told them everything he was able to about each case and its investigation, and the way everyone worked both separately and as a team. He was sympathetic, apologetic, gently spoken, and used as little police jargon as possible. There was actually very little he could say that they hadn't already heard but he managed to make it sound new, and as if he was taking them all into his confidence. It worked. The initial hesitant questions were not aggressive and he did not feel challenged. Mrs Sanders's twin sister said she believed the police had the hardest job in the world, Karen Fletcher asked if there was anything more they could do to help. 'I've racked my brains to think of anything I might know, but I can't. I'd rack them again if it was useful. There's a monster out there. We can't get our own loved ones back but surely to God we can try and do something, anything, to stop this happening again.'

'That's all very well,' Olive Tredwell's son said, 'but it isn't our job, is it? It's theirs.'

Murmurs of agreement.

'You're right,' Simon said. 'The job of catching this extremely dangerous man is ours first and foremost, but this is no different from any other situation – we rely on members of the public for vital information, things people may know or remember that we couldn't possibly be privy to. That's not dodging our responsibility, I assure you. Now as to the resources we're putting into this –'

'Hang on.' An overweight man with a shaven head almost knocked over his chair as he jumped up. 'Anthony Tredwell, Olive Tredwell's grandson. Before you start blinding us with talk about police manning and giving us the sob story about being under-resourced, I don't think you realise just how angry everyone is. You've been let off lightly up to now, people have even asked how they can help you. How *we* can help *you*? And I heard what you just said about not knowing stuff. But it's your job to find it out, not wait to be told. Christ Almighty! I want to know exactly what is being done, line by line, and why these other murders have been allowed to happen under your noses, why this monster, as the lady rightly called him, is still roaming the streets killing inno-cent old people . . . I want to know why you've failed so far. Because you have failed, make no mistake, and if something isn't done, there'll be more. So never mind about us helping, I've got one word for you and that's S-U-E – sue. We'll be suing you for every penny, see what that does to your bloody "resources".'

There was a murmur among the others, though Simon found it hard to tell who was in agreement, who sympathetic to him, but as they were all leaving, Karen Fletcher stood back for a moment.

'Thank you,' she said very quietly. 'And for arranging this. I know you're doing your best, you're doing your jobs. I shouldn't have rung you and spoke the way I did this morning. I wouldn't like to guess how many late nights you're working.'

Simon shook her hand. 'Thank you. And they will pay off. We'll get this man, Mrs Fletcher.'

'Well done, Simon – they're onside now, I think. They listened. And forget the bluff. Nobody's going to sue.'

313

'He needed to get it out of his system. I was surprised there wasn't more anger in the room actually.'

'Grief takes some funny forms. Now – this builders' yard. It's a pretty long shot and I'm never keen on entrapment.'

Simon took a deep breath. 'It's hardly that, ma'am, and frankly, at this point . . .'

'I trust you know what you're doing.' The Chief stood up. 'I'll leave you to it but don't keep me guessing on this one. And it goes without saying that the press mustn't get a whisper.'

Simon waited until he heard her footsteps go smartly down the corridor before he swore. Sometimes, the Chief could make him feel like a first-timer still wet behind the ears.

Sixty

The cards went up on pinboards and were stuck in shop windows all over Lafferton. Simon hoped they wouldn't have to extend to Bevham. The local free paper had a small ad under TRADES VACANCIES which appeared at the top of a column in bold. The paper came out twice a week and it would appear in both editions.

Simon left his car some distance away from Nelson Street and walked round to the garage. He wore jeans, dirty trainers and a faded Guns N' Roses T-shirt under a denim jacket – dressed as unsuitably for the cold weather as most of the males in the area. He had rejected a baseball cap, which looked so wrong that it gave him away, and just gelled his hair back. He had not shaved for the past twenty-four hours. He wasn't going to do more than hang about the yard, listening, on standby, but he couldn't stick out like a sore thumb.

If this had been a bit of TV filming instead of part of a major murder inquiry, he thought as he slouched in through the gates, it would have been fun.

The empty, long-disused repair garage had been transformed into a small, scruffy but fully functioning builders' yard. A pickup lorry and a small truck were parked up, both with 'Cliff Hendry & Son, Building Contractors' on the side. The back of the lorry had been let down and roped-together planks of 4 x 2 were half loaded, with more stacked against the back wall. The rear windows of the van had an ancient Bevham

315

Wanderers sticker, and the doors were held together with string.

Cement mixers, a portable generator, ladders and some random scaffolding, a broken bath and toilet, a couple of stools and a skip half full of rubble had been placed about, and some shavings and general dirt were underfoot. There were also small piles of stones, aggregate and sand, various buckets and spades and bags of cement. At the far end, assorted kindling and wood chippings and an industrial wheelbarrow were available to feed the wood burner in the covered shed area.

Leading off that was the office, built out of old doors and window frames. Behind that, a small area with a rickety sofa and chair, and a notice on the half-open door: 'Waiting Room'. Old trade magazines and the free newspaper going back several weeks were on a bamboo table, together with a sad-looking plant, two ashtrays and a No Smoking sign. On the wall, a couple of Page 3 calendars, and a reproduction of Annigoni's formal portrait of the Queen.

It looked, felt, even smelled like a small builders' yard. It might well have been 'Est. 1950' as was painted, then almost rubbed out, on the front gate.

'Morning, guv.'

Simon shook his head.

Gerry Rathbone grinned. He was one of the old CID, in place before Simon, a sergeant and happy to remain so, hard-working, reliable, imaginative and quicker on the uptake than most. He had four years left in the force and he would hate to go. He relished the job, and in particular he relished a challenge, getting his hands dirty, getting out of the station. He had done some minor undercover work on drugs ops and fitted into the scene perfectly. Simon had told him he could have been an actor in a TV crime series. 'More fun when it's real though.'

Behind the office a small Portakabin stood against the wall. It had no visible door, no windows, was cramped and dimly lit. It contained two straight chairs, a table on which was a mike system, and what looked like CCTV but which relayed live images from the yard itself, the gates and the road immediately outside the gates. There was another console showing close-ups inside the office. Everywhere had been miked; concealed cameras were in place.

The two CID in the small back room each had a laptop, showing the identikit projections of the man they wanted, like a series of postage stamps. Clicking on any one brought it into full-screen. Both men had earpieces to communicate with everyone else on the site.

Serrailler went into the office and sat down on a swivel chair whose polystyrene filler was puffing out of various torn spots like emerging mushrooms.

'Press the grey switch, everyone should hear you. I've tested.'

Simon pressed and looked out of the dirty window into the yard. He could see the gate and a section to the side with the lorry and white van. One of the DCs was lounging against the van smoking, another seemed to be in the driver's cab.

'Listen up, everybody. Gerry will go live on the mobile number in fifteen minutes. We'll also unlock the gate. We'll start booking them in for appointments every thirty minutes, assuming anybody's interested. Cross your fingers. You know the drill, you've had the acting class, I've no worries. Message, basically, is don't overdo it. If we think we've got our man, chances are we'll know when he walks through the gate, but whenever we suspect anyone, Doug sends the Morse code alert to everybody so listen out for the beeps. Pete and Lee will go straight to the gates on this side, Andy will drive the jeep up and block them from the outside. Rest of you stand by for orders. Don't move until I say. We don't want to hit on the wrong guy but, more important, we don't want to lose the right one. He is most unlikely to be armed but, even so, we're not taking that for granted, and we're prepared. Armed or not, remember this is a dangerous man and he'll be cornered. Don't take any chances. One thing I've noticed . . . for a builders' yard this place is as quiet as a cemetery. Get some noise going – general banging about, engine noises, shouting, dropping planks. We'll start up Radio 1 in the office area but we can't afford to drown out the intercom. OK, good luck, guys. Let's make sure that if he does come in here, he won't go out again of his own accord.'

Simon clicked on one of the stamps of Alan Keyes. The ageing

317

was subtle – ten years did not greatly change the features of a man in the prime of life but the cosmetic alterations made a surprising and sometimes dramatic difference. Bald head. Shaven head with a three-day bristle of hair. Hair cropped short and dyed black, blond, ginger. Moustaches, large and small, dropping and straight. Glasses of various shapes changed a face significantly as did a full thick beard. A close-cut beard less so. They had given him a few off-the-wall haircuts – Mohican, ponytail, permed in tight curls, none of which was convincing, all of which made the man stick out like a sore thumb, whereas, in reality, he would want to blend in with the general crowd. Serrailler shrank the more bizarre pictures and put them in a corner as being possible but very unlikely. Keyes, aka whoever, was going to look different but in a rather vague way. He might be recognisable, close up and under careful scrutiny, but there would be things that didn't quite fit. Change of eye colour was one of the things that deceived most easily.

He looked up and saw Pete go to the gates and lift the bar that held them, then the bolts at the bottom, and finally put a key into the heavy padlock.

As he did so, the phone on Gerry's desk rang. Simon went into the cabin via the concealed door. The intercom sound was on low but reception was clear.

'Hendry's.'

'Is that the builders'?'

'Hendry's, yup.'

'Right. I've seen your advert in the free paper.'

'The plumber or the stores manager?'

'Plumber. I'm a plumber, only I left my last –'

'Hang on, let me find a pen and paper . . .'

The iPad was set up with a page on which the list would be made. Gerry's fingers moved quickly about the silent keyboard as he entered name, address, phone number. There was a space for any other essentials which he did not fill in though he let the man drone on with details about his skills, past employment and references. He needed none of them.

'I've had a lot of people enquire.'

'Already? Paper's only just out.'

'Right, only jobs like this are gold.'

'Give us a chance, mate. Give us an interview.'

'Go on then, I had someone just cancel in actual fact. If you can come in at, hang on, what's the time now? Right . . .' Gerry did some muttering along the lines of 'half past, then there's that Polish bloke, eleven, half past . . . OK, can you get in here for one?'

'One when?'

'One o'clock.'

'I mean what day?'

'Today. Tuesday.'

'Oh, fantastic, that's terrific, thanks, mate, I'll be there, on the dot, you won't regret it, you –'

'Cheers,' Gerry said, putting down the phone.

It went on like that for the next hour and a half, until he had people booked in for most of the day. At half eleven the answer-phone was switched on.

'Hendry's Builders. There's no one available to take your call. Leave us a message.'

Simon uncramped his limbs and went out of the cabin into the yard, where he did five minutes of exercises. His long back suffered from a couple of hours spent bent on a low chair in a confined space and his legs were numb.

It was cold but bright, and they sat about on old boxes and benches, eating packed lunches. Two went out on a tea run to the nearest cafe.

Simon had checked through the names on Gerry's list. Nothing out of the way, nothing that rang any bells. Several were Eastern European, which ruled them out before they arrived but the men still had to be seen. P. O'Brien could also be ruled out. Keyes would have been advised not to take an Irish, Scots or foreign name. Anything very unusual or easily twisted into a joke would also be out. If Simon had been asked to guess from the names alone, he would have picked out an N. Taylor or M. Gardener.

The tea boys came back with their orders, plus a bag of jam doughnuts and three copies of that day's red tops.

In the office, Simon phoned Rachel, who was not there, then

319

sent her a text. She was still at the hospital then, still sitting by her husband's bedside, caring for him, looking after him, holding his hand, sponging his forehead. Loving him? He wished he knew. In many ways, he hoped that she did, whatever the present nature of that love. He had never had any relationship with a woman about which he had felt guilty. Now, he did, the more so because of Kenneth's tacit blessing. But he could not give her up.

Twenty minutes later everyone was back at their posts. At ten to one, the gate opened on L. Checkley, over six feet in height, burly, amiable-looking. And black.

Gerry went out, shook the man's hand, brought him into the office and started going through the motions.

Simon felt guilty. How many blokes desperate for this job would come hopefully through that gate, honest, blameless, hard-working men who needed the work? All of them would be told they'd 'hear in a couple of days' and go off, crossing their fingers, touching wood, sending up prayers to the Virgin Mary and the saints that they'd be the one to get the job, never knowing there wasn't one.

The procession of applicants went on through the afternoon. A photograph was taken as they came into the yard and again as they approached the office, and the image beamed through onto every screen. Photofit software worked on trying to find any sort of match with the original picture of Alan Keyes and would send a flashing alert when there was one. But the only two alerts were wide of the mark. Serrailler scrutinised each man's face then checked it against the postage stamps but there were no links. He stretched as much as he could but as the afternoon went on his back ached more painfully.

Three more to go. Earlier, one had appeared without having phoned first. Word had got round about the job and he was in the area. Could they see him? They saw him. No one else had dropped in unexpectedly until ten to five when the gate opened on a bald and rather fat man.

'Heads up,' Simon said. 'We know this guy.'

The overweight man in his early forties walking into the yard was Anthony Tredwell.

320

'Pete, Lee, bar the gate once he's in here. Man is Anthony Tredwell, grandson of the last victim, Olive Tredwell. I can't move out of here unless we have a positive, he knows me. Anyone else thinks they could be recognised, keep out of sight.'

Gerry gave a discreet thumbs up towards the hidden screen.

Simon looked at the monitor. The software had Tredwell's face up and was searching for any match. Nothing. No flashing red light, no arrows. The man had a rubbery, jowly face, with a double chin, stubble, small dark eyes, thick eyebrows. He had a tattoo on his chest, just visible among the hairs sprouting in the V of his T-shirt. Keyes had had no tattoos but could easily have acquired one.

'Gerry, tell him his name rings a bell, see if he mentions his grandmother.'

Gerry gave no indication that he had heard and went on writing notes with a chipped biro taking down what Tredwell told him. 'Right, that's all, OK . . . thanks. You'll guess we've seen quite a few but we'll let you know either way in a day or two.' He stood up and offered his hand. Then he said, 'Tredwell. Your name rings a bell somehow – don't think you've worked for me before, have you?'

'No.'

'Right. Oh well, it happens. Just not your everyday Smith or Jones, and as soon as you said it, I thought –'

'My grandmother was ninety and she was murdered by the same sick bastard who's been knocking off old ladies all over the fuckin' place. Olive Tredwell. Never done any harm to a soul, kindest woman on earth. And why did it happen? Because the fuckin' police are fuckin' useless and he's under their noses, been under their noses for weeks and they haven't got him. If they'd been any use my gran would still be alive, but they do fuck all, and they know it because I've told them. Idle stupid fuckers. I'd like to do to that fuckin' Chief Constable bitch what that bastard did to my grandmother, so help me.'

He turned angrily and walked out, shoulders up, chin jutting. As he went towards the gate he shouted back across the yard, 'So that's where you heard my name, right?'

The gate slammed so hard behind him it jumped off the latch again and swung open.

'Frustrating, I know, but thanks for the good work. Tomorrow's another day and we're here just before eight. Not so many slots filled, but not everybody will have gone through the small ads yet or seen the notices in the shop windows. I didn't realise there were so many out-of-work plumbers – which is a bit baffling, when you can never get one in an emergency. However . . . tomorrow or the next day, he's going to answer this ad and come through the gate; we'll spot him and we'll have him. See you all bright and early.'

These past few days I've been jumpy. And I'm never jumpy. I'm steady. No emotion, no fright, no panic, no being spooked. Save that for other bits of life. This bit, I've never been jumpy. But now I am. Ever since the one in Chalford Road. God knows why I went there. But it was building and building, I was shaking inside, I've never been desperate like that. I've read it's like a junkie needing a fix. I can believe that, though drugs never interested me. Waste of life.

Then ten years went by. That's a bloody long time. TEN YEARS, without wanting to, without needing to, without it even crossing my mind.

But then it did cross and once it had it wouldn't go away of course, it stayed and it nagged and it woke me up and it probed into my head like a worm and then into my dreams and then I knew I needed to get back. Back to who I was. Who I had been. Whichever.

Who am I?

Who was I?

The only way I could find out was start again, and when I started, I found it. I found me. Everything clicked into place. I looked into my own eyes in Elinor Sanders's mirror and I recognised myself for the first time in all those years.

I hadn't meant it to go on but it had to. And then, I got the call out to 17 Chalford Road and saw her in the next-door garden. She watched me leave when I'd finished the job at 17, stood on her front step, pretending to put out milk bottles, but really, feeling lonely, wanting to watch something going on, see someone. On her own too many hours of the day, that was obvious. And the night.

If she hadn't come out onto the step and watched me, maybe I wouldn't have gone back. But I had to.

I had to. I did. And that was that.

And ever since, I've had this feeling in the pit of my belly. Restless. Worried. Bit panicky.

I give myself a bloody good pep talk while I'm driving about. Get yourself together, don't be so stupid. Moment you start panicking you'll make a wrong move. You'll give yourself away. So pack it in.

For now, you pack it all in, d'you hear? Lie low. Keep your head down. There's enough coppers all over town, enough stuff in the papers, enough jittery people about. You be yourself, don't look back, don't think about any of it.

Don't have a moment to think. That's it. Pile the work in. The longer the hours the less time you've got to think.

Sixty-one

Gerry had had a long blank period and then a flurry of calls. There were five men coming to the yard between nine and twelve. Everyone was in place, everything the same as the night before.

The first appointment didn't turn up. The second, who had sent a text to the mobile asking to be seen, arrived ten minutes early. C. Gardener was a young woman, fully qualified, obviously keen, obviously certain that, if she had phoned in, the builder would hear a female voice and not give her an interview.

'I'd have offered her the bloody job,' Gerry said. 'She wouldn't turn up late, she wouldn't let you down, she'd do the job well and she'd tidy up after herself. I feel a right bastard.'

'Take her number, did you? Never know when you'll need a plumber. Best have one handy.'

Various remarks were bandied about the intercom, but Gerry looked sombre. 'Interviewing' perfectly good candidates who needed work, for a job that didn't exist, went against the grain.

Another man came through the gate having seen the sign outside. Gerry brought him into the office.

'Stand down,' Simon said into the intercom, seeing that Jason Hopwood was no more than eighteen and looked even younger.

As Gerry was going through the motions, another man came into the yard.

He was around five seven, his light gingery-brown hair was cropped very short, he had a thin moustache, and as he looked round to find the entrance to the office, and the camera closed in on his face, Simon saw his eyes. Remarkably dark eyes.

'Heads up,' he said tautly. 'We know this one too. Pete and Lee, wander down to that gate.'

Gerry carried on with his interview, aware of the newcomer about to walk into the outer office. When he did, Gerry was there.

'Morning,' he said, 'er – Smith, right? Robert Smith.'

'No.'

'Ah . . . thought you were the next on my list.'

'Came in on the off chance. I suppose you're going to say thanks but no thanks.'

'Keep him talking,' Serrailler was saying into Gerry's ear. 'Get the other guy out without looking obvious, get this one into the office.'

'We've seen a few but there's quite a bit of work on. I'm just finishing off with this lad. I'll see you when he's gone. No one else for twenty minutes. Take a seat.'

'Thanks.'

Gerry went back into the inner office, not quite closing the door. Everyone on the site was now on full alert. Pete was by the gate, Lee was slowly backing the truck towards it.

Simon studied the identikit. Then he switched the image with the cropped hair and a moustache onto the photo of Alan Keyes. His heart lurched. But Keyes's eyes were blue. He fiddled with the image, slotting in dark brown eyes.

'Got you,' he said softly.

One of the two others in the cabin nodded. 'That's him, same mouth, same nose, same funny cheekbones, sort of flat . . .'

'Get rid of the moustache . . .'

'Bingo.'

'Right. You know the drill. Gerry makes a start. He'll leave the door ajar. No one move until my shout, we don't do anything to alert him. Gerry's got to take a bit longer with mi-laddo, not make it look as if he's cutting him short. Now we wait.'

Gerry chatted on. Gave the young plumbing apprentice fatherly advice. 'Stick to your course, don't skive, get your qualifications, come back here when you have, and I could have a job for you, but don't waste my time and yours by claiming to be what you're obviously not. Right? Seventeen and a qualified plumber with a gas-fitting certification? Get out.' He stood up, clapped the boy on the shoulder, shook his hand warmly.

Gerry's ear was full of Serrailler, he could see that the lads were about to block up the gate.

He'd have to escort Jason Hopwood out, shout at Lee for taking the pickup so near the exit, fire regs, how many times have you been told . . .

In the cabin the stuffy air seemed to crackle.

How did I know? I'd been twitchy. I'd been panicky. I had that feeling something was wrong. And what had I done? Given myself a bloody good bollocking, told myself to get it together, straighten up, forget it. You're not him, you're you, so leave it.

Me? I'm me. Yeah. Not him. No.

The work's been falling off a bit. There's always the odd little job in plumbing, blocked sinks, blocked loos, that malarkey. I'm never idle, can't afford to be, can I? But the contract jobs, the big building projects, they're drying up. Those sheltered bungalows, I could have done with a job there.

Yeah.

Then I saw this ad. First off in the newsagent's, then in the paper, then in a different newsagent's. Nearly rang up. But I didn't. And then I was taking a short cut down Nelson Street, and there's this builders' yard. Never seen it before. But then, never come down Nelson Street much. Funny old bit of town.

I stopped because the notice on the gate was big. PLUMBER WANTED. Could see it from the end of the street, near enough.

I clocked straight away it was the same number as on the ads.

I knew there'd be loads of them ringing up so I decided to go in, have a look, try and get whoever to see me then.

Only, at the back of my mind all the time there was something . . . there was just something. Daft.

Walked in. Looked OK. Bit down at heel but you don't expect a builders' yard to be Buckingham Palace.

328

So I'm here. I was right as well. One lad's in there, looks about twelve, no way is he a fully qualified plumber.

I'm in here. Outer office, waiting area, whatever. The usual. One chair, one sofa, magazines out of the ark, yesterday's Sun, holes in the lino. Like something off the telly. Your typical builders' office.

I got the feeling the minute I walked in. Or rather, I had the feeling, only I got it more. A lot more.

There's just something. I can't put my finger on it. Something's buggin' me.

Oh for Christ's sake, get over it. This is work, man, this could be very good work, and they won't find a better plumber than me within fifty miles. They won't.

He's coming out. Twelve-year-old. Ought to be in school.

Slapping him on the shoulder, no hard feelings.

Taking him down to the gate as well.

Having a shout at the guy with the truck and the other guy, looks like a right waste of space. What's he doing employed here?

He's walking back up the yard. Coming in.

'Sorry about that, only that lad, he could talk the talk. Right, now . . . come in the back office. You said you saw the notice on the gate? I'm glad about that because the guys told me it was a waste of paper putting it up, no one'll go by here and see it, whereas in point of fact three have done just that. You're the third. Come in here. Right, what's your name?'

I don't know what it was. Nothing. Just that feeling. Bloody hell.

'Can I have your name?'

Sixty-two

'Harry Fletcher.'

'OK. Come in, let's have a chat, get some details.'

Harry stood up, and as he did so, everything in him gave out the urgent signal. It was like an electric current zapping through him.

GO. GET OUT OF HERE.

RUN.

He ran.

The two guys were at the gate and the van was blocking it, even though it was supposed to have been moved. He swerved, and ran left, dodging a pile of full rubble sacks and a bale of barbed wire. He ran to the back of the yard, all the time working out what was ahead, how to get past it or over it or round it, and he sussed that he could jump onto the cement mixer, and, in one even faster leap, be onto the wall and over the other side. He was good at this. He was very good. He'd had training enough.

He ran, swerved, gathered himself, leapt onto and off the mixer, landed on the wall, where he wobbled for a second or two, put out his arms for balance, and was up and over and down. And running. He'd no idea why but he was running faster than he'd ever run.

'Go, go, go!' Serrailler had yelled into their ears, the second he saw the man taking off out of the office and down the yard.

But he was lightning-fast, ducking, leaping, up and over and off. They pounded down, but they were nothing like as agile getting up and onto the wall. Lee revved the pickup, Pete banged at the iron bars and hauled the gates open, the rest of them poured through and went in every direction, ear-mikes full of Serrailler's shouted instructions.

But he had a head start.

The yard was empty, the gate swinging open. In the office, the phone rang and rang.

Sixty-three

It was every cop's dream chase. The guy trips over a loose kerb. Simple as that. Pete got to him first, Serrailler a minute later. The rest had gone in the other direction.

'Harry Fletcher, I am arresting you for . . .'

Backup was there. The street was half empty. It was all over in seconds.

Fifteen minutes later Harry Fletcher was in front of the desk sergeant; twenty, and he was banged up.

The team were jubilant and Serrailler sent them off in a warm glow after showering them with well-deserved praise. But the clock was now ticking. He could only hold Fletcher for thirty-six hours without applying to the magistrates. He put an urgent application in for a warrant to search Fletcher's house. Ben Vanek would do the initial interview, while he himself watched and listened in. Fletcher was using the duty solicitor.

Simon rang forensics. They had tested the DNA on Olive Tredwell's mirror, and they had found several exhalation traces, all of which were a match for her.

'All but one,' the girl said.

'So someone else had been close to the mirror?'

'And it's fresh. Someone sneezed or coughed or otherwise exhaled in fairly close proximity to the mirror. Mrs Tredwell's weren't fresh.'

'Have you got a match?'

'No. Nothing comes up.'

'Well, stay right there and pray. We're getting a swab in the next five minutes and we'll run it over to you on a blue light. It's urgent. Can you drop everything else?'

'I'll do my best but –'

'Don't say "no promises". Say "I promise". Please?'

The search warrant would be with them in half an hour, and the DNA swab had been taken from Fletcher. Simon put his head round the door of the CID room.

'I'm going for a breather, run round the block. How's everyone?'

Half the room were busy on other cases, several were pent up, as he was, waiting, waiting, knowing they'd got the right man and knowing they had to prove it.

'Luck,' Steph said. 'That's what we need.'

'We're on the home straight, guys, not long. Get your heads into some nice paperwork, keep your minds off the waiting.'

Someone threw a ball of screwed-up paper at him as he went. He put his head back round the door, face grim. There was an uneasy silence. Simon paused, then bent down, picked up the paper ball and chucked it back at the nearest person.

Running in his suit was out so he walked fast four times round the block then went into the Cypriot deli. It was empty. A couple of poached eggs on toast and a double espresso were quickly in front of him, hot, fresh, looking and smelling delicious.

His phone rang. Forensics? Too soon and the search warrant wouldn't have arrived.

'Simon?'

Rachel's voice was very quiet. She was probably in one of the hospital waiting areas.

'Darling?'

'Is it all right to talk?'

'Of course. I'm having a fast food break. How are you?'

He saw her face, her beautifully shaped face, anxious violet eyes, long lashes, the curve of her mouth.

'You should know . . . Ken died . . . twenty minutes ago. Sorry, I can't say any more just now.'

333

The coffee scalded his mouth and he did not remember tasting the eggs. He sat staring out of the window onto the street, seeing nothing, disorientated every time he came to from his focus on Rachel – what had happened, what she would be doing, where she would go, how she felt, if she wanted to see him . . .

Phone again. At least the job would take him over for the next few hours or days.

But it was his sister.

'Hi.'

'Can I talk?'

'Yes.'

'Are you OK?'

Tell her? Don't tell her?

He told her.

'Oh, Si . . . I'm so sorry . . . Are you with her?'

'God, no, I'm just grabbing some food, then heading back to the station.'

'How's it going?'

How was it going? What? How was what going? How . . .

'Looks like we've got him.'

'Listen, do you want to come over here tonight? Have something to eat . . .'

'Yes. Only . . . I'm not sure.'

'Sounds as if you might get an evening off if you've made an arrest, or . . . if Rachel needs you, you should go there.'

'I don't know if she will.'

'Si – come when and if. Got to go, here's the supermarket delivery. See you later.'

He stared at the phone after it had gone silent. Would he go? Did he want to be on his own? Would Rachel need him?

He got up, wandered out, and only heard Nico calling him back to pay when he was halfway down the street.

He texted Rachel, sent her flowers, talked to Ben about interviewing Fletcher, started his report on the builders' yard op, but realised he wasn't focusing.

After that, so many things happened that his focus came back, sharp as a pin.

The team who had gone to search Fletcher's house had found nothing at all of relevance to the murders but in a dustbin they came upon a plastic carrier bag containing trainers and a pair of jeans, both smelling of petrol. They had also found an empty disposable cigarette lighter at the bottom of the bin.

'Thank God for dustbin collections only every two weeks,' Serrailler said to Steph. 'Come back in with this lot and we'll scoot them round to forensics. If they don't find something to link with the Nobby Parks fire I'll go back on the beat. Was the house empty?'

'No, guv. Karen – Mrs Fletcher – was in with two little lads. She's in a bad state. First, her mum is murdered. Now, it's her husband who's the murderer. Well, perhaps he's the murderer. And Heaven knows how any woman could cope with that.'

'Right, I understand. I'll get bods round. One of you stay there until they arrive, the rest get back with the stuff. Sure there was nothing to connect with the old lady murders?'

'Ransacked the place, guv. Garden shed was padlocked like Fort Knox but it was only garden stuff.'

'Steph, you know what we're after. Trophies. Did you find any toenail clippings?'

He heard her stifle a giggle. 'No, sir. And we looked in every jar and tin.'

'No gruesome photos kept as mementos? No electrical flex anywhere?'

'Not that we found – and we took the place apart, to the lady's distress.'

A few minutes later, she was back on the phone.

'Mrs Fletcher wants to see her husband. She's very upset and not taking no for an answer. Says she can get someone for the kids but she's got to see him.'

'No. Get the FLO to her, calm her down. I can't give her access yet. Get that stuff over here as soon as, I want it on hand for the interview.'

Forty minutes later, he went downstairs. The petrol-smelling trainers and jeans had arrived bagged up and were concealed

335

at Ben Vanek's feet in the interview room. Fletcher was sitting at the table, the duty solicitor beside him – Serrailler was pleased to see Michael Spiers, a steady, older pair of hands, fair but no soft touch. Ben Vanek was opposite.

'Cool as a bloody cucumber,' Gerry Rathbone said, getting up.

'Thanks, I'll stand. Is he cool? His eyes are flicking about.'

'He's got a hell of a lot to hold together.'

Ben Vanek had gone through the standard opening lines. Fletcher spoke clearly in answer, looking directly at him, ignoring his brief, not glancing round or fiddling with his hands or shifting in his chair.

Holding himself together was right. It took a lot of concentration. And practice.

Simon itched to be doing the interview but Ben was measured, calm and relentless. They were the qualities that had won him fast promotion, but he also had a spark, a flare, which Serrailler had spotted early on.

'Do you wear trainers?' he asked Fletcher now.

'Sometimes.'

'When? Work? Every day?'

Fletcher shrugged. 'Sometimes.'

'You're not wearing them now.'

'No.'

'How many pairs do you own?'

'A couple.'

'And where are those trainers now?'

'What's that got to do with anything?'

'Just answer the question.'

'In the wardrobe, in the hall, I don't know.'

'What colour trainers are they?'

'White. White and blue. Maybe grey.'

'Which?'

'Don't remember offhand. White and blue. Yes. And there's a grey pair. Think I've still got them.'

Ben bent swiftly and brought the cellophane bag containing the trainers onto the table under Fletcher's nose.

'Are these your trainers?'

'Of course they're not.'

'Why of course?'

'They wouldn't be here in a plastic bag, would they? I said, they're in the wardrobe or somewhere at home.'

'So you don't own these trainers? Grubby but white with a blue flash. Look at them carefully please. Handle them, so long as you don't take them out of the bag.'

Fletcher took the trainers and turned them over and back. Dropped them on the table.

'Could be.'

'What size do you take? Don't bother lying because it's easily checked.'

'Ten.'

'These are a ten. Sure you don't recognise them?'

'I said . . . they're a bit like mine but most trainers are much the same.'

'Our officers searched your house this afternoon and found these in the bin, along with these.' He picked up a second plastic bag. 'Jeans. These are your jeans, aren't they?'

Fletcher stared at them but said nothing.

'Why did you dump a pair of perfectly good trainers and some jeans in the bins, Mr Fletcher?'

'The wife would have. I don't know.'

'Why would your wife do that? She might bin some very old clothes but these aren't old, are they? Look in good nick to me. So why did you bin them?'

'Just didn't want them.'

'So they are yours?'

'I didn't say that.'

'Come on, Harry, don't take the piss. These are your trainers and jeans and you dumped them in your dustbin. Why?'

Fletcher moved about in his chair but did not reply and did not meet Ben Vanek's eye.

'If you don't know, I do. You dumped them because they smelled of petrol, the petrol you used to throw on Nobby Parks's shack before you set light to it. You spilled some and we all know how petrol reeks on your clothes. You could hardly walk home in your Y-fronts so you dumped them in the bin as soon as you got back. Isn't that the case?'

'I've got no idea what you're talking about. Never heard of this Nobby bloke.'

'Have you had a cold recently, Harry?'

Fletcher stared. 'No.'

'Do you sneeze a lot? Rhinitis, allergic to something, that sort of thing?'

'I don't know what you're talking about.'

'Simple enough question, I'd have thought. Just answer.'

'All right – no. I don't.'

'Cough?'

'No.'

'What, you never cough?'

'Of course I bloody cough, everybody bloody coughs, what is this rubbish?'

'Have you had a cough recently? Or maybe you just breathed out a bit hard when you were shifting her body, is that it?'

'What body?'

'That of Olive Tredwell.'

'He's rattled,' Simon said. Fletcher had looked suddenly alarmed, had twitched and swivelled about in his chair, hearing the name.

Someone came in and handed Simon a slip of paper. He looked at it, showed it to Gerry.

'Ben,' Simon said softly into Vanek's earpiece, 'forensics just sent the result through. DNA on the mirror is a match for Fletcher. You don't need to string it out, we've got him. Bang it home now.'

'Either you sneezed or coughed or breathed out heavily when you were close to the mirror in Olive Tredwell's bedroom – maybe when you were shifting her into the chair and strapping her to it? Maybe before? Maybe you don't remember, but it doesn't matter all that much whether you do or you don't, Harry.'

'So what are you banging on about it for? It's all bollocks anyway. You blokes make it up.'

'No. There's nothing made up about this bit of evidence, Harry. The DNA we obtained from a spray of saliva on Olive Tredwell's mirror matches the DNA on the swab we took from you today. You were there, you killed Olive Tredwell. You also set fire to the shack in which Nobby Parks was sleeping, probably because you thought he'd seen you – he was a bit of a nightwatchman was Nobby, he saw a lot of things. You couldn't risk him blabbing about you to us or the newspapers. He liked talking to the papers did Nobby and that panicked you, didn't it? You had to shut him up. Two people dead, Harry, and you killed them both.' Vanek leaned back and looked steadily and calmly at Fletcher. 'So – what have you got to say?'

Whatever Serrailler was expecting – probably denial, bluster, anger, accusations about police methods, all or any of that – it was not what he got.

Fletcher stared at his hands for a moment, glanced at his solicitor, and away again, then said, 'Yes.'

'Yes what?'

'What the fuck do you think? I'm not an idiot. So yes. I killed her and I set fire to his place so I killed him as well. OK?'

Sixty-four

'Result!' Ben Vanek stood in the corridor outside the interview room, his face one big grin.

'Good work, Ben. But I want him for the lot.'

Ben shook his head. 'He's calculated, this one. He knows we've got cast-iron evidence, no point in arguing, but he's worked out that we don't have it for the others. He reckons confession for these will do him some good. Which it won't of course.'

'Call me bloody-minded. I hear what you're saying, Ben, but there's one way we might get him. I've just got to check something with the search team, see if my hunch is right.'

Ben looked dubious.

'Trust me. Then I'll have you back in there. You're a good interviewer, you've got the knack. I bet you can bring this one off.'

The team who had taken apart Fletcher's house were about to go off duty.

'Great result, guys, thanks. Just before you go – can you help me out? Anything strike you about the place – things in it, anything unusual you noticed?'

They were silent for a few seconds, going back over it.

'Nicely furnished, very clean – no, nothing unusual.'

'Keep thinking. Any books, photos, trophies – anything?'

He knew what he wanted, prayed he'd get it.

'He's a Hammers supporter . . . got the scarf, got the sticker on the kitchen window.'

'Anything else?'

'So are his kids, found two Hammers shirts in their room.'

Warm.

It came.

'Those kids . . . two little lads . . . photos of them everywhere, on the walls, on the sideboard, on the window ledges. Way more than you'd expect. There were the usual school photos, but the rest, loads of them, were all taken of them with him, right from babies . . . in fact, there was only one with their mum out of the lot, so far as I remember . . . I've got one of me with mine on the kitchen shelf but that's it, just the one.'

'What I wanted to hear; thanks, guys. Now get off and have a pint, you've earned it.'

He found Ben Vanek. 'Listen up. You can use this.'

'Achilles heel,' Ben said when he'd heard. 'Always is one.'

'Give it a go?'

'Absolutely.'

'Get him back in. It's late, he's tense, he's been on his own for a bit, it's all crowding in on him. He knows the score. Push it.'

Ben nodded.

He's the one you've nurtured, Simon thought, the interviewer born as much as made, trained but with the extra intuition you can never buy with any amount of training. He was going to keep him, make sure he got all the practice but not exhaust him with small stuff, interviewing bottom-of-the-heap dealers in weed and petty shoplifters.

Simon went into the viewing room. Gerry was back, wanting to see this one through. There was the same tension there had been at the builders' yard, the same hope, fear, intense focus, finger-crossing, heightened sense that they could be there. Almost there.

Fletcher came into the room with the solicitor. Serrailler watched him closely. He was not cocky but he had a confidence in the way he held himself, walked, sat, that sent out a message. *I've given you something. I chose to give it. I go on choosing.*

But he could only hope, he could not be certain, that they had no more evidence, nothing to spring on him about the other murders, not even a load of circumstantial. He had calculated the risk. He could be sure that his identity was safe too, that Lafferton would not have been told about Alan Frederick Keyes, and that even if they had linked the MOs of the 'two' men, they couldn't so much as mention the Yorkshire murders. Off limits. Safe.

A calculated risk.

Ben came in, nodded to the solicitor, looked Fletcher in the eye for a second or two. Sat down.

'Let's be clear then, Harry. Let's just be absolutely sure we both know the score. You have confessed to the murder of Olive Tredwell, at her home, on the night of 10 March. You have also confessed to setting the home of Norman Parks on fire deliberately, with the intent to kill Parks. Are we clear about both of these confessions?'

Fletcher glanced at his brief, then nodded.

'Say it, please.'

'Yes.'

'Right. Mrs Tredwell. Do you remember her?'

'No.'

'What, you murdered her in a particularly brutal and cold-blooded manner, and you took time to do it, yet you don't remember her? Odd that. It's not long ago. Why do you think you don't remember?'

A shrug.

'Could it be because you've got mixed up?'

No reply.

'Sorry, let me be a bit clearer. Could it be because you'd already committed several other murders – all of old women, all in their houses, at night, all by strangulation with electrical flex – that you've blurred them all together? You can't remember because there are so many?'

'Are you making a direct accusation? Are you charging my client, Sergeant?'

'Point taken.'

Vanek leaned back, and was still, appearing to think deeply, perhaps to be working out his strategy, perhaps because he felt he was at a dead end. Fletcher watched him.

'He thinks Ben's a bit junior, not difficult to run rings round him. Look – he's got a bit of a smirk on his face somewhere. He's in charge, he's got Ben cornered, not the other way round. He's relaxed a bit, he's the boss in this interview room, is what he's thinking. They sent me a kid who doesn't even shave yet, that's disrespect. I'll eat him up.' Gerry could read criminals. He had the gift plus a lifetime of experience, watching them, listening to them, sussing them out.

Ben leaned back for another thirty seconds, saying nothing, apparently working out what to try next.

'He thinks Ben'll give up on him any minute. Cut his losses. Why not? He's got him for two murders, why bother to struggle for a confession about the rest? Fletcher's pretty sure we haven't got a grain of evidence on the other killings. Look at his face again.' Gerry was right. The expression was only just there, but Simon could see it. The confidence. The arrogance.

Ben lurched forward suddenly and leaned across the table.

'Look at me,' he said to Harry Fletcher. 'Look at me and don't look away. How old are your sons?'

Simon caught his breath.

Ben had taken the man off guard, there had been a flicker across his face and he shifted his body in the chair.

'All right, I guess they're five or six and maybe three? Great lads, you're proud of them and you should be. Do you love them, Harry?'

Fletcher seemed to struggle with the wish to shout at Vanek, or punch him. His body was tense. But he said nothing.

'You love them more than you love life itself, Harry, they mean everything, everything, in the world to you. You're a fantastic dad, they look up to you, they have fun with you, they trust you, Harry. So what's it going to be like for them, never to see you again? That's what you're looking at and you know it. You will never see your lads again until they're grown men with kids of their own and maybe not even then. We'll pin two more murders on you and that makes four. Life, Harry. You've confessed to two murders. You might well get one of those down to manslaughter. You set fire to Parks's home but there's no way you could have been certain he was actually in there. Maybe you felt like a bit of a blaze. Maybe you wanted to teach him a lesson, but you didn't actually plan to burn the poor old bloke to death in his bed. That happened, but I wonder if you meant it to happen? So, you could plead manslaughter on Nobby Parks. One murder, when you were in such a state after you'd found out Nobby was in the shack and you'd burned him to death, one murder committed under such stress that you were out of your mind at the time. You've admitted that murder, you might well get away with manslaughter for Nobby. You're looking at, what, ten, twelve years, time off for good behaviour, maybe eight years? Your lads will be older but they won't be adults who've forgotten you ever existed. But we've got two other murders to pin on you, Harry. You deny knowing anything about them, deny having any involvement in them. Come on, Harry. It's looking like life, isn't it, and for four murders – even if you do get the manslaughter – life will mean life. Your two little lads, those two in all the photographs you've got round the house, the lads you're obviously so proud of and rightly . . . they'll learn the truth and they won't want to know they ever had a dad. Well, would you?'

Fletcher was staring at the table.

'He's with his kids,' Gerry said. 'He's got them here with his arms round them and he's so close to them, closer than he's ever been. It's got to him.'

Serrailler nodded. Not much further. Not much further.

'You weren't in your right mind, Harry. You were someone else. No one in their right mind would break into the bedrooms of frail old ladies who are alone at night and terrify them, drag them out of their beds, shove them down in a chair in front of a mirror so they could see themselves, see you standing behind them, watch you get out the electrical flex, watch you uncoil it and raise your hands to loop it round their necks, watch while you started to tighten it, watch themselves fight for breath, turn blue, start to choke, watch –'

344

'Jesus Christ, what do you think I am? They were dead before I put them in their chairs. What kind of a person would do what you said?'

There was absolute silence.

In the viewing room, Simon and Gerry could barely breathe.

Ben stayed very still, looking intently at Fletcher. 'Only someone not in their right mind, Harry. Someone not themselves. That's what I think.'

Fletcher crumpled, put his head down on his arms and wept. His shoulders shook.

'Yessss,' Serrailler said.

Sixty-five

It was late. They were all knackered. Simon took Ben and Gerry to the Golden Cross and sent Cat a text to say he would be there for supper.

They did not have much energy for chat at first, simply sat with their pints in front of them, grateful that it was all over, that it had worked out. Ben was very subdued, even when Simon congratulated him again.

'To be honest, guv, I feel grubby.'

'You didn't beat him up, you didn't lie, you didn't deceive him.'

'Below the belt though, using his kids.'

'Absolutely not. It made him stop in his tracks.'

'Wiped the smirk off his face,' Gerry added, getting up to go to the bar.

'It was a cheat.'

'No. You're just tired, Ben, and you've got a success hangover. You nailed a man who, as Fletcher, killed four people and, in another life, killed three.'

'He'll play the tricks. Start being a prison altar boy within six months.'

'Ben, he can become a Christian, an altar boy, a flipping Buddhist, he'll have counselling and he'll put in for every psychiatric check going, he'll take up basketball and do his A levels and volunteer to teach reading to those who can't. He can nail himself to a cross. None of it will make a scrap of difference.

He's not coming out. You don't want him out, do you? Given retraining as the warden of an old people's sheltered housing block?'

Gerry brought back the second round. 'What about the Yorkshire stuff?'

Simon shook his head. 'That can never come out. Mind you, the judge may have private info about Alan Keyes. He can't use it, he can't tell the jury about it, but it'll be there to ensure he doesn't let anything daft happen again. If any jury tried to mess about or come in with a not-unanimous he'd instruct them to find Fletcher guilty. No worries. There's something else . . . as Keyes, he was acquitted for those murders but what we've got now counts as new evidence. If I were the Yorkshire police I'd be asking for a retrial on the old killings.'

'There'd be justice,' Gerry said.

Ben shook his head. 'He's not the same bloke. They can't retry a different man – new ID, new person.'

'Doesn't matter. He's breached the law so the protection he was given by a new ID won't apply. Not up to me, of course. Right, the Chief's got the glad news and I'm off to my sister's for a decent dinner.'

Until he opened the front door of the farmhouse and smelled rich savoury meat, hot candle wax, baked potatoes and woodsmoke from the fire, Simon had felt slightly numbed, the good result processed and accepted intellectually but not emotionally. Now, as Cat called out to him and he went in to find her on her own in the warm kitchen, draining vegetables, an unopened bottle of Merlot on the table, he felt a rush of pure pride and happiness. Old people could sleep soundly again, he had tied everything up.

'The only thing is,' he said, pulling the cork on the wine, 'this guy's two men.'

'It happens. You know how often neighbours and friends simply can't believe that old Jim, nicest man on the block, always collecting for charity and going out of his way to do good turns, could be the killer of ten innocent passers-by, but there he is.'

'Fletcher absolutely adores his kids. He's got a nice wife, nice

347

home, he's a good reliable workman. He was a witness on one of the ram raids, gave us a pretty good statement without any trouble. But then he goes walking softly through the streets at night and carries out sadistic murders. Then he goes back home, slips into bed beside the wife, crashes out and wakes up right as rain the next morning to go and fit someone's new back boiler.'

'Jekyll and Hyde. It's been done.'

'Yup. Sorry I'm so late by the way.'

'No prob, you gave me a chance to finish a report and start on my tax papers.'

'So – what's new?'

'Where do I start?'

But she put a large forkful of food into her mouth to delay starting anywhere. Work, Molly's return, the children – those were not what occupied her mind, not what kept her awake, not what troubled her beyond measure. They were not her father and Judith. How did you tell your policeman brother about a crime, of which you have no actual proof, but which you know in conscience you ought to report? You can't.

You can't.

Instead, there was Sam.

'Bad start to the day. I got a call from the film company. They've postponed and won't be filming until the end of next year . . . regretfully, Sam will be too old, so sorry and all that . . .'

Simon groaned.

'The problem isn't so much the film – I'm not sure how keen he ever was to do it actually. But of course it's the humiliation in front of Hannah. If only they could see they're both in the same boat and cling together for mutual comfort, but no.'

'War?'

'Stand-off. You sense the constant low rumble of the drums.'

'I haven't seen them for a while – maybe we can have a day out soon? Haven't seen Dad and Judith either. Have you?'

Cat hesitated. Drank some wine. This was the moment when she ought to say, 'I've got something to tell you about them.'

But she didn't.

'Saw Judith at book group. All fine, I think.'

348

'Perhaps we could all four go out for supper? I'll ask them. The Italian?'

Cat nodded vaguely. 'I've got a lot of work on though.'

'I thought the hospice hours were reduced?'

'And my PhD proposal, and – I've had an idea for a book.'

'Death and dying?'

'That sort of thing.'

'Still, you can spare an evening.'

'I expect so. Do you want another potato?'

Simon held out his plate.

'How does Rachel take it when you're working round the clock and she can't get in touch with you? Not all of them have found it easy to cope with.'

'All of "them"?'

'Girlfriends. Stupid phrase.'

'Yes.'

'So?'

'Her husband died yesterday.'

'I know, you told me. It's tough, whatever she felt about him.'

'She loved him. Don't give me that look.'

'Didn't mean to. So now what?'

'How would I know?'

Cat set her glass down and looked at him hard. 'Now listen. I know you're exhausted, I know you're wound up and I totally understand what an awful state this is with Rachel.'

'Do you?'

'Of course I bloody do. I've seen you in enough messy situations with women to know first that she's different, and second that the guilt and shock both of you feel now Ken has died is massive. I know you, so stop playing games, with me of all people. I want to help you, I'm not trying to interfere.'

'Right.'

'And you know it. Shove your pride where the sun don't shine for once.'

He laughed. 'That doesn't sound like you.'

'No, well, that's Sam for you. Anyway – are you hearing me, Simon?'

He poured them each a fresh glass of wine.

'You staying?'

'Please. Then we can open another bottle.'

'Plan. But just answer the question first.'

'I'm hearing you, Catherine.'

She threw a pot holder at him. But she was filled with relief. They were friends again, he would lean on her while always pretending he was doing no such thing. She didn't think he realised how tricky the next few months were going to be.

They broached the second bottle and sat by the fire, Wookie pressed up close to Simon, Mephisto basking in front of the flames.

Cat looked at her brother, pale with tiredness, hollow-eyed, his blond hair in need of the barber. She loved him dearly, and she wished him not only the usual things, love and security and happiness, a solid home base, but for the prickle hedge that grew round him to be cut, like his hair, or chopped to the ground.

She also realised that, at least for now, and perhaps forever, she must keep knowledge of the situation between Richard and Judith to herself. But she was used to that.

That cop. He kept on saying it until it was like a drill going into my head.

'You weren't yourself. You weren't yourself.'

No.

I wasn't Harry Fletcher because I've never been Harry Fletcher. I've no idea who Harry Fletcher is.

Yes, I have. Harry Fletcher's a decent bloke. Good plumber. Reliable. Hard-working. Honest. Looks after his mother-in-law.

Harry Fletcher has a smashing wife and he has the best two lads in the world. He loves them. He'd die for them. He'd kill for them.

But he didn't. He can't have done. He wasn't himself.

Alan Keyes, now, he's your man. He's a killer. They let him off. Why, I've no idea, I'm not into his secrets or theirs. But they let him off even though he was a killer.

He's the one who liked to do it. Old ladies.

Keyes is your killer, not Harry Fletcher. But Keyes doesn't exist and who's Harry Fletcher? The one who was never born.

'You weren't yourself, Harry.' Spot on.

But it's like this. Harry Fletcher has confessed to the lot. Nobby Parks wasn't a murder. How was anyone to know he was in the shack? He was out all over the town at night. Like me. Only he wasn't, and he died, but that's not murder. An accident isn't murder, it's manslaughter. People often don't get a sentence at all for manslaughter.

Olive Tredwell. Yes, but I wasn't myself. I'd just found out about Nobby. I went mad.

351

'You weren't yourself, Harry.'

So that leaves two. Rosemary. She just had to go because she might have seen something. That's regrettable. Didn't mean to upset Kaz and the kids. Rosemary and Nobby. Not meant to be killed.

So that leaves one.

'You weren't yourself, Harry.'

No. I haven't a clue who I am, to be honest, so they can work with that, psychiatrists, all those people, they can understand and write it up so it's not what people think of as murder. They've got words. Phrases. Jargon.

'You weren't yourself, Harry.'

So the way I see it, it'll be five years in the hospital for treatment, cure, and out. The lads will be a bit bigger but not much. I'll see them. I'll go home to them. They'll understand how much I love them. Everybody will. Like that young cop. He understood. So it'll be all right. I won't lose them after all. And they won't lose me.

Result, then.

Result.

Sixty-six

The phone rang.

'DCS Serrailler?'

He knew the voice. But that was all. Just a voice.

'Yes.'

'Result, then. Pity we're invisible.'

'Sorry?'

'I meant, it would be nice to go public and claim the prize, but we can never do that. So you get the glory. We begrudge you not at all, knowing you won't forget.'

'Forget what?' Simon could barely believe what he was hearing.

'That it was all down to us. If we hadn't given you a piece of vital info, you wouldn't have got on to Fletcher.'

'So what you're saying is, having Harry Fletcher behind bars is all down to you? We didn't play any part in getting this result at all?'

'Oh, come on, Superintendent, we'd never say that, now, would we? Just that you acted on information received. From us. But if there are any medals going, you get them. I'd say that was more than fair. Cheers, then. Nice working with you, Superintendent.'

Simon was incandescent, about to put in a call to the Chief, to make an official complaint, to write an official letter to . . .

But he didn't. He wouldn't.

He went downstairs to take the press conference.

The day petered out, as days after a successful op always did. Everyone had the usual sense of anticlimax and back to routine after the jubilation, no one felt like going to the pub at the end of the shift.

Simon drove home. He would shower, change, drink a Laphroaig, make an omelette and a salad. Go on with reading *The Heart of Midlothian*, lying on the sofa.

It was cathedral bell-ringing practice. He would open the big window to let the changes in. Another whisky. Early bed.

There were a couple of dull-looking letters and a magazine in his letter box. And a white envelope with 'By Hand' written, top left, and 'Simon'.

Dearest Simon

This has been a difficult week, I'm in pieces, not certain how to process what's happened. I knew Kenneth hadn't much longer to live but his actual death has been a devastating shock.

I know – I hope – you will understand that I'm not sure where I am or what I feel otherwise. So I cannot and must not see you, or talk to you – anything. Please don't try and get in touch. I don't know how long it will take, when I will feel I can see you. Or even if I ever will. I don't know who I am just now.

Please, understand all this and forgive, dear Simon.
Rachel

He stood with the letter in his hand, in the light of one lamp, as the bells began to ring.